MURDER ON ICE

Outside, the air was crisp and still. Daisy couldn't resist leaving a footprint or two in the glistening untrodden snow beside the path. It crunched underfoot.

James carried the skating boots down the hill for her as she was laden with camera and tripod. While she set them up, he and Fenella sat on the bench and put on their skates. They circled slowly at the near end of the lake, waiting for her.

"Go ahead," she called, already chilled fingers fumbling at the stiff catch that attached the camera to the tripod. "I'll be with you in half a mo."

Waving to her, they joined hands and whizzed off towards the bridge. As they reached it, James yelled, "Stop!"

They swerved to a halt beneath the arch. James moved cautiously forward into the black shadow cast by the low sun. And then Fenella screamed.

As scream after scream shredded the peaceful morning, Daisy raced along the lakeside path towards the bridge. Stepping down cautiously from the bank onto the ice, she was under the stone arch before she saw what had stopped James and Fenella in their tracks.

In the shadow of the bridge, the ice was shattered, and in the inky water floated a man, facedown . . .

Books by Carola Dunn

DEATH AT WENTWATER COURT

THE WINTER GARDEN MYSTERY
(coming soon)

Published by Kensington Publishing Corporation

DEATH AT WENTWATER COURT

A Daisy Dalrymple Mystery

CAROLA DUNN

KENSINGTON BOOKS
Kensington Publishing Corp.

http://www.kensingtonbooks.com

KENSINGTON BOOKS are published by

Kensington Publishing Corp.
850 Third Avenue
New York, NY 10022

First Kensington Paperback Printing: October, 2000
10 9 8 7 6 5 4 3 2 1

Printed in the United States of America

To Mum, who remembers Liberty bodices and woolly combies

PROLOGUE

Midnight at Ciro's. The strains of the Charleston died away
amid applause for the coloured band. As a babble of
talk and laughter arose, the young man led his partner
from the dance floor. The older man watching him noted
that his well-cut evening togs were slightly rumpled, his
face too red even for the aftermath of the vigorous dance.
The youthful tart hanging on his arm didn't seem to care,
though an excess of face-paint made it difficult to be sure.

Her spangled, low-waisted frock was short, in defiance
of fashion, which this season had sunk hems back to near
the ankle. With her shingled hair and the dangling bead
necklace, she might be either a chorus-girl or a "bright
young thing."

With a contemptuous sneer, the watcher approached
and accosted her partner. "A word with you, old chap."

The young man regarded him with sullen dislike. "Hang
it all, can't it wait?" His words were slurred.

"I have just learned that you are going down to Hampshire tomorrow."

gnor insists on all the family turning up
I'll be back in town in a fortnight. What's

fancy to see your ancestral acres. Invite

't do that! Here, Gloria, you go on back
He gave the girl a light swat on her rear
pink artificial silk—a chorus-girl, then. Car-
outing, she obeyed, but glanced back as she
gave the older man the come-hither look of a
vamp.

pose my sister put you up to this," her escort
ed sulkily.

may suppose what you please. I want an invitation."
e pater'll think it deuced odd."

The pater' will think it something more than deuced
if he should happen to get wind of a certain transac-
n." The note of menace in his smooth voice made the
her's face pale. "I've no ambition to join your family's
Christmas celebrations. Boxing Day or the day after will
do, and I'll stay to see in 1923—a year of great promise,
I feel sure."

"Oh, very well." Now the young man sounded merely
petulant. "Consider yourself invited."

He turned away, pushed through the noisy crowd to his
table, and ordered cocktails. Five minutes later, as the band
struck up again, he took his giggling chorus-girl back to
the dance floor to shimmy away his troubles.

By then, the source of his discomfiture had already left
the nightclub. He gave the chauffeur his orders and leaned
back in the Lanchester, a cold smile of anticipation curving
his thin lips.

CHAPTER 1

"He'll come to a bad end, mark my words, and she won't lift a finger to stop him. It's the little ones I'm worried about." The stout lady heaved a sigh, her old-fashioned mantle, a hideous yellowish green, billowing about her. "Four already and another due any day now."

Daisy Dalrymple was constantly amazed at the way total strangers insisted on regaling her with their life stories, their marital misfortunes, or their children's misdeeds. Not that she objected. One day she was going to write a novel, and then every hint of human experience might come in handy.

All the same, she wondered why people revealed to her their innermost secrets.

When the plump lady with the drunkard for a son-in-law left the train at Alton, Daisy had the 2nd Class Ladies Only compartment to herself. She knelt on the seat and peered at her face in the little mirror kindly provided by the L&SW Railway Company. It was a roundish, ordinary sort of face, pink-cheeked, not one calculated to inspire people to pour out their souls. A confidante, Daisy felt, ought to have dark, soulful eyes, not the cheerful blue that looked back at her.

Near one corner of a mouth of the generous, rather than rosebud, persuasion dwelt the small brown mole that was the bane of her existence. No quantity of face-powder ever hid it completely.

The scattering of freckles on her nose could be smothered, however. Taking her vanity case from her handbag, Daisy vigorously wielded her powder-puff. She touched up her lipstick and smiled at herself. On her way to her first big writing assignment for *Town and Country,* blasé as she'd like to appear, she had to admit to herself she was excited—and a little nervous.

At twenty-five she ought to be sophisticated and self-confident, but the butterflies refused to be banished from her stomach. She had to succeed. The alternatives were altogether too blighting to contemplate.

Was the emerald green cloche hat from Selfridges Bargain Basement a trifle too gaudy for a professional woman? No, she decided, it brightened up her old dark green tweed coat just as intended. She straightened the grey fur tippet she had borrowed from Lucy. It was more elegant than a woollen muffler, if less practical on this icy January morning.

Sitting down again, she picked up the newspaper the woman had left. Daisy was no devotee of the latest news, and on this second day of January, 1923, the headlines she scanned looked very much like those of a week ago, or a fortnight: troubles in the Ruhr and in Ireland, Mussolini making speeches in Italy, German inflation raging out of control.

Opening the paper, she read a short piece describing the latest wonders unearthed from Tutankhamen's tomb, and then a headline caught her eye:

FLATFORD BURGLARY
Scotland Yard Called In

Daisy had been at school with Lord Flatford's daughter, though not in the same form. Shocking how the merest mention of an acquaintance was more interesting than the most serious news from abroad.

In the early hours of the New Year, thieves had walked off with the Flatfords' house guests most valuable jewellery, not yet returned to his lordship's safe after a New Year's ball.

She had no time to read more, for the clickety-clack of the train over the rails began to slow again and the next station was Wentwater. Wrestling with the leather strap, Daisy lowered the breath-misted window. She shivered in the blast of frosty air, heavy with the distinctive smell of a coal-fired steam engine, and wondered whether a cold neck was not too high a price to pay for elegance.

At least the knot of honey brown hair low on her neck, out of the way of the hat, provided a spot of warmth. For once she was glad she had indulged her mother by not having her hair bobbed.

The train rattled and shuddered to a halt. Leaning out, Daisy waved and called, "Porter!"

The man who answered her summons appeared to have a wooden leg, doubtless having lost the original in the Great War. Nonetheless, he made good time along the platform, swept clear of snow. He touched his peaked cap to her as she stepped down, clutching Lucy's precious camera.

"Luggage, madam?"

"Yes, I'm afraid there's rather a lot," she said doubtfully.

"Not to worry, madam." He hopped nimbly up into the compartment and gathered from the rack her portmanteau, tripod, Gladstone bag, and the portable typewriter the editor had lent her. Laden, he somehow descended again. Setting everything down, he slammed the door and raised his arm. "Right away!" he shouted to the guard, who blew his whistle and waved his green flag.

As the train chugged into motion, Daisy crossed the footbridge to the opposite platform. She surveyed the scene. The station was no more than a halt, and she was the only person to have descended from the down-train. Signs over the two doors of the tiny building on the up-platform indicated that one end was for Left Luggage, the other serving as both Waiting-Room and Ticket Office.

The Hampshire countryside surrounding the station was hidden by a blanket of snow, sparkling in the sun. Frost glittered on skeletal trees and hedges. The only signs of life were the train, now gathering speed, the uniformed man carrying her stuff across the line behind it, and a crow huddled on the station picket fence.

"Your ticket, please, madam."

She gave it to him to clip. "I'm staying at Wentwater Court," she said. "Is it far?"

"A mile or three."

"Oh, Lord!" Daisy looked in dismay at her luggage, and then down at her smart leather boots, high-heeled and laced up the front to the knee. They were definitely not intended for tramping along snowy country lanes, and the station was obviously too small to support a taxi service or even a fly.

"I shouldn't worry, madam. His lordship always sends the motor for his guests, but likely it's hard to start in this weather."

"The trouble is," Daisy confided, "I'm not exactly a guest. I'm going to write about Wentwater Court for a magazine."

The porter, cum station master, cum ticket collector looked properly impressed. "A writer, are you, madam? Very nice, too. Well, now, if you was to walk, I can get a boy from the village to bring your traps after on a handcart.

Or I can telephone the garridge in Alton for a hired car to come pick you up."

Daisy contemplated these alternatives, one uncomfortable, the other expensive. Her expenses would be paid by the magazine, eventually, but she hadn't much cash in hand.

At that moment she heard the throb of a powerful motor engine. A dark green Rolls-Royce Silver Ghost pulled up in the station yard, the brass fittings on its long bonnet gleaming. A uniformed chauffeur jumped out.

"I reckon his lordship's counting you as a guest, madam," said the porter with vicarious satisfaction, picking up her baggage.

"Miss Dalrymple?" asked the chauffeur, approaching. "I'm Jones, from the Court. Sorry I'm late, miss. She were a tad slow starting this morning, which she ain't usually be it never so cold, or I'd've got going earlier."

"That's quite all right, Jones," said Daisy, giving him a sunny smile. God was in His Heaven after all, and all was right with the world.

He opened the car door for her, then went to help the porter stow her bags in the boot. Daisy leaned back on the soft leather seat. There were definite advantages to being the daughter of a viscount.

Of course, she'd never have got the assignment to write about stately homes were it not for her social connections. Though she didn't know the Earl of Wentwater, she was acquainted with his eldest son, James, Lord Beddowe; his daughter, Lady Marjorie; and his sister, Lady Josephine. Her editor had rightly expected that doors forever closed to any plebeian writer would swing wide to welcome the Honourable Daisy Dalrymple.

The Rolls purred out of the station yard, down the hill, round a bend, and through the village of Lower Wentwater. The duck pond on the village green was frozen. Shrieking with laughter, several small children in woollen leggings

were sliding on the ice, nothing but bright eyes showing
between striped mufflers and Balaclava helmets.

Beyond the little stone church, the lane wound up and
down hills, past fields and farms and scattered copses. Here
the snow on the roadway lay undisturbed except for two
eight-inch-deep wheel ruts made by the earl's motor on
its way to the station. Daisy was increasingly glad she had
not had to hoof it.

In the middle of a wood, they came to a brick lodge
guarding tall wrought-iron gates that stood open. As they
drove through, Jones sounded the Rolls's horn. Daisy
glanced back and saw the lodge-keeper come out to close
the gates behind them. A moment later, they drove out of
the trees.

Wentwater Court spread before them. On the opposite
slope of a shallow valley stood the mansion. The crenel-
lated and turreted central Tudor block, red brick dressed
with stone, was flanked by wings added in Queen Anne's
time. Virginia creeper, though now leafless, masked the
transition from one style to another, and a pair of huge
cedars softened the rectangularity of the wings. Closer, at
the bottom of the valley, the gravel drive crossed an elaborate stonework bridge over an ornamental lake. The ice
had been swept clear of snow, and skaters in red and green
and blue skimmed its length or twirled in fanciful curlicues.

"Jones, stop, please," Daisy cried. "I must take some
photographs.

The chauffeur retrieved the tripod from the boot for
her. "Do you want me to wait, miss?"

"No, go ahead, I'll walk up." She set up her equipment
on the edge of the drive and adjusted the camera. A frown
creased her forehead.

Most of her photographic experience had been in Lucy's
studio. Peering through the viewfinder, she tried to picture
the scene before her shrunk to half a magazine page. The
skaters on the lake would be mere dots, she decided.

Nonetheless, she took a couple of shots of the entire scene before directing the camera at the mansion alone to take several more. Then she picked up the whole apparatus and trudged down to the lakeside to get close-ups of the skaters and the pretty arched bridge.

The skaters had already seen her, and one or two had waved. As she approached, all five gathered at the nearer foot of the bridge.

"Hullo, Daisy," called Marjorie. "We thought it must be you." Her fashionably boyish figure was emphasized by a tailored cherry red sports coat and matching skirt. Daisy knew that the white woollen hat concealed bobbed hair set in Marcel waves. Her Cupid's-bow lipstick matched her coat, her eyebrows were plucked and darkened, and her eyelashes were heavily blacked. At twenty-one, Lady Marjorie Beddowe was a quintessential flapper.

"Welcome to Wentwater, Miss Dalrymple." Her brother James, a stocky young man some three years older than his sister, wore plus-fours and a Fair Isle pullover patterned in yellow and blue. His face, heavy jaw at odds with an aristocratically narrow nose, was pink from exercise; he had discarded coat, cap, and muffler on the heap piled on a bench on the far side of the lake. "You know Fenella, don't you?"

"Yes, very well. We're from the same part of Worcestershire." Daisy smiled at the shy girl whose engagement to James had recently been announced in the *Morning Post.* "And Phillip is an old friend, too, of course."

"What-ho, old thing, haven't seen you in an age." Fenella's brother, a tall, fair, loose-limbed young man, grinned at her. Good-looking in a bland sort of way, Phillip Petrie had been Daisy's brother's best chum until Gervaise was killed in the trenches. "Taken up photography, have you?" he asked.

"In a way."

He seemed to be ignorant of the reason for her arrival.

She would have explained further, but Marjorie broke in eagerly to introduce the fifth skater.

"Daisy, this is Lord Stephen Astwick." She gazed with patent adoration at the older man. "You haven't met, have you?"

"I've not had that pleasure," he said suavely. "How do you do, Miss Dalrymple." At about forty, Lord Stephen was an elegant figure in a leather Norfolk-style jacket, his black hair pomaded back from his handsome face.

"Lord Stephen." Daisy inclined her head in acknowledgement. She didn't care for the way his cold grey eyes appraised her. "Don't let me interrupt your sport. I want to take some pictures from a bit farther along the bank."

"Let me carry that apparatus for you," Phillip offered, stepping forward. "It looks dashed heavy."

"No, do go on skating, Phil. The more people in the photographs, the merrier."

A flagged path around the lake had been cleared and sanded. As she started along it, Daisy noticed Marjorie taking Lord Stephen's arm in a proprietorial grip.

"Show me that figure again," she said to him with an artificial titter. "I *will* get it right this time, I swear it."

"If you insist, Lady Marjorie," he acquiesced, with a slight grimace of distaste. Daisy's instant dislike of the man was confirmed. Marjorie might be a bit of a blister, but Lord Stephen had no call to show his contempt so plainly.

Finding the perfect position on a short jetty beside a wooden boathouse, Daisy set up her camera. She took several shots of the skaters, with the bridge in the background. Obligingly, they all stayed at the near end of the lake, though she had seen them whizzing under the bridge earlier. It was a pity that colour photography was so complicated and unsatisfactory a process, for the bright colours of their clothes were part of the charm of the scene.

Daisy finished the roll of film. The other rolls were in her Gladstone bag, so she packed up, detaching the camera from the tripod and carefully closing its accordion nose. As soon as she stopped concentrating on her work, she became aware of the biting chill nibbling at her toes and cheeks.

The folded tripod tucked awkwardly under one arm, the camera case slung by its strap over her shoulder, she trudged on around the lake. A path of sanded, well-trodden snow led up from the bench towards the house. Before she reached it, Phillip skated over to her.

"Finished? I'll give you a hand up to the house if you'll hold on half a tick while I take off my skates."

"Thanks, that would be a help."

He skated along to the bench to change his footwear. As she strolled to join him, Daisy wondered if he was about to take up his inconstant pursuit of her. Ever since she had emerged from her bottle green school uniform like a butterfly from its chrysalis, the Honourable Phillip Petrie, third son of Baron Petrie, had intermittently courted her. More for Gervaise's sake than her own, she sometimes thought.

She smiled at him as he relieved her of her burdens. Though she steadfastly refused his periodic proposals, she was fond of her childhood friend and erstwhile pigtail-puller.

"Did you bring skates?" he asked, shortening his long strides to match hers up the hill, slippery despite the sand.

"No, I didn't think to."

"I expect you can borrow some. We could come straight down again. It's a pity to waste such a topping day."

"Yes, but I'm not here as a guest, or at least, not for pleasure. I'm going to be busy."

He looked startled. "What on earth do you mean?"

"I have a commission to write about Wentwater Court for *Town and Country,*" she told him with pride.

"You and your bally writing," he groaned. "Dash it, Daisy, it shouldn't take more than an hour or so to put together a bit of tomfoolery for the gossip column. You can scribble it off later."

"Not a paragraph or two, a long article. With photos. This is serious, Phillip. They are paying me pots of money to write a monthly series about some of the more interesting of the lesser known country seats."

"Money!" He frowned. "Hang it all, my dear old girl, you surely don't need to earn your own living. Gervaise would be fearfully pipped."

"Gervaise never tried to tell me what to do," she said with considerable asperity, "and he'd have understood that I simply can't live with Mother, let alone with Cousin Edgar. He couldn't stand Edgar and Geraldine any more than I can."

"Maybe, but all the same he must be turning in his grave. His sister working for her living!"

"At least writing is a whole lot better than that ghastly secretarial work I was doing. I did enjoy helping Lucy in her studio, but she doesn't really have enough work to justify paying me."

"It was Lucy Fotheringay put you up to this independence tommyrot in the first place. Are you still sharing that Bayswater flat with her?"

"Not the flat." Daisy seized the opportunity to avoid the subject of her employment, though she knew she'd not escape his ragging forever. "We have a perfectly sweet little house in Chelsea, quite near the river."

She went on to describe it in excruciating detail, which Phillip was too well brought up to interrupt. Before her narrative reached the attics, they reached the front door. Phillip being laden with skates, tripod, and camera, Daisy rang the bell.

A footman in plum-coloured livery opened one half of the massive, iron-bound, oak double doors. Stepping in, Daisy handed him her card and glanced around.

"Oh, I can't wait to photograph it!" The early Tudor

Great Hall was everything she had heard. Linenfold wainscoting rose to a carved frieze of Tudor roses, bulrushes, and stylized rippling water. Above, the walls were whitewashed and hung with tapestries of hunting and jousting scenes, alternating with crossed pikes, halberds, and banners. The vaulted hammerbeam ceiling was high overhead.

Daisy despaired of ever doing the vast room justice with her camera.

She shivered. A blazing fire in the huge fireplace opposite her did little to disperse the winter chill rising from the flagged floor. A cold draught blew from the arched stone staircase at one end of the hall. The footman hurriedly closed the front door behind Phillip.

"You'll be the writing lady, miss?"

"Yes, that's right." She had ordered new cards with her profession proudly emblazoned beneath her name, but she hadn't yet received them.

Obviously unsure what to do with her, the footman turned with relief to the stately, black-clad butler who now appeared through a green baize door at the back of the hall. "It's Miss Dalrymple, Mr. Drew." He handed over the card.

"If you'll please to come this way, miss, his lordship will receive you in his study."

"Thank you." She put out her hand as Phillip made to go with her. The last thing she needed was his censorious presence hovering at her elbow when she discussed her work with Lord Wentwater. "Don't wait about, Phil. Go back to your skating in case there's a thaw tonight. I'll see you later."

Quickly powdering her red nose as she followed the butler, she realized that her nerves had vanished. She had never found it difficult to charm elderly gentlemen, and she had no reason to suppose that the earl would be an exception. Half the battle was already won, since he had given her permission to write the article and invited her to Wentwater. Having seen the magnificent Great Hall, she had no doubt that she'd find plenty to write about.

The butler led the way from the Tudor part of the house into the east wing. Here he tapped on a door, opened it, and announced her. As Daisy entered with a friendly smile, Lord Wentwater rose and came round his leather-topped desk to meet her.

A tall, lean gentleman of some fifty years, he did not return her smile but shook the hand she offered, greeting her with a grave courtesy. He had James's straight, narrow, aristocratic nose, and the greying hair and moustache gave him an air of distinction. Daisy thought him most attractive despite his age and the rather Victorian formality of his manners.

The Victorian impression was heightened by the heavy mahogany furniture in the study and the dark red Turkey carpet. A Landseer painting of two black retrievers, one with a dead mallard in its mouth, hung above a superb Adam fireplace.

Still chilled, Daisy gravitated automatically towards the fireplace, pulling off her gloves and holding out her hands to the flames.

"Won't you sit down, Miss Dalrymple?" The earl indicated a maroon-leather wing chair by the fire. Taking the similar chair opposite her, he said, "I knew your father, of course. A sad loss to the House of Lords. That wretched influenza decimated our ranks, and so soon after the War slaughtered the next generation. Your brother, I believe?"

"Yes, Gervaise died in Flanders."

"Allow me to offer my condolences, somewhat belated, I fear." To her relief, he dropped the unhappy subject and went on in a dry, slightly interrogative tone. "I am flattered that you have chosen my home to write about."

"I'd heard how splendid the interior is, Lord Wentwater, and for my January article I couldn't count on being able to photograph outdoors."

"Ah, yes, your editor's letter mentioned that you would be bringing a photographer with you."

Daisy willed herself not to blush. "Unfortunately, Mr. Carswell has come down with 'flu, so I'll be taking my own pictures." She hurried on before he could express his sympathy for the nonexistent Carswell. "It would be most frightfully helpful if you have a small windowless space I could use as a darkroom. A boxroom, or storeroom, or scullery, perhaps? As I'm no expert, I'd like to be able to see how well my photos have come out before I leave, in case I need to take more."

That brought a faint smile to his lips. "We can do better than that. My brother Sydney—he's in the Colonial Service—was a bit of a photography enthusiast in his youth, and had a darkroom set up."

"Oh, topping!"

"The equipment has never been cleared out, though you may find it rather old-fashioned. Is there anything else I can do to facilitate your work?"

"I've read a bit about the history of the house, but if there are any interesting anecdotes not generally known . . . ?"

"My sister's the one you need to talk to. She knows all there is to be known about Wentwater and the Beddowes."

"Lady Josephine is here? Spiffing!"

Again the fugitive smile crossed the earl's face. Lady Josephine Menton was as loquacious as she was sociable, a noted hostess and a noted gossip. No one could have better suited Daisy's purpose.

"I'm sure I can trust your discretion, and your editor's," said Lord Wentworth, standing up. "Come, I'll take you to her and introduce you to my wife. They are usually to be found in the morning-room at this hour."

They crossed the passage and he ushered her into a sunny sitting-room furnished, with an eye to comfort rather than style, in sage green, cream, and peach. As they

entered, a grey-muzzled black spaniel on the hearthrug
raised his head in brief curiosity, twitched his stumpy tail,
then went back to sleep. One of the two women sitting
by the fire looked up, startled, a hint of alarm in her
expression.

"Annabel, my dear, here is Miss Dalrymple. I know you
will see that she is comfortable."

"Of course, Henry." Lady Wentwater's musical voice
was quiet, almost subdued. She rose gracefully and came
towards them. "How do you do, Miss Dalrymple."

Daisy was stunned. She had read in the *Post* that the earl
had recently remarried, but she'd had no idea his second
wife was so young. Annabel, Countess of Wentwater, was
no more than a year or two older than James, her eldest
stepson. And she was beautiful.

A warm, heather-mixture tweed skirt and bulky thigh-
length cardigan did nothing to disguise a tall, slender
figure, somewhat more rounded than was strictly fashionable. Her pale face was a perfect oval with high cheekbones
and delicate features, her coiled hair dark and lustrous.
Dark, wide-set eyes smiled tentatively at Daisy.

"I leave you in good hands, Miss Dalrymple," said the
earl, and turned to depart.

His wife's gaze followed him. In it, Daisy read desperate
unhappiness.

(HAPTER 2

So, Daisy, you have taken up a career?" The stout, good-natured Lady Josephine sounded more interested than disapproving. "I'm sure your mother must be having forty fits."

"Mother's not frightfully keen," Daisy admitted. "She'd much rather I went to live with her at the Dower House."

"A stifling life for a young girl. She should thank her lucky stars you are writing for a respectable magazine, not one of the scandalous Sunday rags. Why, I myself have a subscription to *Town and Country*. I look forward to reading your articles, my dear."

"Thank you, Lady Josephine." She turned to the countess. "It's jolly decent of you and Lord Wentwater to let me come. I felt a bit cheeky even suggesting it."

"Not at all, Miss Dalrymple." Lady Wentwater's response was calm and gracious. Her eyes were shadowed now by long, thick lashes, and Daisy wondered if she had imagined the wretchedness. "Henry is proud of Wentwater," she went on. "He's glad of the opportunity to boast of it vicariously."

"True," observed her sister-in-law, "but I'm the one who knows the place inside out. I'll show you around later if you like, Daisy. I expect you'd like to go to your room for a wash and brush-up now. One always feels shockingly grimy after a train journey, doesn't one?"

Lady Wentwater, slightly flustered at this gentle reminder of her duty, rang the bell.

The housekeeper led Daisy back to the Great Hall, up the stone stairs, along a gallery, and into the east wing. As they went, Daisy enquired about the darkroom Lord Wentwater had mentioned.

"Yes, miss, all Mr. Sydney's machines and such are still there," the woman assured her, "and kept dusted, you may be sure. Down in the sculleries it is. The kitchens are a regular rabbit warren. Just ask anyone the way."

"Is there electric light?"

"Oh yes, miss, his lordship had the electric light put in throughout, being safer than gas, though I will say the generator has its ups and downs. If there's aught else you need in the photography line, just ask me or Drew. Here we are, now. That there's the lavatory, miss, and here's your room."

The square, high-ceilinged bedroom was light and airy, with flowered wallpaper and matching bedspread and curtains. The furnishings were old-fashioned but comfortable, and a cheery fire burned in the grate. A small writing desk stood by the window, which faced south, towards the lake. Daisy was relieved to see her camera and tripod on the chest-of-drawers.

An apple-cheeked young maid, in a grey woollen frock and white cap and apron, was unpacking her suitcase. She turned to bob a curtsy. Daisy smiled at her.

"Mabel will take care of you, miss," said the housekeeper with a swift glance around the room to make sure all was in order. "Anything she can't manage, send her for Barstow, her ladyship's maid. Our girls go off duty at eight, except for one who brings round the hot-water bottles and is on call until midnight. The bathroom's through that door there. You'll be sharing with Miss Petrie—her room's on the other side. Coffee will be served in the morning-room at eleven, and luncheon's at one. Will that be all, miss?"

"Yes, thank you."

Beginning to thaw at last, Daisy took off her hat and coat. She changed boots for shoes, smoothed her pale blue jersey jumper suit, tidied her hair, and powdered her nose.

"Please, miss, I can't open your bag."

"No, it's locked, Mabel. There's nothing in it you need deal with, only photographic equipment."

"You're the writing lady, aren't you, miss?" the maid asked, wide-eyed. "I think that's wizard, reely I do. You must be ever so clever."

Amused, but nonetheless flattered, Daisy admitted to herself that Phillip's disapproval had piqued her, so that even the chambermaid's admiration, added to Lady Josephine's acceptance, bucked her up no end. In a cheerful frame of mind, she went back down to the morning-room.

As she entered, the butler was depositing a tray with a Georgian silver coffee set on a table beside Lady Wentwater.

"Has a flask been taken down to the skaters, Drew?" she asked in her soft voice.

Daisy missed his answer as Lady Josephine greeted her.

"Just in time for coffee, Daisy. You know Hugh, of course."

Sir Hugh Menton, a gentleman of unimpressive stature eclipsed by his wife's bulk, had risen as Daisy came in. "How do you do, Miss Dalrymple," he said, a twinkle in his eye. "I understand you are now an author."

She shook his hand. "Not quite, Sir Hugh, merely a novice journalist, though I have high hopes."

"Ah, Josephine likes to anticipate the splendid accomplishments of her friends," he said fondly, with an indulgent smile at his wife.

"Better than anticipating failure!" she said tartly.

"Much better," Daisy agreed. "I remember last time I saw you in London, Lady Josephine, Sir Hugh was in Brazil and we decided his very presence ensured excellent harvests of both coffee and rubber. I hope your trip was successful, Sir Hugh?"

"Perfectly, thank you, though I can't claim all the credit for the harvests. I put good men in charge of my plantations and leave them to get on with it, with occasional visits to keep them up to the mark. There's a fine line between interference and inattention."

That Sir Hugh knew how to tread that fine line Daisy did not doubt for a moment. Besides his extensive rubber and coffee plantations in Brazil, he was reputed to have made a vast fortune in the City. Yet despite his shrewd decisiveness in business matters, he was as courteous and gentlemanly as Lord Wentwater, though in a more modern, worldly, and approachable way. Daisy liked him.

He asked how she preferred her coffee and went to fetch it for her and his wife.

"Will you have some cake, Miss Dalrymple?" Lady Wentwater enquired. She had provided a large slice of Dundee cake for Lady Josephine without asking, Daisy noted with amusement.

Breakfast seemed an age ago. "Yes, please," she said.

At that moment two young men came in. Lady Josephine took charge of the introductions. "My nephews, Wilfred and Geoffrey, Daisy. Miss Dalrymple is to write about Wentwater Court for *Town and Country* magazine."

"Jolly good show." Wilfred, a year or so older than his sister Marjorie, was as much a typical young man-about-town as she was a flapper. From sleek, brilliantined hair, faintly redolent of Parma violets, to patent leather shoes, he was impeccably turned out. Daisy could imagine him languidly knocking a croquet ball through a hoop, but skating was too energetic a pastime for him. A hint of puffiness about his eyes suggested that he probably saved his energy for living it up in nightclubs. His mouth had a sulky twist.

His younger brother, a large, muscular youth, muttered, "How do you do," and stood there looking vaguely uneasy, as if he didn't quite know what to do with his hands. He headed for the coffee table as soon as Wilfred began to speak again.

"I bet you wish you'd gone to write about Flatford's place, Miss Dalrymple," Wilfred drawled. "What a scoop that would have been! You've heard about the robbery?"

"Just that it happened. Something about a house-party and a ball?"

"That's right. It seems to have been one of a series of burglaries, but of course it's the more interesting for being close to home. In fact, some of us went to the ball on New Year's Eve, you know, but the pater insisted on us leaving early so we missed all the excitement."

"You were lucky to go at all," Lady Josephine told him. "Only a rackety set like Lord Flatford's would hold a ball on a Sunday, New Year or no New Year. I was surprised Henry let you attend. In any case, leaving at midnight made no difference. The robbery wasn't discovered until the morning."

He sighed. "You're right, of course, Aunt Jo. Excuse me while I get some coffee." He drifted off.

"Wilfred is a pip-squeak," said his aunt. "Geoffrey may yet amount to something. He's up at Cambridge, and already he's a boxing Blue though he's only nineteen."

The youngest Beddowe had taken a seat by the coffee table and was silently consuming a huge wedge of cake.

The last crumb disappeared as Daisy watched. She found she had picked the almonds off the top of her slice and eaten them first, a bad habit from nursery days.

"More cake, Geoffrey?" Lady Wentwater asked with a smile.

"Yes, please."

"The bottomless pit," said Wilfred, grinning. Unoffended, Geoffrey ate on.

By the time Daisy finished her coffee and went over to beg a second cup, Geoffrey was on his third slice. He had uttered no more than another "Yes, please." Daisy put his reticence down to shyness.

Lady Wentwater was quiet, too. Wilfred held forth about the *Music Box Revue* with the rather desperate air of one who considers it his duty to keep the conversation going under difficult circumstances. Daisy, who had seen the show, threw in occasional comments, and Lady Josephine asked about the sets.

"If the sets are good enough," she said, "one can amuse oneself admiring them during the dull bits. Do you like revues, Annabel, or do you prefer musical comedies, as I do?" she added in a good-natured attempt to draw her young sister-in-law into the discussion.

"I've never been to a revue, and only one musical comedy, but I've enjoyed the few plays I've seen."

"Of course, you've had little opportunity to go to the theatre," said Lady Josephine and turned back to Wilfred. The critical note in her voice surprised Daisy.

The countess looked so discouraged Daisy tried to cheer her. "Shall we do a matinee together next time you come up to town, Lady Wentwater?" she suggested.

"Oh, thank you . . . I'd love to . . . but I'm not sure . . . Won't you please call me Annabel, Miss Dalrymple?"

"Yes, of course, but you must call me Daisy."

She had noted that Wilfred and Geoffrey both avoided addressing their stepmother by her Christian name. No doubt Lord Wentwater would frown on such familiarity, yet to call her "Mother" was equally difficult. It was altogether an awkward situation, her being so much nearer in age to her stepchildren than to her husband. Sympathizing, Daisy wondered whether that was enough to account for her obvious low spirits.

Lady Josephine finished her coffee and heaved herself out of her chair. "Well, Daisy, shall I give you a tour of the house before luncheon? Why don't you come along, Annabel? I'm sure there are stories you haven't heard yet."

"I'd like to, but I simply must write a few letters," Annabel excused herself.

"Though who she has to write to," Lady Josephine muttered as she and Daisy left the morning-room, "I can't for the life of me imagine. When Henry married her she was utterly friendless. They met in Italy last winter, you know," she explained. "Henry had had rather a nasty bout of bronchitis and was sent there for his health, and she was newly widowed."

Her tone told Daisy a great deal about her opinion of young, beautiful, friendless widows who married wealthy noblemen old enough to know better.

The tour started in the Great Hall, which was still used occasionally for large dinner-parties. "I shan't tell you all the stuff you can get from books," said Lady Josephine frankly. "There's quite a good book in the library about the house and the polite history of the Beddowes—you know the sort of thing, who married whom, and who was minister in whose cabinet—but you won't get the family stories."

"I'm relying on you for those."

"Well, the first Baron Beddowe built the place in Henry VII's reign, a clever chap who ended on the right side in the Wars of the Roses—after several changes of allegiance. His grandson was one of the few noblemen to entertain Queen Elizabeth without being bankrupted."

"How did he manage that?" Daisy asked, scribbling in her notebook in her own version of Pitman's shorthand.

"Rather disgracefully, I'm afraid. She descended on Wentwater with her usual swarm of retainers. The second night, at a lavish banquet in this hall, my ancestor picked a quarrel with one of the courtiers. The Queen had been trying to rid herself of the fellow, without success as he was the son of an influential nobleman. Supposedly in his cups, Wilfred Beddowe stabbed the fellow to the heart with that poniard up there between the halberds." She gestured at a gem-encrusted dagger hanging on the wall, in pride of place over the cavernous fireplace.

"And Elizabeth was so grateful she departed the next day?"

"Yes, expressing shock and censure, of course. However, the Earldom of Wentwater was created not a year later."

Daisy laughed. "That's just the sort of story to make my article interesting. Lord Wentwater won't mind my using it?"

"Good Lord, no. Just don't put the scandals of the last century or so into print." Lady Josephine went on to tell a scurrilous tale of her great-uncle's involvement with Lillie Langtry and Bertie, Prince of Wales. "Henry has rather reacted against that sort of thing," she said. "In some ways he's more Victorian than the Victorians. I do sometimes worry that he won't be happy with Annabel."

"She seems quite a sedate sort of person," Daisy said tactfully.

"But *so* much younger. If only my chump of a nephew had not invited Lord Stephen!"

Daisy made a token effort to avoid the confidences she was dying to hear. "I haven't been able to place Lord Stephen, though the name Astwick is familiar. Who exactly is he?"

"The younger brother of the Marquis of Brinbury. Always a bit of a black sheep, I'm afraid. In fact rumour has it his father disinherited him, but he made good in the City, though Hugh doesn't trust him an inch."

"Sir Hugh jolly well ought to know."

"Hugh is the knowingest man in the City," agreed his proud wife. "He'd have put paid to Wilfred inviting Lord Stephen if he'd been consulted."

"Wilfred invited him? How odd! I wouldn't think they'd have anything in common."

"High living," said Lady Josephine wisely, "but if you ask me, Marjorie put him up to it. She's potty about the fellow, got it into her silly head she's madly in love with him. Thank heaven he don't show a particle of interest in the girl. If only I could say the same of Annabel! But that's beside the point. Let's go up to Queen Elizabeth's chamber. It hasn't been changed since she spent her two nights at Wentwater."

Her curiosity frustrated, Daisy concentrated on matters historical. The notebook filled with mysterious curlicues she hoped she'd be able to decipher later. As they moved up through the house, she learned about the shocking split in the family when an eldest son fought for Parliament against the Royalists; the daughters who had ended up as old maids because their father had spent their dowries on building the new wings; and the Regency bride who had eloped with a highwayman.

Lady Josephine frowned. "On second thought, perhaps you'd better leave that one out, Daisy. It hits a bit close to home. Not that I mean to suggest there's the slightest chance of Annabel's succumbing," she hastened to add. "But one can't deny that Stephen Astwick is a handsome man, with an insinuating sort of charm—and not a scruple in the world. His name is constantly in the scandal sheets, linked with those of ladies who ought to know better."

"Annabel eloping with Lord Stephen?" Daisy asked in astonishment, turning from the turret window where she had been watching a rider on a bay horse canter across the park.

"They were acquaintances some years ago, I gather, and now he is really pursuing her in the most determined and ungentlemanly way, quite blatant. I'm afraid poor Henry is at a loss what to do. He can't throw Brinbury's brother out of the house as if he were some plebeian bounder. They belong to the same clubs!"

"Gosh, what a ghastly mess."

"Mind you, Henry is far too gallant to mistrust his wife. In fact, I'm not at all sure he's aware of what's going on under his nose. My brother has always been the impassive, stoical sort, you know, impossible to guess what he's thinking. I feel I ought to open his eyes, but Hugh has absolutely forbidden it."

Tears had sprung to the plump matron's eyes and her second chin quivered. Daisy patted her arm and said soothingly, if meaninglessly, "I'm sure Lord Wentwater has everything under control, Lady Josephine."

"Oh, my dear, I should not burden you with our troubles, but it is such a relief to get it all off my chest and simply nothing shocks you modern young things. There, now let us forget all about it. Where were we? Oh yes, this is the very room where Charles II was caught *in flagrante* with the then Lady Wentwater's young cousin. He was not invited again."

She prattled on. As Daisy took down her words, she resolved to keep a close eye on the inhabitants of Wentwater Court. To a would-be novelist, the intrigues of the past were not half so intriguing as those of the present.

Some time later, from yet another turret window, Daisy saw the skaters straggling up the hill towards the house. Lady Josephine glanced out and consulted her wristwatch. "Heavens, how time passes. We must go down if you'd like to see the ballroom before lunch."

"Yes, please. Oh, that's odd. Surely Lord Stephen isn't

going off somewhere just before lunch?" A grey Lanchester on its way down the drive had stopped. As Daisy watched, Astwick crossed to it and spoke to the driver.

"I expect he's sending his manservant off on some errand again," said Lady Josephine, irritated. "My maid tells me the fellow is gone more than he's here. I only wish he'd take his master with him!"

Dismissing the unpleasant subject, she took Daisy down to the ballroom, chattering about the splendid formal dances of her youth. The vast ballroom was shrouded in dust covers. Daisy decided not to request that it be exhumed for her to photograph. There was enough of interest in the older part of the house.

Lady Josephine sighed. "Of course, you young things prefer nightclubs these days. Well, my dear, I've shown you the best. Do feel free to wander about by yourself, and I'll try to answer any questions you may have."

"You've been perfectly sweet, Lady Josephine." She riffled through her notebook as they started down the stairs. "I've got loads of material here to start with, and some topping ideas for photographs. I'd like to try a shot of the family in front of the fireplace in the Great Hall, if you think Lord Wentwater will agree."

"I'll speak to him," her ladyship promised.

In the drawing-room, a long, beautifully proportioned room furnished in Regency style, they found several members of the household already gathered. James, with Fenella at his side, was dispensing drinks. He mixed a gin-and-tonic for his aunt, and Daisy requested a small medium-dry sherry.

"I can't drink a cocktail before lunch or I might as well chuck in the towel as far as getting any work done this afternoon is concerned," she said.

"There's no focussing a camera when you can't focus your eyes," James agreed with a grin.

"And it's difficult enough to read my shorthand at the

best of times. Thank you." Taking the glass, she looked around the room.

Nearby Wilfred, his voice a fashionable drawl, was recounting to his stepmother the plot, such as it was, of Al Jolson's musical comedy, *Bombo*. As Daisy watched, he wet his whistle with a gulp from his nearly full cocktail glass. She doubted it was his first. Annabel's sherry glass was also nearly full. She seemed to have forgotten it, standing with bowed head, either listening to Wilfred with more interest than his tale warranted or lost in her own thoughts.

By the fireplace, Sir Hugh and Phillip chatted together—politics, Daisy guessed, hearing mention of Bonar Law and Lloyd George. Marjorie stood by looking bored. She was smoking a cigarette in a long tortoise-shell holder and her cocktail glass held the remains of a pink gin. Daisy guessed that Phillip's glass contained dry sherry. She knew he preferred sweet, but he considered it unmasculine and always asked for dry in company. His nose wrinkled just a trifle as he sipped, confirming her guess.

Lady Josephine went to join her husband, and after a moment Marjorie drifted away from that group. Coming over to the drinks cabinet, she handed her brother her glass.

"Fill it up, Jimmy, old bean."

"It had better be a small one," James warned. "Father will be here any minute."

"Don't be such a wet blanket." She drew ostentatiously on her cigarette and blew a stream of smoke over her shoulder.

Daisy hastily retreated from the prospect of a family squabble. She went over to Annabel and Wilfred. Annabel looked up and smiled absently.

"Have you seen the new show at the Apollo, Miss Dalrymple?" Wilfred asked.

"Daisy, please. No, not yet. Is it good?"

"Oh, pretty tolerable, don't you know. The finale was

rather a"—his voice died away as Lord Stephen entered the drawing room—"rather a nifty do," he finished with an effort, a gaze burning with resentment fixed on the older man.

Making some casual response to Wilfred's words, Daisy watched Lord Stephen. He went up to the drinks table, where Marjorie greeted him with a languishing look.

"Lord Stephen always has a dry martini," she instructed her brother.

"Make it a gin-and-twist, if you don't mind, old chap," Lord Stephen promptly requested.

"Right-oh." James gave his pouting sister a malicious glance and handed over the drink. He sounded malicious, too, as he continued, "I say, Astwick, would you mind asking my stepmama if she'd like a refill?"

"My pleasure." The bland tone was belied by the predatory curl of his thin lips, the gleam in his hard eyes. As he approached, Wilfred blanched. "Must have a word with Aunt Jo," he muttered, and sheered off. Why on earth had he invited the man if he detested him? Daisy wondered.

"Miss Dalrymple." Lord Stephen nodded to her but his attention was already on the countess. "Annabel, my dear, Beddowe sent me to find out if your drink needs refreshing, but I see his solicitude was in vain." He ran his fingertips across the back of her hand, holding the still-full glass.

The amber liquid shimmered as her hand trembled. "Yes, thank you. I have all I want."

"All? Few can claim to be so lucky as to possess *all* that they desire," he said with a meaningful smile. "I know I do not."

"But I do, Lord Stephen." She flashed him a glance under her long lashes. Daisy couldn't tell whether she was just flirting, trying to rebuff him, or deliberately leading him on by playing hard to get.

"Come, now, didn't you promise to call me Stephen? Miss Dalrymple will think you don't count me your friend.

I assure you, Miss Dalrymple, Annabel and I are very good friends from long ago, aren't we, my dear?" He laid his hand on her arm.

"Yes, Stephen." Her voice quivered with suppressed emotion. She neither shook off his hand nor moved away.

CHAPTER 3

To Daisy's relief, Geoffrey came up and broke the charged tension between Annabel and Lord Stephen. His large, solid, unambiguous presence made Lord Stephen's elegant figure appear slight and rather effete. He brought with him a wholesome breath of fresh air.

"Have you been riding?" Daisy asked. "I thought I saw you from one of the turret windows."

"Yes, I had a first-rate gallop," he said with enthusiasm, his face brightening.

"Isn't it dangerous to gallop when the snow lies so deep?" asked Annabel. Lord Stephen's hand slipped from her arm as she turned towards her youngest stepson.

Geoffrey blushed. "Not when you know the country." His tongue once loosened, he continued, "If you know where the hidden obstacles are, ditches and such, it's absolutely topping. The air's so clear you can see for miles. No mud to make for heavy going, and you don't have to worry about crushing crops. Of course, it's not every horse can cope with snow, but my Galahad's a splendid beast."

Half-listening to a recital of Galahad's finer points, Daisy saw Lord Wentwater come in. At once Marjorie furtively put down her drink and stubbed out her cigarette. Wilfred also disposed hurriedly of his glass. Their father didn't appear to notice.

Good manners demanded that Daisy report to him on her tour of the house. She slipped away and crossed to his side. Head bent, he listened with civil interest, then gave his permission to use the stories Lady Josephine had told her.

"No doubt every family has skeletons in its cupboards," he said with a wry smile.

The butler came in just then to announce that luncheon was served. Lord Wentwater escorted Daisy into the dining-room and seated her beside him. Since he was so cordial and approachable, she decided not to wait for Lady Josephine to mention her request to him.

"Would you mind if I took a photograph of you and your family in the Great Hall?" she asked as the soup was ladled out. "I think my readers would like to see who lives in the house now, don't you?"

"Probably," he said dryly and paused for a considering moment. Daisy held her breath, afraid he judged her request mere pandering to vulgar curiosity. "I don't see why not. We'll confine it to those of us who are descended from my disreputable ancestors, thus avoiding the thorny question of whether Miss Petrie ought to appear."

And excluding his wife, Daisy noted. Did he fear that by the time the article was printed, Annabel might have run off with Lord Stephen? If so, he gave no sign of it, asking with unaltered calm, "Will it suit you to take your photograph shortly before dinner? I'll ask everyone to come down early."

"That will be perfect," she said gratefully.

A hush had fallen over the table in tribute to a superb

cream of leek soup. Lord Wentwater announced that he expected his children, and invited his sister, to be present in the Great Hall at half-past seven that evening to have their photographs taken. Amid the nods and murmurs, Daisy thought she saw a hurt expression pass across Annabel's face, at the far end of the table. She couldn't be sure, for Lord Stephen said something to the countess and she turned her head to respond.

The two continued to talk as the soup was followed by Dover sole with lemon-butter. Marjorie, on Lord Stephen's other side, attempted several times to interrupt the tête-à-tête. Rebuffed, she lapsed into sulky silence. Geoffrey, too, had relapsed into taciturnity, devoting his attention to his food.

It was worthy of devotion, and Daisy enjoyed every bite. Soon enough she'd be back in Chelsea subsisting largely on omelettes and bread and cheese.

As she ate, she answered the earl's questions about what he politely termed her writing career. She told him of the bits and pieces published in gossip columns, the two short articles bought by *The Queen*, the daring proposal to *Town and Country* that led to her presence at Wentwater.

"I find your ambition and your industry admirable, Miss Dalrymple," he said, to her surprise. "Too many young people in comfortable circumstances fritter away their time in the pursuit of pleasure." His gaze moved from Wilfred, chattering nonsense rather too loudly to a giggling Fenella, to Marjorie, who had by now set up an unconvincing flirtation with Phillip.

Daisy came to the conclusion that Lord Wentwater was not half so oblivious of what was going on around him as he chose to appear. His children's behaviour disturbed him, but to Daisy the interesting question was what, if anything, did he mean to do about Annabel and Lord Stephen?

*   *   *

After lunch, Daisy spent the short remaining hours of daylight taking interior photographs, a slow business with long exposures. As the early winter dusk fell, she carried her equipment across the gallery above the Great Hall towards her bedroom. By that time, she'd have been jolly glad of Phillip's help to lug it all about.

She heard footsteps below, and then James's voice. "Looking for my stepmama?" he asked, a definite sly malice in his tone.

Moving to the balustrade, Daisy glanced down.

Lord Stephen was regarding James with a saturnine air. "Lady Wentwater is not presiding over the tea table this afternoon."

"You might find her in the conservatory."

"Ah, yes, I expect it reminds her of Italy."

"You knew her in Italy, didn't you?" James's eagerness was obvious. "Won't you tell me what . . . ?"

"That would hardly suit my purpose," Lord Stephen said dryly. He sauntered off.

His mouth tight with annoyance, James strode away in the opposite direction.

Daisy pondered the brief scene as she continued on her way. Their innocuous words had been freighted with meaning, unpleasant meaning. James must bitterly resent his beautiful stepmother to keep throwing Lord Stephen at her, regardless of his father's feelings. Stephen Astwick was amused by James's ploys, but quite content to take advantage of them. He had some end of his own in view, doubtless nefarious.

What had happened in Italy? Daisy regretted that she'd probably never find out.

Skipping afternoon tea downstairs, she settled in her room to transcribe her shorthand notes on the typewriter, before she forgot what they said. Mabel brought her a cup of tea, and Daisy asked the girl to draw her a bath in time for taking photos before dinner. Not that she was not perfectly capable of running her own bath, but it was pleasant to have a maid at her service, like the old days before her father's death. Besides, Mabel would coordinate matters if Fenella also wanted a bath.

Fenella, she mused—what did Fenella think of her fiancé's stepmother? One day shy little Fenella would be Lady Wentwater, having to cope with a dowager countess not much older than herself.

Turning back to her work, Daisy forced herself to concentrate. When she finished her notes, she wearily began to collect the picture-taking gear together again. She was certainly earning the imaginary Carswell's fee.

Someone knocked on the door.

"Hullo, old sport," Phillip called plaintively. "Have you shut yourself up in there for good?"

"No, you're just in time." She opened the door and loaded him with tripod and camera. "I want to set everything up in the hall in advance."

Always obliging, he went down with her and, with the aid of a footman, moved a heavy oak refectory table aside to set up the tripod. Patiently he shifted it from place to place as she chose the best spot for it.

"Those will have to go." She waved at the half-dozen solid, studded-leather seventeenth-century chairs grouped around the fire.

Phillip obliged.

Marjorie wandered into the hall, looking disconsolate. "Have you seen Lord Stephen?" she asked.

"Not for hours," Daisy said. "Would you mind standing over there by the fireplace for a minute while I set the focus?"

Marjorie drifted over and stood drooping, her scarlet mouth turned down. "I can't find him anywhere. I suppose he's chasing my dear stepmother as usual. I can't imagine what he sees in her."

"She's beautiful," said Phillip, surprised.

Marjorie threw him a glance full of scorn. "But he's a sophisticated man of the world and she's so frightfully old-fashioned. Do you know, Daisy, she doesn't smoke, hardly drinks, and doesn't even dance the tango, or fox-trot, or *anything!* Do you think he's trying to make me jealous?"

Phillip snorted and Daisy said hurriedly, "If so, I shouldn't let him see he's succeeding, if I were you. Three inches to the left, please, Phil. That's it, just right. Thanks, Marjorie."

"Sometimes I almost hate him," she moaned. "Maybe he's in the library. I haven't looked there yet."

As she sped off towards the west wing, Phillip said, "Poor little beast, but I'd run for cover if she hunted me the way she does him. A fellow likes to make the pace."

"I hardly think he's running for cover," Daisy contradicted, taking a last look through the viewfinder. "What do you think of him?"

"Of Astwick? He's a good egg, put me onto something very nice in the way of South American silver."

"Oh dear!"

"What d'you mean, oh dear? Confound it, Daisy, you can't pretend you know the first thing about the stock market."

"No." She was too fond of him not to warn him. "It's just that Lady Josephine happened to mention that Sir Hugh doesn't trust Lord Stephen."

"Oh, Menton! The old bird made his pile years ago. He can afford to be conservative, but believe me, one don't rake in the shekels without taking risks," Phillip assured her, but she was glad to see he seemed a trifle uneasy despite his vehemence.

Daisy went upstairs to bathe and change for dinner. The bathroom was immense, at least compared to the cupboard that went by the name in the little house she shared with Lucy. It was dominated by a massive Victorian bathtub, from which rose fragrant steam. Raised several inches above the linoleum floor on feet clawed like the talons of a bird of prey, the bath had brass taps in the shape of eagles' heads.

"They's all different, miss," said Mabel, giggling. "One bathroom has lions, one has dolphins, and there's even one with dragons' heads! I put in the verbena bath-salts, I hope that's all right. The water's that hard we have to use summat."

"I love verbena."

"Me too, miss. Here's your towel, warming on the rail. Will you need help dressing, miss?"

"No, thank you, but I may need help climbing out of the bath!"

"There's a little step stool, see. India-rubber feet it's got, and rubber on top, so's you won't slip. I'll put it right here by the bath mat. But just call out if you needs me, miss. I'll be just through there in Miss Petrie's room soon as I've hung up your frock." Indicating a door opposite the one to Daisy's room, she departed.

Daisy checked the corridor door. It was locked, with a big, old-fashioned key left in the keyhole—probably it was used when there were more guests in the house and not enough bathrooms to go round. She slipped out of her flannel dressing-gown, dropped it on the cork-seated chair in the corner, and plunged into the luxuriously scented hot water.

Getting out was difficult less because of the depth of the bath than because she was enjoying it so much. The water cooled very slowly. At last, hearing Fenella's voice next door, she dragged herself from the heavenly warmth, dried quickly, shivering, and returned to the bedroom. At her request, Mabel had laid out her old grey silk evening frock.

She'd be handling magnesium powder this evening and didn't want to risk stray sparks holing her best dress.

Wearing the grey silk depressed Daisy. Bought after Gervaise was killed in the trenches, it had seen service when her darling Michael's ambulance drove over a land mine, and again when her father succumbed to the 'flu epidemic.

She caught sight of her gloomy expression in the mirror and pulled a face at herself. There was enough despondency at Wentwater Court without her adding to it. Her amber necklace, the colour of her hair, both brightened and smartened the dress. She powdered and lipsticked and went down to the hall.

The Beddowe brothers were already there, all in black-and-white evening togs, yet quite distinct from each other. James, heir to the earldom, though impeccably turned out, appeared very much the stalwart country gentleman in comparison with the elegantly languid Wilfred. Geoffrey, taller and broader than his brothers, seemed constrained by his clothes, as if he'd be more comfortable in safari kit, striding about some outpost of Empire. He asked Daisy about her equipment, and she was explaining the magnesium flashlight when Marjorie joined them.

Marjorie's décolleté dress, violently patterned in black and white, could have been designed—and had certainly been chosen—to stand out in a group photograph. Daisy sighed. She had hoped to portray the dignity of the Beddowe family in their ancestral hall, but the eye of any reader of *Town and Country* would be instantly drawn to that jazzy dress.

It was too late to ask her to change. The grandfather clock by the stairs struck the half hour and the earl arrived.

He looked around, his gaze pausing on his daughter's frock, then moving on. "Annabel's not here yet?" he said. "Nor my sister? We'll wait a minute or two if you don't mind, Miss Dalrymple."

Daisy agreed, surprised. She thought he had deliberately

excluded Annabel, and she was sure Annabel had the same impression. But perhaps he merely meant that his wife had come down before him and he had expected her to be present. At any rate, when Lady Josephine arrived with Sir Hugh, he called to his sister to join the group by the fireplace without further mention of Annabel.

Arranging her subjects, whose height bore no relation to their importance, was no easy matter, but Daisy had worked it out beforehand and soon had them posed. She opened the shutter and detonated the percussive cap in the trough of flashlight powder.

A blinding glare lit the hall to the rafters.

"My hat!" exclaimed Wilfred.

"Drat!" Blinking against an after image of six startled white faces, Daisy hastily closed the shutter. Clouds of magnesium smoke drifted through the hall. "I'm rather afraid that was too much light. The film will be frightfully overexposed."

"The professional touch." Phillip, grinning, strolled in with Fenella. "Try again, old thing, but mind you don't blow up the house."

Daisy gave him a cross glance and se   or a second shot. This time the magnesium powder fizzled damply. Where was Carswell when she needed him?

Her third effort was perfect. "But I'd like to take a couple more, to make sure," she said hastily as everyone began to move.

They settled back into their places. Marjorie looked furious, Lady Josephine distressed, Wilfred nervous, and James smug. Such a range of emotions could hardly be explained by a request to stand still, Daisy thought. She turned her head and saw that Annabel had entered the room, with Lord Stephen.

When she turned back, her subjects' faces had smoothed into the vacuous expressions worn by the vast majority of people having their portraits taken. She shot another picture, wound on the film, and prepared the flash for the final exposure.

Lord Stephen's insinuating voice came from behind her. "You're shivering, Annabel. You are cold."

"No, I'm quite all right."

"Nonsense! There's a beastly gale of a draught in here. Come into the drawing-room."

A pause, then Annabel said in a colourless tone, "Yes, Stephen."

Daisy heard their departing footsteps as she pressed the button.

"Better take one more," James suggested. "My eyebrow twitched just as the flash went off."

"It might be a good idea, if no one objects," said Daisy, though she knew he was just trying to make mischief, to leave Annabel and Lord Stephen alone together for a few more minutes. She was a bit anxious about her photos, and not at all sure the extra money was worth the trouble.

Dinner was as delicious and as uncomfortable a meal as lunch had been. After coffee, Sir Hugh repaired to the smoking-room for a cigar, and Lord Wentwater to his study to write letters.

In the drawing-room, Wilfred said to Phillip, "What do you say to shoving the balls about a bit, Petrie? But you play a dashed sight better than I do. You'll have to give me a hundred."

"All right, old chap," said Phillip with his usual good nature. "Though billiards ain't exactly my game, you know. I rather prefer more active sports."

"Wilfred would look less wishy-washy," said his aunt, dispassionately censorious, "if he took up an outdoor pursuit other than attending the races."

"Oh, I say, Aunt Jo!"

"In my view, keeping fit is of the utmost importance," Lord Stephen put in, running a preening hand over his black hair. "Besides a regular regimen of Swedish gymnastics, I rise every day at dawn, take a cold bath followed by outdoor exercise—skating at present—and then a hot bath before breakfast."

"Dawn's not that early at this time of year," Wilfred muttered in Daisy's ear.

Marjorie gazed up at Lord Stephen with fluttering eyelashes. "You must be frightfully strong," she breathed.

"A cold bath and skating at dawn, eh?" Phillip visibly suppressed a shudder. "Sounds like one's jolly old schooldays and I must say one felt pretty good then, up to anything. I'll give it a try."

Daisy considered it highly unlikely he'd do anything so uncomfortable. He and Wilfred went off to the billiard-room.

Fenella was at the piano, James turning the pages for her. "Why don't you play some dance music?" Marjorie suggested brightly. "Do you know that new fox-trot, 'Count the Days,' Fenella? Or we could see what's on the wireless, or put a record on the gramophone. We can roll back the carpet. Wouldn't you like to dance, Lord Stephen?"

"Certainly, if Annabel will grant me a waltz."

"Oh, no, Stephen, I ... I must not neglect my other guests. I have scarcely had a chance to talk to Daisy all day."

She shot a glance of desperate appeal at Daisy, who promptly moved to a love seat and patted the place beside her. "Do come and sit here, Annabel. I want to ask you about ... about the gardens," she improvised. She was beginning to believe Annabel accepted Lord Stephen's attentions because she was afraid of him.

Marjorie managed to corner Lord Stephen. "The waltz

is frightfully old-fashioned," she said, and prattled on about the latest dances from America, the camel-walk, the toboggan, the Chicago. Geoffrey was talking to Lady Josephine. Daisy overheard snippets of both conversations as she chatted with Annabel. It turned out she had picked a good subject, for Annabel had missed English flowers while in Italy and took a great interest in Wentwater's gardens. Gradually she relaxed and even grew enthusiastic.

The quiet background of piano music changed as Fenella and James sang a sentimental song together, a tentative soprano and a robust baritone.

"Charming," Lady Josephine applauded.

"It's called 'Lovely Lucerne,' Aunt Jo, a new hit that's not from America for a change."

"Do give us another song," she requested.

James set a sheet of music on the stand and they launched into "The Raggle-Taggle Gypsies." Paling, Annabel lost the thread of what she was saying. Lord Stephen stared at her, his gaze at once avid and cold. With a smirk, James began the second verse:

> *It was late last night when my lord came home*
> *Enquiring for his lady-o.*
> *The servants said on every hand,*
> *She's gone—*

"Enough!" commanded Lady Josephine.

The innocent Fenella stopped with her mouth open, bewildered.

Annabel jumped up. "Excuse me," she said in a stifled voice. "I . . . It's been a tiring day. I'm going up now." She fled.

"James, I wish to play bridge," Lady Josephine declared. "You may partner me. Has Drew set out the cards?"

"Yes, Aunt Jo, as always."

Fenella and Geoffrey did not play. Marjorie was roped in, but Lord Stephen begged off. Daisy was afraid she'd be asked to take a hand, but Sir Hugh came in just in time to save her.

As the foursome moved to the card table, Lord Stephen said, "I believe I'll be off to bed, too. Dawn rising, don't you know." He sauntered out, unhurried yet purposeful.

Dismayed, Daisy felt she ought to do something but couldn't think what. Then Fenella turned to her with a plaintive, "I don't understand, Daisy. Why . . . ?"

"I suppose Lady Josephine doesn't like that song," Daisy said quickly, and asked for news of her family at home in Worcestershire.

Phillip and Wilfred returned from the billiard-room shortly thereafter, Phillip having won even with the agreed handicap. He proposed a game of rummy. Geoffrey had disappeared, but the four of them played until it was time for the late weather forecast on the wireless. The bridge game broke up at the same time and they all listened to a promise of another day of freezing temperatures before retiring for the night.

On her way to bed, Daisy went to the library to borrow the book about Wentwater Court recommended by Lady Josephine. Though the evening had ended peacefully, it had been fraught with overwrought emotions, and she hoped a little of the duller kind of history would send her straight to sleep. Through the open connecting door to Lord Wentwater's study she saw the earl sitting in a wing chair by the fire, his face set in stern, melancholy lines. In his hands he warmed a brandy glass and a half-full decanter stood at his elbow.

So perhaps Lord Wentwater was not indifferent to Stephen Astwick's pursuit of his young wife. Daisy wished he would hurry up and decide how to put an end to it.

*   *   *

In the morning, Daisy rose with the sun, which, as Wilfred had pointed out, was not particularly early at the beginning of January. Skipping the cold bath and postponing the outdoor exercise, she dressed warmly and went down to the breakfast parlour, a pleasantly sunny east-facing room. James, Fenella, and Sir Hugh were there before her. Sir Hugh lowered his *Financial Times* momentarily to wish her a good morning before retreating once more behind that bastion.

She helped herself to kedgeree from the buffet on the sideboard and joined them at the table.

"Will you skate with us this morning, Daisy?" Fenella asked. "I know you're frightfully busy but this weather may not last and we don't get such spiffing freezes very often."

"Yes, I'd like to, if I can borrow skates?"

"We have a cupboardful," James assured her. "There's bound to be something to fit you."

"Jolly good. I'll finish off the roll of film in the camera down at the lake, and spend the rest of the morning developing my pictures."

Sir Hugh, emerging from his newspaper, told her he owned shares in the Eastman Kodak company and asked about the developing and printing process. Daisy explained as she ate. James and Fenella lingered over their coffee until she had finished her breakfast, then took her to look for a pair of skates.

Outside, the air was crisp and still. Daisy couldn't resist leaving a footprint or two in the glistening untrodden snow beside the path. It crunched underfoot.

James carried the skating boots down the hill for her as she was laden with camera and tripod. While she set them up, he and Fenella sat on the bench and put on their skates. They circled slowly at the near end of the lake, waiting for her.

"Go ahead," she called, already chilled fingers fumbling at the stiff catch that attached the camera to the tripod. "I'll be with you in half a mo."

Waving to her, they joined hands and whizzed off towards the bridge. As they reached it, James yelled, "Stop!"

They swerved to a halt beneath the arch. James moved cautiously forward into the black shadow cast by the low sun. And then Fenella screamed.

CHAPTER 4

As scream after scream shredded the peaceful morning, Daisy raced along the lakeside path towards the bridge. Stepping down cautiously from the bank onto the ice, she was under the stone arch before she saw what had stopped James and Fenella in their tracks.

In the shadow of the bridge, the ice was shattered, and in the inky water floated a man, facedown.

With a gasp of shock, Daisy turned to Fenella. "Be quiet," she ordered sharply. "Don't look."

The ear-piercing screams ended in a sob, half buried in James's chest as he pulled his fiancée into his arms. He glared at Daisy over her shoulder.

"She's upset!"

"So am I, but hysterics won't help. Send her away."

He nodded sober understanding. "Fenella, I want you to go up to the house and tell Father, or Sir Hugh if you can't find him. Come and take your skates off. I suppose I'd better get a boathook," he added to Daisy.

"Yes, though I'm sure it's too late."

Finding the camera in her hands, Daisy tried to regard the gruesome scene as a problem in photography. The shadow was less deep now that her eyes were accustomed to it, and on the far side the jagged edge of the hole was in sunlight. Her shaking hands steadied as she moved around taking shots from different angles, venturing as close to the dark water as she dared. The ice, roughened by skate blades, felt solid beneath her feet, but of course the man must be much heavier than she was.

The man. Though she kept calling him that to herself, she knew who he was. The tight-waisted, tight-cuffed leather jacket, ballooned with air, supported his torso and arms on the surface. His legs dangled invisible below. His head was just submerged, the slick black hair a darker patch, the nape of his neck white and strangely defenceless in death.

Lord Stephen.

She began to feel sick, picturing him scrabbling desperately at the ice for nonexistent handholds. Though he had been one of the least likeable people she had ever met, she wouldn't wish such a horror on her worst enemy.

James returned from the boathouse. He spread some coconut matting on the ice to give a footing, then, in grim silence, he caught the back of the collar with a gaff, the waistband with a boathook. Awkwardly, one pole in each hand, he hauled the body to the edge of the hole.

"Sorry, I can't manage it by myself."

Daisy hung the camera around her neck, took the gaff pole, shut her eyes, and pulled.

"Lift a bit."

She obeyed. As the body came free, she staggered backwards, slipped, and sat down.

"Oof!"

"Are you all right? I say, Daisy, you're a jolly good sport." James stooped to unhook the gaff and the boathook, and turned the body over. "Astwick, poor brighter. Dead as mutton. I'll get him onto the bank."

Recovering her breath, she gathered herself together and followed. As James dragged him across the ice, Lord Stephen's limp feet in their skating boots flopped pathetically sideways. With a shudder, Daisy averted her eyes.

"Hullo, there's a great gash on his forehead. Look, here on the temple. It's hard to see because his face is all blotchy. He must have knocked himself out on the ice when he fell through. I wondered why the poor devil hadn't pulled himself out."

"He wouldn't have known he was drowning then," she said, saved from her ghastly imaginings. The sound of voices drew her attention up the hill. "Here comes your father."

Lord Wentwater, Sir Hugh, and Phillip joined them. In a solemn circle they stood staring down at the mortal remains of Lord Stephen Astwick, all except Daisy, who watched the men.

The earl must surely feel relief at the very least. His face showed nothing but the natural grave concern of a man whose guest has met with a fatal accident on his premises. Sir Hugh frowned, possibly foreseeing the unpleasantness of enquiries into the victim's City dealings. Had he been more involved in Astwick's business affairs than he was ready to admit?

Phillip regarded the body with the mingled curiosity and distaste of one to whom corpses are nothing new. Of all the young men Daisy knew who had gone through the War in France, he had emerged least affected, perhaps saved by a lack of imagination.

And James, who had done his brief military service safe in a ministry in London, was morose. His plot against his stepmother was now missing an essential part.

Sir Hugh was the first to stir, the first to speak. "We must send for the police."

Lord Wentwater's head jerked up. "No!"

"I'm afraid so, Henry."

"Dr. Fennis will write out a death certificate . . ."

"Precisely: death by drowning. No chance of even you persuading him Astwick died in bed of heart failure. Any unexpected death requires an inquest, especially a violent death, however obviously accidental, and the coroner will require a police report."

"Ye gods, I can't let Wetherby pry into my affairs!"

"Wetherby?" asked Sir Hugh.

"The Chief Constable," James explained. "He and Father have a running feud on every subject under the sun. Colonel Wetherby would revel in a chance to tear us to pieces."

"Surely it needn't go beyond your local johnny," said Phillip. "Your local constable, I mean. One look ought to be enough to get him to swear to an accident at the inquest."

"Job Ruddle?" James laughed. "You've got something there, Petrie. The Ruddles have been family retainers for centuries."

His father shook his head. "He'd have to write a report, and one way or another it would reach Wetherby's ears."

"It's not the kind of thing that can be hushed up," Sir Hugh reaffirmed. "What I could do is telephone the Commissioner of the Metropolitan Police. He's an old friend, and maybe he can send down some discreet C.I.D. officer from Scotland Yard. I don't know what the protocol is, but it might be possible to keep it from the local police."

"Try it." Lord Wentwater's shoulders slumped as he accepted the necessity of calling in the authorities. "Thank you, Hugh. James, see to having . . . this removed to the boathouse. We don't want anyone coming across it unexpectedly."

"Yes, sir."

Sir Hugh looked down at the dead man, sprawled on

his back at their feet. "I believe we ought to have some photographs, before he's moved again. Miss Dalrymple, do you feel up to it?"

"Good Lord, no!" said Phillip, belatedly protective. "Hang it all you can't ask a young lady to do anything so bally beastly. Daisy, you shouldn't be here at all."

His protest erased her qualms. "Don't be a silly ass, Phillip. Of course I can do it. I helped James pull him out."

He stood guard over her like an anxious mother hen until he sent him to fetch the tripod from the other side of the lake. As she finished the roll of film, James returned with a couple of under-gardeners, one all agog, the other timorous. They laid out a tarpaulin like a shroud on the snow beside the path.

The body was a person again, not just a pattern in the viewfinder. Daisy turned away. "I'm going up to develop these now," she said.

"I'll come with you, old thing, unless you need a hand, Beddowe?"

"No, go ahead."

Leaving James and the gardeners to their grisly task, they set off up the path.

"Jolly rotten luck," Phillip observed, "having a guest drown in one's ornamental water. One can't blame Wentwater for being sick as a dog over it. I dare say Lady Wentwater won't be any too bobbish, either. Astwick was an old friend of hers, one gathers."

"So he told me." Daisy marvelled at the way the currents of emotion swirling through Wentwater Court had apparently washed right past Phillip's oblivious head.

"Rather bad form, having the busies in the house," he went on. "I wonder if the mater'd want me to take Fenella home?"

"Don't leave, Phil." She felt a need for his familiar, comforting presence, even if he was a bit of a chump. "I expect the police will want to talk to Fenella, as she was one of those who found the body. She might even have to attend the inquest."

"Lord, wouldn't that just put the cat among the pigeons! The gov'nor will have my head on a platter if I let her appear in court."

"I'm sure they could call her as a witness even if you did take her home. But she didn't see anything that James and I didn't see too. They won't need her evidence."

"Right-ho." He sighed with relief. "I'll ring the parents up on the telephone, but unless they insist or Fenella gets the wind up, we won't leg it."

On reaching the house, Daisy retired to Sydney Beddowe's scullery-darkroom. A narrow, windowless room with whitewashed walls and a stone flagged floor, it was lit by a shadeless lightbulb dangling by its flex from the ceiling. At the far end was a zinc sink with a cold-water tap and slate draining boards. One long wall was taken up by a stained wooden counter where the equipment, old-fashioned but in good condition, was ranged, including an electric lamp with a red bulb. Empty shelves on the opposite wall had doubtless held supplies.

Absorbed in her work, Daisy managed to forget for a couple of hours the unpleasant end of the unpleasant Lord Stephen Astwick.

Sydney's enlarger was still in perfect working order. Daisy decided to make prints of the pictures the police might want to see. As she set them out to dry, some of the horror returned. Nonetheless, she was rather pleased with the way they had come out. She had succeeded in shading the lens from the glare of sun on snow and ice. Most of both close-up and more distant shots were clear, with jolly good contrast. Lucy would be proud of her.

With a puzzled frown, she took a closer look at one of the pictures. Those marks on the broken edge of the ice, almost as if . . .

A knock on the door interrupted her train of thought. "Miss?"

"It's all right, you can come in."

The door opened two inches and an eye appeared. "I don't want to spoil your pitchers, miss."

"Thank you, but really, it's all right now."

Gingerly, a footman stepped into the scullery. "Luncheon will be served in quarter of an hour, miss, and the detective's asking to see you."

"A Scotland Yard man?" Daisy asked, flipping electrical switches to Off. "Here already? Or is it the local police?"

"From Scotland Yard, miss, a Chief Inspector. Seems he was in Hampshire on business anyway. He's already seen Miss Petrie and Master James—Lord Beddowe, that is." He stepped back to let her precede him through the door and along the dimly lit corridor.

"Well, I don't want to keep him waiting, but I'm starved. Is he lunching with the family?"

"Crikey, miss, I shouldn't think so! I mean, a p'leeceman's not a real gentleman, is he? But you better ask Mr. Drew." He dodged past her to hold open the baize door from the servants' quarters.

The butler was in the dining-room, casting a last glance over the table before announcing lunch. "His lordship has not intimated to me that he wishes the detective to join the family," he said austerely.

"A Chief Inspector won't be frightfully happy to be expected to eat in the servants' hall! I suppose you'll give him a tray in . . . wherever he is?"

"The Blue Salon, miss. The detective has not requested refreshment."

"The poor chap's bound to be glad of a bite to eat. I'm sure Lord Wentwater won't mind if you take him some soup and sandwiches. Tell him I'll be with him right after lunch." She would willingly have shared the policeman's sandwiches, but she wanted to see how Lord Stephen's demise affected the company.

Fenella appeared to have recovered from the shock of finding the body. James and Phillip sat on either side of her, treating her like a piece of priceless porcelain. She basked in their solicitude.

Marjorie was absent. "The poor prune came unstrung," Wilfred told Daisy, seated beside him. "Dr. Fennis doped her up. Doesn't know when she's well off," he added in an undertone. "Astwick was a rotten swine."

"I can't say I cared for him myself, but he's dead now."

"*De mortuis,* et cetera." He pulled a face. "Hypocritical bunkum."

Since Wilfred was distinctly cheerful, the smell of gin on his breath was presumably not from drowning his sorrows but from celebrating. Lady Josephine was also in sunny spirits which, whenever she glanced at her thoughtful husband, she tried guiltily to hide behind a more appropriate cloud of solemnity.

Annabel, on the other hand, was even paler and quieter than usual, and seemed to have lost her appetite. The removal of her persecutor ought to have bucked her up no end. Daisy wondered whether she was mistaken in believing that the young countess had feared Lord Stephen. Was she now mourning her lover?

The earl certainly had every reason to rejoice, yet he was as soberly formal, as unreadable, as ever.

After lunch, Daisy declared her intention of skipping coffee and going to see the C.I.D. man. At once Phillip, James, Lord Wentwater, and even Sir Hugh offered to accompany her.

"Heavens, no, thank you," she said, laughing. "I don't imagine he'll use the 'third degree' on me." Leaving Wilfred to explain that American term to his father, she went off to the Blue Salon.

She was eager to meet the detective. The only contact

she'd ever had with policemen was to enquire after the family of the local bobby at home in Worcestershire, and occasionally to ask the way of a London constable. A Chief Inspector was a different kettle of fish, not a "real gentleman," in the footman's words, but a man of a certain power and influence.

Despite her refusal of support, she was a trifle nervous when she entered the small sitting-room. Facing north, decorated in pale blue and white, the room had a chilly atmosphere that the small fire in the grate battled in vain. No doubt that explained why it was little used by the family in winter and could be spared for the police. Daisy shivered.

The man who looked up from the papers on an elegant eighteenth-century writing table was much younger than she had expected, in his mid-thirties, she thought. He rose to his feet. Gentleman or not, he was well dressed in a charcoal suit, with the tie of the Royal Flying Corps. Of middle height, broad shouldered, he impressed Daisy as vigorous and resolute, an impression reinforced by rather intimidating dark, heavy eyebrows over piercing grey eyes.

Daisy was not about to let herself be intimidated. She advanced across the blue Wilton carpet, held out her hand, and announced, "I'm Daisy Dalrymple."

"How do you do." His handshake was cool and firm, his voice educated—though not at Eton or Harrow. "Detective Chief Inspector Fletcher, C.I.D. I understand I have you to thank for my lunch, Miss Dalrymple."

"The servants seemed to think that a policeman is above such mortal needs as food, Mr. Fletcher."

He grinned, his eyes warming, and she noticed that his dark, crisp hair sprang from his temples in the most delicious way. Altogether he was rather gorgeous, she decided.

"This policeman was hungry. Thank you." He became businesslike. "I hope you don't mind describing to me the events of this morning."

"Not at all." Remembering, she changed her mind. "Well, not much. But I shouldn't think I can add anything to what James—Lord Beddowe—and Fenella Petrie have told you." She sat down on the nearest chair, and he resumed his seat.

"You can hardly tell me less." He grimaced. "I'm glad you didn't bring any guardians with you."

"I suppose Phillip—Mr. Petrie—and James insisted on protecting Fenella from you."

"They hardly let her say yes or no."

"And James would have been standing on his dignity, no doubt. I'll see what I can do."

"I'm sorry to put you through this, Miss Dalrymple. Just tell me what happened in your own way."

He picked up a fountain pen and took notes, without interrupting as she spoke until she reached the point where she returned to the house to develop the photographs.

"Thank you, that's very clear," he said then. "You succeeded in developing the pictures?"

"Yes, and printed them. The darkroom has all the necessary equipment."

"I'll want to see them later, but first a question or two. You say you and Miss Petrie and Lord Beddowe went down to the lake right after breakfast."

"After finding skates and collecting my camera and stuff."

"Right, but it was still quite early." He glanced over his notes. "Nine thirty, or thereabouts. Weren't you surprised to find Lord Stephen there before you?"

"No, not at all. I was pretty sure it was him even before I recognized the jacket. You see, he went on and on last night about keeping fit and going out at dawn to exercise."

"Ah, that makes all the difference. I couldn't understand what he was doing there in the first place." Capping his pen, the detective straightened his papers with an air of finality. "Obviously it was just an unfortunate but straight-forward accident."

"Well, I'm not sure." Daisy persevered in spite of his sceptically raised eyebrows. "You'll probably think I'm a complete fathead, Mr. Fletcher, but I wish you'd come and look at the photos."

"I'll have to look at them before the inquest, but I'm down here on another case and I can't really spare the time . . ."

"Please."

"Right-ho," he said indulgently. "I do appreciate your taking the trouble to photograph the body."

"Trouble! It was perfectly beastly." Bursting with indignation, Daisy led the way through the kitchens to the darkroom.

Following her, Alec Fletcher recognized her annoyance and was amused. He smiled at her stiff back.

Even the tailored tweed skirt and blue woolly jumper failed to conceal her shape as she marched ahead of him. Not plump, but not the straight up and down boardlike figure young women strove for these days. Cuddlesome was the word that had sprung to his mind the moment she walked into the Blue Salon. Cuddlesome from gold-brown hair and round face with that delectable mole—"the Kissing," it would have been called as an eighteenth-century face-patch—all the way down to the neat ankles in fashionable beige stockings.

She had been friendly, too, in contrast to young Bed-dowe, who appeared to consider Alec's presence an impertinent intrusion. He found it difficult to think of her as an Honourable, or even simply as a witness to be questioned.

Sternly, he recalled himself to duty. In gratitude for her cooperation he'd give her photos the praise she evidently craved, then get back to the business that had brought him to Hampshire. He'd have to attend the inquest, but luckily Astwick's death was clearly pure mischance.

The local G.P., Dr. Fennis, had assured him that the cause of death was drowning. Astwick must have hit his head on a jagged edge of ice as he fell. The laceration on the temple had probably been caused by a blow sufficient to make him dizzy and weak, perhaps even unconscious, obviously unable to pull himself out of the frigid water. Fennis could not confirm the time of death, since icy conditions retarded *rigor mortis*, always unpredictable in any case. However, since Astwick would hardly have gone skating in the middle of the night, the time was not in question. No autopsy was needed. He had died in an unfortunate accident, thank heaven.

Alec had no desire to tangle with Beddowe's father, Lord Wentwater. Even in this modern day and age an earl had to be handled with kid gloves, as the Commissioner had made quite plain over the wire.

Miss Dalrymple opened a door into a small, stone-floored room with whitewashed brick walls and a sink. The air had a chemical tang. "Don't touch the pictures; they're still damp," she warned. "There's something . . . odd. I won't point it out. See if you notice it."

He studied the photographs. No wonder a well-brought-up young lady had considered taking them perfectly beastly, but the only odd thing he could see was their excellence. He'd expected amateur shots taken from a safe distance, but these could almost have been produced by a police photographer.

"These are very good," he complimented her. "Quite professional."

"You needn't sound so surprised! I worked for a friend in her studio for nearly a year. As a matter of fact, I'm here as a professional photographer."

He stared. "I thought you were a guest."

"Well, not quite. You see, I'm writing an article about Wentwater for *Town and Country,* and Carswell, the photographer who was supposed to take pictures to go with it, is ill." She blushed to the roots of her hair, and went on defiantly, "That is—I suppose I ought to tell the police the truth—he doesn't really exist. My editor doesn't believe women can take good photographs, so I invented Carswell so that I could earn the money."

Alec gave a shout of laughter. "Ingenious. So you are a working woman as well as a scion of the nobility?"

"Yes. Promise you won't tell about Carswell?"

"I promise, unless for some unlikely reason he comes into this investigation." He still hoped an investigation would prove unnecessary, but while he could easily dismiss the fancy of a bored society girl, the doubts of a practical woman deserved serious scrutiny. "Will you show me what has aroused your suspicion?"

"Here, and here." She pointed at a couple of photos of the hole in the ice.

"Those marks?" He took the magnifying lens she handed him.

"When I was down on the lake, I didn't really notice them. I just assumed they were made by skate blades. But you see how short and deep they are? Nicks all along the edge? The sun throws them into relief. I'm fearfully afraid they might be . . . they might be the marks of an axe."

"They might." He frowned. "Are you suggesting that someone deliberately weakened the ice?"

She shuddered. "I don't want to suggest anything."

"I'd better go down to the lake and have another look," Alec said with a sigh. "Will you come with me? Bring your camera and take some more shots of that particular spot."

Donning coats, hats, gloves, and mufflers, they walked together down the path. The dark waters that had taken a man's life gleamed in the sun. Gingerly Alec approached, noting how the ice was roughened by skating. Miss Dalrymple followed him.

"Keep back," he said. "Let me test the ice."

"It seemed to me very solid. That's another reason . . . And wouldn't you expect cracks radiating from the hole?"

"Hmm." He was chary of committing himself, but the ice did in fact feel perfectly safe beneath his feet. Taking out a tape-measure, he went down on hands and knees.

Quite different from the skate-marks, the notches appeared at curiously regular intervals on the very edge of the hole, all the way around. Grimly he confirmed her guess. "They look like the work of an axe to me. But it looks more as if someone cut a hole, rather than simply weakening the ice. There are not nearly enough pieces of floating ice to fill the hole, as if a large central piece was removed or shoved under the edge."

"To save time, rather than chopping it into bits as if it broke? Yes, there is far too little ice floating."

"Surely Astwick would have seen a hole in time to stop. He didn't come down before daybreak, did he?"

"Not as far as I know. This bit of the lake would have been in the shadow of the bridge, though. You remember, in the photos you could only see one side of the hole properly? He was here earlier and the shadow would have been longer. After the dazzle of the sun on ice and snow, he wouldn't have seen anything. I was really close before I made out what James and Fenella were looking at, though the one side was in sunlight and I already knew something was wrong."

"Will you take a few more shots, please?"

"If you like," she said doubtfully, "but the sun is too high now to provide the contrasting shadows. I shouldn't think you'll see much."

"I can get them blown up. They may be useful."

As she moved about with her camera, Alec searched for cracks in the ice around the hole, and for signs that it might have been thinner in that spot. He wanted it to be an accident. He had plenty on his hands with the big jewel robbery at Lord Flatford's place. One disgruntled peer was enough. To affront the Earl of Wentwater with the news that further investigation was warranted would be to risk blighting his career.

Miss Dalrymple finished and returned to his side. "Well?"

"I'm not convinced that it wasn't an accident, but nor am I convinced that it was, I'm afraid. It'd be a dashed peculiar way to commit suicide, so it seems to be a deliberate effort to harm someone, probably the actual victim in view of his known habit of skating at dawn. There will have to be an autopsy—it's involuntary manslaughter at least. But who would have it in for Lord Stephen Astwick?"

"Half the residents of Wentwater Court," Miss Dalrymple informed him unhappily.

CHAPTER 5

Chief Inspector Fletcher looked no happier than Daisy felt. "You'd better tell me," he said resignedly. "You are to some degree an outsider here, so you may not know the inside story but I'm hoping you can be reasonably impartial."

Her heart sank still further. She felt she was betraying the Wentwaters' hospitality, yet it was her duty to help the police. One couldn't let people get away with deliberately drowning other people, however despicable.

"All right. Let's go back to the house. I'm cold."

"So am I, and my knees are wet. Besides, I must telephone my sergeant and the mortuary and the coroner."

"Will I have to give evidence?"

"What I want from you is your impressions, even guesses and hearsay, to give me some idea of where to start. If you have to give evidence it will be of facts only, of what you have actually observed," he reassured her as they trudged up the path.

She nodded, grateful for his understanding. If she had

to assist the police in their enquiries, at least she had a sympathetic policeman to deal with. "I don't know where to begin."

"Astwick must have a friend here, I imagine, or he wouldn't be a guest. Who invited him?"

"Wilfred. Lord Wentwater's second son. But I'm sure they're not friends. Quite apart from Wilfred being twenty years younger, he seems . . . seemed to be afraid of Lord Stephen. He was almost indecently cheerful at lunch today. Come to think of it, he actually told me Lord Stephen was a rotten swine and that Marjorie was well out of it. Admittedly he was rather sozzled."

"Marjorie?"

"His sister. She was madly in love with Lord Stephen and pretty cut up over his death. The doctor put her to bed with a sedative. Of course, she was madly jealous, too. Do you think she might have done it to give him a nasty fright, then been shocked when he actually drowned?"

"Possibly. It would take considerable strength to hack through that ice."

"She's a sporty type, skating, tennis, golf, riding, and so on. As strong as Wilfred, I reckon. He's a stage-door johnny, not good for much more than lifting a glass or a croquet mallet."

"A graphic description! What about Lord Beddowe?"

"James is pretty strong. Huntin', shootin', fishin', you know. Only he had nothing against Lord Stephen, no motive, rather the reverse. Geoffrey, the youngest, is even stronger, but he's just a boy and never paid any heed to Lord Stephen, neither liking nor disliking."

They reached the house. Mr. Fletcher, ignoring Drew's disapproval, went off to make his telephone calls. Daisy repaired to the Blue Salon, where she rang for a footman to build up the fire to dry out the detective's damp knees.

What a ghastly business it was! She couldn't help recalling Annabel's wan face at lunch. Could she have aimed to scare off Lord Stephen with an icy wetting, underestimating the risk of his hitting his head and knocking himself unconscious? No, with the threat of revealing her past to hold over her, he'd only have bullied her even worse afterwards.

Which meant that if Annabel had done it, she had intended his death.

In spite of the roaring fire, Daisy shivered. She wouldn't point out that bit of deduction to the Chief Inspector.

He returned. Standing in front of the fire, steaming at the knees, he said, "Sergeant Tring will be on his way as soon as the locals can get my message to him. The coroner has agreed to adjourn the inquest after evidence of death and identity, which means we need not say yet *where* Astwick died. And the body's off to the Yard's pathologist for post/mortem examination. The Commissioner himself told me to keep the locals out of it as much and as long as possible."

"The less the local people find out, the happier Lord Wentwater will be."

"So I gather. Well, he has to live with them. I'll do what I can. Now, Miss Dalrymple, you said Lord Beddowe had no apparent motive. What about his fiancée's brother, Mr. Petrie?"

"Phillip! Heavens no. At least, he called him a good egg. There was some sort of transaction between them, but he was surprised when I told him Sir Hugh distrusted Lord Stephen. That was last night, so he couldn't have heard in the interim that he'd been cheated, could he? I've known Phillip all my life. He's a bit of a juggins but he'd never do anything underhanded like that."

"I see." Mr. Fletcher sounded rather sceptical. "Who is Sir Hugh?"

"Lord Wentwater's brother-in-law, Lady Josephine's husband. It was he who insisted on calling the police and arranged to have someone discreet sent by Scotland Yard."

"Someone discreet, eh?" He grinned. "I thought it was just because I was already down here."

Daisy smiled at him. "Oh no, your superiors must have a high opinion of your discretion. Sir Hugh is a friend of your Commissioner. He's a big noise in the City, which is how he knew Lord Stephen was not to be trusted. I'm sure he's much too knowing to have let him cheat him. Besides, if he wanted to retaliate, he'd do it financially, don't you think?"

"I certainly hope so. I'd hate a friend of the Commissioner to be my chief suspect." He felt the knees of his trousers and sat down in the chair opposite her. "Lady Josephine?"

"Good Lord, no! She was worried, but she's too good-natured—and far too stout—to take an axe to the ice."

"We can count out Miss Fenella Petrie, can't we?"

"I should think so. Yes, of course. She's just a child and he never showed any interest in her." Daisy was flattered by the inclusive "we," by the Chief Inspector's apparent trust in her judgement. Nonetheless, she dreaded the next few minutes. "That leaves only Lord and Lady Wentwater." And she liked them both.

"Before we tackle them, let me go back a little. You said, or implied, that Lord Beddowe liked Lord Stephen, that Lady Marjorie had cause for jealousy, and that Lady Josephine was worried."

She tried to postpone the inevitable. "You have a very good memory."

"It's part of the job." He paused. His grey eyes were sharp again beneath the heavy brows, as if he had guessed her reluctance. "Would you mind explaining?"

Daisy took in a deep breath and let it out in a sigh. "James didn't *like* Lord Stephen. He *used* him, to further his feud against his stepmother. Not that it was necessary, if you ask me. Lord Stephen was in determined pursuit without any need of encouragement from James."

"You mean Lord Stephen was aiming to seduce Lady Wentwater? It scarcely seems possible!"

"That's certainly what it looked like. She's about my age and quite stunning, you know."

"So naturally Lady Marjorie was jealous. Was Lady Josephine worried that her sister-in-law might . . . er . . . succumb to his blandishments?"

"Yes."

"Did it appear likely to you?"

She hesitated. If she said yes, Lord Wentwater's motive for doing away with Lord Stephen was strengthened and Annabel appeared in a disgraceful light. If she said no, she'd have to explain, which would give Annabel an otherwise absent motive, as well as hinting at something shameful in her past.

The detective's steady gaze was upon her. She sighed again. The truth was the only way. "She hated him and feared him. If she had succumbed, it would have been through fear."

He nodded thoughtfully. "It sounds like blackmail, as does Wilfred Beddowe's invitation. A thoroughly unsavoury character, Lord Stephen Astwick."

"Wilfred was right, he was an absolutely rotten swine."

"Lady Wentwater had a motive, then, as did her husband." He groaned. "So instead of Sir Hugh, my chief suspect is the earl! And now I have to go and tell him I want to interrogate not only his household but himself."

There went any chance of ever making it to Superintendent, Alec thought. In comparison, the indiscreet way he was confiding in Miss Daisy Dalrymple was insignificant. Something about her guileless blue eyes invited confidences, and after two nearly sleepless nights he lacked the energy to resist. Besides, he had reason for trust: if she hadn't drawn his attention to the marks on the ice, Astwick's death would have passed as pure accident.

All the same . . . "I shouldn't be talking to you like this, especially when I'm posing as a model of discretion. I'll be well and truly in the soup if you repeat what I've said."

"As though I would!" she said indignantly. "I haven't told anyone about the photos. I know police business is confidential." Unexpectedly she giggled. "Though I couldn't have guessed it from the way you've been blathering on to me. People do, you know," she consoled him. "It's very odd."

Alec came to a decision. "I'm going to ask a further favour of you. Do you by any chance take shorthand?"

"Yes, sort of. That is, I learned it and I worked for a while as a stenographer, but being in an office all day was simply frightful."

"You've forgotten it?" he asked, disappointed.

"Not exactly. I use it when I'm making notes for my writing, but it's not quite Pitman's any longer. I don't think anyone else could read it. I can, as long as I transcribe it before I forget what it says."

He laughed. "I'll risk it. It'll be better than nothing. I want to interview people while they think I believe the drowning was accidental, but my officers won't be here to take notes for some time."

"You want me to do it?" She sounded astonished and not a little excited, her eyes sparkling.

"A highly irregular proceeding, " Alec admitted. "Expecting a simple accident, I've come ill prepared for a serious investigation. The other case I'm working on, the one that brought me to Hampshire, also involves a number of influential people. We're short-handed and I can't just abandon it."

"I'll help, as long as no one objects."

"Thank you, Miss Dalrymple. I count on you not to repeat anything you hear. I'll see that you're paid for your work, including the photography." Even if he had to pay her himself.

"Spiffing! I'll send for . . . no, I'll go and fetch my notebook. I don't want Mabel messing about with my papers."

She went off, a spring in her step. Alec rang the bell and asked the footman who appeared to inform Lord Wentwater that he desired a private interview.

"His lordship is occupied in the estate office with his agent," the man told him loftily.

Alec turned on the hapless menial the look that made his subordinates jump to attention and crooks shake in their shoes. "Then you know where to find him," he said.

"Yes, sir. At once, sir."

While he waited, Alec planned his approach to the earl. Had he enough evidence to insist on questioning the household if a polite request was refused?

He read over the notes he had made on the thickness and solidity of the ice, the missing piece or pieces, the lack of cracks radiating from the hole, the curious marks on the edge. Glancing at the photographs, he admired again not only Miss Dalrymple's competence, but her perspicacity in noticing something amiss.

His thoughts wandered. From what she said, it sounded as if she was working for living, however cheerfully. At first he'd assumed she was merely amusing herself, like Lady Angela Forbes with her florist's shop off Portman Square, before the War, when he did his years on the beat after University. Surely an Honourable Miss, the daughter of a baron or viscount, could not be so devoid of family as to make employment necessary. Yet she didn't seem the rebellious, or quarrelsome, or shameless sort of girl who might have cast off or been cast off by her family.

He shook his head, rubbing tired eyes. It was none of his business. What he wouldn't give for a pipe!

The footman returned. "His lordship will see you in the estate office, sir, if you'll please to come this way."

The estate office was a small room cluttered with ledgers, monographs on raising beef cattle, silver cups won by prize sows, and the general paraphernalia of running a busy estate. Lord Wentwater, seated at the desk, dismissed his land agent with a nod.

"I trust your investigation is completed, Chief Inspector." He spoke with courtesy but did not invite Alec to sit down.

Alec put him down as an aristocrat of the old school, mindful of his responsibilities and taking his privileges for granted. His son and heir was like him in many respects, but in a changing world Lord Beddowe was less certain of his privileges and therefore more insistent on them. Perhaps that uncertainty had bred the undercurrent of resentment Alec had sensed in James Beddowe. The young man would have to work hard to earn the respect his father received as his due.

"I'm afraid not, sir," Alec said. "I find I must pursue further enquiries. I'd like your permission to ask a few questions of your household, your guests, and yourself."

"What!" The earl gave him a cold stare. "I shall give no such permission."

"I fear I must insist, sir. If you wish, I can report to the Commissioner at Scotland Yard by telephone and ask him to explain the necessity to you."

"I suppose you consider you have sufficient reason for this extraordinary demand?"

"Of course, sir." As though he'd risk his career for a whim! He was not prepared to state his reasons, however, and he prayed Lord Wentwater would not ask. "I need not say that I shall do my utmost not to give offence with my questions, and all answers will remain confidential, with the usual provisos." Unless needed as evidence in a court of law, but he wasn't going to point that out. He hurried on. "I'd be very grateful for your cooperation, sir."

There, with any luck polite but firm should do the trick.

"But you will go your way with or without it," said Lord Wentwater with an ironical look. "Very well, you may tell my family and my servants that I expect them to cooperate with you. For my guests I cannot speak. I am busy at present, but I shall submit to interrogation later this afternoon."

"Thank you, sir." Though he'd rather have interrogated the earl first, he felt he had got off lightly. No use pressing his luck.

He found his way down endless corridors back to the Blue Salon. As he approached the open door, he heard a worried voice he recognized as that of the brother who had so persistently protected Miss Petrie from him.

"But hang it all, Daisy, you've been in here for hours. What's going on?"

The Honourable Phillip Petrie was standing by a window seat where Miss Dalrymple had ensconced herself. Alec remembered that she had known the fellow all her life. Though she called him a bit of a fool, she had spoken of him with affection. He was her elder by two or three years, her equal in rank, and handsome in a rather weak way. They were obviously on the easiest of terms.

"For heaven's sake, don't get all hot under the collar, Phillip," Miss Dalrymple advised him. "Those photos Sir Hugh had me take turned out to be useful, that's all. And now Mr. Fletcher is employing me as a stenographer since his sergeant isn't here yet."

"Employing you? The bounder! What unmitigated cheek."

"Bosh! It's jolly decent of him to offer to pay me when I would have done it for nothing. I'm thinking of writing a detective story some day, instead of any old novel. They're madly popular."

"You and your confounded scribbling," Petrie groaned. "It's beyond me why you won't go back to . . ."

"Here's the Chief Inspector," Miss Dalrymple interrupted, spotting him and greeting him with a cheerful smile.

Alec had the feeling he came as a welcome respite.

"Thank you for coming so quickly, Mr. Petrie," he said smoothly. "I only have a few questions to ask you. Shall we sit down?" His courteous gesture invited the young man to take a seat on a small sofa with his back to Daisy. His face would be adequately illuminated by the next window along, and it wouldn't hurt if he forgot that every word he spoke was being recorded.

Petrie sat down, slightly flushed and looking sheepish. He must be wondering if he'd been overheard describing as a bounder the police officer who was about to question him. "I came to find Miss Dalrymple," he blustered. "I didn't know you wanted to see me."

"A matter of routine."

As usual the soothing formula worked: Petrie visibly relaxed. "Oh, right-ho. Where was I between seven and nine this morning and that kind of rot, eh?"

Alec took the wing chair opposite him. "Between seven and nine?"

"Well, that must be about when the poor fish . . . er . . . chappie fell through the ice, mustn't it? Stands to reason. Too dark before, and he was found not much after nine. I say, you're not going to put Fenella through it again, are you? Deuced upsetting business for a female, don't you know."

"No, I don't expect to have any further questions for Miss Petrie," said Alec dryly. A fat chance he'd have of getting any answers out of her. "Where were you, then, between seven and nine?"

"Swigging down the jolly old early-morning tea, dressing, finding my way to the nose-bag, and so on. You know the routine, old bean . . . er . . . Chief Inspector."

"Finding your way to the nose-bag?"

"The breakfast parlour, I mean to say. Got there about ten minutes before Fenella toddled in with the news."

"You are unfamiliar with the house, Mr. Petrie?"

"By Jove, not that unfamiliar. Just a manner of speaking,

don't you know. I've been down here since the day after Boxing Day, came to keep m'sister company. She's engaged to Beddowe."

"So I understand. You've never been here before?"

"Never. I've often met the Beddowes in town, of course, but we're not particularly pally."

"And you knew the deceased in town?"

"Astwick? More in the City. He put me on to a good thing just a few weeks ago."

To Alec's ears, Petrie sounded distinctly uncertain about the good thing. If he were brilliantly acting the part of the upper-class twerp he appeared to be, surely he'd have hidden his doubts. It couldn't be an act, though. Miss Dalrymple had known him all her life.

After a few more questions, Alec let him go and rang the bell. As he instructed the footman, Daisy glanced through her notes, clarifying an odd squiggle here and there.

"Please ask Geoffrey Beddowe to spare me a few minutes."

"I don't b'lieve Mr. Geoffrey's come home yet, sir."

"Come home?"

"Mr. Geoffrey went out riding early and telephoned to say he was going to spend the day with a friend, sir."

"All right, I'll see Lady Josephine next."

The footman left and the detective came over to the window seat.

"Did you manage to get it all down?" he asked.

"I think so. Why Lady Jo? I'm sure she can't possibly have had anything to do with it."

"I expect you're right, but having begun by chance with Mr. Petrie I might as well get the least likely out of the way first."

"Then you don't think Phillip did it?" she said, relieved.

"He doesn't seem to know the place well enough to lay his hands on an axe without poking about or asking the servants a lot of awkward questions, which we'll soon find out if he did.''

"So that's what you were after. Frightfully clever.''

"Somehow I can't picture him packing an axe in his luggage.''

She laughed. "If he did, you may be sure the servants would know all about that, too.''

"I must say, it wouldn't suit me to have my every sneeze discussed in the servants' hall. The trouble is, even with servants swarming about, no one's going to have an alibi.''

Daisy nodded. "The ice could have been hacked at any time between nightfall and daybreak. I wondered why you wanted to know about seven to nine.''

"I didn't, but he wanted to tell me,'' said Mr. Fletcher. "In fact, it led to the business of his being unfamiliar with the house, so it was worthwhile. What about the married couples? No chance of eliminating them, I suppose.''

"I don't know about their sleeping arrangements,'' Daisy said, blushing, "but Lord Wentwater spent most of the evening in his study, Annabel went to bed early, and Sir Hugh disappeared to the smoking-room after dinner. I don't know if he was gone long enough to do it.''

"You were in the same room as Lady Josephine all evening?''

"From about half past seven. It was dark long before that.'' While she was enjoying her leisurely bath, anyone could have been down at the lake. "Most of the maids go off duty at eight, though there would have been a few servants around until midnight or so. It wasn't till after dinner that Lord Stephen talked about skating early.''

"He'd been here a week and the lake's been frozen for three days, I gather; the servants must have known,'' said the detective with a sardonic look. "Which means anyone could know. Well, we're getting nowhere fast. Are you comfortable there, Miss Dalrymple? It's a good, unobtrusive spot.''

"That's why I chose it," she said smugly. "Watching someone write down my words would jolly well shut me up. Phillip had forgotten I was here by the time he left." To herself she admitted to being a bit piqued.

As if he guessed, Mr. Fletcher said consolingly, "After all, that's just what we want." He glanced at his wristwatch. "Where has Lady Josephine got to? You know, it's odd that Geoffrey is out, in the circumstances."

Daisy considered the matter. "I hadn't even noticed that he didn't turn up to lunch. He's big, but so silent he's easily overlooked. He must have left before the body was discovered."

"Surely whoever spoke to him on the 'phone would have told him."

"Not if he just left a message with a servant, and even if he was told, he might not see any reason to return. It was nothing to do with him."

"True. But if he left the house early, he may have seen Astwick skating, or on his way down to the lake. Every little scrap of information helps. If he doesn't put in an appearance soon, I'll have to see if I can get hold of him on the telephone. Incidentally, what about the servants? Might any of them hold a grudge against Astwick?"

"I haven't the foggiest. I only arrived yesterday, remember. I could have a chat with the chambermaid who waits on me, if you like."

"By all means have a chat about the general feeling in the servants' hall, but I don't want you asking specific questions. We'll leave that to Sergeant Tring."

At that moment Lady Josephine put in an appearance, followed by her husband. Alec sighed, inaudibly he hoped, and went to meet them.

"You won't mind if I sit in on this interview, will you?" Sir Hugh asked, affable but with a determined edge to his voice.

"Of course not, sir. I need to speak to you as well."

He needn't have worried that Sir Hugh's presence would render his wife monosyllabic. A large lady of uncertain years, clad in bulky tweeds and superb pearls, she gushed, "This is all most frightfully exciting, Chief Inspector. A dreadful business, of course," she added hastily. "Why, Daisy dear, I almost didn't see you hidden in that corner."

"I'm acting as Mr. Fletcher's stenographer, Lady Josephine, since he's come without one."

"How clever you young women are nowadays! You want us to sit here, Mr. Fletcher? Do be seated, won't you? It must be quite wearying asking questions all day. That's better." She beamed at him. "Now, how can we help you?"

Alec found himself warming to the earl's sister in a most unprofessional way. He understood why Miss Dalrymple refused to believe her guilty, whether or not she was physically capable of chopping a hole in the ice. "Perhaps you would begin by telling me what you know of Lord Stephen Astwick, ma'am," he said.

"He was an utter cad!" she declared forthrightly. "He was paying the most objectionable attentions to my sister-in-law, which is only what one might expect of a man who is a byword in the most scandalous weeklies. Not that I read them! But I've heard him linked with a dozen names: Lady Purbright, Lady Amelia Gault, Mrs. Bassington-Cove, Gussie Warnecker . . ."

"Just a moment!" Three of those names were familiar to Alec. "Miss Dalrymple, are you taking this down?"

"Names are tough."

"Would you mind repeating them, Lady Josephine, and continuing a little more slowly?"

"I'm not telling you anything you couldn't find out from past issues of *Tittle-Tattle*," she said anxiously.

"Of course not, ma'am. You are simply saving me time and trouble, and everything you say will remain confidential." As hearsay it was not allowable in evidence, however useful he might find it.

She looked to Sir Hugh, who nodded, faintly amused, to Alec's relief. He was very much interested—and puzzled—by the names she reeled off. She recalled another five of Astwick's presumed conquests before her memory ran dry.

"There are more, Mr. Fletcher, but they have slipped my mind."

"You've been extremely helpful, Lady Josephine. If any more occur to you, be so good as to write them down for me. I don't suppose you happen to know—by reputation or through staying in the same house as Lord Stephen on a previous occasion, perhaps—whether he was also in the habit of, er, paying his attentions to, er, females of the lower orders?"

"Did he run after the maids, you mean? I don't believe so. In a sense, you might say that he was fastidious, though that is far too complimentary a word for the rotter. But he did demand a certain breeding in his mistresses."

Alec bit back a smile at her frankness. "I see. Now, one more question, if you please. Did you know, before Lord Stephen spoke of it last night, that he was in the habit of skating before breakfast?"

Her ladyship snorted. "Pure bunkum! As though there were something positively virtuous about exercising at dawn. Yes, I did know. My maid told me it was quite a joke in the servants' hall."

"Thank you, ma'am. I need not trouble you further for the present." Alec rose to his feet.

"No trouble, Chief Inspector. It's our duty to help the police. A most worthy group of men, I'm sure. Hugh, shall I stay?"

"No, no, my love, no need." Her husband patted her hand. "I've a feeling we'll be talking business, and you know how anything to do with the City confuses you."

"Yes, dear. I'll be off then." Halfway to the door, Lady Josephine turned. "Just one thing, Mr. Fletcher," she said earnestly. "My brother didn't realize Lord Stephen was chasing after Annabel. I'm sure he didn't. He can't have. He never showed any sign that he knew."

"I shall take your opinion into consideration, ma'am," Alec assured her. Damn! he thought. People read too many detective novels these days.

"Yes, Chief Inspector," said Sir Hugh with a mocking smile, "even my wife has worked out that you think Astwick's death was no accident."

The keen-eyed baronet was going to be a worthy opponent, if opponent he proved to be. However, he was the one who had called in the Met, Alec reminded himself.

"I'm afraid I can't discuss that, sir," he said. "Will you tell me about Astwick's business dealings?"

"Stephen Astwick was a swindler, Mr. Fletcher. He never did anything straight if he could make a penny more by doing it crooked. I could give you particulars of dud investments, the names of many men he cheated, a few ruined, but I won't, unless you really need them."

"Not at present, thank you, sir, except that I'd like to know if he ever cheated you."

"I cut my eyeeeth long before he arrived in the City. And before you classify that as an evasive answer—no, he never attempted to embroil me in his fraudulent schemes, and I have no investments in any of his companies."

"Anyone else here now?"

"I've wondered about young Petrie. He's been nosing about the latest nonexistent South American silver mine, but if he's been bitten I don't believe he's aware of it yet."

"Hmmm," said Alec noncommittally.

"I ought to tell you, perhaps," Sir Hugh continued, "that in my opinion Astwick's holding company is a hollow sham which will collapse in shards when news of his death breaks. It couldn't have lasted much longer anyway."

"Good Lord!" Alec drew in a long breath and thanked

heaven he'd never had the money to invest in stocks and shares.

"That, of course, is a secondary reason why I asked your Commissioner to send down a discreet man, the first being my concern for my wife's family."

"Lady Josephine's description of Astwick as an utter cad seems scarcely adequate."

"Adequate to his social misdeeds, I dare say, which is all that concerns my wife."

"May I ask, do you and Lady Josephine share a bedroom?" Seeing Sir Hugh stiffen, he added, "I should prefer not to have to ask the servants."

"We do."

"I understand you went down early to breakfast."

"I like to read *The Financial Times* in peace, so I am often the first to arrive in the breakfast-room. The footman on duty gave me to understand such was the case this morning."

"You saw nothing of Astwick?"

"Nothing."

"Then I think that's all I need ask you for now. Thank you for your patience, Sir Hugh."

He nodded acknowledgement of Alec's thanks and started to leave the room. Like Lady Josephine, he turned halfway to the door. "It's my turn for a parting word. My wife is as at home in society as I am in the City, Chief Inspector. What she has told you may be hearsay, but she'd not have repeated it had she not been convinced of its truth."

"Whew!" Miss Dalrymple exclaimed as the door closed behind him. "I suppose it must have been someone in residence here who chopped that hole? It sounds as if there are countless deceived husbands and swindled businessmen all over the country with excellent reasons to be out for Lord Stephen's blood!"

CHAPTER 6

Alec sent the footman for Lord Beddowe before responding to Miss Dalrymple. "It certainly would appear that Astwick was heading for a sticky end sooner or later. We'll check with the lodge-keeper whether he admitted anyone last night. However, I'm pretty sure someone in this house reached him first."

"Then why were you so interested in the names Lady Jo gave you?"

"You never miss a trick, do you? It's probably just an odd coincidence, but eight out of ten of those names are connected with the other case I'm working on."

She flipped through her notes. "She only remembered nine."

"Seven out of nine, then. A significant proportion, you'll allow."

"Yes, but connected how? What is your other case?" She stood up and stretched, then moved to the fire and held out her hands to its warmth. "Come on, Mr. Fletcher," she said when he didn't answer, turning her head to look back at him. "I know it's none of my business, but you can't leave me dangling."

Alec shrugged. "A big jewel robbery. I'm sure you must have read about it in the papers."

"I saw a headline in the train yesterday, but I didn't have time to read any further."

"It looks like one of a series of burglaries of country houses, all over the south of England. In each case, the thieves have taken a huge haul of jewellery, chiefly from house-party guests, while ignoring other valuables."

"As if they knew what to look for."

"Exactly. We've recovered a lot of the smaller pieces from fences, but none of the major stones has turned up."

"Those seven women who were involved with Lord Stephen are all guests who were robbed at one time or another? The latest burglary was near here? And Lord Stephen turned up in the neighbourhood, having practically invited himself? It does sound vaguely fishy."

"Only vaguely, I'm afraid. But I would like to know his manservant's whereabouts."

"Isn't he back yet? I saw him drive off yesterday, before lunch. Perhaps he came back last night and chopped that hole in the ice, only you'd think he could come up with an easier and more certain way to dispose of his master if he wanted to."

"He might have wanted merely to inconvenience him."

"There must be a hundred thousand easier ways for a servant to inconvenience his employer!"

"True," he admitted.

"Lord Stephen might have met someone else there, though, by arrangement," Daisy suggested. "Someone who biffed him on the head and happened to have an axe in his motor-car."

"Interesting that he went down to meet this mysterious someone wearing his skates."

She grinned. "Well, perhaps not. No, a rendezvous with

an outsider is out, and anyone in the house would have found somewhere inconspicuous to meet him indoors."

"Unless it was a moonlight tryst, a romantic skating party for two."

Daisy didn't care for that line of thinking. "It was far too cold to be romantic, and . . . Wait, he wouldn't have walked down there with skates on in the morning, either. What happened to his ordinary boots?"

"Now that is a very good . . ." Alec paused as the door opened. "Ah, Lord Beddowe."

"What's all this about?" the young man demanded aggressively. "I've told you all I know."

"I find further enquiries are necessary. Lord Wentwater was good enough to assure me of his family's cooperation."

"Oh, very well." Crossing the room towards the sofa Alec indicated, he suddenly stopped. "What the deuce are you doing in here, Daisy?"

She had slipped back to her window seat. With a reproachful glance at Beddowe, she picked up her pad and pencil, leaving Alec to answer.

"Miss Dalrymple is my stenographer."

"You can't expect me to answer your bally questions in the presence of a young lady."

"I admit that it is somewhat irregular. If you strongly object, we can go to the local police station to find an officer able to take down your statement."

"Good Lord, no! I suppose a Chief Inspector considers himself too important to take shorthand," he sneered.

"You need not write that down, Miss Dalrymple," Alec said dispassionately.

Beddowe noticed her shocked stare and had the grace to look a little ashamed of himself. Taunting one's inferiors was not part of the code of a gentleman. He didn't apologize, however, and he showed no sign of shame when he started talking about Astwick and his stepmother.

"It's too obvious for words," he said contemptuously.

"Like a cheap, sordid melodrama. They were lovers in Italy, and then my father comes along, a wealthy peer infatuated enough to offer marriage, and she drops Astwick like a hot coal. Here she is, living on velvet, when who turns up but her lover, threatening to reveal all and wreck the cosy nest if she doesn't jump back into bed with him."

"Have you evidence that Astwick and Lady Wentwater were lovers?" Alec regretted that Miss Dalrymple had to hear such an outpouring of venom. Like the others, Beddowe appeared to have forgotten her presence.

"Not exactly evidence, but anyone could tell he had a hold over her, knew some nasty secret from her past. She had every reason to get rid of the bounder."

Alec couldn't resist a dig. "Naturally, for your father's sake, you did all you could to prevent Astwick's persecution of your stepmother."

"Protect that scheming adventuress, after she wheedled her way into my father's confidence! Of course, I'm sorry he's going to be disillusioned, but divorce isn't such a ghastly business nowadays, is it? As the guilty party, she wouldn't get a penny out of him. Oh yes, she hadn't much choice but to dispose of Astwick."

He seemed prepared to carry on endlessly in a similar vein. Alec stopped him with a question about Astwick's boots.

"Boots? I haven't the foggiest. They must have been by the bench at the bottom of the path, where we sit down to change, but I can't say I noticed them. I was carrying my own skating boots, and Miss Petrie's and Miss Dalrymple's."

"Who carried everything back up to the house?"

"I told the under-gardeners who moved the body to the boathouse to clear everything up. I suppose they put away the boathook and gaff and brought the rest back to the house. I wouldn't put it past them to swipe Astwick's boots. After all, he didn't need them any longer."

Much as he disliked Beddowe's attitude towards his servants, Alec silently agreed that the theft was possible, and if that was the case, the boots might very well remain unaccounted for. Miss Dalrymple hadn't seen them, or she wouldn't have raised the point. Miss Petrie might have, though he'd think twice about believing anything she said with her overbearing guardians beside her. He'd have Tring question the under-gardeners, but it looked like another dead end.

He asked for the names of the gardeners, put a few more questions to Lord Beddowe, then let him go.

"What an absolute beast!" Daisy burst out as Mr. Fletcher rang the bell. "I know James egged Lord Stephen on, but I never would have guessed he had such a foul mind. And so frightfully vulgar! Annabel isn't at all . . ." She broke off as the footman came in.

"Mr. Wilfred, please," the detective requested.

"Mr. Geoffrey's come home, sir."

"Thank you. I'll see him first. By the way, is Lady Marjorie still out of circulation?"

"Yes, sir." Having abandoned disdain in favour of obedience, the footman now became communicative. "Cora, that's Lady Marjorie's maid, said as how Lady Josephine had her take another dose of that stuff the doctor left. Crying and carrying on something awful, she was."

"Mr. Geoffrey, then." He waited until the servant left before saying to Daisy, "You see what I mean about the servants discussing every sneeze! Dash it, I must see Lady Marjorie some time. What was it I wanted to ask Geoffrey?"

"Whether he saw Lord Stephen on his way to or at the lake," she told him, pleased that she remembered. She was glad she had taken on the job. It was fascinating, though she'd just as soon not have heard James's diatribe. "I can understand James resenting his father's second wife," she said with a frown, hunting through a drawer of the writing table for a pencil sharpener. "Annabel has taken his mother's place and diverted his father's attention from him. But why should he loathe her so bitterly?"

"In a word, money." He took the sharpener and her three pencils from her.

"Money? I don't believe she's at all an extravagant sort of person. She cares more for flowers than for fashion."

"Nonetheless," he explained, "she represents a drain on the estate that's liable to continue as long as Lord Beddowe lives. Also, there's always the possibility of children who would, I presume, be provided for out of his inheritance. He has motive enough to wish to break up the marriage."

"Enough to risk someone else's life in order to blame Annabel for it?" Daisy demanded, sceptical yet hopeful. As a villain, James was greatly to be preferred to Annabel.

"It's conceivable. On the other hand, a mere wetting would hardly have suited his purpose. I can't imagine Lord Wentwater divorcing his wife for playing a trick on the man who was trying to seduce her."

"No, but if James made Lord Stephen believe Annabel was responsible, he might well have been angry enough to tell Lord Wentwater whatever his nasty secret was. Thank you." She took the three perfectly sharpened pencils he held out. "You won't let James influence your view of Annabel, will you?"

"I'll try not to," he promised, adding gently, "but you must be aware that it's difficult to blackmail someone who has led a blameless life."

"I know." Daisy's despondency was quickly overcome by curiosity. "I wonder what Wilfred did to give Lord Stephen a hold over him?"

"I hope to discover very shortly. Nothing, I trust, to shock a young lady."

"Nothing could possibly shock me as much as James's malevolence. I wonder if I ought to warn Phillip that he's not at all a suitable husband for Fenella."

"I shouldn't interfere, if I were you."

"I'll have to think about it. I expect Wilfred's misdeeds are innocent in comparison, gambling debts and borrowed money probably. He's that sort. Here he is," she said as the door opened. "Oh no, I forgot, Geoffrey first."

The large, stolid youth entered, still in riding breeches, his colour high from cold air and exercise. "You wanted to see me, sir?" he enquired, in the apprehensive tone of a schoolboy called to the headmaster's study.

"I shan't keep you a moment. What time did you leave this morning?"

"Eightish. Maybe a bit earlier."

"After breakfasting?"

"No, there's a farmhouse on the way to Freddy's that does a jolly decent spread. That's Freddy Venables. I was at school with him."

"I assume you've been told by now what has happened. Did you see Astwick this morning, either in the house or out-of-doors?"

"No, sir. The stables are at the back of the house and I went off that way, nowhere near the . . . the lake."

Daisy was surprised by the tremor in his voice. She wouldn't have thought he was so sensitive as to be shaken by the drowning he had not witnessed of a man he did not care about. Though possibly he was just disappointed to have missed all the excitement, she thought with sympathy. Finding a body would have been a ripping story with which to regale his pals at Cambridge.

"Chief?" A shining pink dome appeared around the door, its pristine glory set off by the luxuriant grey walrus moustache below. A massive body followed, clad in a regrettable suit of large yellow and tan checks. Stunned by this apparition, Daisy scarcely spared a glance for the wiry young man in modest brown serge who entered after him.

"Sergeant! I was beginning to think you lost in a snowdrift. Thank you, Mr. Beddowe, that will be all for now."

Geoffrey departed, and Mr. Fletcher introduced Detective Sergeant Tring and Detective Constable Piper to Daisy.

"Miss Dalrymple has been helping me," he explained. "I'd intended to have one of you take her place when you arrived, but I've other things for you to do. Piper, you'd better get down to the lake right away before it starts getting dark. Have a hunt around, for anything out of the way but especially for a pair of boots. I didn't see anything, but you never know. Have a word with the lodge-keeper. Ask if he opened the gates to anyone between dusk and dawn. And if not, see if you can find footprints approaching the lake from any direction other than the house."

"Sir!" The constable saluted and went out.

"Tom, let me explain what's going on. Miss Dalrymple, I count on you to interrupt if I leave anything out."

Mr. Fletcher's précis was rapid but comprehensive. Daisy admired his ability to bring all the necessary information together in a clear and concise account.

"Ah," said Sergeant Tring ruminatively when he finished.

"So I want you to tackle the staff. You're good at that."

"Ah." The sergeant winked at Daisy and preened his moustache. She gathered he had a way with female servants. Extraordinary, though no more extraordinary than the slimy Lord Stephen's conquests. "It's a rum thing," Tring elaborated on his monosyllable in a rumbling bass, "that there man of Lord Stephen's being missing. I've a notion he's the one could blow the gaff. You see, Chief, there's been developments." He glanced sideways at Daisy.

"You can speak before Miss Dalrymple, Tom. She knows about that case, too."

"Well, 'tain't much to go on, but we've picked up a fellow driving a motor that's been seen lurking about near the Flatford place on and off the last few days. Rang a bell, it did, and I went through the reports of the other jobs.

Seems there's been a grey Lanchester spotted in three out of four."

"A grey Lanchester!" Daisy exclaimed. "Lord Stephen's car was a grey Lanchester."

"Is that so, miss. Don't happen to know the number-plate, do you?"

"I was too far away to read it, and I don't suppose I'd remember if I had. Jones, Lord Wentwater's chauffeur, is certain to know."

"Very true, miss. The one we've got is a London number, Chief. Inspector Gillett wired for identification. Obscured by mud, it was—a right laugh, that, with the paintwork gleaming, the brass bright as gold, and no mud this side of the Channel that's not froze solid. We're holding chummie on that and on not having no driving license on him. The inspector sent his dabs up to the Yard, too."

"Dabs?" Daisy queried.

"His fingerprints, miss. To find out if he's got a record."

"I take it he's not talking?" Mr. Fletcher asked.

"Dumb as the knave of diamonds, Chief." Sergeant Tring's little brown eyes twinkled as Daisy laughed. He was brighter than he looked, she decided.

"Astwick may turn out to have been the king of diamonds," said the Chief Inspector dryly.

"Not to mention king of hearts!" Daisy put in.

"Miss Dalrymple and I already had a vague inkling of some connection. If the number-plates match, well and good, but it wouldn't surprise me if the plates turn out to be faked or recently stolen. Either way, we'll search his room before we go, Tom. Let's get the interviewing done first. On your way to the servants' quarters, you'd better ring up Gillett and tell him on no account to let the chummie go; and tell the footman to send in Mr. Wilfred."

"Right you are, Chief." He removed his bulk from the room with an unexpectedly light, swift tread.

Daisy was bursting with questions. "Why would they

bother to cover a stolen number-plate with mud? It just made it conspicuous."

"I'd say that was the servant's idea, not Astwick's, if he is in fact involved. He strikes me as too canny a man to do anything so stupid."

"But a Lanchester is a pretty conspicuous motor-car to use in the first place. I'd use a Morris, or a Ford, something people wouldn't look at twice."

"Astwick would have looked pretty conspicuous rolling up to Wentwater Court in a Morris Oxford," Mr. Fletcher pointed out patiently. "Admittedly his man could have switched vehicles before he approached the burgled house, but that would complicate matters no end. Whereas a Lanchester is not likely to be stopped, short of an outright breach of the law, because it can only belong to a man of wealth and therefore of influence."

"So . . . Oh, botheration!" Daisy scurried to the window seat and took up notebook and pencil as Wilfred breezed in.

"What-ho, my dear fellow!" he greeted the detective airily. "What can I do to help the jolly old coppers? Hullo, hullo, playing the scribe, are you, Daisy?"

She nodded and gave him a small smile, but left it to Mr. Fletcher to answer.

To Alec's ears, the slight young man in his natty suit sounded distinctly nervous. Seated, he fidgeted constantly, crossing and uncrossing his legs, straightening his tie, smoothing his sleek, pomaded hair. When Alec took a moment to shuffle a pile of irrelevant papers, Wilfred Beddowe burst into speech again.

"Rotten business, this, what? Gave me a nasty turn when my man brought the news with my tea. I mean to say, a guest here, not just any old passing tramp."

"More particularly your guest, Mr. Beddowe, I understand."

"Yes, I invited him," he agreed with a hint of his elder brother's belligerence. "What of it?"

"May I ask why you invited Lord Stephen Astwick to join a small family party?"

"Happened to run into him in town just before Christmas. I thought he might fancy a glimpse of the old homestead."

"Let me get this straight. You happened to run into Astwick in London—in your club, perhaps, or in the street?"

"At Ciro's."

"Ah, in a nightclub—and you thought he might like to see Wentwater Court, so you invited him down for a few days. You and he must have been very good friends." He gave Wilfred an enquiring look which elicited silence. "Interesting, when he was nearly twice your age. No doubt he was in some sort a mentor?" Silence. "A pity you should choose a rogue to guide you."

"I didn't! He wasn't! We weren't even friends."

"You invited a rogue who was not your friend to stay with your family?" Alec asked with feigned incredulity.

"Yes. No. I didn't want to but he insisted," he said sulkily. "Dash it, I knew Marjie would be pleased at least."

"But you were not pleased."

"Pleased to be stuck in the same house with that infernal fellow!" Wilfred exclaimed, shuddering.

"Then why . . . ?"

"All right, if you must know, I owed him money."

"Gambling debts?"

"How I wish it had been! I'd've gone to the gov'nor sooner than let Astwick blackmail me. He'd have read the riot act, maybe cut my allowance and gated me, but he'd have paid up. He's a bit of a fossil, my father, but not such a bad old stick."

"Then what was it you couldn't tell Lord Wentwater?"

Wilfred crimsoned. "Breach of promise," he confessed.

"Whispering sweet nothings to a shopgirl, eh?" Alec hoped his voice had covered the muffled snort from Miss Dalrymple.

"A chorus-girl."

"Letters?" He shook his head as Wilfred nodded. "Silly young chump. So Astwick lent you money to buy her off and then threatened to tell your father."

"The pater would have blown me sky-high. I'm *glad* Astwick's dead," said Wilfred defiantly. "They're all sitting around trying to pretend nothing's happened, but I want to break out the champagne."

"Yet it gave you a nasty turn when you heard of his demise."

"Gad, yes. I mean to say, not the sort of thing a chap likes to hear first thing in the morning when he's not feeling too bobbish."

"First thing? What time was this, Mr. Beddowe?"

"Oh, half past tennish." His confession over, he was regaining his insouciant air. He took out a chased silver cigarette case and offered it to Alec, who shook his head. Wilfred lit up.

"You had a late night last night?"

"Not at all. Went to bed early as a matter of fact. There's nothing to do in the country. I daresay I was all tucked up cosy by one, but my man has strict instructions never to wake me before ten-thirty."

"You didn't retire immediately after the weather forecast?"

"No, Jimmy—my brother—and Petrie and I went to the smoking-room for a nightcap. But Jimmy's a yokel at heart and Petrie had this asinine notion of skating with Astwick at dawn, so we weren't long."

Alec pricked up his ears. "Mr. Petrie told you he intended to go skating at dawn?"

"He told everyone, when Astwick was blathering on about Swedish exercises and fitness, after dinner. Said it sounded like a ripping idea. All rot, if you ask me. I take it he came to his senses, or he'd have been there to pull Astwick out.''

Unless he'd been the one to fall in, Alec thought. This put an altogether different complexion on things. Who knew Petrie planned to skate early? Did someone not care if they injured the wrong victim? Or could that amiable ass possibly be the intended victim?

CHAPTER 7

I completely forgot about Phillip's pronouncement," said Daisy, full of remorse. "It changes everything, doesn't it?"

"It does alter matters somewhat," the Chief Inspector agreed tiredly, rubbing his eyes.

"You see, I know him jolly well and I was pretty sure he wouldn't turn out at dawn, so it didn't make much impression on me. No one else knows him so well, though, except Fenella, so everyone else may have expected him actually to skate with Lord Stephen."

"Does your memory agree with Wilfred's as to who constitutes everyone?"

"Lord Wentwater and Sir Hugh weren't in the drawing-room. I can't say whether the rest were all listening." She thought hard. "The only others who joined in the conversation were Lady Josephine and Marjorie, and Marjorie was so busy fluttering her eyelashes at Lord Stephen she may not have heard what Phillip said."

"Marjorie! I *must* speak to that young lady but I can't wait about for the sedative to wear off. I suppose tomorrow will have to do. Let's see, that means Lord Wentwater and Sir Hugh were unaware of Mr. Petrie's plans, and Lord Beddowe, Geoffrey, Lady Marjorie, Lady Josephine, and Lady Wentwater may or may not have known."

"It doesn't help much, does it?" Daisy said with a sigh. "I can't believe anyone would have deliberately risked hurting Phillip instead of Lord Stephen—he's such an inoffensive idiot!—but we can't be sure who heard him."

"It shouldn't be difficult to . . . Ah, Piper. Any luck?"

Detective Constable Piper entered the room with the heavy tramp of a policeman on the beat. Daisy saw Mr. Fletcher wince, remembered Tring's catlike tread, and deduced that Piper had only recently joined the plain-clothes branch.

"Nothing, sir. No boots nor nothing out of the way. The bloke at the lodge didn't let anyone in, nor did his missus. And there weren't no footprints, 'cepting on the paths and the drive." The young man appeared bitterly disappointed. "Couldn't someone've come up behind the house, sir, and walked round by where the snow's trampled?"

"A good thought, Constable. Would that be possible, Miss Dalrymple?"

"Possible, certainly, but it's miles to any road other than the lane by the lodge. And from the lane you'd have to walk miles around to come up behind the house without leaving footprints near the drive."

"I suppose someone could have left a vehicle outside the park wall, climbed over, and tramped for miles through the snow in the dark just to play a trick," the Chief Inspector mused, "but it seems highly improbable. Besides, it's not likely any outsider would know Astwick had taken to skating at dawn since the lake froze, let alone that he'd be on his own. No, I think the mysterious someone is out. Any other ideas, Piper?"

"Just that, seeing the hole in the ice is evidence, sir,

p'raps I ought to report as the wind's in the south and like as not there'll be a thaw afore morning."

"Thank you, that's certainly worth knowing. Luckily we have excellent photographs, thanks to Miss Dalrymple. Well, there's no sense in your looking for an axe. I'm sure there are several about in the outbuildings, and no one would have gone out without gloves last night just to provide us with fingerprints. You'd better relieve Miss Dalrymple."

"Sir!" Pad and pencil appeared on the instant.

"I don't want to be relieved," Daisy protested.

The daunting stare he turned on her, intensified by dark, baleful eyebrows, made her quail. It vanished in a moment and he grinned. "I'd almost forgotten you're not one of my officers. I appreciate your hard work, Miss Dalrymple, but at present the best thing you can do to help is to begin transcribing your notes. I promise I'll not leave without letting you know what's going on."

She pulled a face. "Oh, very well. I'll try and get them done before you go. Do you mind spelling mistakes? I type faster if I don't have to worry about spelling."

"Just as long as you think I'll be able to make a guess at what the garbled words are supposed to be."

"I'm not *that* bad! Cheerio for now, then."

As she moved towards the door, Piper hurried forward to open it for her. Before he reached it, it opened and Lord Wentwater appeared. He held the door for her with his usual grave politeness. Turning towards the stairs, Daisy decided she was after all quite glad to be relieved of her note-taking duties. She respected the earl and didn't want to listen while he explained or defended—or incriminated—himself.

Alec would have been happy to avoid that duty. Not for a moment did he believe in the innate superiority of the aristocracy. The malignant James Beddowe would have disabused him of that notion if he had. What concerned him was their perceived superiority, the influence they wielded by virtue of their birth and their belief in their own importance.

Lord Wentwater had never doubted his right to special treatment, Alec was certain. Nonetheless, he had to admire the earl's calm dignity and iron self-control. Impossible to imagine this distinguished gentleman on his knees hacking at the ice with an axe.

Yet Alec knew from experience that a man in the throes of jealousy and hate is capable of actions he'd never dream of otherwise.

Buoyed by that knowledge, he gently steered Lord Wentwater towards the seat where he wanted him. Even more than with his other suspects, it was essential to be able to read every nuance of expression on the earl's face.

Piper slipped inconspicuously into the window seat favoured by Miss Dalrymple, and Alec sat down opposite the earl, not waiting to be invited. Here, he was in charge. "Would you please give me your opinion of Stephen Astwick, sir?" he requested.

"As I am sure you have heard by now, Chief Inspector," Lord Wentwater said in an even voice, "the man was an unmitigated blackguard."

"Yet you entertained him in your home."

His mouth tightened. "No doubt you have discovered that Astwick is the brother of the Marquis of Brinbury. Brinbury and I went to school together, are members of the same clubs, sit in the House of Lords together. Astwick also belonged to some of those clubs. While I would never have invited him to Wentwater, it would have been an intolerable insult to ask him to leave."

"I understand his own family had disowned him. Have they been informed of his demise?" Alec ought to have seen to that long ago. If only there were more hours in a day! Two nights' lack of sleep was suddenly catching up with him at just the wrong moment, and he saw no prospect of a full eight hours tonight.

"I telephoned Brinbury."

"And?"

"He asked me to let him know when his brother was safely underground," Lord Wentwater said dryly. "Perhaps you find it difficult to understand, Chief Inspector, but the views of his family in no way altered my obligation towards Astwick as a member of that family. No doubt you have colleagues at Scotland Yard with whom you are obliged to associate against your wishes."

True, but he didn't take them home, Alec silently protested, and even the most objectionable had never chased his wife, let alone blackmailed her. Was it possible the earl had been as blind to Astwick's conduct as his sister believed?

"The laws of hospitality supersede the natural desire for a faithful wife?" he asked, trying to make the question sound like simple curiosity rather than impertinent prying.

"Astwick was not my wife's lover!" The anger in Lord Wentwater's tone was unconvincing, and for the first time in the course of the interview he did not meet Alec's eyes. A muscle twitched twice at the corner of his mouth.

An outright lie seemed out of character. As Alec murmured an apology for his crassness, he wondered whether the earl might be attempting to convince himself, as much as his interrogator, of Lady Wentwater's faithfulness. A proud man, he'd not easily admit to himself that he had been cuckolded. Possibly he was also a charitable man, eager to give his wife the benefit of the doubt. Possibly he was simply an old man with a young wife who accepted as inevitable that she would take lovers.

No, not an old man. He must be about fifteen years older than Alec, still the erect and vigorous product of an active, healthy country life. He looked quite robust enough to satisfy a young wife—or to hack a hole in the ice.

Alec rubbed his eyes. God, what he'd give for a pipe and a cup of coffee, or even tea, but he couldn't ask Lord Wentwater for it any more than he could ask him whether he shared a bedroom with his lady. Thank heaven Tring would be finding out that most pertinent bit of information from the servants.

No doubt the sergeant would also be wallowing in tea and cakes. He had that effect on cooks for some inscrutable reason, witness his waistline.

Doggedly Alec continued questioning the earl. He felt as if he'd lost the thread of the investigation, or rather, as if he'd never found it. His questions and the answers seemed equally irrelevant, and he wished Miss Dalrymple were there to discuss them with him. With any luck everything would fall into place when he talked to Lady Wentwater, though it was still conceivable that her only connection with Astwick's death was as the object of the gallantries that roused Lady Marjorie's jealousy.

Why had that death so shattered Lady Marjorie that she needed several doses of a sedative? Was she truly broken-hearted over the loss of a man she was deeply in love with? Or was she appalled that her vengeful mischief, intended to discomfort, had killed him?

"I take it this farce is at an end?" said Lord Wentwater impatiently.

Alec realized that he had failed to follow up an answer with another question. "I have nothing more to ask you for the moment, sir," he said. "May I have your permission to search Astwick's bedroom?"

"If you must."

"Also, I still need to speak to Lady Wentwater, and to Lady Marjorie, who, I gather, is not to be seen today. I shall have to return tomorrow. My constable will remain here. I'm afraid I must request that no one leave Wentwater before my return."

"Very well." Lord Wentwater appeared to be resigned to the continuance of the investigation.

Either innocent or very sure of himself, Alec decided as the earl left the room. Right at that moment, he didn't care which. He only hoped he'd make sense when he was talking to Lady Wentwater.

The footman took a confounded time to answer the bell. When he arrived, he preceded a parlourmaid bearing a heavily laden tea tray.

"Miss Dalrymple's orders, sir," he announced.

"Bless the woman!" Alec fell upon the teapot like a fox on a hencoop.

Piper was not far behind. "No lunch, sir," he explained, putting away dainty, triangular, crustless Gentleman's Relish sandwiches by the fistful.

"At least you had more than two hours sleep last night," Alec grunted, pouring his second cup. The tea was no wishy-washy Earl Grey but a strong Darjeeling brew, which he put down to Tring's presence in the kitchen. It was wonderfully revivifying.

Resuscitated, he felt ready for anything by the time the footman ushered in Lady Wentwater. Nonetheless, her loveliness took away his breath.

Miss Dalrymple had said she was young and beautiful. He had not expected the figure of an Aphrodite, undisguised by her fashionably shapeless crêpe-de-Chine teadress, and the exquisite face of a sorrowing Madonna. Her dark, melancholy eyes cried out for sympathy. Alec knew he'd have to fight to maintain a balance between favouring her and reacting too far the other way.

No wonder the earl had married her, Astwick had pursued her, and Lady Marjorie was jealous of her. Lord Beddowe's antipathy might be based more on sheer sexual jealousy than he himself realized. Fenella Petrie was a candle to her sun.

But Lady Wentwater was more moon than sun. Pale from

weariness of climbing heaven and shining on the earth . . .
Shelley, wasn't it? Daisy Dalrymple was really more to Alec's
taste. Pretty rather than beautiful, but cheerful rather than
tragic, she reminded him of Joan, who had never let slender means nor the hazards of war dampen her spirits.

Surely Lady Wentwater ought to have perked up a trifle
now that her persecutor was gone. Was it possible Miss
Dalrymple had misinterpreted the situation, that the young
countess had been Astwick's willing lover and now grieved
for his death? She didn't look strong enough to chop a
hole in the ice, though she was taller than average and
desperation could augment a person's strength in the most
amazing way.

As Alec greeted her, she looked around the room distractedly. "I thought . . . someone said Daisy was here. Miss
Dalrymple." Her voice was low and soft, with a pleading
note.

"She was, but my constable has taken over from her.
Would you like someone with you? Another lady, or your
maid?"

She bit her lip. "Miss Dalrymple, please, may she come
back?"

"Of course, Lady Wentwater." He sent the footman to
fetch her, and while they waited he asked with considerable
curiosity, "You have known Miss Dalrymple long?"

"I met her for the first time yesterday, but she is very . . .
simpatica, the Italians say. I feel she is already my friend."

If a stranger so quickly became a friend, she must feel
herself friendless indeed in her husband's house, and who
could blame her? Her husband and his sister suspected
her fidelity; her stepson hated her; her stepdaughter
regarded her as a rival. Whatever she had done, Alec pitied
her.

He had to warn her. "You are aware that Miss Dalrymple
has been actively aiding me in this investigation?"

Nodding, she managed a hesitant smile. "I believe Daisy

would throw herself wholeheartedly into whatever situation she came across. She's not the sort to stand by and let things happen."

A trait that might prove awkward at times, Alec thought.

Daisy hurried in, breathless, a few minutes later. "Mr. Fletcher, you need me? I haven't quite finished the typing."

"Lady Wentwater requested your presence."

"Oh, Annabel, I didn't see you. Of course I'll stay if you want me." Sitting down on the sofa beside the countess, she impulsively took her hand. It was cold, and trembled slightly. Annabel had cause to dread the coming inquisition, whether she had anything to do with Lord Stephen's death or not.

The detective, at his most formidable, went straight to the point "Was Stephen Astwick blackmailing you, Lady Wentwater?" he asked abruptly.

"Oh, no, he never demanded money."

"Money is not always what a blackmailer seeks to extort."

"I suppose not. Yes, you could call it blackmail. He threatened to . . . betray me if I refused to . . . to . . ." She faltered, clutching Daisy's hand.

"To become his mistress. Did you?"

"No! I put him off and put him off. It was horrible! He didn't even really want me so much as he wanted revenge. He wanted to ruin my life, one way or another."

"Revenge?"

"I had refused him before. Once, when I was a girl, he asked me to marry him, and then later, in Italy, he tried . . . but my . . . my first husband forced him to leave me alone. I think Rupert knew something about Stephen he couldn't afford to have known."

"Birds of a feather," Mr. Fletcher grunted, and Daisy glared at him.

To her surprise, Annabel straightened and flew to her first husband's defence. "Oh no, Rupert would never have blackmailed anyone. He just used his knowledge to defend me."

"I beg your pardon, I spoke out of turn." He passed his hand wearily across his brow. "I plead fatigue. What was it Astwick threatened to reveal to Lord Wentwater?"

"That has not the least relevance to your enquiry," Annabel said with dignity. She had recovered her composure—and Mr. Fletcher had lost the initiative.

"As you will. Let it pass, for the moment. You will not deny that you loathed and feared Astwick?"

"How can I? He was a fiend."

"You hated him enough to kill him?"

A tremor ran through her and her grip on Daisy's hand tightened again. "Perhaps. I don't know. If I had known how. Do you mean you suspect that his death wasn't an accident?"

"It seems probable that the hole in the ice was deliberately cut."

"Why should I do that? He'd be as likely just to take a wetting as to drown. I tell you, he wanted to wreck my life far more than he wanted to . . . seduce me. The first thing he'd do would be to go to Henry. I'd have gained nothing."

Ay, there's the rub. The only bit of *Hamlet* Daisy remembered from school trickled through her thoughts. Whether 'twas nobler in the mind to suffer the slings and arrows of outrageous fortune, or to take arms against a sea of troubles, and by opposing end them . . . but Annabel's troubles would not have ended if Lord Stephen had merely been soaked to the skin. In Daisy's view, she was in the clear.

Mr. Fletcher asked her a few more halfhearted questions, then let her go with thanks for her frankness. "Piper, find out how Sergeant Tring's getting along," he ordered, and slumped back into his chair.

"Not enough sleep?" Daisy queried.

"Just a couple of hours, two nights in a row."

"Well, make sure you have at least eight hours tonight,"

she said severely, "or you won't be fit for anything tomorrow. How can you solve one case, let alone two, if you can't think straight?"

"I can't," he admitted with a rueful smile. "I feel as if I've run headfirst into a brick wall and I'm not sure whether it's an extraordinarily confusing case or I'm just confused."

"I'm confused too, though after all it is my first case."

"And your last, I sincerely trust!"

"Probably," said Daisy, sighing. "It's very interesting but rather painful. Annabel couldn't have done it, could she? It wouldn't make sense."

"Not much. The weather wasn't exactly suitable for her to lure him to a romantic midnight tryst by the lake, sock him on the head, and drop him in."

"Besides, he wouldn't have been wearing skates."

"Damn those missing boots!" said Mr. Fletcher explosively. "I beg your pardon for the language, Miss Dalrymple, but it's enough to try the patience of a saint. What happened to them?"

"I don't mind the language," she assured him, "but won't you call me Daisy? I rather fancy calling you Chief."

"My name's Alec."

"Alec in private, Chief when your officers are around. Perhaps Sergeant Tring has found the boots."

"Them boots?" The stout sergeant had entered the room unnoticed with his peculiarly silent tread, which Piper, following, appeared to be trying to imitate. "Sorry, Chief, the gardeners don't remember how many pair they carried up. Albert, the bootboy, thinks he cleaned a pair of Astwick's, but it might've been the day before and he hasn't a clue if they was his only boots. And they might've been someone else's. Not too bright, our Albert. The vally can tell us that, if he'll talk, which it's my belief he will when he hears about his master's nasty end."

"If your chummie is in fact Astwick's manservant. Any luck with the number-plate?"

"The number we got on the Lanchester is quite different from what Jones remembers on Astwick's, and Sir Hugh's chauffeur, Hammond, agrees with him. But this vally-chauffeur Payne's description matches chummie." He grinned. "I couldn't have put it better meself. 'Ferret-face,' says the cook. 'More like a weasel,' says her ladyship's maid."

"Do the earl and countess share a room?"

"They do, but his lordship's vally hemmed and hawed and allowed as how his lordship's been known to sleep in his dressing-room. I couldn't pin him down as to the last few days, Chief. A cagey laddie and I didn't want to push too hard in case he shut up altogether."

"Quite right. We'll have another go tomorrow if it seems necessary."

"I talked to the chambermaid while I was gone," Daisy put in. "She said none of the staff much liked Astwick, but no one had a specific grievance against him, either. He never said a pleasant word, but nor was he actively unpleasant."

"That's what I heard, too, miss," said Tring. "He was indifferent to them and they was indifferent to him's the impression I got."

"No help there, then," the Chief Inspector sighed. "It looks like one of the family. If only we could pin down the time the hole was made to something less than twelve hours! No one has an alibi for the whole period. At least, did you find out anything else useful, Tom?"

"Nowt vital. I'll give you the rest of the dope on the way back to Winchester, to save time, shall I? Now why don't you let me and Piper search Astwick's room while you have a bit of a kip, Chief?"

"Is it so obvious I'm running out of steam? All right, Tom, go ahead. I'll put my feet up, if Miss Dalrymple will excuse me."

"There's a footstool by the fireplace," said Daisy. "That will be just the thing."

Piper sped to fetch it, saluting with a blush when Daisy thanked him. He and Tring went off and Alec settled back with a sigh, loosening his necktie, his booted feet on the crewelwork footstool.

"You'd be more comfortable without your boots," Daisy suggested.

"But how embarrassing if someone came in to make a confession and found me shoeless."

"When I leave, I'll tell the footman not to let anyone in without warning you first. And I *will* leave you to sleep, but you did promise to tell me what Lord Wentwater said."

Alec bent down and untied his bootlaces. "He denied that Astwick was his wife's lover."

"You didn't expect him not to, did you?"

"Not really." Slipping off the boots, he wiggled his toes as he leaned back again.

"So what it comes down to is whether you believe he believes she's not." Daisy noticed that the toes of his navy socks were neatly darned. Had he mended them himself, or was there a woman in his life? She quickly looked up.

He was already asleep, his head drooping to one side. Daisy fetched a cushion and gently stuffed it between his ear and the wing of the chair. He didn't stir.

Before going upstairs to finish the typing, Daisy asked the way to Lord Stephen's bedroom. It was at the far end of the east wing, in a corridor parallel to the one where her room was located. The two corridors were connected by a third, off which were situated the earl and countess's suite on one side, the linen-room and more bedrooms on the other.

As Daisy reached the corner, a housemaid came out of a room carrying a coalscuttle.

"Was that Lord Stephen's room?" Daisy asked her.

"No, miss, Mr. Geoffrey's. That one next to the end,

t'other side o' t'bathroom, were Lord Stephen's. Them p'leecemen's in there now, miss.''

"Thank you.''

The maid bobbed a curtsy and disappeared through a swing-door in the opposite wall, presumably to the back stairs. Daisy went on to the door she'd pointed out, knocked, and entered.

Tring looked round, his frown clearing as he saw her. "Ah, it's you, miss. Does the Chief want summat?''

"No, he's fast asleep. I just wondered if you've found anything yet.''

"We only just started, miss. I 'spect the Chief'll tell you if we comes across owt of interest. A real help, you've been, and no mistake.''

"Oh, well, it was just lucky that I took those photographs and . . .''

"Sergeant!'' Piper emerged backwards from the ward-robe, waving a Manila envelope. "Beg pardon, miss. Look here, Sarge, I found it in a sort of a hidden pocket in the lining of his overcoat.''

"You'll go far, laddie, you'll go far,'' said Tring benevolently, taking the envelope and opening it. "Now what have we here. Ah, the Chief'll want to see this. Two passports and . . . well, knock me down with a feather! So Lord Stephen Astwick and his ferret was planning to scarper, was they?''

"Was . . . I mean, were they?'' Daisy demanded.

"Booked on the S.S. *Orinoco,* sailing from Southampton 3:00 P.M. day after tomorrow, for Rio.''

CHAPTER 8

"Do you have to wake him?" Daisy gazed down upon the semirecumbent Chief Inspector. His face relaxed in sleep, he looked years younger.

"Bless you, miss, he'll have me hide if I don't, and quite right, too. I'll see he gets a decent kip tonight, but we got to get back to Winchester first."

"He said I'm to stop here, Sarge," said Piper apprehensively. "No one's to leave, but if they try, what'm I s'posed to do?"

"He don't expect the impossible, laddie. You're a reminder, that's what you are, a reminder of the majesty of the law."

The constable's shoulders squared and a determined light shone in his eyes.

Daisy laid her hand on Alec's shoulder and gently shook him. "Chief? *Chief,*" she said softly. "Time to wake up."

Muscles tensed beneath her hand and he sat up straight as his eyes flickered open. "Wha'?" he mumbled, thick-tongued. "Daisy?"

"I finished typing the notes." She had been politely but firmly dismissed from Lord Stephen's room while Tring completed the search. "I put them with your other papers. But the sergeant has something much more exciting for you."

"Tom?" Alec was already alert, kicking away the footstool and fumbling for his boots as Tring waved the Manila envelope at him. "What have you found?"

"Young Piper here found a ticket to Brazil, Chief, and there's this, too." He flourished a dark brown leather despatch case, then set it on the stool. "Locked with a fancy combination lock, it is."

Alec groaned. "I don't suppose Astwick left the number lying about."

"No, Chief, but it just so happens as we found a scrap of paper with a number on it in the pocket of the laddie in the Lanchester. Inspector Gillett kept it, of course, but it just so happens as Detective Constable Piper has a habit of memorizing stray numbers."

"The first part's me auntie's birthday, sir," Piper explained eagerly, "and the last bit's the number of inches in an elf. Forty-five sir," he added as they all looked at him blankly.

Shaking his head in wonderment, Alec gestured at the despatch case. "Give it a try, Ernie."

"Yes, *Chief!*" Beaming, he started rotating the lock.

Alec and Tring exchanged a significant nod. A rite of passage had taken place: Piper had earned his place on Alec's team.

The lock clicked open. Alec leaned down, unfastened the brass catch, and opened the case. On top lay another Manila envelope, larger than the first. He removed it, opened it, and slid a sheaf of papers halfway out.

"Bearer bonds," he said, but the others were staring at

the case, which was filled with small drawstring bags of yellowish chamois leather.

Alec reached for the nearest. Loosening the drawstring, he tipped the contents onto the palm of his hand. As he tilted his hand this way and that, the electric light struck blue fire from the huge cabochon-cut star sapphire.

A vast contentment filled him. "Mrs. Bassington-Cove's Star of Ceylon." From a second pouch he spilled out six glittering diamonds, smaller than the sapphire but perfectly matched. "We've got the goods, Tom. Let's get going. I find myself eager to have a little chat with your Lanchester driver."

"Right, Chief. I'll drive so's you can kip, but we'll take your motor, shall we? You won't want to risk young Ernie having to use it in an emergency."

"Hey, what d'you mean!" Piper protested.

Alec grinned. "I'll have to risk it. You're right, Tom, you'd better drive, and you'll never fit behind the wheel of mine. It's an Austin Seven," he explained to Daisy, slipping the sapphire and diamonds back into their chamois bags, depositing them and the envelope with the rest, and relocking the despatch case. "Tom can barely squeeze into the passenger seat. More to the point, this lot will be safer in the official car till we can lock it up in the safe at the station."

"I wish I could come," she said wistfully. "I'm dying to know what the ferret has to say. Don't look so worried, I know I can't."

"You may learn something useful here," he consoled her. "Keep your eyes and ears open, won't you? We'll be back tomorrow. Tom, will you bring the car round, please? I must leave Lord Wentwater a receipt for the loot in case Astwick's family kicks up a fuss about the disappearance from his room of a fortune in gems and bonds."

As Tring left the Blue Salon, the dressing gong sounded through the house. Reluctantly Daisy followed him.

On her way to her room, she stopped to see how Marjorie was doing. Awake, though dopey, she clung to Daisy's hand and wept. Nonetheless, Daisy received the impression that her grief was not profound, in fact that the tears were a mask. If Marjorie was capable of deep feeling, Lord Stephen had not evoked it.

She was growing cynical, Daisy reproached herself as she went on to her own room. Just because she had put him down as a nasty specimen the moment she met him, she refused to believe anyone could fall in love with him.

On the other hand, Marjorie didn't need to be desperately in love for his indifference to make her furious, a matter of hurt pride rather than spurned love. She might have wanted to punish him, or she might have hoped to win him over by lavishing sympathy on him after his wetting. Either way, chopping up the ice made much more sense for Marjorie than for Annabel.

Running late, Daisy hurriedly changed. She put on her old grey dress again, since there had after all been a death just this morning and her best dress was rather on the bright side.

Drew announced dinner two minutes after she reached the drawing-room, so she had no time for the cocktail she felt in need of. A glass of wine with the hors-d'oeuvres and a second with the soup perked her up no end, and she refused a third with the fish. She noticed that wineglasses around the table were being refilled with abnormal regularity. Yet everyone was sombre, speaking in low voices to next-door neighbours or not at all. Having the police in the house was as sobering as if the death had been in the family. Daisy was glad she was seated between the urbane Sir Hugh and the silent Geoffrey, neither of whom was likely to embarrass her with questions about the investigation.

Coffee, brandy, and liqueurs were served in the drawing-room. Everyone was present, perhaps feeling there was safety in numbers.

Lady Josephine, her colour high, said defiantly, "I don't see why we shouldn't have a quiet rubber of bridge." She looked around for players.

"Do you play bridge?" Daisy asked Annabel.

"Badly."

She lowered her voice. "Do you *like* to play?"

"Not at all. It's the sort of thing a hostess can't always escape."

Daisy took her arm. "Then quick, come over here and tell me about the gardens in Italy. Are they all as formal as what we call an Italian garden? Patterns of square box hedges and dreary cypresses like ninepins?"

Annabel smiled. "I take it you play bridge but hate it."

"I wish I'd never learned," said Daisy with a shudder.

They sat down on a sofa at some distance from the fireplace. Sir Hugh, Phillip, and James joined Lady Josephine at the card table; Wilfred chatted brightly with Fenella, the taciturn Geoffrey sitting with them though not taking part in the conversation as far as Daisy could see; Lord Wentwater sat by the fire reading *The Field*.

Daisy kept an eye on them all as Annabel described the garden of the ramshackle villa near Naples where she had lived. A wilderness of pink oleanders, purple bougainvillea, pale blue plumbago, and scarlet hibiscus, it had been anything but formal.

"It was gloriously colourful, and Rupert loved to paint it," she said in a low voice, "but I missed forget-me-nots and daffodils."

"Rupert was an artist?"

"Yes. He wasn't at all like what the detective seemed to think. He was gentle, and vague, and not very enterprising, and he didn't care about money, which was just as well as he hadn't much. My aunt—the aunt who brought me up—deeply disapproved of him and refused to let me marry him."

"So you ran away with him?"

"He had a weak chest and he was advised to go to a warmer climate. I couldn't bear never to see him again, so I went too."

"How often I wish I had taken the bull by the horns," Daisy exclaimed bitterly. "Even if we had only had a few days together . . ." Her throat tightened and she blinked hard.

Annabel laid a comforting hand on her arm. "Your parents disapproved of the man you loved? Or his circumstances?"

"Oh, his income was adequate and his family socially acceptable, but he was a Quaker, a Conscientious Objector. Instead of doing the proper thing and getting blown up in a trench, he joined a Friends' Ambulance Unit and got blown up with his ambulance."

"My dear, I'm so sorry."

Daisy was unused to wholehearted sympathy. "You don't despise him?" she asked.

"Despise him! He laid his life on the line to help others, so his physical courage was as great as any soldier's, and besides that he had the moral courage to stand up for his beliefs. How could anyone despise him?"

"It's obvious you've been living abroad. People still speak sneeringly of conchies and some of them were in prison for years. There were over a thousand in Dartmoor, shut up with the worst felons."

"That makes their courage the greater," Annabel said gently.

"My parents didn't see it that way. We decided to wait until the War was over in the hope that . . ."

"More brandy, anyone?" James had pushed back his

chair from the card table, where Phillip was dealing in the methodical way Daisy remembered from childhood games. "Benedictine or Drambuie? Whisky?"

"Benedictine, please, dear boy," said Lady Josephine, handing him her liqueur glass. Daisy asked for the same. Under Phillip's stern eye, Fenella shook her head, and Daisy saw the wheels turning in Phillip's head as he decided he needed to keep it clear for the card game. Sir Hugh requested a brandy and soda. Geoffrey's brandy glass was barely touched, unless he had at some point replenished it himself.

"Father?" James enquired.

"Yes, a drop more brandy, please, neat. Annabel, my dear, what will you have?"

"Nothing, thank you."

"G-and-t for me, old bean," said Wilfred as his brother passed behind his chair on the way to the drinks cabinet. He turned back to Fenella. "No, I'd not do anything so dashed uncomfortable as bashing ice about in the middle of a bitter winter's night," he said, obviously continuing what he had been saying, "if I wanted to do away with someone, which of course I don't."

James stopped beside Fenella. "There's only one person here who had good reason to want to do away with Astwick," he said loudly, with venomous intensity, staring at Annabel. "What better motive than to rid oneself of an importunate lover?"

"Shut up!" Geoffrey rocketed from his seat, his left arm swinging as his solid length unfolded. James stepped back, but Geoffrey's fist caught him on the side of the jaw, staggering him. He tripped and fell on his back, and Geoffrey was upon him, grabbing his shoulders and banging his head on the floor while he, dazed, feebly tried to push his brother off.

"Here, I say!" Wilfred jumped up, seized the back of Geoffrey's collar and hauled ineffectively.

Fenella screamed. Phillip sprang to his feet, sending the card table flying, and rushed to help Wilfred.

"Stop it!" Lord Wentwater's cold, incisive voice cut through the bedlam.

Geoffrey's shoulders slumped. He stood up and brushed vaguely at his clothes. With Wilfred's aid, James sat up, clutching his head.

"Geoffrey, go to your room. James, to my study, and wait for me."

"It's not true!" Geoffrey turned to his father, pleading, hands outstretched. "He's lying. You mustn't believe him. Stop him saying such things!"

"You may leave me to deal with your brother."

"Yes, sir." His head bowed, Geoffrey trudged towards the door, cradling his left fist in his right hand. His face was pale and to Daisy's eyes he looked utterly exhausted.

As he neared her, his steps hesitated. He raised his head and shot a glance of heartrending entreaty at Annabel, before he plodded on out of the drawing-room.

Daisy realized that Annabel was quietly weeping, huddled in the corner of the sofa with her hands over her face. Sitting down, for she too had jumped to her feet, Daisy took Annabel in her arms. She glared at James as he stumbled after his brother, tenderly feeling the puffy red swelling on his chin.

Quietly Lord Wentwater apologized to his guests and thanked Wilfred and Phillip for their intervention.

Wilfred brightened, then visibly braced himself. "It was nothing, sir, but I say, Geoff was right. Jimmy shouldn't keep spouting off like that, not quite the article, don't you know."

"Thank you, Wilfred, I do . . . Annabel!"

Annabel, who had been sobbing on Daisy's shoulder, had broken free and was hurrying from the room. Her husband's appeal failed to slow her pace. He strode after her.

"Oh dear," said Lady Josephine, and turned to Sir Hugh, her plump chin trembling.

With Sir Hugh comforting his wife, Phillip comforting his bewildered sister, and Wilfred righting the card table, Daisy decided she had had enough for one evening. Even her promise to Alec to keep watch was insufficient to detain her in the drawing-room.

"I believe I shall go to bed now," she announced and, receiving no response, did a bunk.

Yet she was too het up to concentrate on her neglected writing, or even to read, let alone to sleep. Instead, she went to the darkroom-scullery. Though it was absolutely freezing, at least concentration on the mechanical process of printing her photos kept her mind off the Beddowes and their problems.

She was astonished when a knock on the door presaged the arrival not, as she half hoped, of a kitchen maid offering hot cocoa, but of Lord Wentwater.

He apologized again for the scene in the drawing-room.

"How is Annabel?" Daisy asked. She refused to enquire after James, and thought it unwise to enquire after Geoffrey.

"She is asleep. I persuaded her to take half of one of the bromide powders Dr. Fennis left for Marjorie." Standing there with unfocussed eyes fixed on her pictures, he said absentmindedly, "You are very diligent, Miss Dalrymple."

"I haven't worked on my article all day."

"No, I suppose not. The policeman didn't believe me, did he?"

"I beg your pardon?" she said, startled.

"Chief Inspector Fletcher." The earl's harrowed gaze met hers. "He thought I was lying when I told him I didn't believe Annabel was Astwick's mistress. It's true. I know her. I trust her. But she's keeping something from me."

Obviously the secret Astwick used to threaten her, Daisy

thought. Did he imagine she knew it, or that she'd tell if she did? Did he even know Annabel was being blackmailed? Daisy wasn't going to be the one to tell him. "I'm glad you trust her," she said. "I like her, very much."

"She needs a friend." He hesitated, then went on sombrely, "I expect you feel I've handled everything badly. Besides the sheer impossibility of demanding Astwick's departure, I never realized—I swear I did not realize!—that James was behaving so abominably."

Reflecting on the past two days, Daisy said, "No, as I recall he always did his worst when you weren't there. Geoffrey told you what he's been up to?"

"Yes. It is true, then? I find it so very difficult to credit that my own son could be so cruel."

"I can't honestly blame Geoffrey for attacking him."

"Nor I, though it's past time he learned that fists are rarely an effective solution."

"He's the strong, silent type. He takes after you."

"After me?" Lord Wentwater exclaimed, startled. "Good Lord, is that how you see me?"

"Not resorting to fisticuffs," Daisy hastily assured him.

He shook his head, frowning. "Perhaps I have been too silent, and not strong enough. Since their mother died I've not had much interest in society or entertaining. I have divided my time between estate business and the House, leaving my children very much to their own devices. I suppose I relied on their schools to form their characters, and on Josephine to chaperon Marjorie after she left school."

"Marjorie's no sillier than a hundred other debutantes with nothing to occupy their time or their minds but their amusements and their emotions. I must say I jolly well admired Wilfred when he stood up for Geoffrey this evening."

"Yes, possibly Wilfred is not without redeeming traits."

"If you ask me, they both need an occupation," she said

severely, then bit her lip. "But you are not asking me. I beg your pardon, Lord Wentwater."

"There's no need." He smiled ruefully. "I've been rattling on at you about my troubles, so how can I resent your advice? I can't imagine why I've disburdened myself into your patient ears. It's for me to beg your pardon."

"Not at all." Daisy decided it would be untactful to tell him that he was by no means the first to confide in her.

"No doubt you will feel obliged to repeat what I've said to the detective."

"Not unless it's relevant to Lord Stephen's death. If you wish, I'll tell him you really do trust Annabel."

The earl put on his mask of hauteur. "He chose to disbelieve my statement. Reiteration will not make him believe."

"Probably not," she conceded. "I'll have to tell him about Geoffrey, though I'm sure he'd hear about it one way or another even if I didn't."

"And James's filthy accusations?"

"Didn't you know? James himself made Mr. Fletcher a present of those."

Lord Wentwater looked stunned. Then, his jaw set, his mouth a stern line, he strode from the darkroom.

He had had three purposes in coming to her, Daisy realized: to assure her of his trust in Annabel, to find out whether what Geoffrey told him of James's conduct was true, and to persuade her not to repeat James's accusations to the Chief Inspector. But any damage James could do was done.

Suddenly exhausted, Daisy cleared up the darkroom. Heading for bed, she was returning along the servants' wing corridor when a footman came through the green baize door from the Great Hall.

"Oh, miss, I was just coming to find you. There's a telephone call for you, a Miss Fotheringay."

Hurrying to the hall, Daisy picked up the apparatus from the table in the corner and sat down in the nearest chair.

"Lucy? Hello, is that you, Lucy? Darling, how too heavenly of you to ring up. Are you in a call box?"

Lucy's voice came tinnily over the wire. "No, I'm at Binkie's flat and he's treating me to the call so we can blether on forever. Don't worry, it's perfectly proper, Madge and Tommy are here too. We had supper at the Savoy. Daisy, darling, you sound positively desperate. Is Lord Wentwater too frightfully stuffy for words?"

"Good lord, no!" "Stuffy" was now about the last word she'd think of applying to the earl, but she couldn't possibly tell Lucy all that had been going on. Quite likely a switchboard-girl or two was listening in, but in any case, what she had learned in confidence was not to be betrayed even to her dearest friend. "The earl's been quite friendly," she said lamely.

"And what about that mysterious new wife of his? Who *is* she?" Though living independent of her family, Lucy was inclined to dwell on family trees.

As far as Daisy knew, Annabel had no noble connections. "Annabel's a dear," she said. "Guess who's staying here. Phillip Petrie."

"Oh yes, his sister's marrying James Beddowe, isn't she? Has Phillip taken up the pursuit again?"

"In a desultory way. He's fearfully disapproving of my writing. But Lucy, I've met a simply scrumptious man."

"Darling, how spiffing! Who is he?"

Too late she realized the trap she had dug for herself. "He's a detective."

"A 'tec? An honest-to-goodness Sherlock Holmes? My dear!"

"No, a Scotland Yard detective."

"A policeman! Surely not a guest at Wentwater?"

"He's investigating Lord Flatford's burglary. You must have read about it. The people here were at the New Year's ball." Daisy congratulated herself on telling the truth without giving away the real reason for Alec's presence at Wentwater.

"Too, too exciting, but there must be something wrong with the line. I thought you said the policeman was scrumptious."

"He is."

"But Daisy darling, isn't he frightfully common? I mean, people one knows simply don't go into the police."

"He's not at all common," she snapped, then sighed. "But for all I know he has a wife and seven children tucked away in some horrid semi-detached in Golders Green."

"Cheer up, darling." Lucy sounded relieved. "I'll find someone for you yet. Just a moment—yes, Madge, I'm coming. I have to go, Daisy. Madge and Tommy are giving me a lift home. They send their love, and Binkie, too. When will you be back?"

"I'm not sure, I'll send a wire. Thanks for ringing, Lucy, and thank Binkie for me. Toodle-oo."

"Pip-pip, sweet dreams."

Daisy hung up the receiver and put down the set. Talking to Lucy had brought a welcome reminder of the outside world, but had done nothing to dispel the day's tensions.

She went up to bed. Tired as she was, she lay awake for what seemed hours, memories, doubts, and speculations racing through her mind. The drama in the drawing-room that evening played itself out on the screen of her closed eyelids. Why had Geoffrey violently attacked his own brother in defence of his stepmother? Why had he begged his father not to believe James? The anguished look he had cast at Annabel as he left the room suggested an all too reasonable answer.

Geoffrey was in love with his beautiful young stepmother. Nor was it a selfish infatuation such as Marjorie had felt for Astwick. The quiet youth doubtless saw himself as a chivalrous knight, worshipping his lady from afar yet always ready to rush to protect her.

Which added Geoffrey to the list of those with excellent motives for wishing Astwick harm. Moreover, he might well have considered a ducking sufficient punishment and warning, without seeing any need to dispose permanently of his beloved's persecutor. Yes, if Astwick's death was the result of mischief gone wrong, Geoffrey was definitely a suspect. Who else?

Lord Wentwater? Impossible to imagine a haughty gentleman, so bound by convention that he refused to ask an unwelcome guest to leave, doing anything so undignified as wielding an axe on the lake at midnight. The earl had confessed himself stymied, unable to deal with the situation, yet he seemed too dispassionate to resort to such desperate measures.

Phillip? Daisy couldn't believe it. If he knew he'd been defrauded, Phillip would grumble ineffectually and convince himself that the next silver mine he invested in would turn into a gold mine. If he did go so far as to hunt out an axe and cut a hole in the ice, he'd have been there to see no serious accident occurred. Surely not Phillip!

Marjorie? Wrapped up in her emotions, the silly girl would never consider the possible dire consequences. Marjorie had to be considered a likely suspect.

The Mentons? Dismissing Lady Josephine and Sir Hugh out of hand, Daisy plumped up her pillow and turned on her other side. James was really the most satisfactory villain, she thought drowsily. She wouldn't mind at all if James went to prison for manslaughter for a few years.

Sleep still evaded her as the image of Lord Stephen's drowned body came to haunt her. That frightful gash on his temple—if it hadn't been for that he might have pulled himself out. What was it Alec had said? Something about a romantic tryst by moonlight and Annabel biffing him on the head—the weather kiboshed that—no, it was Daisy herself who had said perhaps the manservant met him and biffed him, but he wouldn't have been wearing skates. Whatever had happened to his blasted boots, he must have drowned when he went down to skate in the morning.

His death was mischance—Annabel couldn't have risked his surviving—Annabel wasn't responsible—so it must be one of—

Daisy slept.

CHAPTER 9

I'm sorry, sir, I can't let you leave." Detective Constable Piper, barring the open front door, sounded nervously determined.

"Bosh, my good fellow, you can't stop us." That was Phillip, at his most pompous. Dressed in his drab motoring coat, he slapped his gauntlets impatiently against his hand. Beside him stood Fenella in a blue travelling costume, the dust veil of her hat thrown back, plucking timidly at his sleeve.

As Daisy reached the bottom of the stairs, she called to him. "Phillip! What's going on?"

He swung round. "This confounded chappie is bally well trying to stop me taking Fenella home. You have a word with him, Daisy. You're in cahoots with the ruddy coppers."

"Do be reasonable, Phil. He's only doing his duty. I heard Chief Inspector Fletcher tell him not to let anyone leave. Will you shut that door, please, Officer? There's a frightful draught through here, though at least it's a bit warmer today, thank heaven."

"Right away, miss!" Piper threw her a look of worshipful gratitude and turned to close the door.

"Mr. Fletcher's coming back this morning," Daisy assured the Petries, "and I expect he'll let you go, but I do think you ought to wait till he arrives."

"The pater said to take Fenella home," Phillip said obstinately. "I didn't catch him on the 'phone till quite late last night, after that nasty mix-up, and he said to bring her home straight away."

"It's fearfully early still. Have you had breakfast? Why on earth do you want to leave so early?"

"It's a deuce of a way."

"The roads will be perfectly ghastly with this thaw. You're sure to get bogged down on the way. Haven't you some relative or other a bit nearer than Worcestershire where Fenella can stay for a few days?"

"There's Aunt Gertrude and Uncle Ned, Phil. Reading isn't far, is it? I'd like to stay with Aunt Gertrude, and I'd like more than a cup of tea before we leave. You rushed me so." Fenella took off her gloves, and Daisy noticed her engagement ring was missing.

"Oh, right-ho," Phillip grumbled. "I'll have to ring up Aunt Gertrude and make sure it's all right. Hang it, Officer, you'd better tell Lord Wentwater's man we'll be leaving later and he's to put the car back in the garage."

"Yes, sir." Piper saluted and opened the door just wide enough to slip out, closing it firmly again behind him.

"Come on, Fenella," said Daisy, "to the breakfast-room. I'm starving."

Already on his way to the telephone table in the corner of the hall, Phillip turned, frowning. "You'd better order a tray in your bedroom, Fenella."

Daisy raised her eyebrows quizzically. "I promise I'll not let her be either murdered or corrupted at the breakfast table, and she can stick to me like a leech till Mr. Fletcher comes. You'll join us, won't you, when you've finished telephoning?"

"Yes. As a matter of fact, I only had a cup of coffee and a muffin and I'm still dashed peckish," he admitted with a sheepish grin.

Daisy and Fenella found Sir Hugh in the breakfast-room, ensconced behind *The Financial Times*, which he lowered briefly to bid them good morning. His plate and cup were already empty, Daisy was glad to see. By the time the girls had helped themselves from the sideboard, he was folding the paper and standing up.

"Nothing about this business in the papers yet," he said approvingly. "That's a good man they sent down from Scotland Yard."

"Is there any more news of the jewel robbery at Lord Flatford's?" Daisy asked.

"Just a paragraph in my paper, saying the police are holding a man for questioning and expect an imminent arrest. *The Financial Times* doesn't go in for that sort of news, though. You'll find the *Daily Mail* on the table in the hall."

Daisy thanked him, but she knew she'd find out more from Mr. Fletcher than from the *Mail*. Besides, at present she was itching to discuss Fenella's departure.

The moment Sir Hugh left the room, she said, "So your parents want you to go home?"

"*I* want to go! I simply can't marry James after all."

"Very sensible of you. He is not a nice person."

"Phillip called him a deuced rum fish," Fenella revealed, glancing over her shoulder at the door. "What shall I do if he comes in?"

"You'll say good morning and then preserve a dignified silence," Daisy advised, spearing a piece of sausage. "Did you love him very much?"

"I don't really know. I think not, because I am more

shocked than upset. He was always perfectly polite and kind, and when Mummy told me he wanted to marry me I thought I should like to be a countess one day. Only, he was quite horrid to Lady Wentwater, so I could never be sure that one day he might not be horrid to me, too, could I?"

"Quite right. These are jolly good sausages."

"The cook makes her own. James showed me the pigs on the home farm. He's frightfully keen on farming, and I like animals. I did think we might be happy together." She sniffed unhappily. "Suppose no one else ever wants to marry me?"

Daisy hastened to support her resolve. "I'm not married and I'm perfectly happy," she pointed out. Seeing Fenella blanch, she quickly added, "But I'm sure you'll easily find a husband. The boys your age weren't in the War, after all. You haven't even spent a season in London yet, have you?"

"No. James and I met at a house-party last summer."

"There, you see? Engaged before you're even out. You don't need a brute like James."

They had nearly finished breakfast before Phillip came in to report that all was well. "Aunt Gertrude will be pleased to see Fenella, and I talked the parents into agreeing. Actually, Daisy old bean, it was a dashed good idea of yours, because I'll be able to get back here this evening to look after you. I was pretty worried about leaving you on your own for the best part of two days."

Daisy did her best not to snap at him. "Thank you for the kind thought, though I assure you I can look after myself."

"Come to think of it, old thing, I expect the inspector chappie would let you go, too. You'd be better off buzzing back to town out of this fishy business."

"I'm not leaving, Phillip," she informed him through gritted teeth, "so you might as well save your breath to cool your porridge. Fenella, I'm going to the darkroom. Do you want to come or will you hang about with Phil?"

Fenella chose to accompany her and fiddled quite happily with magnifying lenses while Daisy printed a few more shots. Some kindly soul had put a paraffin heater in the scullery so they were reasonably comfortable once their noses grew accustomed to that smell on top of the developing chemicals.

Finishing her printing, Daisy studied the prints she had made last night, thoroughly dry by now. They included the shots she had taken by magnesium flash, and she was anxious to see how they had come out.

"I didn't print the two disastrous ones, of course," she explained to Fenella. "The one where your beastly brother accused me of trying to blow up the house, and the one that fizzled. But look, this isn't bad, nor this."

As she had expected, Marjorie's black-and-white dress inevitably drew the eye. Though she couldn't do anything about that, the background of the Great Hall fireplace, carved frieze, tapestries, and ancient weapons had come out surprisingly clearly. Even Queen Elizabeth's dagger was plain to see. Through a magnifying glass, she could make out the details of the frieze and the solemn faces of the family group.

"They're jolly good," said Fenella. "Are they really going to be in a magazine?"

"Yes, though I don't know which ones the editor will choose." She picked up another of the Great Hall shots. Studying it through the lens, she gasped, then threw a quick glance at Fenella.

"James doesn't *look* like a rum fish," Fenella was saying. She hadn't heard Daisy's gasp. "I don't see how I could have guessed."

"You couldn't. Just be thankful you found out in time." Daisy remembered James's smug expression after she had taken the first flash photograph that worked right. Wilfred had looked apprehensive, Lady Josephine upset, and Marjorie angry, and when Daisy had turned her head she'd seen Annabel and Lord Stephen.

What she hadn't realized at the time was that while those four of her subjects had reacted after the shot, the other two had reacted quicker. Lord Wentwater's and Geoffrey's faces had been impassive by the time she looked up from the camera. Dazzled by the flash, she had not noticed the turbulent emotions of father and son, so quickly hidden, so clearly visible now in the print.

"It's just another of the same," she said as Fenella reached for the photograph in her hand. She shuffled it into the pile Fenella had already examined.

As they returned through the kitchen passages towards the main part of the house, they met a footman.

"Miss Dalrymple, her la'ship says if you'd be so kind as to step up for a word wi' her in her boodwah when you has the time." Well trained, the man was as expressionless as if nothing had ever occurred to disturb the peace of Wentwater Court.

"Lady Wentwater? Of course. Fenella, I'll just see you safely back in Phillip's care first."

"Mr. Petrie's in the billiard-room, miss."

Fenella delivered to her brother, Daisy headed for the stairs.

Annabel's boudoir-dressing-room was beyond the Wentwaters' bedroom. Daisy heard no response to her knock, but Annabel might be too miserable to call out loudly, she decided. In view of her invitation she went in.

No one was there. From beyond a door on the opposite side of the boudoir from the bedroom came the sound of running water. Daisy hesitated on the threshold, glancing round the room.

The near end held chests-of-drawers, wardrobes, a cheval glass, and a dressing table. At the far end, under the window, stood a small table and two cane-backed chairs, with a roll-top bureau in one corner, a matching glass-fronted bookcase in the other. In the centre of the room, grouped around the fire, were two armchairs and a chaise-longue covered in light brown chintz with tiny butter cup yellow flowers. The walls were hung with a Regency stripe wallpaper in cream and brown, colours picked up by the Axminster carpet. A pretty, cosy room.

Daisy crossed to the fireplace to examine the picture hanging over the mantelpiece. It was an impressionistic oil painting of a dark-haired girl in a yellow dress descending a flight of steps in a garden full of flowering shrubs and vines.

She swung round as a door closed behind her.

"Yes, that's Rupert's work." Annabel's red eyes were conspicuous in her pale face. She wore a simple coat-frock of turquoise jersey, so beautifully cut it must be straight from Paris. "Henry insisted on my keeping some of his paintings. Oh Daisy, he's been so kind, so sympathetic. I can't seem to stop crying."

"Isn't it funny how sympathy does that, much more than someone being beastly? It was Geoffrey's defence that made you cry last night, not James's attack, wasn't it?"

Annabel nodded, joining Daisy by the fire, and they both sat down. "Henry feels terrible about it. He keeps apologizing for not being the one to protect me, for having been blind to James's spite."

"James took pretty good care not to let him see it, until last night. And I imagine Geoffrey was brought up not to tell tales on his brothers."

"Henry says *I* should have told him, but I couldn't, could I? I didn't want to worry him, or to make trouble between him and his son. I hoped in time James would realize I really do love Henry, and then he'd grow accustomed to having a stepmother. But instead I've ruined his life. You know Fenella has broken off the engagement?"

"Yes, I've been hearing about it all morning."

"So I've ruined her life, too."

"What rot, Annabel. It's a good thing she discovered in time what James is like." Daisy looked up as the silvery chime of the Dresden china clock on the bureau began to play. "Quarter to eleven. Are you coming down for coffee?"

"I don't know. Should I? Henry said he'd go down with me, but he doesn't usually join us for morning coffee and I didn't want everyone to think I'm afraid to face them without his support."

"Are you? Are you afraid of meeting James?"

"No, he's confined to his room. As soon as the police go, he's to be sent to live in Northumberland. Henry owns a small property there, and James is to run the farms. You see why I say I've ruined his life," Annabel finished despairingly.

"What tommyrot! It's entirely his own fault, and besides, James likes farming. Everyone will think he's buzzed off to the wilds because Fenella jilted him." Unless he ended up on trial for manslaughter. "What about Geoffrey? Will meeting him upset you?"

Hesitating, Annabel studied her hands as she answered. "I ought to thank him, but he's confined to his room too. Henry's grateful to him for standing up for me, but he's also angry about the brawl in the drawing-room."

"It certainly wasn't a display of what my governess used to call drawing-room manners!" Daisy wondered whether Annabel was embarrassed because she knew Geoffrey was in love with her. Yet she hadn't talked of ruining *his* life. Was Lord Wentwater aware that his son was in love with his wife? Another ghastly situation, but fortunately not one Daisy felt called upon to deal with. "Come on, I could do with coffee and a biscuit. I've been working hard this morning."

Annabel managed a smile as she stood up. "I miss my work. In Italy I used to arrange things for English people who came to stay in the area—you know, hiring servants and interpreting and so on. That's how I met Henry." She stopped by the dressing-table and peered at herself in the mirror. "Oh Lord, I can't go down with my eyes like this. The cold water didn't do any good."

"They're not as bad as they were when I came in. It's the contrast with your pale cheeks. Try a bit of rouge."

"I'm not very good at it. I hardly ever bother with anything but powder."

"Nor do I, because I always look frightfully healthy. I've always wanted to be pale and interesting like you. But I've watched Lucy put on rouge and she always looks marvellous. Shall I give it a go?"

"Please do."

Daisy's efforts met with her own and Annabel's approval. "Now lipstick," she said. "There. Your eyes aren't at all noticeable now."

They both powdered their noses and went down to the morning-room. The elderly spaniel, who seemed to live there, ambled over to greet Annabel. Wilfred, nobly entertaining his aunt with the latest gossip from the theatrical world, stood up.

"Good morning, Daisy. Good morning ... er ... Mother." He turned pink and gave a self-conscious laugh. "I feel like a dashed idiot ..."

"Please, call me Annabel." She blinked hard and bit her lip, fondling the dog's head. Afraid she was going to burst into tears again at Wilfred's touching gesture, Daisy squeezed her hand.

"The gov'nor wouldn't like it," Wilfred objected diffidently, smoothing his hair with a nervous hand.

"Never mind that. I'll talk to him. Please?"

"Right-oh, Annabel."

"That's better," said Lady Josephine, her plump face benevolent. "It's so very awkward when no one knows what to call anyone. You modern young things are delightfully casual about proper forms of address. In my youth it was unthinkable for any gentleman to address a lady other than his sister or wife by her Christian name.''

She chattered on as the morning coffee was brought in and Lord Wentwater and Sir Hugh joined them. Phillip and Fenella came too. Coffee was poured, cakes and biscuits passed around, polite small talk exchanged, just as if Lord Stephen had not drowned and James had not disgraced himself. The only reminder of recent events came when Phillip grumbled to Daisy, in a hushed mutter, because the Chief Inspector had not yet returned.

He moved on to a lengthy story about his car, an elderly Swift two-seater which, Daisy gathered, he kept running with spit and string. It was a pity his noble antecedents ruled out employment as a motor mechanic, she was thinking, when Marjorie came in. Soberly dressed, the scarlet lipstick missing, her wan, hollow-eyed presence was a sudden reminder of unpleasant reality. A momentary silence fell.

Wilfred broke it. "Feeling better, old bean? I'll get you some coffee."

"Thanks, Will," she said gratefully as the buzz of conversation resumed.

Lord Wentwater crossed to her and took both her hands. They spoke to each other in low voices, Marjorie nodding once or twice, assuring her father she was recovered, Daisy assumed. Wilfred took her a cup of coffee. The earl put his arm about her shoulders in a brief embrace before he left them, going to Annabel.

Daisy heard him say, "I have work to do, my dear," as he stooped to kiss her cheek. She gazed after him with a look of devoted gratitude mixed with a yearning in which Daisy read something of hope—and something of dread.

Before Daisy had a chance to ponder Annabel's curious expression, Marjorie approached.

"Phillip, if you don't mind, I'd like a word with Daisy."

He sprang to his feet with gentlemanly alacrity and took himself off. Marjorie sat down in his place, then seemed to lose steam.

"I'm glad you're feeling well enough to come down," Daisy said in an enquiring tone.

"I've been the most frightful fathead!" Marjorie's exclamation was a masterpiece of suppressed violence. "Poor Daddy, watching me make an ass of myself when he has so much else to worry him. But even worse . . . Daisy, you're chummy with Annabel—my stepmother—aren't you?"

"Call her Annabel. She just asked Wilfred to. Yes, you could say we're chummy."

"Will you tell her I don't hold her to blame because Lord Stephen liked her better than me? I know I acted as if I thought she was trying to take him away from me, but he never really wanted anything to do with me even before he came down here. He was . . . he was rather a scaly character, wasn't he?"

"A real snake in the grass," Daisy agreed. "Won't you tell her yourself?"

"Oh, I couldn't!"

"Try. She's not very happy and it might cheer her up."

"She must be in a fearful huff at me."

Daisy shook her head. "I think you'll find she understands. She's not much older than you. Go on."

A few minutes later she had the satisfaction of seeing Marjorie and Annabel embrace each other. Marjorie, like Wilfred, was turning out to be not half such a blister as she had made herself out to be. The trouble was, the more her resentment had been directed at Lord Stephen rather than Annabel, the more likely that she had decided to give him a ducking.

Daisy slipped out of the room. She wanted to think about what she was going to tell Alec. It was beginning to dawn on her that, whoever was responsible for Astwick's death, the whole family was going to be dragged through the courts. Her increasing liking for Annabel made her quail at the prospect.

However, her duty as a citizen to cooperate with the police was unchanged. Besides, what they didn't learn from her they'd probably dig up anyway, perhaps with more disruption of everyone's feelings. Alec was a good detective who would leave no stone unturned. Even exhausted by lack of sleep, he had jumped on a coincidence of names leading to the recovery of a fortune in stolen gems!

Where was he? She was dying to know what Astwick's ferret-faced manservant, Payne, had to say about the burglaries.

As she reached the Great Hall, a footman came towards her. "The detective's back, miss. I was just coming to tell you he's asking for you."

"In the Blue Salon again? Thank you." Daisy was taken by surprise by the lightening of her heart. Alec was back, and he wanted to see her—purely for professional reasons, she reminded herself.

"The Blue Salon?" Phillip had overheard as he arrived in the hall, Fenella in tow. "The Chief Inspector's here? It's belly well about time, too." He and Fenella followed Daisy to the Blue Salon, where he instructed his sister to wait outside.

Alec, flanked by Tring and Piper, glanced up and smiled as Daisy entered. He looked as if he had slept well, his eyes restored to brightness, no longer hollow beneath the fierce eyebrows.

"Good morning, Miss Dalrymple. Ah, Mr. Petrie." The eyebrows rose, giving him a sardonic air. "I understand you wish to leave us."

"Not me, my dear chap, my sister. My people want me to take her to her aunt's, near Reading. It's an infernally awkward situation, here, don't you know."

"It is indeed," said Alec gravely, but Daisy would have sworn he was hiding a smile. "I take it you're referring not only to my investigation but to Miss Petrie's broken engagement.''

"How the blazes do you know about that already?" Phillip was properly impressed by this evidence of omniscience. "Hang it all, one can't keep much from you chaps. Yes, that's right. Deuced uncomfortable for the poor old thing being stuck in the same house with the blighter she's handed his papers.''

"You don't feel the same discomfort?"

"What, me? By Jove, I've been in worse holes, I can tell you. You were up above it all, I see." He nodded at Alec's Flying Corps tie. "Ever meet von Richthofen?"

"I never had that honour." Alec patiently returned him to the point. "I gather you intend to return to Wentwater Court after leaving your sister with your aunt?"

"Oh yes, can't leave Daisy—Miss Dalrymple—in the lurch. Have to keep an eye on her. Dash it, I've known her since she was no higher than my knee.''

"What rot, Phillip! You're only two years older than me. I was higher than your knee when I was born.''

"No, you weren't, old bean. Not until you were old enough to stand up," said Phillip triumphantly.

Sergeant Tring managed to turn a guffaw into a muffled snort. Ernie Piper frankly grinned.

Alec preserved his countenance. "May I have your word on that please, Mr. Petrie?" His lips twitched at Phillip's blank stare. "No, not on the height of your knee, on your return to Wentwater.''

"My hat, I believe you still suspect me!" Phillip fidgeted under Alec's suddenly piercing gaze. "Yes, confound it, you have my word.''

"Thank you, Mr. Petrie. I regret to say that so far only Miss Petrie and Miss Dalrymple have been eliminated from my enquiries. Everyone else at Wentwater Court is still under suspicion of having caused Lord Stephen Astwick's death.''

CHAPTER 10

With a subdued "toodle-oo," Petrie departed. Alec sent Tom Tring off to the servants' quarters to ask the questions they had discussed on the drive from Winchester, then he turned to Daisy.

"I must thank you, Miss Dalrymple, for supporting Piper this morning."

All the same, he thought, he must have been more tired than he had realized yesterday to put such trust in her, to treat her almost as another police officer under his command. Had he really called her Daisy, or was it a dream? He had been too happy to see her when she walked into the room a moment ago. He must keep reminding himself that she was the Honourable Miss Dalrymple and he was merely a middle-class copper, doing his job.

"I'm sure Phillip didn't do it," she said, her smile becoming uncertain as if she recognized his withdrawal, "but I reckoned if he walked out you'd be mad as a wet cat. Do you really still suspect him?"

"I must. The lodge-keeper's statement together with the

skates Astwick was wearing virtually rule out an outside agency connected with his financial shenanigans or the jewel robberies.''

"Have you found out anything more about the robberies?" she asked eagerly. "Has Payne talked? I suppose the man you picked up in the Lanchester really is Payne?"

"Chummie admitted to being Astwick's 'personal gentleman,' and that's about all we got out of him. He only admitted that much after we told him we'd found the loot, the passports, and the tickets to Rio, and had arrested his lordship."

"Arrested!"

"One of our little tricks that often works. They're so keen to put the blame on the other fellow that they spill the beans."

"I can't imagine Lord Stephen claiming his servant was the brains of the show," said Daisy. "Too, too humbling."

"Nor can Payne, apparently. He remained unmoved. Still, a few more hours behind bars and we'll see what news of Astwick's death does to his tongue. In the meantime, there are blocks on the roads around the area where he was found lurking, and half the Hampshire force combing the countryside. That business is under control. I wish I could say the same of this. Have you anything new to tell me?"

"If you know about Fenella's engagement being broken, then you know about James's outburst, which means you know about Geoffrey sloshing him. I take it Piper found out from the servants . . ."

"Yes, miss," young Ernie confirmed proudly.

". . . though I'd swear none of them was in the room at the time and I can't think how they found out."

"The footman on duty was just about to go in to make up the fire, miss, when it all happened."

"What did I say about servants and sneezes?" Alec teased, momentarily forgetting his good resolution. "Still,

I'd like to hear the story from you to make sure what I heard is accurate."

The tale she told was essentially the same as Ernie's report, and once again Alec marvelled at the servants' espionage system. One difference caught his attention.

"You say Geoffrey cast a *heartbreaking* glance at Lady Wentwater as he left the drawing-room. What exactly do you mean by that?"

She hesitated. "I wish I hadn't said that. After all, I might have imagined it. One can't draw conclusions from a passing expression."

"Not conclusions, but inferences, or my job would be impossible. Tell me."

"I'll show you," she said with a sigh, "or at least show you something which seems to confirm my inference. A photograph. It's in the darkroom." She started to rise.

"Can you describe to Piper where to find it? Good." He sent the constable off to fetch the photo. "We'll leave the subject of Geoffrey until he comes back. I understand Lady Marjorie has emerged from seclusion. Have you talked to her?"

"Yes." Again Daisy seemed reluctant to continue. "Or rather, she talked to me. She wanted me to tell Annabel she doesn't really believe Annabel tried to take Lord Stephen away from her."

"Which suggests she realizes that Astwick was the villain of the piece."

"She called him a scaly character," Daisy admitted. Clearly she recognized—and deplored—the strengthening of Lady Marjorie's motive. "I'm sure James did it," she hurried on. "If you'd heard his beastly attempt to put the blame on Annabel . . ."

"He's already tried that on me, remember, and I'll be speaking to him again. I assure you, he's high on my list."

"Good! Wilfred's turned out to be a bit of a brick, you

know. Besides standing up for Geoffrey last night, he made a special effort to be friendly to Annabel this morning.''

"He's low on my list.'' Alec smiled at her. "Didn't we decide he'd more to lose than to gain from making Astwick mad as a wet cat?''

"Yes, like Annabel,'' she agreed with a grateful smile. "I'm so glad Annabel is out of it. I've been talking to her a lot and I like her awfully.''

Alec didn't disillusion her. True, Lady Wentwater had had nothing to gain from angering Astwick, and she knew it, but would she have considered that in a passion of desperate hate and fear? Or might she not somehow have ensured that the ducking should end in drowning?

Except that he couldn't think how.

"She didn't say anything helpful?'' he asked.

"Helpful to you? No.''

"To you?''

Daisy nodded, a haunting sadness crossing her face. If Lady Wentwater had said something to comfort her, Alec prayed fervently that her ladyship would not be implicated.

Piper returned, breathless, with a stack of photographs. Skimming through them, Daisy picked out four, discarded three, and handed Alec the fourth. "I shot it just as Annabel and Astwick came into the hall together.''

"A family group, yet Lady Wentwater wasn't included?'' He took out his magnifying glass.

"I'm not sure whether she was left out on purpose or by accident. I think it was a misunderstanding.''

The figure in the centre of the photo, her boldly patterned dress standing out, was a young woman he recognized only as a type. Her boyish figure, marcelled bob, and sharply defined lips were the current uniform of fashion. "So that's Lady Marjorie? A bright young thing bent on grabbing the limelight.''

"It's a bit thick, isn't it? I was pretty fed up when she bobbed up wearing that frock, but she's really quite sweet.''

"And there's Geoffrey." He studied the large youth's face. "Good Lord, don't tell me the lad's in love with his stepmother!"

"That's what it looked like to me," Daisy agreed. "And if he loves her, he wouldn't have wanted to hurt her by getting Astwick in such a dudgeon he'd make trouble for her."

"He might not have thought so far ahead," Alec pointed out, scanning the rest of the photographed group, "or he might not even have realized Astwick was threatening Lady Wentwater with . . . Great Scott! To think I put Wentwater down as one of those stoic gentlemen incapable of violent emotion! He's practically foaming at the mouth."

"Yet just a moment later, when I looked up, he seemed as unruffled as ever. He came to the darkroom to talk to me last night. I'd done a bunk after all the fuss and bother," she explained apologetically.

"I don't blame you. It must have been a deuced awkward situation." In her place most girls would have fled the house, like Fenella Petrie, but Daisy soldiered valiantly on, doing her best both to aid the course of justice and to protect her friends. Alec wished he had never enlisted her, dividing her loyalties. It was his job, though, to make use of anything and anyone who could help him solve the case. "What had Lord Wentwater to say to you?"

"He wanted to convince me that he trusts Annabel."

"So he has already assured me," said Alec cynically.

Daisy chuckled. "He advised me in his most earlish manner not to bother to pass it on to you as repetition wouldn't make a believer of you."

"Then why . . . ?"

"I think he came to me for Annabel's sake, in case James's beastliness had influenced me against her. He swore he hadn't realized what James was up to. I'm almost sure he also hoped to persuade me not to pass on the slander to you. When I said James had already flung the dirt, he was absolutely appalled."

"I'm not surprised. If I don't nab that young brute for manslaughter, I sincerely hope he'll get his comeuppance from his father." He held up his hand as she opened her mouth to speak. "Wait a minute, didn't you tell me Sir Hugh insisted on sending for the police? I was in a bit of a fog yesterday and I didn't catch the significance, but I assume that means the earl himself objected to calling us in."

"Only because he didn't want the Chief Constable poking his nose in. He and Colonel Wetherby are at daggers drawn, I gather. Didn't the Commissioner explain?"

"He just said to keep the local people out of it as much as possible. I didn't realize Wetherby himself was the problem. They're incredibly lucky that I was down here in Hampshire already, you know. No one from the Yard could have come without a request from the Chief Constable, or at least his consent."

"I don't think Sir Hugh can have known that. He did say something about not being sure of the protocol."

"Had it turned out to be an accident, the Commissioner might have been able to hush it up, I dare say. As it is, the only reason I haven't had to notify Wetherby yet is the connection with the case I'm already working on."

"He'll have to know eventually?"

"Oh yes, he'll get a copy of my report. It can't be kept from the press forever, either. Tring and Piper are good men and haven't breathed a word to the local chaps. Only Gillett, the Inspector knows my whereabouts or you'd have had swarms of reporters here by now."

"Too ghastly!"

"Fortunately they're quite happy at present. The conservative papers want to know when the police are going to start protecting delicately bred ladies from the scum of the earth. The left-wing rags are inveighing against the poverty that drives men to steal the purely ornamental wealth flaunted by the fashionably useless.''

''You haven't told the press about recovering the gems?''

''No, partly because of the link with Astwick's death, mostly because I'd like to keep it out of the papers until we've recovered the latest haul. Too many people know, though. I give it twenty-four hours at most, and then another twenty-four before they're onto Astwick.''

''Golly, forty-eight hours before ravening hordes of reporters descend on Wentwater Court?''

''At most.''

''Don't tell Lord Wentwater!''

''Don't you, either,'' he recommended, smiling. ''Well, unless you have anything more to report, I'd better go to work on Lady Marjorie to start with. Thank you, Miss Dalrymple. I'll see you later. Are your pencils sharpened, Ernie?''

Daisy left the Blue Salon with mingled disappointment and relief. Alec had no need of her shorthand today. Though she disliked being excluded after feeling herself part of his team, she was also quite glad to be spared the second interview with James. Besides, she hadn't done a stroke of work on writing her article yesterday. It was her only excuse for staying at Wentwater, and she wanted to stay until everything was cleared up.

On the way to her room, she met Geoffrey on the stairs, togged out in riding kit. She didn't think he'd defy his father so he must have been released from confinement. He stopped three steps above her, his tall, solid-muscled frame looming over her.

She wouldn't want to make him angry, but his violence was the violence of a hot temper. Though Geoffrey would strike out in a fury, she simply couldn't imagine him coolly planning a nasty trick.

''Miss Dalrymple—Daisy—I must apologize for the dustup last night,'' he said, shamefaced.

"I don't blame you," Daisy told him warmly. "James was asking for it." Finding herself with a choice of craning her neck or addressing his waistline, she continued up the stairs, halting a few steps higher.

He turned to face her. "I shouldn't have started a rough-house in the drawing-room. I didn't think, I just wanted to stop him spouting such filth. You don't believe what he said, do you?"

"Certainly not, and your method was jolly effective, if not quite the thing. Are you going riding? I don't think you should, you know. Mr. Fletcher's going to want to talk to you."

"To me?" Geoffrey blanched. "Again?"

"I shouldn't worry, I don't expect he'll have you up for assault," she said with a smile. "Why don't you ask if he can see you right away, then you can ride afterwards."

He nodded, but in the moment before his stolid mask shut down, Daisy saw that her words had not reassured him. Despite his size and strength, he was awfully young and vulnerable.

How perfectly ghastly for the poor prune to be in love with his stepmother!

When Daisy reached her room, Mabel was dusting. "I haven't touched your papers, miss," the maid assured her. "I'm that sorry I'm not done yet but things is all at sixes and sevens what with the p'leece in the house and all."

"Have you been talking to the sergeant again?"

"Not today, miss." She giggled. "He's a right caution, that Sergeant Tring. 'Smorning he just wanted to see Dilys, she's the girl did my lord's room that drownded. On about boots again, he is, but our Dilys don't know nothing about them. Mr. Payne's the one to ask, being as Albert the bootboy's thick as two planks. Is it true, miss, Mr. Payne's been nicked?"

"How on earth do you know that?" Daisy suspected Mr.

Tring's questions must have given it away, but perhaps Alec had no reason to keep it quiet.

"Summun told me," said Mabel vaguely. "A nasty piece of work, Mr. Payne, that's what Cook says. He done it, for sure."

"Done . . . did what?"

"Why, done his lordship in, miss, or at least swiped them boots. That's what we all thinks, or why'd the p'leece pinch him?"

"Did Payne have a reason to want to get rid of Lord Stephen?" Daisy asked hopefully, though she was sure Tom Tring must have asked already. That was the trouble with being on the fringes of the investigation: she'd missed the sergeant's report to Alec.

"Didn't seem like it, miss. He wasn't one to talk but summun asked him what it was like working for Lord Stephen and he said his lordship was a good master and ever so generous. But he clammed up after that, and you never know, do you? A good pair of boots costs a pretty penny, after all. Well, you'll be wanting to do your writing, miss. I'll leave you be, and beg pardon for chattering on."

Shaking her head at the notion of Payne stealing a pair of boots when he must have been aware of the despatch case full of priceless gems, Daisy settled at her typewriter. If only the manservant might turn out to have killed Astwick, for reasons that had nothing to do with the Beddowe family. But she couldn't work out how he'd have managed it, and he'd have to be barmy not to have pinched the jewels.

She shrugged her shoulders and turned to her notes on the history, architecture, and furnishings of Wentwater Court. Who killed Astwick was Alec's problem not hers, thank heaven.

* * *

At that moment, Alec would have been quite happy to shrug his shoulders and turn over the problem to someone else. Lady Marjorie was proving as unhelpful as the rest of his suspects. At least, somewhat to his surprise, she hadn't brought guardians with her.

She sat opposite him, too demure to be true in a dark blue tweed skirt flecked with pink and a long, pale blue, knitted V-neck jumper over a pink silk blouse. With no more than a dusting of powder on her face, her lips their natural shape and colour, she looked much younger than in the photograph, and defenceless, as if cosmetics were her armour.

"Yes, I knew Lord Stephen in London. He didn't go to deb dances much, or afternoon teas and that sort of thing, but we were introduced at a dinner party. I used to see him at nightclubs and . . ." she hesitated.

"And?"

"And gambling-rooms," said Lady Marjorie defiantly.

Alec was careful not to react as new possibilities opened before his eyes. Had she, like her brother, owed Astwick money? Or had he introduced her to a life of vice? Could she even be a cast-off mistress, clinging to the hope of winning him back, rather than the foolish, infatuated girl everyone believed her?

"You enjoy gambling?" he asked in a casual tone.

She relaxed. "Not much. An occasional rubber of bridge and half a crown each way on the Derby and the Oaks is enough for me. But one's escorts . . . you know how it is." She regarded him with doubt. "Or perhaps you don't."

"I can imagine. How long had you known Astwick?"

"About a year. Since Aunt Jo stopped insisting on chaperoning me everywhere."

Alec waited. Silence sometimes brought more results than questions.

"You only saw him . . . dead," she said. "He was frightfully handsome and sophisticated. He made the fellows who took me out seem like silly boys playing at being grown-up. And he was always escorting older women, the really smart set, married women usually. I never thought he'd take any notice of me."

"But he did?"

"Yes, in a sort of teasing way, as if he considered me a little girl."

"When? When did he start paying attention to you?"

"It was at Henley. Ronnie—the chap I was with—was cheering on his college crew, and I was bored, and Stephen took me to get strawberries and champagne. It was ripping. All my friends were fearfully envious." She frowned in thought, then looked up at Alec with stricken eyes. "Oh gosh, I've just realized, that was the first time I'd seen him since Daddy and Annabel were married. What an awful, unmitigated, hopeless chump I've been. He was after her all the time wasn't he?"

"He may have been. You have every right to be angry for the way he made use of you."

"Well, I was pretty fed up, I must say, when Will invited him down and he actually came, and then he ignored me. In fact, if you want to know the truth, I was jolly peeved— not enough to kill him!" she added hastily, aghast.

"Just enough to want to pay him out," Alec suggested.

"Is that what you think? That someone arranged for him to fall through the ice, just to make him suffer a bit?"

Alec decided it was time to admit his suspicions. "It was no accident," he said.

"Obviously, or you wouldn't still be here. But I reckoned that meant it must be murder, and you were trying to find out if anyone had seen a tramp, or a sinister stranger, or something. It was a practical joke that went wrong?" She considered the matter, then said candidly, "Well, I might have done it, if I'd thought of it. But I didn't."

Rather than disarming Alec, her candour rang alarm bells. Misleading frankness was one of the oldest tricks in the book and immediately made him wonder whether he was facing a clever actress.

Though she claimed to have failed to see through Astwick, Lady Marjorie was clearly quite bright. Presumably she had played the innocent to her father and aunt with such success they didn't realize she was frequenting gambling dens in Astwick's company. Her hysterical reaction to Astwick's death savoured more of acting than of a natural response. And just why had she chosen not to wear her usual sophisticated make-up today, when she must have guessed she was bound to be interviewed by the police?

Alec made a mental note to consult Daisy. Not that he considered her an infallible judge of character, let alone unbiased, but her insights were definitely useful to a confused detective. With a dearth of clues and alibis, and a plethora of motives and opportunity, character might yet turn out to be the only key to this case.

In the meantime, the girl sat there in her modest skirt and jumper, her pale-faced innocence a startling contrast to the fashionable flapper in the photograph. Which was the real Lady Marjorie?

CHAPTER 11

It wasn't me, honestly," said Lady Marjorie, earnest and uneasy.

"If it was," Alec said in his most fatherly manner, "and if you were to make a confession, I'm sure you'd get off lightly. There's nothing a jury likes better than a pretty young girl, especially with a title, who's been led astray by a rascally older man. I shouldn't be surprised if . . ."

The door opened, interrupting him. The footman stuck his head into the room. "Beg pardon, sir, it's Mr. Geoffrey wants to know, if you has to see him, can you do it soon, please, being as he's all set to go riding?"

Alec suppressed a sigh. "Tell him I'll see him next, in a few minutes." As the door closed, he turned back to Lady Marjorie. "You see, I don't believe for a moment that you meant to kill Astwick, so you'd very likely get a suspended sentence."

"But you really believe I'm the one who played the trick on him?" She shook her head violently. "I'm not! Why me?"

"I didn't say that, Lady Marjorie. You are by no means the only person I have reason to suspect. I'm just pointing out that confession inclines the courts to take a lenient view, and in the circumstances you need not fear severe consequences."

"I can't confess to something I didn't do!"

"Just bear my words in mind. Tell me . . ."

"I wish I had let someone come with me."

"We can send for someone now." He had no desire to figure as a bully. "Whom would you like? Your father? Your aunt?"

"Daddy? Oh no, nor Aunt Jo. I wouldn't want them to hear . . . Could Daisy come? She won't get upset."

"Certainly, assuming she's willing." Surprised and a little amused by her choice, he rang the bell. His efforts to detach Daisy from his enquiries appeared to be doomed to failure.

While they waited, he ventured one question. "Did anyone other than Astwick ever skate so early in the morning?"

"Heavens, no. Skating is supposed to be fun. Stephen did it as part of a fitness regimen that included cold . . . Wait a bit. Someone—Phillip Petrie, was it?—said something about trying it. It wasn't Wilfred, that's certain. I wasn't really listening, and I certainly don't know if Phillip actually went down to the lake. He would have seen Stephen fall in, wouldn't he? He could have pulled him out."

"Or fallen in himself."

"Golly, yes. How frightful if the wrong person had drowned! I mean, no one wanted Stephen to drown, but better him than Phillip. He's such a sweet old fathead."

"An amiable gentleman," Alec agreed gravely. Her answer to his query was no more helpful than he had expected.

Daisy came in, her face suitably solemn except for the sparkle in her blue eyes. Whatever her misgivings, she enjoyed being involved in the investigation, Alec realized.

She flashed him a mischievous smile as she sat down beside Lady Marjorie and said, "Is he being beastly to you?"

"Gosh no. Not really. He's just asking awkward questions, but that's his job, isn't it? I hope you don't mind my asking you to come and hold my hand."

"Not a bit. One would so much prefer one's relatives not to hear the answers to awkward questions." Daisy spoke with such heartfelt sympathy that Alec couldn't help wondering about her own relatives.

Lady Marjorie turned back to him. "Right-oh, fire away, Chief Inspector."

"Thank you. I'd like you to explain why you were prostrated with grief on learning of Astwick's death. You have recovered remarkably fast if true love was the cause of your distress."

She flushed. "You know quite well it wasn't true love. It was a stupid pash. I was flattered that he noticed me, and I liked having my friends envy me. I was already disillusioned when he . . . died."

"Then how do you account for your state prompting Dr. Fennis to prescribe a bromide?"

Her pink cheeks turned crimson and she looked wildly at Daisy.

"I can guess," Daisy said gently. "Tell him."

"I wanted everyone to believe I was frightfully upset," she said in a low voice. "I'd been making such a fuss over him, I'd have looked a fearful idiot if I'd just said good riddance."

"I see." Alec nodded. "Instead, everyone is sorry for you."

"That was the idea. Of course, in fact everyone thinks I'm an idiot anyway, for loving such an absolute cad."

Again the suspicious candour. What was more, Lady Marjorie admitted to feigning hysteria well enough to deceive a medical practitioner. Yet her embarrassed flush was real.

Alec asked a few more questions, then dismissed her and said to Daisy, "I want to discuss that interview with you, Miss Dalrymple, but it had better wait. Young Geoffrey is champing at the bit."

"Yes, he wants to go riding. I told him he must speak to you first."

"So that was your doing? I might have guessed. Thank you."

"Are you going to see Annabel again? I'll find out if she wants me with her today, before I go toddling back up all those stairs to my typewriter."

"Yes, I'll see her, and everyone else, though I did manage to ask most of the necessary questions yesterday in spite of being half asleep. Now I'm wide awake, watching them tell their stories may suggest new lines of enquiry that I missed before and that aren't apparent in the written report. I don't have much hope of breaking new ground, other than with Lady Marjorie and Geoffrey, of course, and perhaps Lord Wentwater."

"Marjorie's just . . ."

"Later, if you please." He smiled at her indignant look. "Sorry, but I'm sure to have more to discuss with you by the end of the day, and if we put it all together, we're more likely to see connections."

"Oh, all right. Anyway, I absolutely *must* get some work accomplished today."

She departed and Geoffrey came in. His impassive face gave no hint of the emotion which had driven him to attack his brother in his father's drawing room. Yet the evidence said that love and fury seethed beneath the calm exterior.

"Tell me about last night," Alec invited.

The lad's jaw tightened and his hands clenched on his thighs, then loosened slightly as though he forced himself to relax. "Last night? You must have heard every detail by now," he said dully.

"I'd like your side of the story."

"James started spewing filthy lies about An . . . my step-mother. I had to stop him."

"Do you often lose your temper and resort to fisticuffs?"

"No! Good Lord, no. I box for my University, and one can't box scientifically if one's always losing one's temper. Last night, I . . . I just saw red."

"What exactly was it that infuriated you?"

Geoffrey's mouth set in a stubborn line. "I won't repeat the vile things James said."

"No, no, that's not necessary. I meant something more on the lines of: Was it just because you believed he was lying?"

"I *know* he was lying. Annabel's an angel. She'd never do anything mean or underhanded. What got my goat was that James was deliberately trying to hurt her. To say such things in front of everyone, in front of my father!"

"You were afraid Lord Wentwater might believe his lies?"

"Yes. He doesn't. He told me so."

"I've been informed by several people that Lady Went-water was a good deal in Astwick's company. How do you account for their apparent intimacy?"

His face, which had grown animated, closed down again. "There was nothing in it. She knew him years ago and he took advantage of old acquaintance. She was too kind to give him the boot when he kept pestering her."

"So you tried to help her."

"I interrupted their tête-à-têtes whenever I could, but he was a guest here. It was up to my father to ask him to leave."

"And when he didn't, you took matters into your own hands and decided to warn him off by giving him a ducking in the lake."

Geoffrey's expression altered not an iota. "I might have, if he had been harassing her on the bank on a summer day. It never crossed my mind to crack the ice and wait for him to fall through. Anyway, he'd have presumed it an accident so it wouldn't have served as a warning. It wouldn't have helped my stepmother."

"Unless you told him afterwards and threatened more to come," said Alec halfheartedly. Geoffrey did indeed appear far more likely to biff Astwick in public as he had his brother than to plot a delayed vengeance or make threats. Time to move on to his other suspects. "Does Lady Wentwater know you love her?"

"No!" The denial exploded from his lips as his face first paled and then suffused with blood.

For the first time, Alec was certain he was lying. He didn't blame the boy. As long as his love was secret, his situation was merely miserable. Once his stepmother knew, it became impossible, for both of them. Whatever his faults, he was a chivalrous youth and no doubt hoped a pretence of her ignorance might make matters easier for her. Only time could ease his own heartache, but, being young, he wouldn't believe that.

No wonder his eyes were filled with apprehensive wretchedness. Geoffrey Beddowe's life was in a hell of a mess.

"Don't tell my father," he begged.

"I shan't, unless it should become absolutely necessary, and I don't foresee any such circumstances. Let me give you a word of advice. As much as you possibly can, stay away from Wentwater Court, and when you must be here, avoid Lady Wentwater's company."

"Yes, sir."

"And watch that temper, or your fists will land you hock-deep in the soup one of these days."

Geoffrey made a strange sound, halfway between a bitter laugh and a strangled sob, as if worse trouble than he was already in was beyond his imagining. Alec let him go.

"Whew!" breathed Piper from his window seat. "There's that song says a policeman's lot is not a happy one, but I reckon most people makes their own unhappiness, don't you, Chief?"

"As often as not, Ernie," Alec agreed. "As often as not."

He had been going to request the earl's attendance next, but, remembering that Daisy was postponing her work in case the countess wanted her, he called Lady Wentwater in next. To his professional relief and personal disappointment, she came alone. In a plain straight, turquoise woollen dress with ivory buttons down the front and an ivory sash about her hips, her figure was no less ripely inviting than in last night's silk. However, today the Madonna face was masked by cosmetics in the modern fashion.

The reverse of Lady Marjorie's transformation—why? Alec's searching gaze detected signs of pink puffiness around the dark, soulful eyes. Lady Wentwater had been weeping.

Weeping for a lost lover, a hopelessly devoted boy, or a publicly supportive husband's privately expressed doubts? Lord Wentwater must surely have suffered moments of mistrust, though Geoffrey's absolute belief in her innocence was understandable. In the way of the young, he had put her on a pedestal.

"Why did Geoffrey attack his brother last night?"

"To protect me against James's false accusations," she said quietly. "He is a gallant, unselfish, and courageous young man."

"He is in love with you."

She flushed. "What makes you say that?"

"I've been talking to him."

"He told you . . . ?" The brief colour fled from her face, leaving two patches of rouge on her high cheekbones. She clasped her slender hands to her breast. "You mustn't tell Henry! Oh, please, you won't tell Henry?"

"Not unless it becomes unavoidable, which I don't foresee." He was interested to discover that Lady Wentwater, like Geoffrey, was afraid of the earl's reaction. Lord Wentwater must be a formidable man when roused. Alec hoped against hope that he himself was not going to be the one doing the rousing.

He might at least be able to knock her ladyship off his list of suspects. He continued, "Nor do I see any need to pass on to your husband any disclosure you may make to me regarding your relationship with Astwick."

"You want to know what he was holding over me? I *cannot* see that it matters."

"Probably not, if there actually was a secret. You do realize that if in fact you were enjoying an amicable affair with him, your motive for wishing him dead would vanish?"

"I suppose it would," she said despairingly. "Since I'm caught between Scylla and Charybdis, I might as well stick with the truth. I was never his mistress. I hated him."

With that, Alec had to be satisfied. Lady Wentwater preferred to be suspected of causing Astwick's death rather than to be revealed as an unfaithful wife. He admired her for it.

He had to wait until after lunch to see her husband. Alec and Piper were provided with veal-and-ham pie, coffee, and bottled beer, and after eating Alec ventured to light his pipe. As he went over his notes of yesterday's interview with Lord Wentwater, he decided he must stop holding back in deference to the earl's social status. Certain questions needed asking. If his lordship chose to complain to the Commissioner, so be it.

Alec was knocking the dottle from his pipe into the grate when Lord Wentwater arrived. Piper hastily tossed his Woodbine into the fire and retreated to the window seat.

Once the earl was seated with the light from the window on his face, Alec spent a moment studying him. No sign of the passionate emotion of Daisy's photograph showed on those aristocratic features. Even his eyes met Alec's with calm gravity. Alec felt he'd never get anywhere unless he could shake the man's self-possession.

"I understand you and Lady Wentwater do not have separate bedrooms," he opened.

"That is neither a secret, nor unusual." Lord Wentwater seemed faintly amused.

"However, you have been known to sleep in your dressing-room. Did you do so the night before Astwick's body was found?"

"If you want an alibi, I have none." The trace of amusement was gone. "As it happens, I learned that my wife had retired early that evening, so I did not disturb her."

"Astwick also retired early. You claim to trust her, yet you must have wondered why she made no vigorous effort to repel his advances."

"Not at all. I am sure you are aware that my wife's life for some years was somewhat ... Bohemian. She is still unused to the role of hostess to a house party and undoubtedly feared insulting a guest."

"And that was the only reason?"

"It was sufficient." If Lord Wentwater had had any inkling of blackmail, he didn't betray it by so much as the flicker of an eyelid.

"Are you so sure Astwick's pursuit was unwelcome? I'm not suggesting, at present, that there was any question of her permitting him to seduce her, but the most respectable of ladies may enjoy a light flirtation."

"Respectable in some eyes, perhaps," he said coldly. "It was perfectly obvious that my wife neither encouraged nor enjoyed the scoundrel's attentions."

"Then why did you not intervene to protect her?" Alec rapped out.

A faint tinge of pink coloured the earl's cheeks but his voice was still more frigid. "I suppose I am obliged to put up with your prying. However, this was a matter of some delicacy which I doubt you would understand."

Alec fought to suppress his annoyance. "I may not understand the gentlemanly code that obliges you to entertain a *scoundrel,*" he said pointedly, "but I'm not entirely insensitive, I hope. Try me."

"I felt she might interpret any interference on my part as a lack of trust." Though his positive tone expressed belief in the rightness of his course of action, or rather inaction, his form of words suggested uncertainty.

"It's possible," Alec conceded, but he envisioned the unhappy young wife feeling herself abandoned to the unscrupulous snares of a vengeful blackmailer. If she was indeed innocent, he pitied her with all his heart. He found himself pitying the earl, too, for all his wealth and position. "You did nothing, yet you must have been distressed and angry."

The flash of anger in Lord Wentwater's eyes could have been remembered wrath or offence at Alec's suspicions. "Not so angry as to descend to playing a childish trick upon Astwick, I assure you," he said dryly.

"You knew his habit of skating at dawn."

"I did?"

"Your valet recalls mentioning it to you."

"Chief Inspector, I don't listen to, let alone remember, whatever nonsense my valet may babble when he's shaving me."

"A pity. You might have caught wind of Lord Beddowe's persistent spite towards Lady Wentwater."

And now the façade briefly cracked. For just a moment, fury, hurt, and despair chased each other across his face. Then he regained command of his features and spoke with icy calm. "My son's conduct was unforgivable. You may be sure I bitterly regret not having been aware of it."

"You give no credence to his accusation, I take it?"

"That Annabel was responsible for Astwick's drowning?

If you knew her, Mr. Fletcher, you'd not ask. My wife is the gentlest of souls. She hesitated to repulse him verbally, so how can you imagine she'd resort to violent measures to discourage him?"

"Stranger things have been known. Has it crossed your mind that Lord Beddowe might have engineered the accident in order to blame his stepmother?"

Lord Wentwater's calm shattered with a cry of aghast incredulity. "No! Oh God, no!" He dropped his head into his hands. "If I ever obtain the slightest evidence of that, you shall have it on the instant."

Which was precisely what Alec wanted. Though he regretted the effect of his question, it told him a good deal. In his experience, men who successfully hid their feelings were rarely capable of dissimulation once forced to reveal them. Lord Wentwater loved his wife; and he'd not have shown such horror at the possibility of his son's guilt had he himself caused Astwick's death.

Yet Alec could not quite write him off the list. "We're always grateful for evidence, of course," he said, "but I own I'm a bit surprised by your offer of assistance. You strongly objected to calling in the police, didn't you?"

"I did." Once again the earl quickly recovered his dignity. "I was satisfied that it was an accident. In fact, I've yet to hear of any proof to the contrary, though I presume you are convinced of deliberate intent to cause harm if not death."

"We are."

"But believing it an accident, I saw no need to have the local constabulary prying into Astwick's business at Wentwater Court. Whatever the truth, inevitably innuendos would fly. No doubt you've heard that Wetherby, the Chief Constable, and I are not on good terms."

" 'At daggers drawn,' " Alec quoted Daisy.

"Near enough," his lordship said with a wry smile. "Now if you had found Wetherby dead in the hall with Queen

Elizabeth's dagger in his back . . . Naturally, when Menton persuaded me that the police were inevitable and offered to consult Scotland Yard, I accepted."

Unable to credit that anyone could think the Met less likely than a mere county force to solve a crime, Alec was inclined to believe him. On the other hand, he might have counted on being able to sway Menton's friend at the Yard, whereas Colonel Wetherby was beyond his influence. Lord Wentwater remained on the list.

James Beddowe still topped it, a matter of wishful thinking for want of evidence. Alec sent for him.

The earl's heir was by no means the cocky, vitriolic young man he had appeared yesterday. He came in with a hangdog air, accentuated by the purplish bruise on his chin, and slumped into the seat Alec indicated.

Alec wasted no sympathy on him. "Do you wish to add to or amend your statement?" he enquired.

"Statement!" James looked distinctly rattled. "Here, I say, what I told you yesterday was pure speculation. If you're calling it a statement, I'll withdraw the whole bally thing. Tear it up."

"I'm afraid I can't do that, though I'll note that you have changed your mind since last night."

"I suppose you've heard all about last night," James said sulkily, fingering the bruise.

"I understand you more or less accused Lady Wentwater to her face, in your father's presence, of having murdered her lover. Is that correct?"

"I was kidding! If Geoffrey hadn't cut up rough, no one would've taken what I said seriously because Astwick's death obviously wasn't murder. It was an accident. People are always falling through weak ice. The silly ass should have checked it, and it's sheer folly to go skating alone, anyway."

"The ice was firm, and overnight temperatures were well below freezing."

James managed a sneer. "Ice varies in thickness, you know. Astwick hit a thin patch. Just bad luck. It was an accident."

"An 'accident' which you attempted to blame on your stepmother. An 'accident' which you caused in order to blame it on your stepmother?"

"Good gad, no! You can't believe that!"

"I have evidence that the ice was tampered with."

"Not by me! You must be mistaken. It was pure chance."

Alec shook his head.

"Then how can you be sure *she* didn't do it? *I* didn't, I swear it. I had no motive for harming Astwick."

"Except to lay the blame on Lady Wentwater," Alec pointed out inexorably.

James reverted to insisting that the police had misinterpreted the evidence, that Astwick had simply struck a weak patch of ice. "It might have happened to anyone," he maintained.

"Phillip Petrie, for instance."

He grimaced at the mention of his ex-fiancée's brother. "Or me. But someone would have been there to pull us out."

So he hadn't heard Petrie's boast. Another mark against him. On the other hand, he had taken Fenella skating with him when he found the body. Was he so callous he'd subject the inoffensive girl to such an experience? His behaviour to his stepmother argued that he was.

Alec took him again through the story of the discovery of Astwick's drowned body, hoping for a slip of the tongue indicating prior knowledge. He learned nothing new.

Wilfred was next. Breezing into the Blue Salon, he said at once, "You mustn't believe what my brother's been saying about Annabel. Jolly poor show, I'm afraid. The poor old pater's pretty shattered."

Alec found himself liking the natty young man, who was unashamedly relieved by the removal of the threat Astwick had presented to him. Unless he was very devious indeed, it seemed unlikely that he had had a hand in that removal. Nonetheless, he could not be crossed off the list.

Nor could the Mentons, though a second interview with them gave no new cause for suspicion. Altogether, though the weight of Alec's suspicions had shifted somewhat, the list remained unchanged. Even a full night's sleep had shed no light on the confusion. He requested Daisy's presence.

When the footman knocked on her bedroom door, Daisy was gazing out of the window. The sky was overcast and a few drops of rain were beginning to fall. By morning, she guessed, the snow would be gone, the grim evidence of the hole in the ice a thing of the past.

She hurried down to the Blue Salon.

Greeting her with flattering pleasure, Alec said, "I'm hoping you can straighten out my thoughts, which are going round and round in circles."

"So are mine," she admitted. "I've hardly done any work on my article. Yet at the same time, I'm beginning to find it hard to believe anything really happened. How I wish it hadn't!"

"If you'd rather not . . ."

"Oh no, I'll help if I can."

"Thank you. Let's go back to Marjorie, for a start. She feigned hysteria well enough to convince the doctor, but I'd swear her embarrassment was real when she told me why. Surely it's impossible to blush deliberately?"

"Heavens no. Lucy, the friend I share a house with, can blush at will just by turning her mind to something frightfully embarrassing. She claims it's an essential part of flirting. It doesn't work for me," Daisy added mournfully.

"So even that could have been acting, which makes me think she left off her cosmetics in order to look the part of an innocent."

"She might have, but if you ask me, she just felt too

wretched at the prospect of having to face everyone to bother."

"Maybe. Lady Wentwater did the opposite, trying to disguise with make-up that she'd been crying."

"That was on my advice."

"Oh. All the same, it's odd that she's so miserable when she no longer has anything to fear from Astwick."

"She's not miserable, she was crying because Lord Wentwater was so kind to her." She wrinkled her nose at Alec's sceptical face. "I don't expect kindness makes men want to cry, but I assure you . . ."

"All right! The earl was especially kind to his wife and it made her cry. Does he know Geoffrey is in love with her?"

"I can't see that that's relevant."

"Who knows? I'm at a loss and clutching at straws."

"Well, I wondered myself. He didn't see Geoffrey's look at Annabel in the drawing-room, nor the photograph. The earl could well suppose that Geoffrey attacked James just from a general sense of chivalry, towards Annabel or even towards their father. After all, James's accusations hurt him, too."

"True. Did—does—Lord Wentwater know Astwick was blackmailing his wife, or was his violent emotion in the photo caused simply by jealousy?"

"I don't know. He did say Annabel was withholding something from him, but as far as I could tell he didn't appear to guess that it might be a secret from her past. Certainly he was more sad and worried than angry with her, as if he wished she'd bring herself to confide in him."

"To trust him as much as he trusts . . ." Alec broke off as the door opened and the footman's head appeared. "Yes? What is it?"

"A call for you on the telephone, sir. It's from Inspector Gillett in Winchester."

"Thank you, I'll come at once." Alec sprang to his feet.

"Ernie, go and tell Torn I want him in the Great Hall. If this is what I think, we'll be off."

Daisy trailed after him to the hall and waited at a discreet distance to find out whether he was about to leave. He listened, spoke briefly, listened again, then hung up the receiver as his sergeant and the constable came in.

"Gillett told chummie Astwick's dead and he's ready to talk. Let's hope we can get there before he changes his mind, Tom. Ernie, you're on duty here as last night. Miss Dalrymple, thank you for your help. We'll be back."

He and Tring strode off by the back way to the garages. Daisy stepped out onto the front porch for a breath of fresh air, and a few minutes later watched the yellow Austin Seven disappear down the drive into the rainy dusk. When she returned to the hall, the disconsolate Piper was still there.

"I expect you'd like to be in on Payne's interrogation," she said.

"Yes, miss, wouldn't I just."

"You're needed more here, or Mr. Fletcher wouldn't have left you," she consoled him. "Have you worked with him before?"

"Not on an out-of-town case, miss."

"Is he sent out of town often?"

"Pretty often, miss. He's been in charge of all these jool burglaries, besides other cases where there's nobs involved. He's got a degree, see, he knows how to talk to them sorts of people."

Daisy gathered that Piper no longer numbered her among "them sorts of people." Fishing for information about Alec, she remarked casually, "It must be hard on his family, having him away from home so much."

"All coppers has irregular hours, miss," he told her, unintentionally unhelpful, "and it's worse for us detectives. My girl, she knows what she's in for."

Before Daisy had to pretend to a polite interest in his

girl, the telephone bell rang and Drew appeared as if by magic to answer it. "For the Chief Inspector," he announced.

"He's left," said Daisy, dismayed.

"I'll take it," Piper said importantly, taking the apparatus from the butler, who disappeared as magically as he had appeared. "Hullo, hullo, this is Detective Constable Piper, C.I.D."

The receiver squawked at him in an irascible tone, cutting off his attempted explanation of his superior's absence. Piper felt in his pocket and produced his notebook and pencil. Daisy removed the elastic band holding it shut and opened it for him. He scribbled desperately for a few minutes.

"Yes, sir, I think I've got that but . . . Hullo, operator? Bloody hell, he's gone!" He blushed. "Beg pardon, miss."

"Oh, never mind that, who was it? What did he say?"

The constable studied his notes with an air of bemusement. "It were Dr. Renfrew, miss, the pathologist. Best I can make out, he's saying the deceased drowned not more'n two hours after he ate his dinner."

CHAPTER 12

Daisy and Detective Constable Piper stared at each other. "So Astwick died that evening?" Daisy said. "Not in the morning?"

"That's what it sounds like to me, miss. Everyone seems sure he didn't eat no breakfast, and anyway, by what I heard them doctors can tell pretty much what a body's ate recent by what's in the stomach."

"Ugh! What on earth was he doing going skating in the dark? It seems a frightfully peculiar thing to do, and I distinctly heard him say he was going to bed." She recalled wondering whether he was aiming towards his own or Annabel's bed, but Piper didn't need to know that. A sudden longing for Alec's competent presence swept over her. "Oh Lord, this does complicate matters," she exclaimed. "You'd better ring up the police station in Winchester and leave word for the Chief. He may want to come back tonight."

"Dr. Renfrew said he telephoned there first, miss, and

left a message. That's why he chewed my ear off, like it were my fault he couldn't find the Chief nowhere."

"Too unfair," Daisy commiserated. "Did he tell you anything else?"

"Summat about confusions and cold water." Piper eyed his notes dubiously. "And imaging?"

Daisy racked her brains. "Contusions and haemorrhaging? Bruises and bleeding?" Not for nothing had she done a brief stint in a hospital office during the War.

"I couldn't say for sure, miss, 'cepting he's doing some tests as he'll have the results of come morning. Such long words them doctors use, you can't rightly make head nor tail of 'em."

"Right now, I can't make head nor tail of anything. Confusions is about right. I simply can't believe Astwick went down to the lake after dinner."

"If 'tweren't for them skates he had on, you'd think he'd gone to meet Payne, or one of his burglar chums. Lumme, miss, you don't think the skates were kind of like a disguise, in case someone saw him there?"

"He could just as well have said he was out for a stroll and a breath of fresh air."

"I s'pose so," Piper agreed, disappointed. "And it's true there weren't no sign I could find of anyone coming in from outside. So it was still someone here done him in. The time's narrowed down to a couple of hours, though, and some on 'em has alibis. I can't remember who, off-hand, but it'll please the Chief."

Almost everyone had been in the drawing-room for two hours after dinner. Almost everyone. Lord Wentwater had been alone in his study, and Annabel had left shortly before Astwick. Unless her maid could give her an alibi, she had to be considered a chief suspect.

"No," Daisy cried, shaking her head, "it's not so simple. It gets dark so early, anyone could have made the hole before changing for dinner, expecting Astwick to fall in in the morning."

"True, miss, but it still leaves just a few hours to account for. We didn't look for alibis for before dinner, reckoning there was all night to do the job in. Some on 'em'll be in the clear. Just knocking two or three off the list'll cheer the Chief up."

At that moment, the Chief was in dire need of something to cheer him up. His pipe clenched grimly between his teeth, he peered out through the open upper part of the windscreen into the darkness. The headlights illuminated silver needles of rain slanting across the lane, and the drumming of rain on the raised roof-hood vied with the drone of the engine. The little car sloshed bravely through the slush. The surface beneath was still frozen, and every now and then Alec had to correct a skid as the narrow wheels hit a patch of ice.

Squeezed into the seat beside him, Tom Tring reported on his questioning of the servants. "Nothing new on Astwick's boots, Chief."

"Blast the boots. Payne may tell us whether there's a pair missing or not, but I can't see it's going to help us much. What else?"

"Talking of boots, Lady Wentwater's boots and other outdoor clothes didn't show no signs of having been worn for a day or two, nor Lady Josephine's, nor Mr. Wilfred's. That's according to their personal servants. All the others, we know they was out at some point, when the body was found if not before."

"Hmm, interesting. And?"

"Ah, let's see now. The housemaid that did Astwick's bedroom, Dilys her name is, and a neat, perky little baggage as I wouldn't mind . . ."

"Spare me the rhapsodies, Tom. What did she have to say?"

"Well, as a rule she didn't have owt to do with Astwick's clothes and that, but being as Payne was gone she tidied up a bit. Snooping, if you arst me," said the sergeant tolerantly. "A good job he'd locked the despatch case. Anyways, there's two things she noticed that morning she thought was a bit fishy. It seems Astwick's dressing gown was damp. Hanging on the back of the bathroom door, it was, and she took it down to the kitchen to dry."

"Some men put on a dressing gown before they towel themselves dry," Alec pointed out. "Or perhaps he dripped on the floor when he got out of the bath, and dropped his dressing-gown in the puddle. We know he was in the habit of taking a bath before his dawn exercise. A cold bath, wasn't it?" Shivering, he braked as they reached an unsignposted fork in the road.

"Right, Chief. No, go left here," he contradicted himself as Alec turned the wheel. "I meant, you're right, a cold bath was what he took."

A flurry of cold raindrops hit Alec in the face as he swung left, narrowly missing the ditch. "Silly ass," he growled around the stem of his pipe. "Didn't know when he was well off. What else did your pretty housemaid notice?"

"Astwick's bed hadn't been slept in," said Tom bluntly. "The covers was turned back neat, the way she left them. No wrinkles in the sheets, no hollow in the pillow."

"Oh hell. It looks as if he spent the night with Lady Wentwater, then."

"Looks like it, Chief. Her ladyship's maid, Miss Barstow, was the only one as went upstairs between dinner and the chambermaid putting hot-water bottles in the beds at half ten. Lady Wentwater ordered her to draw a bath and then dismissed her for the night."

"But the earl might have walked in on them at any

moment! Perhaps Astwick didn't care. He was doing a moonlight to Rio anyway, so the social consequences wouldn't bother him, and he'd have his revenge on Lady Wentwater one way or the other. I must admit, whatever it was she did that gave him a hold over her, I'm sorry for her."

"His lordship didn't walk in on them, though," Tom reminded him, "at least by his own account. And she couldn't've chopped a hole in the ice if she was having a bit of nooky with the victim, so it lets her out."

"Except that her only witness is dead. We've no proof he was with her, after all. He might have been exploring your Dilys's charms in some garret. There's a lamppost. Damn it, where the devil are we?"

The sergeant glued his nose to the bespattered side window, then let it down and stuck his head out. "Alresford," he announced. "Next right, then straight ahead. Not *my* Dilys, Chief, not but what she'd hardly've told me about his bed if he'd been in hers."

"He could have been in any other female servant's," Alec said with a sigh, trying to find a way out for the countess. He turned right into the broad main street of the little town.

"Don't think so. Fact, I'm pretty sure not. Like Lady Josephine told you, I haven't picked up the slightest hint he was interested in the maids. Someone'd've tattled if there was owt to tattle about, I'll be bound. There's always jealousies belowstairs like you wouldn't believe, Chief. No, Astwick only fancied upper-crust ladies and at Wentwater he hadn't eyes for nowt but her ladyship."

"Nonetheless, we've no evidence he spent that night in her bed. I'm not quite ready to dismiss the possibility of his having spent it in Lady Marjorie's, if not in a maid's. We're really no further forward than before. I don't see how I'm ever going to clear up this case unless Payne comes up with something startlingly new, which seems unlikely."

"He may lead us to the loot from the Flatford job, and even if he don't, we picked up the good stuff from the other burglaries," Tring reminded him cheerfully.

"True."

"That's a feather in your cap, Chief, even if chummie's no help with the Wentwater business, if it's all in the family, like."

"As seems probable." Gloom returned. "It'll take a sheaf of peacock feathers to make up for arresting the earl, if that's what I end up having to do. Suppose he overheard Astwick and his wife making love? His dressing-room's right next door to the bedroom. He might have reckoned that setting up an accident would allow him to get his own back without ever admitting to knowing he'd been cuckolded."

At the police station in Winchester, a stout, grizzled constable who looked well past the age of retirement was nodding off on a high seat behind the front desk. His blue uniform jacket strained at the seams, as if resurrected from slenderer days.

The telephone at his elbow rang just as Alec and Tring entered the station. Startled to wakefulness, he blinked at them, then turned his head to regard the shrilling instrument with deep suspicion. Taking the receiver from its hook, he held it at arm's length and turned back to Alec.

"What can Oi be a-doin' fer 'ee, zir?" he enquired in a slow country voice, ignoring the chittering coming from the telephone.

"Deal with your 'phone call first."

"Don't 'ee moind that, zir. Truth to tell, Oi can't roightly foller what folks be zayin' on the machine," he confided. Suddenly raising the receiver to his mouth, he bellowed into it, *"Yes, zir!"* and hung up. "If it be important, they'll zend round or step by come marnin'. What can Oi be a-doin' fer 'ee?"

Wondering how many messages had been lost or delayed, Alec exchanged an exasperated glance with Tom.

"I'm Chief Inspector Fletcher, Scotland Yard," he announced.

The constable lumbered down from his stool and saluted, with the genial, placid air of one doing a favour. "Constable Archer, retired, zir," he introduced himself.

He had been recalled to duty because all able-bodied men were out hunting for the stolen jewels, at Alec's request, so there was no point making a fuss about his incompetence. Alec asked for Gillett and was told that the Inspector had gone out to call off the search for the night.

"Did he leave any message for me?"

Archer pondered. "Come to think on it, he did zay to tell 'ee he'd step home fer a bite o' supper afore he come back."

"I could do with a pie and a pint meself, Chief," the sergeant rumbled behind him.

"I suppose we'd better wait for Gillett, as he was the one who nicked Payne," said Alec resignedly. "All right, Tom, we'll go and get something to eat. At this rate, we might as well have stayed to dine on the fat of the land at Wentwater."

Dinner at Wentwater Court was as delicious as ever, but Daisy paid her food the scantest attention. The postmortem discovery dismayed her. The more she considered the changed time of Astwick's death, the less she was able to imagine any reason for him to be skating at that hour. Yet how else could he have ended up drowned in the lake? It didn't make sense.

Desperate for someone to discuss the matter with, she wished Alec would return. In fact, she was rather surprised when he didn't. Surely the news was of sufficient moment to bring him back!

Payne's revelations must be of still more interest to him. Of course, the recovery of Lord Flatford's guests' jewellery would bring grateful applause, whereas the arrest of Astwick's killer, presumably a member of the earl's family, meant nothing but trouble.

One of Lord Wentwater's family was a killer. The word reverberated in Daisy's mind. The simple change of a few hours in the time of death had somehow changed everything. Now she found it difficult—nearly impossible—to believe in a prank gone wrong. What had Astwick been doing down at the lake after dinner?

Surreptitiously she glanced around the table. With Phillip and Fenella gone, she was the only non family member. Except for James, all of them were there. Not one looked like a killer. They were subdued, even Wilfred, the weight of the continued police presence in the house making itself felt. Lady Jo, never one to despise her victuals, was eating as if it were her last meal. Annabel was pale and withdrawn. She jumped visibly when Sir Hugh asked her to pass the salt.

James? He had been in the drawing-room the whole of that evening. Daisy started to build a fantasy in which he had broken up the ice before dinner and forged a note from Annabel to Astwick inviting him to meet her to skate by moonlight. Astwick would have skated about to keep warm while he waited for her—but he'd never believe she'd issue such an invitation in the first place.

Somehow James must have managed it. Daisy couldn't bear to think that any of the others were guilty.

She was glad to find Phillip in the drawing-room when they all repaired thither for coffee. He looked a bit down in the mouth, but he bucked up when he saw her. "What-ho, old thing," he greeted her. "Bearing up all right?"

"I'm perfectly all right," she said crossly, annoyed by his tactlessness.

"Have you dined, Mr. Petrie?" Annabel asked.

"Yes, thanks. I stopped at a little place on the way when I realized I was going to be rather late. The roads are absolutely foul." He launched into a tale of motoring through rain and icy slush and narrow escapes from ditches. Daisy hoped Alec's continued absence wasn't due to a motoring mishap.

Coffee and its alcoholic accompaniments were served and consumed. Lady Jo invited her brother to partner her at her inevitable bridge, playing against Sir Hugh and Wilfred. Occasional dismayed exclamations of "Oh, Henry!" suggested that the earl's mind was not on his cards. Geoffrey drifted off in his unobtrusive way and Annabel and Marjorie talked quietly together by the fire.

"Fancy a game of snooker?" Phillip asked Daisy. "Lord, we haven't played together in years. Do you remember when you and I used to team up against Gervaise? He usually beat both of us." He rambled on in a sentimental vein as they made their way to the billiard-room. "Things just haven't been the same since Gervaise bought it," he concluded. "Well, my dear old thing, what about it?"

Daisy, who had been trying to remember Gervaise's instructions on choosing a cue, said absently, "What about what?"

"You and me, old girl. Teaming up. Tying the knot. Making a match of it."

"Oh, Phil, it's awfully sweet of you to ask me again, but I still think we shouldn't suit."

"Hang it all, I don't see why not."

She tried to let him down lightly. "For a start, neither of us has a bean. Setting up a household costs pots. What would we live on?"

"I'm bound to make money soon," he said, incurably optimistic. "It stands to reason, bad luck can't last forever. You have that bit from your great-aunt, haven't you? If you go back to live with your mother until we get married, you can save up enough for a rainy day."

"Phillip, I am *not* going to live with Mother. You know what she's like. She's never forgiven my cousin for inheriting Fairacres and she never stops complaining, as though poor Edgar had any choice in the matter!" She held up her hand as he opened his mouth. "And yes, Edgar and Geraldine have invited me to make my home with them at Fairacres but I'd be mad within a fortnight."

"They are rather stuffy," he admitted.

"Stuffy! They're absolutely mediaeval. Geraldine considers the tango debauchery and lipstick the sign of the devil. And I'd always be a poor relation. Thank you, I prefer to work for my independence."

"What about your sister? You always got on well with Violet. Surely she and Frobisher would take you in."

"I'd still be a poor relation, though Vi and Johnnie are dears. Even though Violet earned Mother's approval by marrying young, she supports me when Mother starts ragging me about working."

"You wouldn't have to, if you married me."

"I *like* earning my living, Phil. I like writing. I wouldn't stop just because I married. You don't understand that, and you'd hate it."

"Dash it, Daisy, I know I'm a frightful idiot, but I am deuced fond of you."

"You're an old dear, but it wouldn't work, believe me."

"You're not still mourning your conchie, are you?"

Daisy flared up. "Don't call Michael that!" With an effort she smothered her anger. "You see, we disagree about practically everything. Let's agree to disagree. Are you going to set up the balls, or shall I?"

"We can still be chums?" Phillip enquired anxiously, collecting the red pyramid balls within the triangular frame.

"Of course, you silly old dear. You have the white ball, you go first."

They played an amicable game, Daisy sternly holding her tongue when he let her win by a couple of points.

He'd have been hurt and baffled if she'd insisted on losing honestly.

Later, lying in bed, listening to the blown rain spatter against her window, she pondered his question. Was she still mourning Michael? She'd never forget him, never forget the breathless joy of being with him, of knowing he loved her. Yet the biting pain of her loss had dulled. Was it Annabel's sympathy, her respect for Michael's courage and dedication, that allowed Daisy to begin to let go?

Annabel, too, had loved a man disdained by society, and lost him. Daisy vowed to do all in her power to protect her new friend from the further troubles Astwick's death was certain to bring upon her.

For the moment, Daisy didn't want to think about the mystery of the drowning. If she tried to work out an answer to the latest complication in the riddle, she'd never fall asleep. Instead of speculating, she proposed to wander through memories of happy hours with Michael.

Somehow Alec's dark brows and keen grey eyes kept intruding.

After a restless night filled with agitated dreams, Daisy drifted into a sound sleep shortly before dawn. She woke later than usual. When she went down to breakfast, Detective Constable Piper was talking on the telephone in the hall.

Not so much talking as listening and frantically scribbling, Daisy saw. She lingered, just out of earshot.

At last Piper hung up the receiver. His face was taut with excitement as he stared down at his notes, oblivious of Daisy's presence. "Gorblimey," he said on a long, exhaled breath. "This'll put the cat among the pigeons, right enough."

"What is it?" Daisy demanded, her heart in her mouth. "Who were you talking to?"

Startled, he looked up. "Dr. Renfrew, miss, the pathologist." He was bursting with news. "I got him to tell me in
ord'n'ry words this time. That bruising and bleeding? You
was right about that. Seems the gash on Astwick's forrid
and the bruise on his chin . . ."

"He had a bruise on his chin?" Daisy recalled the horribly blotched face of the drowned man.

"That's what he says, miss. Seems they didn't look right
for if Astwick got dumped in icy cold water right away, so
Dr. Renfrew did some more tests, like I told you last night."

"And?"

"And"—Piper paused dramatically—"he found stuff in
Astwick's lungs as looks to him like soap and bath-salts."

"Soap and bath-salts!" She sank onto the nearest chair.
"So he couldn't have drowned in the lake, could he?"

"Reckon not, miss."

"He drowned in the bath, and his body was carried down
to the lake."

"That's the way I sees it, miss."

"To make it appear to be an accident." Daisy shuddered
and, with the utmost reluctance, acknowledged, "But he
can't have drowned accidentally in his bath or someone
would have found him and reported it, not moved him.
It must have been murder."

CHAPTER 13

"I wish the Chief was here," Piper groaned.

"Oh yes!" Daisy dragged her mind from contemplation of the awful fact of murder. "Did Dr. Renfrew ring up Winchester?"

"No, miss, he said he's too busy to go telephoning all over the country leaving messages with morons."

"How rude!" She was growing quite fond of Ernie Piper and didn't care to have him insulted. Besides, she was glad of the distraction from her imaginings.

"He didn't mean me, miss. He said so. The bloke he talked to at Winchester last night was"—frowning, he consulted the notebook—"a congenial idiot."

"Congenital, I expect."

"Could be. Anyways, I wish he told me yesterday. D'you think the Chief might not've got that message?"

"I've been wondering why he hadn't come back yet."

"So've I, miss. I ought to've rung up meself, I know I ought." The young detective looked ready to weep.

"Too late to worry about that now, but you'd better call up the police station at once with the latest."

Eagerly Piper turned back to the telephone. Without consulting his notebook he gave the operator the Winchester police number.

Daisy listened intently to the cryptic half of the conversation she could hear, trying to guess what was being said on the other end of the wire.

"Hullo? Hullo, give me Chief Inspector Fletcher. It's urgent ... Detective Constable Piper here. Where did he? ... He did? ... You don't ... Couldn't you send a messenger after? ... I *can't* tell you what's so ... No, I haven't, but ... Yes, I know the numbers ... Yes, I will, but if they comes back or calls up, you better be bloody sure you ask the Chief to give me a ring! Operator? Operator!"

He gave the exchange another number, and then a third, asking each time for the Chief Inspector. At last he hung up the receiver and turned back to Daisy, his face disconsolate.

"You can't find him?"

"I tried his hotel, miss, and Lord Flatford's place, on the offchance. The copper on duty at the station says Payne's come clean and the Chief and Sergeant Tring went off after them jools—Inspector Gillett, too—but he don't know zackly where. He won't send someone to find 'em acos I won't tell what's so urgent."

"Quite right," Daisy approved. "It's to be kept from the local force as long as possible."

"I'll have to go after 'em meself, miss. The Chief'll want to know right away, for sure. Will you tell him what's what if he telephones?"

"Of course."

"But don't you let on to anyone else, miss. We don't want to warn the bloke who done it and have him scarper. 'Sides, it might be dangerous if he knows you know there's a murderer in the house."

Daisy discovered she had lost her appetite. As the constable went off to get the police car from the garages, she started up the stairs. She'd ask Mabel to bring her tea and a bit of buttered toast in her room, and try to get some work done.

A murderer in the house! Who was it? Bits and pieces began to come together in her racing mind.

Stephen Astwick had been drowned in his bath, not long after dinner. Why had he taken a bath in the evening, since he was accustomed to two, one cold and one hot, every morning? Was he preparing for a seduction?

He had shared a bathroom with Geoffrey. Suppose he had failed to lock the connecting door to Geoffrey's bedroom. Geoffrey had left the drawing-room shortly after Astwick and might have accidentally walked in while he was in the bath. But Daisy simply couldn't imagine Geoffrey cold-bloodedly pushing him under the water and holding him there while he struggled, blew bubbles, and finally grew limp.

In hot blood, then? Could Astwick have boasted about his intention of seducing Annabel, taunting the youth, perhaps, until Geoffrey attacked in a fit of overwhelming fury?

That was a more likely scenario. Not unlikely, in fact, yet Daisy sought for other explanations. She liked Geoffrey and didn't want to believe he was a murderer.

Astwick might not have bothered to lock the other doors. Perhaps someone else had entered the bathroom, through the door to the corridor or through his bedroom. Someone who knew he was there and went deliberately to confront him, if not intending to kill.

James, for instance, might have wanted to press him to reveal Annabel's secret and have been angered when he refused to speak. It seemed an inadequate motive for murder, however, even for the loathsome James. Worse, Daisy had to admit that he couldn't have done it. He'd been in the drawing-room that entire evening, playing bridge with his aunt.

Phillip and Wilfred had gone to play billiards. How much time had passed between Astwick's leaving the drawing-room and their return? Long enough for Astwick to draw a bath and get into it, and for one of them to drown him? How long did it take to drown a man? Daisy wasn't sure.

Either Wilfred or Phillip could have excused himself from their game for a few minutes without the other thinking to mention it. It hadn't been important as long as Astwick was supposed to have died in the morning. They could even have been in collusion, Phillip cheated, Wilfred blackmailed, finding a common grievance. But neither had been in the drawing-room when Astwick retired. They didn't know he'd gone upstairs.

Conceivably both or either might have gone up to his bedroom, expecting to find it empty, with some sort of mischief in mind, and seized the chance to dispose of him. Not that Daisy believed for a moment that Phillip was guilty. As for Wilfred, was he strong enough to hold down a man who prided himself on his fitness, and then to carry his body all the way to the lake?

The same argument applied to Annabel. She had motive and opportunity; though Daisy was sure she'd never voluntarily go to Astwick's bedroom, he might have forced her; but surely she hadn't the strength to carry a body all that way!

Which left Lord Wentwater: alone in his study or upstairs drowning his rival?

Without conscious volition, Daisy's footsteps had carried her past the end of the passage leading to her room. Lost in speculation, she passed the Wentwaters' suite, turned the corner, and found herself before the door to the fatal bathroom. She turned the handle.

Locked. She hadn't meant to come, but since she was here . . .

She glanced quickly around. No one in sight. The wall behind her had two doors. One, she worked out, must be to Annabel's bathroom, for use when the house was full of guests. The other was to the back stairs. A maid or footman might pop out at any moment.

Daisy ducked into Astwick's bedroom, closing the door swiftly and silently behind her. The room looked just as it had when she'd seen it before: the bed made up with a chocolate-and-cream-patterned coverlet, a gentleman's toilet articles arranged on the chest-of-drawers, a couple of chairs, the wardrobe where Piper had found passports and tickets. He and Sergeant Tring were neat, efficient searchers, or else a housemaid had tidied after their search.

There was the door to the bathroom. On tiptoe, holding her breath, Daisy made for it. A moment later she was contemplating a vast Victorian bath with brass taps in the form of the heads of a lion and a lioness. Were they the last things Astwick had seen as water filled his lungs?

Tearing her gaze from the gruesomely fascinating sight, she noted the jar of bath-salts on a low shelf above the tub. The crystals were green—pine or herbal for the gentlemen instead of flower scents. Within easy reach of a bather, a heated towel rail bore an assortment of thick, white towels, matching the bath mat that lay on the green linoleum floor. A rubber-footed and -topped stepstool stood in one corner, a cork-seated wooden chair in another.

It was just like the bathroom she had shared with Fenella, an innocent setting for a horrible crime. She turned her attention to the doors.

None of the three doors had keys in the keyholes. The one to the corridor was fastened shut with a bolt, but neither of the connecting doors to the bedrooms had a bolt. Geoffrey had easy access at any time. Things looked black for the chivalrous young man.

Daisy frowned as an overlooked snag struck her. Astwick had a jagged gash on his forehead and, according to the pathologist, a bruise on his chin. The latter had immediately reminded her of the bruise on James's chin after its unexpected encounter with his brother's fist. But a blow used to fell a standing opponent made no sense against a man in a bathtub.

She returned to the bath and stood gazing down into it, trying to picture the scene. Even if Astwick had sat up rather than reclining in the hot, scented water, his shoulders would scarcely have cleared the rim of the deep tub. Biffing him on the chin seemed a peculiar thing to do, especially for a tall chap like Geoffrey. His nose would have made a more obvious target.

Still, Daisy knew nothing about boxing. What about the laceration? She didn't see how either Geoffrey's fist or the smooth, enamelled bathtub could have caused an irregular wound. Probably the ice had done it, when Astwick's body was dropped into the hole. Dr. Renfrew had implied that it was caused before death, but she wouldn't be at all surprised if Piper had misunderstood his . . .

Click. The latch of the door behind her. The hinges gave a faint squeak as the door opened. Daisy froze.

"Miss Dalrymple!" Geoffrey's voice, startled, not threatening. Not yet.

Turning, Daisy summoned up a bright smile. "Hullo! This is your bathroom, too, is it? I just asked the way to the one Astwick used. Mr. Fletcher wanted me to . . . to check that his . . . his missing boots hadn't somehow hidden themselves in here." Of all the feeble excuses! "I expect the maid would have taken them away by now, though. I can't see them, can you?"

"No." He glanced around distractedly, his normally ruddy face pale. "His boots! I forgot . . ."

She took a step backwards.

His voice shook. "You think I killed him, don't you?"

The dangerous words escaped her against her will. "Did you?"

"I didn't mean to!" he cried, slumping against the door-post and covering his face with his hands. "I didn't mean to! It was like a nightmare I couldn't wake up from."

There was no anger in him, only despair. Daisy no longer feared him. She crossed the bathroom to lay a gentle hand on his arm. "Do you want to tell me about it?"

"The police will find out anyway, won't they?" he said drearily.

"If I can work it out, you can be sure Mr. Fletcher will."

"The boots . . . I forgot he couldn't have walked down to the lake in skates."

"It seemed unlikely." She didn't tell him that particular error had led the detectives nowhere. "But there's also new evidence, from the autopsy. Astwick died soon after dinner, and he drowned in his bath, not in the lake."

"Not in *his* bath. Not in here."

"Where else?" Daisy asked, bewildered. If Astwick hadn't drowned in this bathroom there was no reason to suspect Geoffrey more than anyone else—except that now he had practically confessed.

He stared at her in horror. "You think I just walked in here and drowned him in his bath? Without provocation? In cold blood?"

"No, I was sure he must have provoked you," she assured him. "I mean, with something more immediate than his general nastiness. What happened? If it wasn't here, where was it?"

"I'll tell you. I'll explain it all, but I . . . The detective hasn't come back yet today, has he?"

"The Chief Inspector? Not yet," said Daisy warily. "He's expected at any moment."

"Let me tell *you*, before he comes. But I want Father to hear, too. Please!"

"Of course. Let's go and see if he's in his study."

Without speaking, they traversed the corridors together. Geoffrey had regained his self-control, though his face remained colourless. Daisy thought it had grown thinner since she first met him.

At the top of the stairs, he paused and said in a low, pleading voice, "Will you explain to Mr. Fletcher for me? I don't think I can bear to tell the story twice. If he already knows, he can simply ask questions."

"I will if you'd like me to, but I can't promise he won't want to hear the whole thing in your own words."

"I suppose so."

"Are you sure you wouldn't prefer to wait till he arrives?"

"No! I can't let Father find out from someone else." His gaze beseeched her. "And . . . and I'd rather you were there when I tell Father."

"I shan't desert you." Whatever he had done, now he was just an unhappy, defenceless, motherless boy. Her heart filled with pity.

They went on down the stairs and across the unoccupied Great Hall. The earl's study was empty, but for Landseer's retrievers gazing down from the wall with aristocratic indifference. No one was in the library next door. Geoffrey turned to Daisy with a lost look.

"There's no need to get any servants involved," she said firmly. "You wait here and I'll go and find Lord Wentwater."

Nodding dumb acquiescence, he crossed to the window and stood staring out at the drizzling gloom beyond the glass.

As the study door shut behind her, she hesitated. She hadn't wanted to ring the bell in the earl's private study and have a footman find herself and Geoffrey there obviously wishing to speak to his father together. Not that the servants wouldn't eventually find out everything—Alec had made her very much aware of that—but the later the better.

On the other hand, to hunt all over the house for Lord Wentwater would raise eyebrows and pique curiosity. No one would think twice if she enquired for him and then requested a private word. She hurried to the hall.

The footman on duty was making up the fire in the vast fireplace. He stood up as he heard her footsteps approaching. "Can I help you, miss?"

"Do you know where Lord Wentwater is?"

"In the estate office, miss." His eyes gleamed inquisitively in his otherwise impassive face. "Can I take a message to his lordship for you?"

"Thank you, I'll go myself, if you'll be so kind as to direct me."

In her haste, the corridors seemed endless. She preferred not to leave Geoffrey in suspense any longer than necessary. Aside from his misery, he might get cold feet and decide not to confess. She had a feeling that in the end everyone would be best served if she knew the whole story before Alec returned to Wentwater Court.

She found the office at last. The door was ajar and she heard the earl's voice. When she knocked, he called, rather impatiently, "Come in!"

The small room reminded her of her father's estate office at Fairacres. Shelves contained an orderly jumble of agricultural books and magazines, prize ribbons and cups, and account books. Maps hung on the wall. On the desk lay a pile of papers and a spike of paid bills, an open ledger between them. A man she didn't know sat behind the desk. The two chairs on the near side were occupied by Lord Wentwater and his eldest son. They all rose to their feet as she entered.

James gave Daisy an uncertain smile. She ignored it. For him she felt no pity.

"Lord Wentwater, may I have a word with you?"

His grave eyes, searching her face, grew sombre. "Of

course, Miss Dalrymple." He rose and accompanied her into the corridor, closing the door behind him.

What on earth was she going to say to him? Was there any way to prepare him for the frightful shock to come? Daisy's mind was a blank.

"Will you come to your study, please? Right away?"

He gasped. "Not another body?"

"No!" Filled with remorse, she touched his hand. "No, nothing like that. But I think you'd better come."

"Very well." He returned momentarily to the office to tell his heir and his agent to carry on without him. Then, in silence, he and Daisy made their way back to the hall and on to the study.

Geoffrey still stood by the window, a drooping figure, his forehead now resting wearily against the glass pane. He swung round, straightening, as his father followed Daisy into the room.

"Sir, I . . ." His voice wavered. "I have something to tell you."

"My dear boy!" Forgetting Daisy, the earl strode past her, his hands held out to his youngest child in a gesture almost of entreaty.

They clasped hands, two proper English gentlemen incapable of giving each other the embrace both needed. Then Lord Wentwater led Geoffrey to the maroon-leather wing chairs by the fire, made him sit down, and poured him a glass of brandy from the tantalus on a corner table. He took the other chair. Daisy retreated to a ladder-back chair by the desk. Turned away from her, the earl seemed unaware of her continued presence, but Geoffrey's eyes sought her out before he took a swallow from his glass.

He squared his shoulders, ready to confess to his misdeeds and take his punishment like a man, as he had been taught. "Father, I must explain . . ."

"Wait!" Annabel appeared in the doorway.

Geoffrey started to his feet. "No! You have nothing to do with this!"

With swift steps she crossed the room to stand beside her husband, face to face with her stepson. "My dear boy," she said passionately, "you *cannot* imagine I shall let you shoulder all the blame."

CHAPTER 14

I went up to bed early that night," Annabel began in a low voice, staring down at her clasped hands. Geoffrey had seated her in his chair, with an ardent solicitude that made Daisy blink hard.

In turn, Lord Wentwater had set a straight chair for Geoffrey between them and made him sit. As he fetched it from the desk, his gaze had passed over Daisy unseeingly, his mind on his wife and son and the disclosures he must fear were about to bring his world tumbling in ruins about his ears. He listened with bowed head. Daisy saw only his aristocratic profile and one thin but strong white hand, resting in tense stillness on the maroon arm of his chair.

"I was tired," Annabel continued, "and I had a slight headache."

Geoffrey interrupted her. "It was that horrible song of James's that drove you away! The one about . . ."

"That's enough, Geoffrey," she said sharply, raising her head with a protective glance at her husband. Her eyes met Daisy's. Daisy tried hard to convey sympathy and encouragement, and hoped she was right in thinking Annabel looked a little comforted. "No matter why, I went upstairs and had Barstow draw me a bath, then I dismissed her. All I wanted was peace and quiet.

"I stayed in the bath for ages. The warmth and the rose scent of the bath-crystals were so soothing, just what I needed. Then the water began to cool. You know how you feel after lying in a hot bath, relaxed and languorous and indolent. It was quite an effort to get out and I was glad of the little stool. I was stepping down from it to the floor and reaching for my towel when I heard behind me the click of a latch.

"I flung the towel around me and turned. The door to the corridor was opening. That man"—Annabel's voice cracked—"Lord Stephen swaggered in.

"He held the key dangling from the tip of his finger in front of him, like a sort of Open Sesame talisman. He boasted that he'd stolen it. That door was always kept locked and I hadn't noticed the key was missing. He pushed the door to behind him and came towards me.

"He was wearing his dressing-gown, a frightful crimson velvet thing embroidered with gold dragons, with a gold-tasselled cord. As he came he untied it. Underneath, he was nude. I cried out, 'Go away,' and clutched the towel tighter around me, and retreated backwards. He smiled. Oh, it was a cold, evil smile! It made me cringe. He said, 'Oh no, my dear. Not when at last we have our chance.'

" 'Go away,' I cried out again. I couldn't move any farther back. The edge of the bath pressed into the back of my thighs. I told him I'd scream if he came a single step closer. 'Someone will hear!' I threatened, praying I was right. 'Someone will come!'

"He laughed. He said that would suit him almost as well, though he'd be sorry . . . to miss the seduction scene. It was revenge he wanted, you see, as much as he wanted m-me, revenge because I refused him years and years ago.

"That was when he touched me. He stroked my shoulder and I hit his hand away. Then he told me he was leaving the country very soon anyway, so scandal could not touch him. He didn't care if he was caught with me, not that he'd ever paid much attention to the gabbling of envious geese, he said.

"He tore the towel from my grasp," Annabel continued with a dry sob. "He tossed it on the floor and reached for me. I did scream then. I was terrified. But at that moment the door crashed open and Geoffrey rushed in."

"I heard her," Geoffrey said simply. "I heard his laugh. I'd been suspicious when he left the drawing-room so soon after she did. I followed him upstairs and saw him go into his room. I went to mine, but I left the door open just a crack and kept an eye on the corridor.

"The trouble was, my door hinges on the wrong side. I couldn't see towards Astwick's room without sticking my head out. I didn't think it mattered because I assumed he'd have to go past my room and round the corner to the boudoir or bedroom door. I didn't see him sneaking across the corridor to the bathroom. I heard a door close, though, and voices. I went to listen at his bedroom door. That was when he laughed and she screamed.

"Oh, God, I was so afraid the bathroom door would be locked. I'd have knocked it down, but it would have wasted time. But it wasn't even properly latched. It slammed open with a crash and he swung round, still gripping her by the arm. As I charged at him, she wrenched free and escaped.

"I hit him." Geoffrey couldn't keep a vestige of pride out of his voice. "It was a ripping left uppercut to the chin. Of course, I did catch him unawares. Anyway, he lost his balance, tangled his feet in the bath mat, and tripped over the stool. I didn't wait to see any more than that. I grabbed a towel from the rail and her dressing-gown from the chair and dashed into the boudoir after her.

"I didn't want her to take a chill," he explained earnestly

to his father. "I wanted to comfort her, and to promise I'd never let that beast go near her again. I didn't look, I swear it. Besides, I had to watch the door in case he came after us."

"He kept his back turned to me," Annabel confirmed shakily, "until I had dried myself and put on my dressing-gown, and a cardigan over it. I was cold, so very cold. Henry?" The word held a desperate plea.

Lord Wentwater leaned forward and clasped her outstretched hands. "My dear, no blame can attach to you for that blackguard's actions, nor are you responsible for my son's gallantry. If I am silent it's because I don't wish to interrupt what I know to be a painful narration."

Reassured, she took up the tale. "We talked for a few minutes, not long. There was no sign of Lord Stephen, no sound, so Geoffrey returned to the bathroom to make sure he had left."

"He was still there all right," Geoffrey said harshly, pressing the heels of his hands to his eyes as if to shut out the memory. "He was bent double over the edge of the tub, his head and shoulders underwater. I hauled him out but there was no heartbeat, no pulse, no breath. He was dead."

In the tense, almost palpable hush that filled the study, a coal falling in the grate made Daisy jump.

"Geoffrey didn't come back," said Annabel, "and I heard such odd noises. I was frightened. I peeked into the bathroom and saw him crouching by the body. Lord Stephen lay sprawled on the linoleum in a spreading pool of water, with blood oozing in droplets from a gash in his forehead. I thought I was going to be sick.

"Geoffrey's face was stark white, horror-stricken, anguished. He cried out that he hadn't meant to kill him. I knew it, and I pulled myself together enough to reassure him. He stood up and glanced at the bathtub. I saw that the water was stained pink. There was blood on one of the taps.

"The taps in my bathroom are cockatoos," she said in a monotone. "When Lord Stephen tripped and lost his balance, he must have somehow spun round, falling, and hit his head on a cockatoo's crest. Between that and Geoffrey's blow, he must have been unconscious, or at least too dazed to pull himself out when he fell head down in the water. And perhaps before he recovered he was weakened by loss of blood.

"Geoffrey wanted to go to you, Henry. I stopped him. Maybe I was wrong. Maybe I should have let him go. But I couldn't bear to bring any more trouble upon you! You should never have married me!"

In an instant the earl was out of his chair and bending over her. "Never say that, my love." He took her face tenderly between his hands and kissed her forehead. She clutched his sleeve, tears trembling on her dark lashes.

Daisy hurriedly looked away. Geoffrey, scarlet to the tips of his ears, was staring with intense concentration at the window. His chin quivered pitiably.

After a moment, he gasped out in a strangled voice, "I promised. I promised not to tell you, sir, but when Miss Dalrymple guessed . . ."

Lord Wentwater threw a vague glance over his shoulder at Daisy before turning to Geoffrey and laying a hand on his shoulder. "You saved the woman I love from rape. How can I thank you? What more can I ask of you?"

"I love her too," said Geoffrey, almost inaudibly.

As though struck by a physical blow, Lord Wentwater sank back into his chair. "I see." He sounded old and very tired.

"She loves *you*, Father!"

Before the words had left Geoffrey's mouth, Annabel was kneeling at her husband's side, pressing his hand to her cheek. "Oh, my love, my love, don't look like that. There is no one in my world but you. Geoffrey knows it. He has my affection as your son, and my eternal gratitude for what he has done for me, but you are all I want or need."

And Geoffrey, to Daisy's silent applause and admiration, moved his chair close to his father's for her. She sat down, her hand in the earl's, and Geoffrey retreated to lonely exile on the far side of the fireplace.

With an obvious effort, he returned to his story. "We couldn't leave Astwick lying there for the maid to find in the morning. Lord knows what sort of scandal that would have led to. We had to get him out of there. I thought it would be best just to move him into my bathroom, the one I shared with him."

"I couldn't let him do that," his stepmother said. "If anyone had guessed more was involved in Lord Stephen's death than a simple accident, Geoffrey would inevitably have been implicated. We had to make it appear obvious that Lord Stephen had been alone, that the accident was entirely his own fault, but we weren't even sure whether he had bled to death or drowned.

"I suppose I was beginning to recover from the shock, because I began to notice things I'd overlooked. There was a strong smell of roses and I discovered the entire jar of bath-salts had dropped into the bath and broken. He must have knocked it with a flailing arm when he fell. The salts were bright pink, so presumably part of the tinge of the bathwater was from that. Then I saw the red rivulets trickling from his dressing-gown—it was sodden from the waist up—into the pool on the floor. The dye was running, and must have started to run when it was in the bath, colouring the water.

"So I realized he had not necessarily lost a great deal of blood. It seemed more likely he had drowned. We needed to stage a drowning accident and the lake was the obvious place."

"I didn't want her involved in the gruesome business, Father. I said I'd do it myself. She insisted on helping."

"While I dressed, Geoffrey went to change into outdoor clothes and to fetch Lord Stephen's skating clothes. I put them on the body." Annabel shuddered. "It was ghastly. My stomach heaved the whole time."

"And in the meantime," Geoffrey explained, "I sneaked down the backstairs and out to the woodshed. I found an axe. The moon was rising, which made it quite easy to move about outside and not to stray from the trodden path. A beautiful night! If I'd been seen I could have concealed the axe and said I was just out for a stroll.

"Once I got down there I was pretty safe in the black moon-shadow of the bridge. I hacked a hole in the ice, took the axe back to its place, and went back up to the bathroom.

"She was struggling to force Astwick's limp feet into the skating boots. I helped her, and we laced them up tightly." He looked across at Daisy. "It never crossed my mind that he would have worn ordinary boots to walk down to the lake. That was what aroused the detectives' suspicions, wasn't it? That one stupid mistake was what made them guess it wasn't an accident."

"As a matter of fact, no. Later they wondered about the missing boots, but no one could remember whether they'd been under the bench when we went down or not. The gardeners cleared everything up afterwards, so anything might have happened to them."

"Then what was it?"

"A silly little thing. There were axe-marks in the ice around the hole. If I hadn't taken those photographs, they'd probably have passed for the marks of skates, but they showed up distinctly different on my pictures. I pointed them out to Mr. Fletcher. How I wish I hadn't!"

All three rushed to reassure her.

"It was your civic duty," the earl reminded her with stern kindliness.

"You mustn't blame yourself, Daisy," Annabel cried.

"You didn't know—how could you?—where it would lead."

"It's all my fault," Geoffrey said desolately. "If I hadn't lost my temper, I could have stopped him without hitting him. None of this would have happened. The whole thing's like a bad dream. The worst was carrying him down the back stairs, then down the hill. A nightmare! His feet kept knocking against the walls."

"I went first down the stairs," Annabel said, "to make sure the coast was clear, but I didn't go out. I went back up to clean up the bathroom. I wrung out the wet dressing-gown and draped it over the towel rail to dry, cleaned the bloody tap, and mopped the floor. I left the broken glass in the tub and in the morning I told Barstow I'd knocked it off the shelf reaching for it to add more to my bath. Would you believe it, she was very relieved that I hadn't cut myself!

"Meanwhile Geoffrey was struggling down the hill with that ghastly burden on his back."

"He weighed me down, upset my balance. I kept slipping and sliding on the packed snow and I was terrified of letting him fall, leaving an inexplicable hollow in the untrodden snow to either side of the path.

"I got him down to the bank, though he seemed to grow heavier and heavier. I had to lay him down to take a breather, and I thought I'd never be able to lift him up again. The moon was high by then, reflecting brightly off the snow. I felt as conspicuous as a beetle on a sheet of white paper. If anyone had looked out . . .

"I picked up the body in my arms, heaved myself to my feet, and set out across the frozen lake. Beneath the double weight the ice creaked and groaned, and I kept thinking how ironic it would be if *two* drowned bodies were found in the morning.

"I didn't dare go right to the edge of the hole. I knelt down and rolled him towards it. I couldn't believe everyone for miles didn't hear the splash when he fell in." Geoffrey faltered. "He sank, and I thought he'd stay down, but that leather jacket of his—with the belt and tight cuffs and fastened up to the chin—it trapped air like a balloon. I nearly fainted when he bobbed to the surface. Thank God he was facedown. Thank God!

"Somehow I made it back up to the house, through the side door, and up the back stairs. By then her bathroom door was locked. I went to bed and tossed and turned for hours before I fell asleep. Yet when I woke in the morning, I didn't remember any of that horror until I went into my bathroom and saw Astwick's crimson dressing-gown hanging on the back of the door.

"All I wanted was to get away from the house. I went riding—and when I came back, the police were here."

"We didn't talk about it," Annabel said. "Not even once. It was too risky, and I suppose I wanted to pretend it hadn't happened. Besides, there really wasn't anything to say. We had done all we could to keep scandal from your family, Henry. It wasn't enough." She hid her face in her hands. "Now we'll all be dragged through the courts. The whole world will be convinced of your wife's . . ."

"No!" cried Geoffrey. "You need not come into it at all. We'll make up a story. We'll tell them I quarrelled with Astwick over money or something, and he drowned in his own bath, not yours."

"The police know Astwick was pursuing Annabel," said Lord Wentwater, passing a weary hand over his face. "They know you attacked James to defend her, Geoffrey."

"They know he's in love with me," whispered Annabel.

The earl groaned. "I still cannot bring myself to believe that my son is in love with his stepmother. I'm not sure which appalls me more, that, or his killing a man, a guest in my house."

Huddled in the wing chair, Geoffrey seemed to shrink.

"Remember, Henry, he did it for me!" Annabel reproached her husband.

"And not on purpose," Daisy reminded him, "and Astwick was a villain."

"Yes. Yes, of course. I'm sorry, my boy, I'm having difficulty trying to take it all in. Of course, it was unintentional, and Astwick richly deserved punishment, if not to meet his end."

"Will I have to go to prison, Father?" Geoffrey asked fearfully.

"I don't know. It can't be called murder, surely, but manslaughter . . . ? I don't know the penalties. Criminal law has never been one of my interests. I'll stand behind you all the way, you may be sure. You shall have the best lawyers in the country. We'll ask Hugh's advice. He will know who's best, what we ought to do first, whom to approach." Lord Wentwater stood up and moved towards the bellpull, cheered by the prospect of a practical course of action.

Not murder, Daisy thought, but would the police believe it? Would a jury believe it?

Even if Geoffrey was found innocent, or convicted of manslaughter, would sensation-hungry journalists believe the verdict and persuade their readers of its truth? There would always be those who were certain that the earl had used the influence of his title to save his son from the gallows. Mud always stuck.

Not only to Geoffrey. Suppose some reporter, not satisfied with scandal easily acquired, dug up the secret from Annabel's past that had allowed Astwick to blackmail her. Annabel would be ruined, her marriage and her life destroyed.

Overwhelmed with guilt, Daisy couldn't bear the possibility that she might be responsible for so much misery. If only she had more time to think up some way to prevent it! Once Alec came back and arrested Geoffrey it would be too late.

CHAPTER 15

I have it!" To Daisy, her plan appeared gloriously inevitable in its simplicity, the solution to every problem—as long as Alec didn't come back too soon.

Lord Wentwater's hand hesitated on the bellpull.

"Listen!" Daisy jumped up from her chair. Three faces harrowed by emotion turned to her. "Listen! I have the most utterly spiffing idea you've ever heard. Do go ahead and send to ask Sir Hugh to join us, please, Lord Wentwater. We shall need him, and we must hurry."

"Hurry?" asked the earl with a frown, ringing the bell. "I fear a hasty and ill-conceived scheme can only lead to further disaster."

"At least let Daisy tell us her idea, Henry," Annabel proposed, a light dawning in her dark eyes.

"I can't see how things could possibly be any worse," said Geoffrey dully.

"Let me explain," Daisy begged.

"Of course, Miss Dalrymple." Lord Wentwater's habitual courtliness prevailed over his mistrust. "I beg your pardon if I seemed to reject your assistance. We are in need of any help anyone can offer."

"Everything comes together so neatly it must be Fate," said Daisy. "Geoffrey must . . ."

She was interrupted by the arrival of Drew himself. The butler's outward stateliness was unimpaired by the troubled times the household was passing through. Yet Daisy sensed a certain commiseration in the swift glance that swept over the gathering in the study.

Nothing but deference was apparent in his tone. "Your lordship rang?"

"Please tell Sir Hugh I should be glad of a word with him in here." The earl looked at Daisy and shrugged slightly. "At his earliest convenience. And, Drew, bring glasses."

"At once, my lord." Bowing, the butler withdrew.

Reminded of the brandy his father had poured him, Geoffrey reached for the glass and finished it at a gulp. A tinge of colour crept into his pallid cheeks. "What must I do, Miss Dalrymple?"

"Go abroad. I suppose you have a passport?" she asked anxiously as the others gasped.

"Yes, I went climbing in Austria last summer." He stared at her, hope restoring the vitality and resolution to his youthful features. "But . . ."

"You would have my son running from justice?" said Lord Wentwater harshly, hauteur in every inch of his tall, stiff-necked figure. "He will stay and take his punishment like a gentleman."

"Henry, no!" Annabel protested. "He didn't mean to kill Stephen, and it was all for my sake, for *your* sake."

"It's not only Geoffrey," Daisy reminded him. "Can you stand aside and let your private life be made public? Let James's conduct become common knowledge?"

"James!" he groaned.

Inexorable, she continued, "Let Annabel be pilloried in the papers?" She was rather pleased with her rhetoric.

His shoulders sagging in defeat, he returned to his chair, took Annabel's hand, and said remorsefully, "Forgive me, my love."

"Never mind that," she soothed him. "Let's just think of how to send Geoffrey abroad in a hurry."

"I'll do whatever you say, Father," Geoffrey promised.

"I'd say go, but it's impossible. However fast we move, the police will have plenty of time to close the Channel ports, and I believe the French police work closely with ours these days. If you somehow escaped the net here, you would simply be arrested in France."

"Not France," said Daisy, impatient with his pessimism. "Not the Channel. Not *Europe*." She stopped with a frustrated sigh as Drew came in again.

"I sent a footman to request Sir Hugh's presence, my lord." He set a tray of glasses, bottles, and decanters on the desk. "Shall I pour the drinks, my lord?"

"No, thank you, Drew."

"Does your lordship desire anything further?"

"No!" the earl snapped impatiently, then retrieved his calm courtesy with an effort. "No, thank you, that will be all for now."

"Very good, my lord." A hint of reproach in his bow, the butler once again departed with his ponderous tread.

As the door clicked shut, three eager faces swung towards Daisy. "Where?" they demanded as one.

"Brazil." Daisy savoured their astonishment. "It just so happens that I know the S.S. *Orinoco* sails from Southampton this afternoon, for Rio, and there will be at least two empty berths aboard."

"This afternoon?" Lord Wentwater pulled a gold hunter from his fob pocket.

"At three."

Annabel and Geoffrey turned to look at the clock on

the mantelpiece. Though Daisy felt as if a century or so had passed since she stepped out of bed, it was not yet noon.

"Southampton's only about thirty-five miles," said Geoffrey, and added wonderingly, "Brazil! But what shall I do when I get there?"

"That's the beauty of my plan," said Daisy with pride. "Sir Hugh owns vast plantations of rubber and coffee in Brazil. I'm sure he'll be able to give you a job."

"I will, will I?" said Sir Hugh's dry voice behind her. He entered the study, followed, to everyone's dismay, by Lady Josephine.

"What's going on, Henry?" she asked plaintively, her plump face alarmed.

"It's all right, Jo," said her brother as he and Geoffrey rose to their feet. "Nothing that need concern you. I'll tell you about it later."

"You needn't think you can hoodwink me." Not to be fobbed off, she settled in Lord Wentwater's chair in a determined way and patted Annabel's hand. "Maybe I can help."

While they argued, Daisy whispered to Geoffrey, "There's no time to waste. You'd better go and find your passport and pack a few things."

Nodding assent, he whispered back, "Is it all right if I say good-bye to Marjie and Will?"

She frowned. "I suppose so. Yes, of course you must, but for heaven's sake try not to tell them anything. Don't let them ask you questions."

"Right-oh." He slipped out, oddly enough no less unobtrusive for being the centre of the present storm.

Lady Josephine had won the argument simply by refusing to budge. "So you might as well just tell me what's going on," she reiterated.

Lord Wentwater sighed. "Miss Dalrymple, will you be

so good?'' Abandoning the floor to her, he moved to the desk to pour drinks.

Daisy turned to Sir Hugh. The baronet had watched with mild amusement his wife's quarrel with her brother. ''Yes, do please explain, Miss Dalrymple,'' he invited, his tone affable but with an authoritative note.

''First, Sir Hugh, let me ask if I'm right in thinking you can employ Geoffrey in one of your South American concerns. Because if not, there's no need to trouble you further.''

''It's possible,'' he said cautiously.

''Of course you can, Hugh,'' Lady Josephine insisted. ''Only a few months ago you found a position for Mr. Barnstaple's cousin, and Geoffrey is your own nephew. Or mine, which comes to the same thing.''

''Very true, my love, but young Barnstaple was not fleeing the law, which, unless I'm greatly mistaken, is young Geoffrey's problem.''

Lady Josephine's round, pink face crumpled. ''Oh, Daisy, is that what it is?''

Daisy decided candour was the best policy, though she had no intention of revealing the full story. If Annabel and Lord Wentwater wanted the Mentons to know all, they could tell them at a later date.

''I'm afraid so, Lady Jo. He was responsible for Lord Stephen's death, though it was entirely unintentional. He was just trying to protect Annabel.''

''The dear boy! Breaking up the ice was a simply marvellous scheme. If only the rotten bounder hadn't drowned, he'd certainly have left Wentwater with his tail between his legs after falling into the lake. Too too mortifying, like a careless schoolboy!''

Daisy didn't disillusion her. The fewer people who knew that Astwick had drowned in the bath, the better. ''So, you see, if Geoffrey doesn't go away, there will be a trial and the newspapers will make up the most frightful stories.''

"As sure as night follows day," Lady Josephine agreed with a shudder.

"And if he does go away ..." Sir Hugh began in an ominous voice.

"I'm sure the police will decide to let the matter drop, to treat it as an accident," Daisy hastily interrupted, her fingers crossed behind her back and a prayer winging its way heavenward. So far she'd been too busy putting her plan into action to dwell on possible consequences. "But he must be gone before Chief Inspector Fletcher returns, which he may at any moment. Luckily there's a ship sailing from Southampton at three."

Everyone turned to consult the clock. The hands stood at a quarter past twelve.

"It could be done," said the baronet reluctantly.

"It *will* be done," Lady Josephine declared. "Don't be difficult, Hugh dear. Astwick was an absolute wretch and the world should be grateful to Geoffrey."

"Very well." His decision made, Sir Hugh was all business. "I'll take the boy to Southampton in my motor. Henry, would you send a message to Hammond to bring the Hispano-Suiza round at once, please? I must telephone my agent in Southampton to arrange passage, and write a letter of credit for Geoffrey. He'd better carry a recommendation to my Rio agent with him, too, though I'll send full instructions by wireless later. May I use your desk?" He was already moving towards it, taking his fountain pen from his pocket.

"There's notepaper in the second drawer on the left." Lord Wentwater had rung the bell. Now he cleared the desk of the tray of drinks and stood holding it, looking rather helpless. "Miss Dalrymple, where did Geoffrey go?"

"I thought he ought to go and pack." She took the tray from him and in turn deposited it in the hands of the butler as he entered. "Please get rid of this, Drew."

"Yes, miss."

She glanced back. The earl had turned away to listen anxiously as his brother-in-law asked the telephone operator to look up his agent's number and connect him.

"And, Drew," Daisy continued, "tell Sir Hugh's chauffeur to bring the Hispano-Suiza to the front door. At once."

"At once, miss."

"There's no sign of the Chief Inspector, is there?"

"No, miss."

"Thank heaven."

The imperturbable butler's eyebrows twitched. "Will there be anything else, miss?"

"No, thank you. But tell Hammond to *hurry.*"

As Annabel and Lady Jo were talking quietly together, Daisy followed Drew out of the study and sped off upstairs to find Geoffrey.

She knocked on his bedroom door and entered in response to his subdued invitation. The room was sparsely furnished, its most notable feature a shelf displaying gymkhana trophies: blue, red, and white rosettes and engraved silver cups. A Stubbs horse and groom hung on the wall opposite the bed, and several lesser paintings, drawings, and photographs of equine beauties completed the décor.

Geoffrey had retrieved two large, brass-studded, leather portmanteaux from the boxroom. They lay open on the bed, half filled with coats and trousers. Tactfully ignoring his reddened eyes, Daisy helped him stow away the contents of his chest-of-drawers.

"You needn't worry about when you arrive in Rio. Sir Hugh is writing a letter to his agent, and he'll wireless him, too. You'll have a job to go to."

In a strangled voice, Geoffrey blurted out the thought that tormented him. "I'll never see her again."

"No." She had no comfort to offer.

"I'd almost rather go to prison, if it weren't for dragging her through the courts."

"You couldn't do that," said Daisy urgently. "You absolutely must go."

"Yes, I know." He blinked hard. "It's best, really, that we don't meet again, isn't it? I put her in an impossible situation."

Her throat tight, Daisy nodded. She had been no older than Geoffrey when she fell in love with Michael, not much older when the telegram came announcing his death. Though he now existed only in her memory, the memories still hurt. How would Geoffrey ever begin to heal when the woman he worshipped still lived, so far away? She couldn't dismiss his pain as a youthful infatuation he'd soon get over.

In silence they continued the hasty packing. Daisy had just folded a warm pullover—he'd need it on board if not in Brazil—when she heard a sound.

"Listen!"

Footsteps in the distance rapidly approached along the corridor. Just outside the bedroom door they halted. Geoffrey froze, his hands full of balled socks, and Daisy sank onto the bed, her heart in her mouth. Too late! The police had come back.

The bedroom door edged open. Marjorie's face peeked around it. In her relief, Daisy felt positively light-headed—and increasingly aware of a sense of desperate urgency.

CHAPTER 16

Marjorie came into the bedroom. "Geoff! It's true, then. You're leaving?"

Wilfred was close behind her. "So it was you who bumped him off, old fellow. A spiffing piece of work. Congratulations!"

Marjorie tearfully hugged her brother and Wilfred shook his hand with a vigour astonishing in so languid a young man. Daisy regarded them with exasperated resignation.

"I hope you two can keep your mouths closed," she said crossly, dumping a last load of shirts into one of the portmanteaux and closing it. "Come on, quick, we must get these down to your uncle's car."

Geoffrey fastened the other and effortlessly set both on the floor.

"I'll carry one," offered Wilfred, and attempted to lift the smaller of the two. With an effort, he raised it an inch or so. "Too many late nights," he said with an uneasy laugh. "Well, boxing's not for me but perhaps I'll take up riding."

"Take care of Galahad for me," said Geoffrey abruptly, his head down as he picked up the portmanteaux and made for the door.

"I will, old man, I will." Wilfred's eyes were suspiciously bright. "I expect I'll be spending more time down here, don't you know. Town palls on one after a while."

"Now I know Annabel better," said Marjorie, "I'll come home more often, too."

Daisy followed Geoffrey and Marjorie out into the corridor. Behind her, Wilfred drew in a sharp breath and groaned. "Oh Lord, what now!"

He was looking ahead down the corridor. Daisy peered past Geoffrey's bulk. James stood in the doorway of his bedroom, watching them, his heavy jaw set, his face stony.

Coming abreast of him, Geoffrey hesitated. Then he put down a portmanteaux and offered his hand. James simply stared for a moment before, with obvious reluctance, he gave his brother's hand a brief shake. Without further ado, he stepped back into his room and closed the door.

However unsatisfactory, Daisy was glad for Geoffrey's sake that he had made the gesture of reconciliation. Among the regrets that would haunt him, he'd not have to remember parting from James in anger.

"I'll jolly well have to spend more time at Wentwater," said Wilfred quietly as they turned into the cross-passage. Thoughtful and rather pale, he looked daunted by the prospect of trying to compensate his father for the loss of two sons.

"Lord Wentwater told me he believes you are not without redeeming traits," Daisy informed him. She knew what it was like to be compared with a sibling and found inadequate.

"High praise," he snorted, but he seemed relieved.

As they descended the stairs to the Great Hall, a footman rushed to relieve Geoffrey of the portmanteaux. "The motor's out front, Mr. Geoffrey. Mr. Drew just went to tell his lordship." With a quick glance behind him, he leaned forward and hissed, "Us in the servants' hall all wants to wish you Godspeed, sir." Straightening, his nose in the air in proper footmanly fashion, he lugged the portmanteaux across to the front door.

The Wentwaters and the Mentons came into the hall from the east wing. With a cry of distress, Lady Jo swooped on her erring nephew and enveloped him in her substantial embrace, to his uneasy embarrassment. Daisy moved back, out of the way of the family's farewells. She had intruded enough—more than enough—on their troubles.

Kissing Geoffrey's cheek, Lady Josephine allowed her husband to tear her away. Geoffrey turned to Annabel.

"I'm sorry," he muttered, head hanging.

She took his hand in both hers and whispered something in his ear that made him raise his chin and stand tall and proud as he faced his father.

"I'm sorry, sir."

"My dear boy, if you hadn't . . ." Lord Wentwater left his sentence unfinished. He shook his son's hand with the grave propriety of a gentleman parting from an acquaintance he expects to meet again at no distant date. But then he turned away from the others and Daisy caught a glimpse of the deep sorrow he couldn't quite conceal.

Geoffrey distracted her, coming up to thank her heartily for her help.

"I do hope all goes simply swimmingly from now on," she said, reassured that her interference was valued. He was not yet out of the woods, though. "You really must buzz off before it's too late," she urged.

Behind him, she saw Hammond in his chauffeur's uniform, peaked cap in hand, consulting with Sir Hugh. A sudden alarm sent her hurrying to join them.

"We are ready to leave, Miss Dalrymple," said the baronet dryly. "Have you any further instructions for carrying out your enterprise?"

"Yes," she said, unabashed. "For heaven's sake avoid the Winchester road." Not wanting to explain before the chauffeur, she was relieved when Sir Hugh nodded his understanding, with a wry smile.

It would be altogether too frightful if, on their way to Southampton, they met Alec on his way back to Wentwater.

Everyone went out to the front steps to wave good-bye. Sir Hugh and Geoffrey stepped into the long, sleek, midnight blue Hispano-Suiza with the silver crane in flight on its bonnet. Hammond took the wheel. Smoothly swift, the motor-car swept down the drive, over the bridge across the lake, and away.

He was gone. Daisy breathed a deep sigh as the silent group returned into the house. She had got him safely away and his fate was out of her hands now. Thank heaven Alec had not come back too soon!

But now she had all too much leisure to wonder how on earth she was going to face Alec after thwarting him of his prey. However justified she felt herself, he was bound to be absolutely livid. The whole scheme had been hers; she couldn't leave it to someone else to tell him that Geoffrey was well on his way to Brazil.

Dreading Alec's arrival, nonetheless she was beginning to worry about his continued absence. Constable Piper had left hours ago to find him. Surely the arrest of a presumed murderer must take precedence over the recovery of even the most valuable loot? He ought to be here by now. Suppose he had caught up with the burglars, and they turned out to be a gang of violent ruffians, and he had been hurt?

Ghastly images flitted through Daisy's mind as she dropped onto a chair by the hall fire, drained of energy.

Phillip wandered in, disconsolate. He brightened when he saw her. "What's going on, old bean?" he asked. "Hang it all, where has everyone disappeared to?"

"As a matter of fact," said Daisy, "Geoffrey has disappeared to Brazil, but keep it under your hat, won't you?"

"You're ragging me," he said without resentment.

"No, Phil, I'm far too fagged to rag you."

"Brazil, eh? Plenty of good opportunities out there."

"I hope so, though that's not quite why he's gone."

"Oh, I see. I think. The poor prune left in a bit of a hurry, what? The busy's not back yet?"

"If you mean Detective Chief Inspector Fletcher," she said reprovingly, "no, he's not. I can't help wondering whether something dreadful has happened to him."

"Not to worry, old dear. Coppers have nine lives, like cats. I just hope he doesn't turn up to bring a hornet's nest about our ears until after lunch."

"Lunch!" Daisy sat up straight. "Of course, that's what's wrong with me! I didn't have any breakfast. I'm starving."

Fortunately she didn't have to wait long before Drew came in to ring the gong for lunch. Despite her hunger, before dashing to the dining-room she remembered to entreat the butler, "I know it's not correct, but *please* let me know the *moment* Chief Inspector Fletcher arrives. Before you tell his lordship or anyone else. I know what to say to him."

"Very good, miss," Drew promised, with what almost might have been an approving look.

Throughout lunch, Phillip, Lady Josephine, Wilfred, and Marjorie kept up a flow of social chitchat, though now and then one of the latter pair would fall silent for a few abstracted minutes. Both Annabel and the earl were conspicuous by their absence.

So was Alec when coffee in the drawing-room brought the meal to a conclusion. Daisy's concern for him warred with the hope that he wouldn't turn up until after the *Orinoco* had safely put out to sea. She was prepared to employ delaying tactics, but she'd much prefer not to have to try to mislead him. Remembering his piercing gaze, she wasn't at all sure she'd succeed.

Four of the five in the drawing-room kept glancing surreptitiously at the clock. When Daisy caught herself at it for the third time (five past two), she decided to go and see Annabel. However, when she left the room she met in the passage a footman sent by Lord Wentwater with a request for a few minutes of her time. She entered the study with some trepidation, afraid that he might have changed his mind and decided his son must face the music, regardless of the consequences to his wife.

He was seated at the desk, writing. When he looked up, she was shocked by the deep lines in his drawn face. His hair and moustache seemed to have grown much greyer, aging him by ten years since she first met him just three days ago. He rose to his feet with a visible effort.

"Miss Dalrymple, I just wanted a few words with you. I hope I haven't interrupted your work."

"I haven't even tried to work today. I'd never be able to concentrate. Actually, I was on my way to see Annabel."

Whatever he had intended to say was forgotten. He leaned heavily on the desk with both hands, staring down at the papers he had been writing on, though Daisy was sure he didn't see them. "Annabel needs your friendship more than ever," he said painfully. "She still doesn't trust me. There is still something she won't confide to me."

"Do you want me to talk to her about it? I will, if you will come up and wait in your dressing-room. I can't promise anything, but if she chooses to make a clean breast of it, I'll fetch you."

They went upstairs together. Lord Wentwater retreated into his dressing-room and Daisy went on to Annabel's boudoir. She found her pacing the floor, white-faced and distraught.

"Daisy, I don't know what to do. Perhaps I should go away. I've brought Henry nothing but disaster and I can't bear it, waiting for the next blow."

Daisy drew her to the chaise-longue by the fire and sat down beside her, an arm about her waist. "Henry loves you, and Astwick's gone for good. There won't be a next blow."

"There might be." Tears trickled down Annabel's face. "That's the awful thing. Other people know what he knew, and any one of them could take it into his head to tell Henry."

"Then why don't you tell him? Your fear of confiding in him hurts him far more than anything you did in the past possibly could."

"Do you think so?"

"I'm certain. He's waiting in his dressing-room. Will you let me bring him to you?"

Annabel clutched Daisy's hand. "You'll stay? You won't desert me?"

"If that's truly what you want," she demurred though by now she was dying of curiosity.

"It is, oh, it is."

She went to fetch the earl. His face brightened as she said, "Annabel has agreed to speak to you."

"Miss Dalrymple, how can I ever thank you?" He was already past her and into the corridor.

She scurried to keep up with his long strides. "She wants me to be there with her."

"Anything!"

"She's more afraid of giving you pain than anything else, but I think she's also afraid you might cast her off."

"Never!" He burst into the boudoir and went straight to sit down beside Annabel, pulling her to him with a possessive arm about her.

Daisy retreated to a chair by the window as Annabel clung to her husband, sobbing into his shoulder. "Oh, Henry, it's all my fault, all this misery . . ."

"What utter nonsense. Haven't I already said that you're in no way to blame for Astwick's villainy and its consequences?"

"But I am! If I'd been brave enough to tell you, then he couldn't have blackmailed me . . ."

"Blackmail!" thundered Lord Wentwater. "The devil was blackmailing you? If I'd known, I'd have cut his throat with the Queen Elizabeth dagger, without a qualm."

She raised an adoring face to him. "Then thank heaven you didn't know. But if I'd never done anything to be ashamed of . . ."

"My darling, I doubt there are any in this world can truly say they have never done anything they regret. And I think I can guess . . . What a fool I've been!"

"You can't have guessed, Henry." Annabel once more buried her face in his shoulder. Daisy barely caught her words. "I wasn't a widow when you met me. You see, Rupert and I were never married."

Daisy suppressed a gasp of shock. In all her wildest imaginings about Annabel's secret, it had never crossed her mind that she and Rupert might have lived together for years without being husband and wife. Few misdeeds could have been calculated to offend more deeply against Lord Wentwater's Victorian view of morality.

But he was saying tenderly, "I know. I've known from the first, or very soon at least. As soon as I began to court you, some expatriate busybody made it her business to reveal the worst."

"You never said!"

"And how I wish I had. I didn't want to cause you any discomfort, but if I'd spoken, Astwick would have had no hold over you. Can you ever forgive me?"

"Oh, Henry." Annabel sighed.

Unnoticed, Daisy crept from the room.

On her way down the stairs, she considered what Annabel had told her about Rupert. He had sounded likeable but far from practical. Add his poor health and the difficulty of finding a Protestant minister in southern Italy—

Daisy could picture time drifting by without a wedding until it was too late.

Reprehensible, of course, but after all, artists were expected to lead a Bohemian life, as she and Lucy had discovered when they moved to Chelsea. Lord Wentwater had known, and had married Annabel anyway. He wasn't as frightfully old-fashioned as Daisy had feared.

Her thoughts elsewhere, she was stunned when, just as she reached the foot of the stairs, the front door opened and Alec walked in. And she'd forgotten to powder her nose in all the excitement!

Her eyes flew to the grandfather clock. Ten to three.

Alec's grim face was decorated with a square of sticking plaster on the forehead. Behind him, Tring limped slightly and Piper's arm was in a sling. Crossing the hall to meet them, Daisy saw that all three had damp overcoats and filthy turnups to their trousers.

"I've been so worried about you," she exclaimed. "What happened? Did the burglars attack you?"

"Nothing so dramatic," Alec grunted sourly. "The lanes are knee-deep in mud. I skidded into a ditch and Ernie, who was following me, tried to dodge and went through a hedge."

"Thank heaven none of you was badly hurt."

"And both cars still running," Tom Tring informed her genially. "A couple of cart-horses put us back on the road."

"That's good, but you look as if you got pretty wet in the meantime. Take off those coats and come and sit by the fire. Have you lunched? Yes? I'll order something hot to drink, at least."

Alec shook his head, winced, and raised his hand to feel the plaster on his brow. "Not now." He watched the footman bear away their coats before he continued, "This has turned out to be a case of murder, as you know. I've a fair idea of what happened but it's just guesswork so far. We'll have to do a bit of investigating before I can make an arrest. Stay out of it, Daisy. I don't expect things to get dangerous but I can't be sure." He started towards the stairs.

She caught his sleeve. "Wait, Chief. I simply *must* talk to you first. I can tell you exactly what happened."

He gave her a hard stare, then sighed wearily. "All right, Five minutes."

"Come to the Blue Salon, where we shan't be disturbed." Leading the way, she asked, "Did you find the jewellery?"

"Yes, we nabbed the lot," he said, cheering up, "and the two chummies who did the job. What's more, Payne gave us leads on the previous burglaries. Astwick had him find local housebreakers in each case, as a way to vary the *modus operandi* and so that no one had a chance to learn too much about him. It was a clever racket. I suspect he'd be safely on his way to Rio if he hadn't ended up dead."

"No, you'd have caught him once Sergeant Tring picked up the clue of the grey Lanchester." She glanced back to smile at Tom Tring and he winked at her.

Daisy's nerves caught up with her as she reached the Blue Salon. How on earth was she going to persuade Alec that Geoffrey had deserved the chance to make good in a distant country instead of going to prison? He was not going to be pleased.

Her knees felt wobbly. She sat down on one of the blue-and-white brocade chairs, leaving places nearer the fireplace for the men. But Tring and Piper took straight chairs at a distance and Alec stood with his back to the fire, looking alarmingly formidable. He frowned down at her.

"It was Geoffrey, wasn't it? He left the drawing-room early; Tom says he shared a bathroom with Astwick; and he may well be the only one strong enough to have carried the body down to the lake."

"Yes," she admitted, "only ..." She paused as somewhere in the distance a clock chimed three. Within her a tense spring began to uncoil.

"I was afraid of it," Alec said. "I liked the boy. I can't picture him murdering even that blackguard in cold blood. There was immediate provocation?"

"Plenty. Only it didn't happen in his bathroom. Astwick assaulted Annabel in *her* bathroom and Geoffrey heard her cries for help."

"Good Lord, provocation indeed. I'll be sorry to take him in." He groaned. "And no doubt Lady Wentwater helped him dispose of the evidence."

"You can't arrest him," said Daisy with more trepidation than triumph. "It's too late. You see, I remembered that the S.S. *Orinoco* was leaving for Rio today, and Sir Hugh has plantations in Brazil where Geoffrey can work. He sailed from Southampton at three."

Alec stared at her with an expression of utter disbelief. "He *what*? And you . . ." His quiet voice was somehow more terrifying than any shout. "You little idiot, don't you understand? That makes you an accessory to murder."

CHAPTER 17

How the blazes was he going to save her from the consequences of her folly?

As Alec glared down into Daisy's face, frightened yet defiant, he realized that he was not about to play the part of a stern police officer with a misbehaving citizen. He was going to have a blazing row.

Young Piper was gaping at him with fascinated dismay, while Tom's eyes twinkled with sly amusement in an otherwise stolid mask.

"You two," Alec snapped, "go and find yourselves a hot drink." He waited in grim silence until the door closed behind them, then turned on Daisy. "I must have been raving mad to trust you!"

Guiltily she protested, "But I . . ."

"Or have *you* gone raving mad, to try to help a murderer go scot-free?"

"He's not going scot-free. Besides he's . . ."

"You're damn right he's not. I'll wireless the ship before it reaches the three-mile limit and have him put ashore."

His wits, scattered by outrage, returned to him. "In fact, the sooner the better." He started forward.

"Wait!" Aghast, she jumped up and put out her hand. "Let me . . ."

"I'll be back in a minute."

"For pity's sake, will you stop interrupting and listen to me?" she demanded angrily. "Geoffrey's not a murderer. Just let me explain what happened!"

"All right." With a weary sigh he subsided into the nearest chair. His head ached where he had bashed it as the Austin slid into the ditch. "The *Orinoco*'s a British ship. I can always have her ordered to turn back."

Daisy sat down rather suddenly. "Can you really? I thought he'd be safe once the ship had sailed."

"We don't let killers go unpunished so easily."

"He won't be unpunished. He's going into exile, leaving his family and friends and the woman he loves. And he's not going to the French Riviera for a rest cure. He's going to Brazil, which is full of beastly snakes and natives with poisoned blowpipes and those frightful fish that reduce you to a skeleton in less than a minute."

"I'm surprised he didn't opt for Dartmoor," said Alec sardonically, "if, as you claim, he's not a murderer in danger of hanging."

"He almost did, but a trial would have exposed Annabel to the worst excesses of the scandal sheets."

"His absence wouldn't prevent a trial, you know. Lady Wentwater's guilt as an accessory after the fact, if not before, is even clearer than yours."

"Oh, it all seemed so simple!" she wailed.

"Far from it. I'm surprised a canny old bird like Sir Hugh went along with your wild scheme."

"Is he an accessory too? He still believes Geoffrey only mucked about with the ice. We never told him the rest."

"It's time you told me. How did you find out, by the way?"

"When Constable Piper left ... You won't blame him for telling me what the pathologist said?"

"How can I, when he was only following my example?"

"Good. It seemed as obvious to me as it did to you that Astwick had been drowned in his own bath. Though it seemed all too likely that Geoffrey had done it, I couldn't be sure. I went up to the bathroom to try to work out if someone else could have got in."

Alec's heart skipped a beat. "My dear girl, have you no common sense at all? Didn't it occur to you that you were putting yourself in deadly danger?"

"I was just a bit scared when Geoffrey came in," she confessed, "but there wasn't really the least chance of his hurting me. He was really quite keen to get it off his chest."

"And you believed every word," he said sceptically.

"I might not have, I suppose, if it had been only Geoffrey's word, but he and Annabel told the story together without the least disagreement. I refuse to believe they conspired to invent such a perfectly dreadful business."

"They conspired to dispose of the body."

"Just listen, will you? Astwick pinched the key from the corridor door to Annabel's bathroom. It's right opposite his bedroom door, you know. He went in and assaulted her as she stepped out of her bath. Geoffrey heard her cry out. He rushed in and biffed Astwick one on the chin, just as he did to James. Then he followed Annabel into her boudoir to promise her his protection. When he went back into the bathroom he found Astwick doubled over the edge of the bath with his head underwater, drowned. They decided he'd tripped when Geoffrey hit him, bashed his head on the taps, and been too dazed to help himself. So, you see," she said earnestly, "his death was completely unintentional."

"That's the whole story?"

"Apart from how they tried to make it look like a skating

accident. I gave you the bare bones, not all the beastly details I'd rather forget."

He couldn't resist. " 'Corroborative detail intended to add verisimilitude to an otherwise bald and unconvincing narrative'?"

She spread her hands in a gesture of helplessness. "I can't force you to believe it wasn't murder."

"I was teasing you. At an inappropriate moment, I admit. On the whole, I'm inclined to credit their account. However, manslaughter is still a felony, with serious penalties. The law is the law."

"Do you believe the law always serves justice?" Her blue eyes demanded honesty.

"Perhaps not always," Alec said cautiously, "but without law there would be no justice, only the strong preying on the weak. And I serve the law."

"Do you never make exceptions? When you were on the beat—were you on the beat?"

"Yes, all detectives have to spend some time on the beat. No exceptions."

"Did you never let anyone off with a warning? Under extenuating circumstances, or if you were pretty certain they'd never do it again?"

"Now and then," he conceded with a wry grimace. She was doing her best to back him into a corner. "But a kid lifting a bar of chocolate is hardly on a par with a killing."

"Unintentional. To save Annabel from a fate worse than death. Hasn't she suffered enough?"

"Have you discovered what misdeed Astwick was using to blackmail her?"

"Yes, though I see absolutely no reason to tell you. It wasn't so dreadful. In fact, Lord Wentwater knew all along and married her anyway, so she suffered for nothing."

Alec recalled the sorrowing Madonna, the moon pale from weariness. Yes, Lady Wentwater had suffered. And

Geoffrey had gone into exile, a chivalrous knight protecting his fair lady.

And his victim had been an out-and-out rotter.

"I can't just ignore the whole thing," he said pettishly. His head hurt.

"Can't you simply say you were mistaken in thinking he didn't just fall through the ice by accident? Geoffrey, Annabel, and Lord Wentwater are the only ones who know about the axe-marks and that Astwick didn't drown in the lake. Besides Sergeant Tring and Constable Piper and the pathologist, of course, unless you told anyone else?"

"No, no one. Tring and Piper will do as I say. Dr. Renfrew never expresses any interest in a case once he's finished cutting up the body."

Daisy wrinkled her nose in disgust but said cheerfully, "Then you can easily claim it was a skating accident after all."

"Easily!" he exploded. He sprang to his feet, wincing as the bump on his brow sent an arrow of pain shooting through his skull. "I'm a police officer. I have a duty to uphold the law. I'm going to send a wireless ordering the *Orinoco*'s captain to turn back to port."

"Alec, wait!" She looked at him with concern. "Is your head aching? Do sit down for just one more minute. There's one thing you haven't considered. If the *Orinoco* has to turn back so that you can arrest Geoffrey, you're going to have the shipping line and all the passengers after your blood, not to mention Lord Wentwater, Sir Hugh, and very likely your own Commissioner, who, you may recall, is a friend . . ."

He groaned as her voice trailed off. "True, but my duty must come first."

"That's it! Telephone your Commissioner, tell him everything, and ask him what to do. He's your superior. If he orders you to drop the case, you will have done your duty, won't you?"

"And if not?"

"Well, I suppose I'll have to stop trying to persuade you," she said, disconsolate. "At least you can make him wireless the ship, so that no one blames you."

Gazing down at her upturned face with its scattering of freckles and the tiny, bewitching mole, he did not doubt that she was genuinely concerned for him. All her efforts to talk him out of chasing down Geoffrey were due to concern for her friends, not herself. She had already forgotten that she was an accessory to the crime. He'd keep her out of this, he vowed, whatever the Commissioner decided.

"Not a bad idea," he admitted.

"I expect you can use the telephone in Lord Wentwater's study. The last I saw of him, he looked as if he'd be busy upstairs for some time."

She saw him settled in the study and tactfully disappeared. Alec had less difficulty being put through to the Commissioner than he had expected, because of Sir Hugh Menton's involvement, no doubt. In guarded terms, avoiding names where possible, he explained the situation.

He had nearly finished when Daisy reappeared, bearing a tray with a pot of tea and a plate of biscuits. He smiled at her and continued, avoiding all mention of the fact that Geoffrey's departure was her idea.

"So you see, sir, we can have the *Orinoco* turn back, or wait till he reaches Tenerife or even Rio and have him extradited."

"No need for that, Chief Inspector," the Commissioner's voice boomed down the wire. "Send the Coast Guard out and have him taken off."

"Yes, sir. I hadn't considered that possibility."

"All sounds to me like a vast waste of public monies. The boy was protecting a certain lady from rape, wasn't he?"

"Yes, sir. I'm willing to accept their story, based on what I've learned of Geoffrey's and Astwick's characters."

"Hmm. Whole thing was an unfortunate accident. Astwick's family likely to give us any grief?"

"I doubt it, sir. Lord Brinbury seems to have been anxious only to hear that his brother was underground."

The Commissioner's bellow of laughter rocked his head. "What about the coroner. Reasonable man?"

"I'd say he knows his duty, sir—and which side his bread is buttered. He is Lord Wentwater's solicitor. If you and his lordship were both to advise his directing the jury to find accidental death . . ."

"Done, Chief Inspector. Accidental death it is. I'll have a word with Lord Wentwater later but my secretary is pulling faces at me now. Good job. Good-bye."

Alec also pulled a face. At least Daisy was safe but . . . Good job? Well, he had been chosen for his discretion. He hung up the receiver and gulped the tea Daisy had poured for him. "It's all settled," he said as she refilled his cup. "Wealth and rank win again. It leaves a sour taste in my mouth."

She regarded him uncertainly. "When I came up with the plan I was thinking mostly of Annabel, but I hoped I was solving a problem for you, too. I must say I expected you to be delighted not to have to arrest the son of an earl."

"Delighted!"

"Well, relieved, at least."

She was right, to his chagrin. He was relieved to have avoided running foul of Lord Wentwater and Sir Hugh. Despising himself as a craven toady, he was irritated with her for guessing.

"Are you sure you weren't simply trying to shield your own kind, people of your own class, Miss Dalrymple?"

"No," she said, hurt. "Why should I champion a class that includes James and Lord Stephen? I wanted to protect

Annabel because she's become a dear friend and hadn't done anything really wrong. All the same, I wouldn't have intervened to prevent a trial if I hadn't considered Geoffrey's actions justified."

"It's quite possible he would have got off with a warning anyway," Alec admitted reluctantly. Her eyes brightened and she beamed at him. She was too pleased with herself, too satisfied with the success of her scheme to outwit the law. He couldn't let her get away with it so easily, or the Lord alone knew what she'd be up to next. "Nonetheless," he continued in his most severe official voice, "that decision was for police, coroner, judge, and jury to make, not you. You could have been in extremely serious trouble."

Her face fell. "I know. Thank you for not telling the Commissioner it was my idea."

"The fewer people who know, the better. And now, if you will excuse me, I must speak to Lord Wentwater, prepare a statement for the press, and write my reports." Three reports, he thought with a mental groan, one on the Flatford affair and two for this Astwick mess: one for the records, and the eyes of the Chief Constable of Hampshire; and one for his own superior, the Assistant Commissioner for Crime, who had to know the whole thing, even Daisy's part in it.

Filled with regret, he watched her trail despondently from the study. He had dished his chances of seeing her again. Not that there had ever been a future for a friendship between the Honourable Daisy Dalrymple and a common-or-garden police detective.

Daisy turned towards the drawing-room. Alec had every right to be furious, she thought mournfully. Though everything had worked out for the best, that didn't make up for her letting him down. She couldn't blame him for dismissing her so coldly, stern policeman to erring citizen.

Her reception in the drawing-room bucked her up a bit. Wilfred rushed to meet her, his usual nonchalance abandoned. "We heard the police are back," he said. "What's up?"

"Everything's all right," she assured him, joining Marjorie, Lady Jo, and Phillip by the tea trolley. She'd been too upset to share Alec's tea. "Mr. Fletcher was going to have the *Orinoco* called back but instead he telephoned the Commissioner at Scotland Yard and persuaded him that Lord Stephen's death was an accident."

"Oh, good egg!" Wilfred exclaimed.

"I knew he'd come through," said Marjorie dreamily. "He's really rather scrumptious, don't you think, Daisy?"

Her aunt regarded her with considerable misgiving. "A most worthy officer," she said repressively. "This is good news, Daisy. Now dear Geoffrey will be able to come home again."

"He might as well stay in Brazil once he gets there," said Phillip. "All sorts of opportunities for the right sort of fellow, what?"

"I daresay he will," Daisy agreed. "He always seemed to me the sort to go off to bring civilisation to some benighted tropical country." If he had any sense he'd stay, for Annabel's sake.

"I say, Daisy, does this mean we're free to leave?" Phillip asked. "The detective chappie doesn't want to see us again, does he? I've already outstayed my welcome."

"It's nearly dark. You mustn't leave until the morning," said Lady Josephine, and Marjorie and Wilfred assured him that he was more than welcome at Wentwater.

"Very kind and all that, but after the fuss and botheration with m'sister, I'd better toddle off, don't you know. It's stopped raining and the old bus buzzes along quite happily in the dark. Daisy, old girl, can I give you a lift back to town?"

She was tempted. Driving up to London in his nippy little Swift two-seater, even at night, would be much more fun than going by train. But she wasn't certain whether she had enough material for her article, and besides, she wanted to make sure Annabel didn't need her anymore. "Thanks, Phil, but my work here has been rather interrupted and I still have quite a bit to do."

"Work!" he grumbled. "Oh well, right-oh."

He went off to pack and to make his farewells to his host and hostess. Daisy went up to her room to try to reacquaint herself with her article before dinner. Seated at the little desk by the window, she read over her notes and the pages she'd already written. Phillip, in his motoring coat, found her there.

"I say, I haven't got your new address. You won't mind if I drop round? I haven't given up hope, you know, old dear."

"I shan't marry you, Phillip, but I'll always be happy to see you."

Writing down the address for him, she wished it was Alec who was asking. She wondered whether he had already left Wentwater. She wanted to apologize to him, though she was not sorry for what she had accomplished—but one didn't apologize to a policeman for breaking the law, did one? To do so would imply that she regarded him as a friend. Which she did, but there wasn't much chance he reciprocated the feeling after she'd aided his quarry's escape.

Gazing glumly out of the window into the deepening dusk, she saw his Austin Seven proceeding down the drive, the police car close behind. They crossed the bridge over the fateful lake and their red taillights disappeared into the woods at the top of the opposite slope. A fat chance she had of ever seeing Alec again.

Not long after, Phillip's jaunty two-seater followed them. Apart from Daisy, only a diminished family remained at Wentwater Court. She'd better leave tomorrow, she decided. Her presence would be a constant reminder of

the frightful events of the past few days. She drew the
curtains and turned back to her work.

Dinner was more cheerful than any of Daisy's previous
meals at Wentwater. The departure of the police had raised
everyone else's spirits. Marjorie, Wilfred, and Lady Josephine were all buoyant, James's disgrace forgotten for the
moment. Sir Hugh, back from Southampton, was relieved
to hear his friend the Commissioner had come to the
rescue. He vowed to write a commendation of the Chief
Inspector's common sense and discretion.

Lord Wentwater looked nearer forty than fifty. His habitual gravity had given way to an air of contentment punctu-
ated by fond smiles, and Annabel positively glowed. To
Daisy, their happiness made everything worthwhile.

They were all embarrassingly grateful to her. She was
quite glad to claim pressure of neglected work and retreat
to her room after dinner.

In the morning, a windy day with the sun coming and
going between clouds, she went down to breakfast quite
early. Only Sir Hugh was before her, ensconced as usual
behind his *Financial Times*. Emerging, he folded the paper
to show her a modest headline: FINANCIER DEAD. Underneath, in smaller letters, it said: "Astwick dies in skating
mishap. Company expected to fail, say experts."

"There's a paragraph or two about Flatford's burglary,
too," said Sir Hugh, "but you'll find more about it in the
other papers."

Daisy dashed out to the hall. A selection of daily newspapers was spread on the table by the front door. Alec had
made the front page of most of them, under headlines
such as: YARD MAN RECOVERS LOOT. Two or three had
photographs of him, recognizable only by his dark, thick
eyebrows.

The demise of Lord Stephen Astwick, City mogul and

bon viveur, in an unfortunate skating accident was relegated to the inside pages.

Taking all the newspapers to the breakfast-room, Daisy read every word as she consumed Cook's homemade sausages, toast, and tea. Though Lord Stephen's connection with the burglaries must surely come out at Payne's trial, for the moment the reporters were apparently unaware of the makings of a spectacular story. Alec being discreet again, Daisy thought. He was the hero of the hour, the articles full of gushing quotations from grateful ladies whose diamonds, pearls, and emeralds were to be returned to them.

Daisy wondered whether he enjoyed being a celebrity. She rather thought it would bring out his sardonic side.

With a sigh, she went off to the darkroom to sort out her pictures.

By three o'clock that afternoon, having shot a few more photographs and filled in a few gaps in her information about the house, she was ready to leave. She had sent a wire to Lucy to say she'd be home for dinner. The dark green Rolls stood gleaming at the front door with her luggage already stowed away. In the Great Hall, she took her leave of the family. As they pressed her to visit again soon, she found it hard to believe she had been at Wentwater Court for less than a week.

They all came out to the front steps to wave good-bye. Jones handed her into the backseat and took his place at the wheel. The Silver Ghost rolled smoothly on its way.

When Daisy glanced back for a final look as they started down the hill, the Mentons, Marjorie, and Wilfred had gone in. Annabel and the earl still stood on the step, locked in a loving embrace.

A pang of envy stabbed at Daisy's heart. With a wistful sniff, she settled back in the seat.

The sodden countryside was dun and depressing. When they reached the station, Jones and the one-legged porter carried her luggage onto the up-platform. As the Rolls drove off, she waited beside the pile of stuff, gazing down the track towards Winchester, hugging her coat around her. Though the wind had dropped and it was much warmer than the bitter day of her arrival, she felt chilled.

She heard another car pull up in the station yard but she didn't turn until a voice behind her called, "Miss Dalrymple!"

Alec! His neck swathed in an orange-and-green-striped scarf, he was leaning on the fence where the crow had huddled. A curl of smoke rose from his pipe, hiding his expression.

She went across to him, a spring in her step. "I thought you'd have gone back to London by now," she said.

"One or two bits and bobs to clear up."

"I didn't know you smoked a pipe."

"Not when I'm on duty, except in my own office."

"I suppose you don't wear that natty scarf when you're on duty, either."

He smiled around the stem of the pipe. "Do you like it? My daughter, Belinda, knitted it."

"Your daughter?" Her heart sank. "What a clever child. How old is she?"

"Nine. Not bad, eh? Listen, will you trust your life to my driving? I know a nice little place in Guildford where we could stop for tea. I telephoned my mother and she's not expecting me home till after six."

"Your mother?"

"She lives with Belinda and me, takes care of us. Here comes the train," he said as an approaching whistle sounded. "Can I give you a lift?"

"A lift? Tea in Guildford? Yes, *Chief!*"

"Oh no, not Chief!" He shook his head determinedly. "Never again. If our acquaintance is to continue, it will be on a strictly nonprofessional basis."

"Right-oh, Alec," said Daisy.

Please turn the page
for an exciting sneak peek
at Carola Dunn's
THE WINTER GARDEN MYSTERY
coming in paperback in March 2001
from Kensington Publishing!

CHAPTER 1

o you're Maud Dalrymple's daughter." Lady Valeria's
tone did not suggest she found any cause to congratulate
the Dowager Viscountess on her offspring.

Under the critical gaze, Daisy wished she had put on
her grey frock with its high neckline and left off her lipstick
and face-powder. She wasn't sure the basilisk stare did not
penetrate straight through to the frivolous artificial silk
cami-knickers she had donned in place of her practical
combies.

At least she should have made sure someone else had
come down before joining Lady Valeria in the drawing-
room.

She was a professional woman, not a dependent, she
reminded herself sternly, taking a seat on one of the
fringed, tasselled, antimacassared Victorian chairs. She had
no reason to wither beneath that withering eye. No mere
imperious presence swathed in imperial purple could cow
her unless she allowed it to. Even a voice horribly reminis-

cent of her headmistress's was insufficient to reduce Daisy to an erring schoolgirl.

"You know my mother, Lady Valeria?" she asked politely.

"She and I were presented in the same year, though we lost touch long ago. In those days young ladies were properly brought up. Emancipation! We did not know the word. I am shocked that Maud should permit her daughter to seek employment."

"Mother does not control my actions."

"Well, she ought to. Still, Maud never did have any backbone."

Daisy held on to her temper with an effort. Her mother might be a querulous grumbler with a permanent sense of grievance, but it was not for Lady Valeria to criticize her.

"Mother is quite well," she said through gritted teeth, "considering her circumstances. I shall tell her you enquired after her. I must thank you for inviting me to write about Occles Hall." There, let her stick that in her pipe and smoke it. "Both the house and the village are charming."

Smugness chased censure from Lady Valeria's heavy, high-coloured features. "Everything was in a shocking state when I married Sir Reginald, but I flatter myself you will seldom find another estate so perfectly restored and maintained."

Revenge was irresistible. "Except for the smithy."

Lady Valeria scowled. "You will not write about the smithy," she commanded harshly.

"No, it's not the sort of thing *Town and Country* subscribers want to read about," said Daisy with regret. "I'm sure I'll find heaps to say without it."

"I have ordered Sir Reginald's secretary to give you every

assistance. I suppose it will not take you more than a day, two at most, to gather material for your article. Naturally you may ring Mr. Goodman up on the telephone after you return to town, should you have any further questions."

Neatly dished, Daisy had to admit. She had been jolly well and truly given the raspberry. On the other hand, she had abso-bally-lutely no desire to accept Lady Valeria's reluctant hospitality any longer than she needed.

She smiled at her hostess and murmured, "Too kind."

Lady Valeria looked disconcerted. Honours even, thought Daisy, and awaited the next thrust with interest.

She was rescued from the fray, at least temporarily, by the arrival of a small, chubby gentleman in an old-fashioned crimson velvet smoking-jacket.

"Oh, there you are, Reggie," said Lady Valeria. "Why on earth aren't you wearing a dinner-jacket?"

Sir Reginald looked down at himself in vague surprise. "Your pardon, my dear. I was thinking about clover and quite forgot we have a guest." He smiled at Daisy. "Won't you. . . ."

"What do I pay your valet for?" thundered his wife.

"He has a bad cold," said the baronet placidly. "I sent him back to bed this morning and told him to stay there until he feels better. Won't you? . . ."

"I have told you before, Reginald, that nothing good ever came of cosseting the servants."

"I'm sure you are right, my dear, but I didn't want to catch his cold and perhaps give it to young Goodman. Now, won't you introduce me to our guest?"

"Miss Dalrymple, my husband, Sir Reginald. Miss Dalrymple is a magazine writer."

"Welcome to Occles Hall, Miss Dalrymple. May I pour you a glass of sherry?" His eyes, as blue as Sebastian's, twinkled mischievously. "I'm afraid we haven't got the ingredients for these American cocktails you modern young ladies favour."

"Thank you, Sir Reginald, I shall be perfectly happy with sherry."

"I should hope so," snorted Lady Valeria, not quite sotto voce.

He poured three glasses of sherry. As he handed Daisy hers, he said, "You are Edward Dalrymple's daughter? I regret to say I didn't know your father well, but he once gave me some sound advice about Holsteins. Very sound. A sad loss to agriculture. You were at school with Bobbie, were you not?"

"Yes, but she's two years older and frightfully good at games. I'm a hopeless duffer so I was utterly in awe of her."

"Ah, but I gather the positions are reversed now that you are an independent woman, earning your own way by your pen. I am delighted that you have chosen Occles Hall to write about. May I hope you will spare a sentence or two for my dairy?"

"What piffle, Reggie. Miss Dalrymple's article will be about the Hall and the village."

"I shouldn't dream of leaving out the dairy, Sir Reginald. I consider it a patriotic duty to support British agriculture. You will be kind enough to show me around yourself, won't you?"

Lady Valeria turned as purple as her frock and choked on a sip of sherry.

Bobbie and Ben Goodman came in together. Lady Valeria glanced with obvious dissatisfaction from her daughter to Daisy and back. Daisy was sorry she had worn the rose charmeuse, which made Bobbie's olive sack look drabber and less becoming than ever.

On the other hand, she was glad to see that Mr. Goodman dined with the family. She wouldn't be the only outsider among the Parslows, and besides, from what she had seen of him, she liked him.

"Mr. Goodman!" Lady Valeria summoned the secretary to her side and started complaining about some letter he had written for her earlier.

Bobbie joined Daisy and Sir Reginald. She kissed her father with obvious affection, then turned to Daisy. "Did Mummy rag you terribly?"

"Oh no," Daisy nobly lied, racking her brain for something good to report. "Apparently she and my mother made their curtsies to Queen Victoria the same year. It was kind of her to arrange for Mr. Goodman to tell me the history of Occles Hall, and she even suggested I should telephone him if I have more questions after I go back to town."

"I hope you will stay until all your questions are answered," said Sir Reginald with quiet firmness. "Bobbie, Miss Dalrymple has kindly promised to squeeze a few words about the dairy into her article."

"Good-oh!"

They chatted for a few minutes about Daisy's writing, until the butler, Moody, came in.

He looked around the room and his dismal expression became downright lugubrious. "Dinner is *ready,* my lady," he announced.

"Mr. Sebastian is not down yet," said Lady Valeria sharply. "We shall wait."

"Very well, my lady."

Sebastian breezed in five minutes later. Daisy caught her breath at the sight of him in evening clothes. In the hours since she last saw him, she had managed to persuade herself he could not possibly be as handsome as she remembered, but he was.

"Sorry I'm late, Mater," he said. "Thomkins couldn't find the cufflinks I wanted."

"My dear boy," Lady Valeria's voice was a mixture of

indulgence and exasperation—"if you will insist on not sacking the fellow despite his carelessness. . . ."

"Oh, Thomkins suits me well enough. Sorry to keep you from your soup, Miss Dalrymple." When he smiled at Daisy, it was easy to see why his mother doted on him—and feared to turn him loose among the ladies.

Moody reappeared, walking as if his feet hurt. "Dinner is *served*, my lady."

Dinner was served by the butler and a parlourmaid; since the War only the grandest houses had footmen. Daisy recognized the girl who had brought the tea earlier, a plump brunette who moved awkwardly, with frequent whispered directions from Moody. Every dish she handed around seemed about to slip from her nervous grasp, but all went well until the end of the main course. Then Lady Valeria snapped at her for removing the plates from the wrong side.

The plate she had just collected crashed to the floor, knife and fork flying. With a wail of despair, she ran from the room.

"Really," said Lady Valeria angrily, "if she's still incapable of doing the job properly after three weeks, she will have to go. Moody, I can't imagine why you and Twitchell find it impossible to hire and train an adequate parlourmaid. You will have to do better than that."

"Yes, my lady," gloomed Moody. "Very well, my lady."

Dessert was consumed in fraught silence, except by Daisy and Sir Reginald, who struggled to carry on a conversation about cheese. At least she was able to congratulate him sincerely on the Cheshire cheese that closed the meal.

Lady Valeria rose to lead the ladies out. "The vicar and Mrs. Lake will be joining us in the drawing-room," she announced, adding in a tone of surprised displeasure, "He was not at home when I called at the vicarage to reprimand him about his sermon. All equal in the sight of God indeed! Anarchist piffle."

"Bolshie piffle, Mater," Sebastian drawled. "The Anarchists are passé—in fact, quite exploded."

Daisy, Sir Reginald, and Ben Goodman laughed. Bobbie looked so puzzled Daisy wondered whether she'd ever heard of Bolsheviks or Anarchists.

"Very clever, Sebastian," his mother said with a thin smile. "Don't linger over the port, now, Reggie."

"No, Valeria," murmured the baronet.

The Reverend and Mrs. Lake were already waiting in the drawing-room. They were very alike, both thin, spectacled, and anxious looking. However, the look Mrs. Lake cast at Lady Valeria when her ladyship began to dress down her husband was one of loathing. And Daisy was surprised to overhear the vicar arguing his side of the question. The Lakes were not such meek rabbits as they appeared, then.

Bobbie explained when the gentlemen came in and relieved them of the responsibility for entertaining Mrs. Lake. "They are absolutely dying to leave St. Dunstan's, so Mr. Lake often preaches sermons he knows Mummy will disapprove of, hoping she'll persuade the Bishop to replace him. It'll work, too. We've never had a vicar for longer than two years since old Mr. Peascod, who practically asked permission to breathe."

"It doesn't sound as if your parlourmaids last long, either."

"We've had three in two months," Bobbie said with a grimace. "They're promoted from housemaid and then reduced to the ranks again when Mummy gets fed up with their incompetence. There are two more housemaids to go, and then I suppose it'll be the kitchen maid."

"But they don't get the sack?"

"Gosh, no. It's far too difficult to find anyone willing to work in the house."

"Everyone seems to have trouble with servants since the War," said Daisy, who could not afford a maid if she could find one. She and Lucy made do with a treasure of a woman

who came in daily. "The girls are used to more freedom
and higher wages than they can get in service."

"And jolly good for them, I say."

Moody shuffled in with coffee. Daisy accepted a cup but
only drank half of it before making her excuses and retiring
to bed. She was tired after the journey; more important,
she had a lot of work to accomplish and, unless by some
miracle Sir Reginald prevailed, she had only two days to
do it in.

Daisy was wakened in the morning by a flood of sunshine
pouring in through the pink-check gingham curtains. In
the rosy light, she couldn't think for a moment where she
was. Then remembrance returned. She trounced out of
bed.

The house faced east. This was the ideal time of day to
photograph it, and for once the weather was cooperating.
Any moment clouds might roll in. She flung on a pullover
and skirt and her coat, grabbed camera and tripod, and
set off.

She only lost her way twice. The first time a housemaid
bearing a coal scuttle directed her. The second time, she
found a door opening into a sort of cloister in the courtyard
around which the house was built, so she went out that
way. Hoping the sun would rise high enough later to allow
photography within the courtyard, she hurried across to
the tunnel under the east block and a moment later
emerged, blinking, by the moat.

Conditions were perfect. The February sun rose far
enough south to make for interesting shadows. The frosty
air was diamond-clear and so still the water reflected every
detail of the intricate black-and-white façade. Daisy shot a
whole roll of film before deciding that the next important
item on her agenda was breakfast.

Bobbie and Ben Goodman, already in the breakfast-room, bade her a cheerful good morning.

"Help yourself," said Bobbie, waving at the sideboard. *The Times* lay beside her plate, unopened. "Isn't it a simply spiffing day?"

"Top-hole." Investigating the covered dishes, Daisy avoided the eggs, on which she existed at home, and served herself with smoked haddock, hot rolls, and tea. "I've already been out taking pictures," she said, sitting down at the table.

"Good-oh. Do you play golf? I have to take Ranee to the smithy first, but I thought we might pop over to the links and bash a ball around a few holes later."

"I can't," said Daisy, glad of an excuse. "I must get to work. Your mother made it rather plain my welcome is limited to two days."

"Two days? Bosh! I don't believe she meant it. Ben, what do you think?"

"I think I had better not offer an opinion," he replied with the smile that transformed his plain face. "I'm at your service any time, Miss Dalrymple."

"I'd like to see a bit of the gardens while it's fine."

"Certainly, though there's not much to see at this time of year, of course, except in the Winter Garden."

"There's a winter garden? Spiffing." She was about to ask him to explain how to find it, not wanting to drag him around at her side with his gammy leg, when Sebastian came in.

He looked sleepy. Pouring himself a cup of coffee, he sat down as his sister said in surprise, "You're up early, Bastie."

"Beautiful day, and we have a beautiful guest." He grinned at Daisy and her heart fluttered. "Do you ride, Miss Dalrymple? I'll show you a bit of the countryside."

"Thank you, but. . ."

Bobbie interrupted, "Bastie, Daisy says Mummy told her she can only stay two days."

"Not in so many words," Daisy put in hastily.

"Do you think she meant it?"

Stirring his coffee, Sebastian pondered. "Who knows? Stay longer and we'll find out."

"Don't be a hopeless ass! Daddy invited her to stay as long as she likes."

"A fat lot that has to say to anything," he said cynically.

"And Mummy knew Daisy's mother back in prehistoric times."

"Oh well, then, I should think you're safe, Miss Dalrymple, unless they had a frightful set-to?"

"Lady Valeria didn't mention one."

"She would have. Will you ride with me?"

"Thanks, but all the same I think I'd better see the gardens while it's fine, in case we get sleet tomorrow."

He nodded and did not press her, nor offer to tour the gardens with her.

"I expect I can find my way about without your aid, Mr. Goodman," Daisy suggested, "if you have work to do indoors."

"I'm glad of an excuse to be outside on such a glorious day," he assured her.

"It's bally cold out," said Sebastian abruptly, getting up and going to the sideboard. "I saw frost on the lawn. For heaven's sake, don't get chilled."

"I've already been out with my camera. It is a bit nippy." Daisy had a feeling his admonition was addressed more to Ben Goodman than to herself. She liked him the better for his concern for the secretary's dicky health.

"We'll wrap up well," Mr. Goodman promised.

When they set off together, he had on a knit balaclava helmet under his hat, covering his mouth and nose, and a heavy Army greatcoat with the shoulder straps removed.

"A sight to scare the crows," he said, a smile in his voice. "I hope you don't mind."

"I'm not a crow. The cold air hurts your lungs?"

"If I breathe too deeply. But the sun feels warm already. I'll take the balaclava off in a few minutes."

He took her first out onto a terrace on the south side. From there wide stone steps led down to an Elizabethan knot garden. Within the elaborate pattern of low box hedges, the beds were bare, but Daisy decided it would make a good photograph later in the day. She hadn't brought her equipment, not wanting to lug it around unnecessarily.

They went on along a gravel walk with a high yew hedge on one side, an ivy-grown wall on the other, till they came to a door in the wall. Pausing to take off the balaclava, Mr. Goodman pointed along the walk. "This turns into a footpath across the park, a shortcut to the village. I don't know if you'd care to walk down to the Cheshire Cheese with me for a nip before lunch?"

"I'd love to, but ought you to walk so far?"

"A certain amount of exercise is good for my leg, otherwise it stiffens. You lost a brother in the War, I gather?"

"My only brother . . . and my fiancé."

"I'm sorry. It was a beastly show. Both Army?"

"Gervaise was." She didn't usually talk about Michael, but a depth of compassion she sensed in him made her go on, defiantly. "My fiancé was a driver in a Friends' Ambulance Unit."

"A conchie?" The way he said the hateful epithet was quite different from Phillip's—most people's—absolute, unhesitating contempt. "It was one of those units pulled me out. Brave men, going into Hell with no weapon to defend themselves."

Tears pricked behind Daisy's eyelids. The need to bottle up her feelings unless she was prepared to defend him had kept the wound of Michael's loss raw and painful. Ben

Goodman's understanding quickened the healing process recently begun by another rare, sympathetic soul.

He had turned away to open the door. As it swung open, the sound of running footsteps, boots on gravel, made them both turn. A dark, wiry lad in gardening clothes dashed up.

"Mr. Gootman, sir, a telephone call for you there is," he announced in the musical accents of Wales. "A trunk call."

"Blast. Still, never mind. Miss Dalrymple, this is Owen Morgan, who is undoubtedly much better able to show you the Winter Garden than am I, but I'll be back as soon as I can. Excuse me." He limped hurriedly away.

Daisy smiled at the blushing youth. "Good, an expert guide."

"But I don't know all the Latin names yet, miss," he blurted out. "Mr. Bligh, the head gardener, he knows."

"To tell the truth, I'd much rather have the common names. Come on, Owen." She preceded him through the door, and stepped into instant spring.

The garden was protected from cold winds by walls on all four sides. In the middle, in the centre of a paved square, stood a classical statue, a winged figure of a burly, dishevelled man with a conch shell held to his lips: *Boreas, the North Wind* according to the pedestal. And surrounding the paving, along the walls, was a wide raised border ablaze with colour.

There were evergreens—Daisy recognized laurel and variegated holly—and plants with gray-green foliage. Flowering vines and shrubs hid the walls, yellow cascades of winter jasmine, white honeysuckle and wintersweet scenting the air, the coral blooms of Japanese quince. In front, vying with snowdrops and aconites, grew scylla and irises, crocuses, violets, multihued primroses, purple-blue anemones, lilac periwinkles, crimson cyclamen.

"It's beautiful!" cried Daisy. "How I wish someone

would invent an efficient way to take colour photographs. Even if I learn the name of every plant, words will never do it justice."

The young gardener led her around, pointing out delicate Christmas and Lenten roses, daphne, orange Chinese lanterns, and fluffy yellow hazel catkins. She enjoyed his voice as much as the flower names.

"Which part of Wales are you from?" she asked.

"Glamorgan, miss. Merthyr Tydfil."

"That's in the south. You're a long way from home."

"Oh yes, miss, and it's dreatfully I miss it."

"You have left your family there?"

His story came pouring out. "My pa wass killed down the pit—the coal mine. Mam wouldn't let us boys be miners. Fife brothers we are, scattered all ofer. Two's in the Nafy; one's a gentleman's personal serfant in London. Rhys iss a schoolteacher," he said with shy pride, "and so's one of my sisters. Married the other two are, at home in Merthyr."

"I expect you're lonely here, being used to a big family."

"I wass walking out with a young woman." His face crumpled in misery. "Nearly engaged we wass, look you, but she ran off to London."

"Then she didn't deserve you," said Daisy firmly as they turned the last corner, coming to the bed to the right of the entrance. Owen looked less than comforted. "Are these daffodils here, just coming up between the snowdrops?" she asked to distract him, though she recognized the green shoots perfectly well.

He blinked hard, sniffed, and answered, "Yes, miss, and narcissus. They come out here earlier than anywheres."

"And that bush?" She gestured at an unhappy-looking shrub in the middle of a bare patch of ground. "What's that?"

"Azalea, miss." He frowned, puzzled. "They bloom early in here, too, but. . . ."

.

"What's wrong?"

"It's terrible it looks. And where's the irises around it? Myself I planted them, the kind that's flowering now, and hardly any hass come up." He stepped over the low kerb and picked his way carefully to the small bush. Most of its few remaining leaves were brown, except for one bronze-green sprig.

Daisy saw that the dark soil of the bare patch was broken by a few scattered iris shoots. "Perhaps a dog got in and dug them up and buried them again too deep," she proposed, though there was no sign of the earthworks usually left by an excavating canine.

"The azalea iss dying." Owen Morgan turned, panic-stricken. "All the buds are dead. What'll her ladyship say? Please, miss, I must find Mr. Bligh."

"Of course, Owen. I'll just wait here until Mr. Goodman comes back."

She wandered around, trying to work out whether it was worth taking photos when all the marvellous colours would be lost. The knot garden, however dull in fact, would turn out better on film, but Boreas deserved a picture, she decided.

Presumably he was supposed to be exhaling a gale from his conch, though hair, beard, and tunic were all streaming in the opposite direction and he actually faced north-east. Moving from side to side, she tried to work out the best angle for a shot. She was wondering whether to go and fetch her camera or wait for Mr. Goodman when Owen returned.

He brought with him a wheelbarrow, spade, and fork, and a bent, weatherbeaten ancient. Mr. Bligh wore a drooping tweed deerstalker of an indeterminate colour, breeches tied at the knees with string, and woolly gaiters in startling pink-and-blue stripes. He tipped his hat to Daisy, revealing a hairless scalp as weatherbeaten as his face, and brown eyes as bright and knowing as a sparrow's.

"Fine marnin', miss," he remarked, and went to examine the patient.

Owen followed him, looking anxious. Daisy hoped he wasn't going to be blamed for whatever disaster had overtaken the azalea and the irises. The poor boy was unhappy enough already.

"She's dead," said Mr. Bligh. "Dig 'er out, lad, an' we s'll find summat else to put in afore her la'ship takes a fancy to come by. I s'll take kindly, miss," he added unexpectedly to Daisy, "if 'ee'll not tell her la'ship, being she don't foller as you can't lay down the law to plants like you can to people."

"I shan't say a word," Daisy promised as Owen took the spade and started digging, watched by the old man propped against the wheel-barrow. Returning to the statue, she realized the sun was just right for the pose she wanted. "I'm going to fetch my camera," she said to the head gardener. "If Mr. Goodman comes, tell him I'll be back in a jiffy."

"Right, miss. What is it, lad?"

"There's something in the way, Mr. Bligh. 'Bout a foot and a half down. Like a mass of roots it feels."

"Try the fork, but go at it easy like. Don't want to do any more damage."

Daisy left them to the new puzzle and sped back to the house. She had already put a fresh roll of film in the camera. Returning laden with equipment through the Long Hall, she met Ben Goodman on his way to rejoin her.

"You won't mind if I dash ahead?" she said. "I have to hurry to catch the light."

He nodded. "I'll follow at my own pace."

When she reached the Winter Garden, she was surprised to see that Owen had dug a trench right across the bare patch of soil. He and Mr. Bligh stood at one end, gazing down with fascinated revulsion.

"Go on, have a look," urged Mr. Bligh.

Owen knelt in the dirt. Reaching down, he moved something at the bottom of the trench.

"Oh God! Oh God!" He flung himself backwards onto his heels, his arms across his face. "It's her. It's my Grace."

ABOUT THE AUTHOR

Born and raised in England, Carola Dunn now lives in Eugene, Oregon. Her next Daisy Dalrymple mystery, THE WINTER GARDEN MYSTERY, will be published by Kensington Publishing in March 2001. You can visit her Web site at: http://www.geocities.com/CarolaDunn

Running with the Kenyans

Running with the Kenyans

Discovering the Secrets
of the Fastest People on Earth

ADHARANAND FINN

faber and faber

First published in 2012
by Faber and Faber Limited
Bloomsbury House
74–77 Great Russell Street
London WCIB 3DA

Typeset by Faber and Faber Limited
Printed and bound by CPI Group (UK) Ltd, Croydon, CRO 4YY

A CIP record for this book
is available from the British Library

ISBN 978–0–571–27405–5

10 9 8 7 6 5 4

To my fellow collaborators Marietta, Lila, Uma and Ossian

When the divine is looking for you, that's a pretty powerful force.

PREM RAWAT

Prologue

I hear someone else's alarm go first. I've been waiting for it, in my half-sleep. A shallow, impatient slumber under the thin sheet, the name of the hotel stamped across it in green ink. BOMEN. The light from the corridor makes the room visible. Bare walls. A dark pink colour in this light, but in the day an intoxicating bright peach. An energy-saving light bulb hangs from its wire above my head.

A phone rings. Godfrey, in the other bed a few feet away, answers it immediately, as though he's been holding it in his hand, waiting for it to call. He speaks in calm, wakeful Kalenjin, and then hangs up.

'Chris,' he says in the darkness. He knows I'm awake. 'You know Chris. He wants to go down for breakfast.'

My alarm starts off, buzzing on the bedside table. I reach over and turn it off. 4 a.m. Time to get up.

The hotel is a clatter of pots and pans and people talking. Some of the guests must be turning over in their beds and wondering what is going on, checking their watches. I head out along the corridor. The leaves of a palm tree bristle at one end. At the top of the stairs I meet Beatrice, standing in the shadows, unsure whether to go down. She smiles, her teeth white against her black skin.

'Let's go,' I say.

Without replying, she follows me down.

In the dining room the waiters are ready. They've been pulled out of their beds in the middle of the night and pressed into their waiting suits. They don't look pleased.

'Tea, coffee?' asks the head waiter, walking over to us with a tray of pots and cups. We both shake our heads. I sit down at the table. Beatrice follows, sitting down opposite me. Outside the street is silent. I look at Beatrice.

'Ready?' I ask her.

She smiles. 'I will make it,' she says, nodding.

Japhet and Shadrack walk into the room. Two young men in their early twenties. Neither of them has ever been this far from home. Japhet is all big toothy smiles, excited, while Shadrack looks permanently as though he has just seen something both shocking and incredible, his eyes pointed, bulging from his head. The head waiter is at the table with his tray.

'Tea, coffee?'

'Chai,' says Shadrack so quietly he has to repeat it twice before the waiter understands. Japhet just nods. The waiter, pleased, pours out the tea.

'You both feeling ready?' I ask. Shadrack looks at me confused, as though I've just asked him if he has ever been in love.

'We're ready, yes,' says Japhet, grinning. The waiter, on a roll now, brings us all a plate of fruit. Shadrack pokes his watermelon nervously with a fork and offers it to Beatrice. Then the waiter brings us all plates of bread and fried eggs.

'Whatever you do,' Godfrey told us the night before, 'don't eat eggs for breakfast.' I look at the others.

'You like eggs before a race?' I ask them. But they're already tucking in. I decide not to make a fuss, but I leave mine untouched. Two slices of bread and butter is enough. I eat up quickly and return upstairs to my room.

I had planned to go back to sleep after breakfast, but I'm too awake, so I pack up my bags and sit on the bed. My foot feels fine. I rub it to make sure, pressing my thumb into the sole where the injury was. I pull out a bottle of Menthol Plus, a balm from the pharmacy back in Iten. I rub it on my foot, then pull my socks on and sit back on the bed. Slow, deep breaths. An hour later, it's time to go.

The dawn is casting a faint light across the parking lot as we all stand around beside the minibus, waiting for Godfrey. I left him combing his hair in the bedroom. He has a grade-one crew cut, but still spends five minutes combing it each morning. The others stand quiet, patient. Finally he turns up.

'Sorry, guys,' he says, sliding open the minibus doors. The junior members of the team, Japhet, Shadrack and Beatrice, climb into the back of the bus. Chris, Paul and Philip, all veteran runners, take the middle row. And as the sole mzungu, white man, I'm given the front seat next to Godfrey, our trainer and driver.

We bump our way out of the drive and along the dirt street to the main, paved road. People are up walking around, herding goats, carrying large sacks across their shoulders. Crowded matatus, small buses, pull over and more people squeeze in. The day is already under way.

Inside our bus nobody speaks. Godfrey fiddles with the radio, but he already knows it doesn't work. He drives on, the road straight, rising up along the edge of the savannah, which spreads out vast and empty on one side. On the other side are makeshift houses, small fields of maize, kiosks painted in bright colours advertising phone companies.

After about twenty minutes we reach the main entrance gate to Lewa, a 55,000-acre wildlife conservancy 170 miles north of Nairobi. A long line of 4×4 cars is filing through. People are walking beside the road. We join the queue of traffic. The savannah spreads out on both sides now, filling the world. This is the classic African landscape. Dry grassy plains, dotted with spiky acacia trees.

In the back they're all getting excited suddenly, pointing out of the window.

'What is it?' I ask.

'Look,' says Godfrey, pointing to one side, where an elephant is standing, as still as a statue, just a few feet away.

'Is it real?' Philip asks, craning over my shoulder to see.

We bump on through the clouds of dust from the other cars. The elephant has lightened the mood in the bus. Godfrey starts out on his pep talk.

'OK, guys. Here we are. I know we have a winner in this car. You've all done the training, now it's time to run. Remember that this is a marathon. You mustn't go too fast at the beginning. But you need to stay in touch with the leaders. You know you can do it.'

Godfrey pulls the bus to a halt. Even though it's still barely past 6 a.m., hundreds of people stand lined up behind a rope, being pushed back by security guards. Runners in shorts and vests, numbers pinned to their chests, are streaming along the track towards the start. Before I know it everyone is out of the bus and has disappeared.

'They've gone straight to the start,' says Godfrey. 'You go,

I'll meet you there.' It's already warm, so I strip off my track-suit and throw it in the bus. Underneath is my yellow vest. My number, 22, is pinned to the front. Along the back are the words 'Iten Town Harriers'.

The start is buzzing with over a thousand runners. Among the mêlée I spot a group of yellow vests, the rest of the team. They're with my wife, Marietta, and my two-year-old son, Ossian. My daughters are somewhere watching from the sidelines. Marietta's waiting for me so she can take a group photograph.

We huddle together. Godfrey doesn't want to be in the picture, but we haul him over. We couldn't have done this without him. He stands at the back, his face lost under the shadow of his hat.

'OK, thank you,' says Marietta, releasing us from our pose. 'Good luck.' And with that we're lining up. We all shake hands, but there's nothing left to say. This is it. Months of training on the line. The wild plains of Africa lying before us. Waiting. Still. Helicopters hover overhead. The man with the microphone doesn't say it, but we're waiting for some lions to move off the course. The helicopters are swooping low over them, trying to force them on. It seems a long time to stand there. I stretch my arms. Twenty-six miles. Forty-two kilometres. But they're just numbers. One step at a time. One breath at a time. The morning heat rising from the spiky grass. My children, big smiley faces, waving at me from the side. And then we're counting. Five. I feel my breath filling me with life. Four. People hold their watches, crouching. Three. Two. This is it. One. Go.

1

In my mind I am a Kenyan.
1980s Nike advertising slogan

We're running across long, wavy grass, racing for the first
corner. I'm right at the front, being pushed on by the
charge of legs all around me, the quick breathing of my
schoolmates. We run under the goalposts and swing down
close beside the stone wall along the far edge of the field.
It's quieter now. I look around. One boy is just behind me,
but the others have all dropped back. Up ahead I can see
the fluttering tape marking the next corner. I run on, the
air cold in my lungs, the tall poplar trees shivering above
my head.

We go out of the school grounds, along a gravel path
that is normally out of bounds. My feet crunch along,
the only sound. An old man pushing a bicycle stands to
one side as I go by. I follow the tape, back down a steep
slope onto the playing fields, back to the finish. I get there
long before anyone else and stand waiting in the cold as
they come in, collapsing one after the other across the
line. I watch them, rolling on their backs, kneeling on the
ground, their faces red. I feel strangely elated. It's the first
PE class in my new school and we've all been sent out on
a cross-country run. I've never tried running further than
the length of a football pitch before, so I'm surprised by
how easy I find it.

'He's not even breathing hard,' the teacher says, holding me up as an example to the others. He tells me to put my hands under my armpits to keep them warm as the other children continue to trail in.

A few years later, aged twelve, I break the 800m school record on sports day, despite a few of the other boys attempting to bundle me over at the start in an effort to help their friend win. Five minutes later, I run the 1500m and win that too. My dad, sensing some potential talent, suggests I join the local running club and looks up the number in the telephone directory. I hear him talking to someone on the phone, asking directions. From that point on, a course is set: I am to be a runner.

It all begins rather inauspiciously one night a few weeks later. I put on my shorts and tracksuit and walk across the bridge from our suburban housing estate in the town of Northampton to the nearby shopping centre. The precinct is half-deserted, save for a few late shoppers coming out of the giant Tesco supermarket. I head down the escalator to the car park, and then across the road to the unmarked dirt track where the Northampton Phoenix running club meets. It's a cold night and all the runners are crammed into a small doorway in the side of a huge red brick wall. Inside, the corridor walls are painted blood red and covered in lewd graffiti. Further down the corridor are the changing rooms, where men can be heard laughing loudly above the fizz of the showers. I give my name to a lady sitting at a small table.

Rather than head onto the track, as I had imagined, I'm taken back across the road with a group of children around my age to the shopping centre's delivery area, a stretch of covered road with shuttered loading bays all along one side. The road itself is thick with discharged oil. A man in tights and a yellow running jacket gets us to run from one side of the road to the other, touching the kerb each time. Between each sprint he makes us do exercises such as press-ups or star jumps. I begin thinking, as I lie back on the cold, hard tarmac ready to do some sit-ups, that I've come to the wrong place. This isn't running. I had imagined groups of lithe athletes hurtling around a track. My dad must have got confused and called the wrong club.

I'm so convinced it isn't the running club that I don't return for another year. When I do, they ask me if I'd like to train in 'the tunnel', which I take to mean the shopping centre loading bays, or head out for a long run. I opt for the long run and am directed over to a group of about forty people. This is more like it. As we set off along the gravel pathways that wind their way around the council estates of east Northampton, I feel for the first time the sensation of running in the middle of a group of people. The easy flow of our legs moving below us, the trees, houses, lakes floating by, the people stepping aside, letting us go. Although most of the other runners are older and constantly making jokes, as I drift quietly along I feel a vague sense of belonging.

I spend the next six years or so as a committed member of the club, running track or cross-country races most weekends, and training at least twice a week. Much of my formative years I spend out pounding the roads. Even when I grow my hair long and start playing the guitar in a band, I keep on training. The other runners nickname me Bono.

One night, when I'm about eighteen, I pass a bunch of my school friends coming back from the pub. We are in the last mile of a long run and are going at full pace. My school friends stare at me open-mouthed as I charge by, one shouting incredulously: 'What are you doing?' as I disappear into the distance.

I first become aware of Kenyan runners sometime in the mid-1980s, around the same time I join the running club. They seem to emerge suddenly in large numbers into a running world dominated in my eyes by Britain's Steve Cram and the Moroccan Said Aouita. I'm a big fan of both these great rivals, Cram with his high-stepping, majestic style, and the smaller Aouita, with his grimacing face and rocking shoulders, who is brilliant at every distance from the short, fast 800m right up to the 10,000m.

But by the 1988 Olympics in Seoul, it is all Kenyans, winning every single men's middle-distance and long-distance track gold medal except one. What impresses me most about them is the way they run. The conventional wisdom is that the most efficient method, particularly in the longer distances, is to run at an even pace, and most races are run that way. The Kenyans, however, take a more maverick approach. They are always surging ahead, only to slow down suddenly, or sprinting off right from the gun at a crazy pace. I love the way it befuddles the TV commentators, who are constantly predicting that a Kenyan athlete is going too fast, only for him to suddenly go even faster.

I remember watching the World Championship 5,000m final in our living room in Northampton on a warm mid-

August evening in 1993. My mum keeps coming in and out, suggesting I go and sit outside in the garden. It's a lovely evening. But I'm glued to the TV. The pre-race favourite is the Olympic champion from Morocco, Khalid Skah, while the television cameras also focus in on a young Ethiopian called Haile Gebrselassie who won both the 5,000m and 10,000m at the world junior championships the year before. The athletes stand beside each other on the start line looking back into the camera. They smile nervously when their names are announced, and give the odd directionless wave.

The race sets off at a blistering pace, with a succession of African athletes streaking ahead one after the other at the front. Skah, who has taken on and beaten the Kenyans many times before, tracks every move, always sitting on the shoulder of the leader. Britain's only runner in the race, Rob Denmark, soon finds himself trailing far behind.

With seven laps still to go, the BBC television commentator, Brendan Foster, is feeling the strain just watching. 'It's a vicious race out there,' he says. Right on queue, a young Kenyan, Ismael Kirui, surges to the front and within a lap has opened up a huge gap of about 50 metres on everyone else. It's a suicidal move, Foster declares. 'He's only eighteen and has no real international experience. I think he's got a little carried away.' I sit riveted, screaming at the TV as the coverage cuts away to the javelin for a few moments. When it switches back, Kirui is still leading. Lap after lap, Skah and a group of three Ethiopians track him, but they aren't getting any closer. The camera zooms in on Kirui's eyes, staring ahead, wild like a hunted animal as he keeps piling on the pace. 'This is one savage race,' says Foster.

Kirui is still clear as the bell sounds for the last lap. Down the back straight he sprints for his life, but the three Ethiopians are flying now, closing the gap. With just over 100 metres left, Kirui glances over his shoulder and sees the figure of Gebrselassie closing in on him. For a brief second everything seems to stop. This is the moment, the kill is about to happen. Startled, frantic, Kirui turns back towards the front and urges his exhausted body on again, his tired legs somehow sprinting away down the finishing straight. He crosses the line less than half a second ahead of Gebrselassie. But he has done it. He has won. Battered and bewildered, he sets off on his lap of honour, the Kenyan flag, once again, held aloft in triumph.

That evening I head down to the track for a training session with my running club. I try to run like Kirui, staring straight ahead, going as fast as I can right from the start. It's one of the best training sessions I ever do. Usually, if you run too hard at the beginning, you worry about how you'll feel later. You can feel it in your body, the anticipation of the pain to come. Usually it makes you slow down. It's called pacing yourself. But that night I don't care. I want to unshackle myself and run free like a Kenyan.

The night I spend hurtling wide-eyed around the track after watching Ismael Kirui turns out to be one of the last sessions I ever do with my running club. Just over a month later I pack my belongings into my parents' car and drive up to Liverpool to begin university. Although I join the college running team, my focus on training is soon lost amid the whirlwind of university life. Like most teenage students

I'm unleashed into a new world where anything is possible. Running seems to belong to a previous life, although I never completely let it go.

The extent to which my training peters out becomes clear by the time the British Universities Cross Country Championships come round the following March. The night before the race, I take off on a spontaneous road trip to Wales with three friends, clambering onto the team bus the next morning ready for little other than sleep. It's a miracle I make it at all.

A hundred miles away in Durham it's a cold, blustery day. I lace up my spikes and go through the familiar routine of jogging and stretching, but once the race starts, my legs, sucked down by the thick mud, give up without a fight. I jog around, unable to rouse myself to run any faster. I finish in 280th position. My good friend and rival from my days running in Northampton, Ciaran Maguire, comes second. Just a few years before we battled neck-and-neck all the way in the county cross-country championships, until he edged past me on the line to win. And now here we are separated by almost 300 people. I see him after the race. 'All you need is to give yourself one good year of training,' he says consolingly. I nod, but deep down I know it is not going to happen.

Over the years I've met others like me: former runners who still, every now and then, dig out their old trainers and start lapping the local park in the vague hope of remembering what it felt like. We sign up to a local 10K or half-marathon, determined to get back in shape. But something – life, an injury, a lack of dedication – always gets in the way, and we stop training. But the embers refuse to die. We refuse to chuck our old mouldy trainers away. We know we might need them again, that the urge to run will return.

After I have children, it becomes even harder to find the time to train, that is until I manage to land a freelance job writing race reports for *Runner's World* magazine. Although it doesn't pay much, it makes the running feel less self-indulgent. It isn't just me doing something for myself in an effort to revive some lost childhood fervour. It is now work.

With regular assignments from *Runner's World*, over the next few years I start training more frequently, although with young children it's still hard to get out more than twice a week. I descend the stairs from my office to find Marietta with little Ossian hanging off her hip, struggling to get the lunch ready, my two daughters, Lila and Uma, screeching at each other as they tussle over a book. The garden is overgrown, the bins need taking out and the phone is ringing. It's not easy to say, 'I'm just popping out for a long run. See you in an hour or so.' So even though I start racing regularly, my times barely improve. I run my first half-marathon when I'm twenty-nine in 1 hour 30 minutes. Seven years later I've run three more in exactly the same time.

I keep telling myself that one day I will train hard and run really fast. I'm not sure what that would mean exactly – a sub-3-hour marathon, perhaps? But the years are slipping away. Every time an athlete over thirty-five wins a big race on television I tell myself that there is still hope. It isn't that I want to achieve any specific goal; I just don't want to one day look back and regret that I never gave myself a decent chance to see what I could do.

2

So we sold the house and fled from the gloom of the English summer, like a flock of migrating swallows.

Gerald Durrell, *My Family and Other Animals*

I sit looking out of the car window on the way to a 10K charity race near our home in Devon. It's a blustery September morning and I'm not feeling well. If I wasn't writing about it for *Runner's World*, I probably wouldn't run. I make myself feel better by resolving to start at a slow pace and to just enjoy the scenery. The course loops around the grounds of the lovely Powderham Castle, past deer and along the Exe estuary. It will be nice to take in my surroundings as I run for a change. As we park the car, I have no idea that something is about to happen that will make me rethink my whole approach to running.

Once I get to the start line, I seem to forget about my illness, instinctively snaking my way to the front. I can't let myself start behind with all the fun runners, no matter how bad I feel. There are almost a thousand people in the race, but most of them are here purely for the fun of the event or to raise money for charity. The actual running is just the excuse. For many, it's the chatter of friends, the picnics on the grass, and the general sense of occasion that brings them out.

It occurs to me afterwards, though, when we've all finished, that perhaps, secretly, it's the other way around. Afterwards, the race is all anyone wants to talk about. What time did you do? I couldn't get going. I went off too fast. People beam as they tell each other how tired they feel, their faces flushed, their bodies tingling as they pull their tracksuits back on. Perhaps, really, all the other stuff is the excuse. If it comes disguised as a charity event, with team T-shirts and picnics, then people will have a good excuse to run. In fact, they'll come flocking. A thousand people, and nearly all of them feeling better for it afterwards. Perhaps the running really is the main attraction. One woman tells me, as we sit on the grass afterwards, that she thinks running is like getting drunk in reverse. With drinking, it feels great at first, but then you start feeling awful. With running, you feel awful first, but then, after you finish, you feel great. That sounds like a much better deal.

As the starting gun fires, we surge forward across the grass. I'm near the front as we reach the first corner. A sharp bend leads us onto the gravel drive up towards the castle. As we run, a man beside me asks me what my personal best time is. 'I don't know,' I say. I did run a 10K a few years before, in 47 minutes, but I'm sure I'm faster now.

We clatter in under the arched entrance to the castle and across a small courtyard. My daughters, Lila and Uma, are standing there with my mother-in-law, Granny Bee.

'Here he is,' she tells them, pointing me out among the sea of charity T-shirts. 'Come on, Dhar,' she shouts. My daughters just stare at me as I run by. I smile at them, to reassure them it's OK, it's still me. And with that we head out under the arch and off into the countryside.

The course dinks down a short hill and then along by the Exe estuary, the sailing boats bobbing and clinking out on the water. I'm still near the front, and decide to stretch my legs to make use of the wind blowing behind us. No one else seems to have the same plan, and they let me go, racing off at the front, blown like tinder along the path. The 2 km marker seems to appear almost instantly. Surely they've put it in the wrong place – we haven't run that far already, have we? I look back. I'm now a good 40 metres clear at the front. If I keep this up, I think, I could finish in the top ten. In my mind I'm already rehearsing how I'm going to tell the story afterwards. 'I was still in the lead at 3 km.'

As the 3 km marker comes and goes, I revise my story. 'I was still in the lead at 4 km.' Then 4 km becomes 5 km.

I keep expecting a stream of runners to pass me at any moment. Where are they? What is going on? It's strange being out on my own. It's almost as though I'm not in a race at all, but on a solitary training run, except for the fact that there are a thousand unseen runners massing behind me, chasing me. Like some fugitive, each time I feel my legs slowing I force myself on, bursting up hills, tumbling down grassy banks. I'm running more on some primal survival instinct than any fierce desire to win.

In the end I finish well clear of the field in a huge personal best time of 38 minutes 35 seconds. My daughters run over as I cross the line and give me a big hug. A reporter from the local newspaper comes up and starts asking me questions. I feel like I've won the Olympics.

As I sit in Granny Bee's car on the way home, I wonder again, for the millionth time since I left school, what would happen if I trained properly. If I did what Ciaran said, and gave myself one year of real training. But how could I fit it in?

As the car purrs along, the wipers swishing back and forth, the girls both quiet in the back, tired from a morning of running around outside, I begin devising a crazy plan. A few months earlier, Marietta's sister, Jophie, suggested I came to Kenya, where she lives, to run the Lewa marathon. Famous as one of the toughest marathons in the world, the race is run across a wildlife conservancy.

'There are lions roaming around,' she said, as if that somehow made it more tempting. 'But there are helicopters in the sky to make sure they don't come too close.'

I wasn't really listening. I wasn't ready to run a marathon, and besides, I couldn't travel all the way to Kenya just for a race. Life doesn't work like that. Right? But now, sitting here weaving our way along the A379 back to Exeter, it seems like a great idea.

For years I've been telling people the story of Annemari Sandell. She was a talented junior athlete in Finland when, in 1995, she travelled to Kenya. She spent six weeks training in the Rift Valley in the lead-up to the world cross-country championships, which were held in Durham, England. I was there, watching, on a cold, rain-drenched afternoon as the sixteen-year-old Sandell ran away from the Kenyans and Ethiopians to win the title. What had happened to her out there in Kenya? What did she find that had turned her into a world champion? Could I find it too?

Quite simply, the Kenyans are the greatest runners on Earth. Considering that running, and in particular long-distance running, is the most universal, accessible and widely practised sport in the world, it is remarkable that one tiny corner of the planet can dominate so much. In virtually any elite road race anywhere in the world, within minutes a group of Kenyans will break away at the front of the field.

The facts and figures attesting to their running dominance are incredible. Of the top twenty fastest marathons ever run anywhere in the world, seventeen were run by Kenyans. (The other three, incidentally, were all run by athletes from Kenya's East African neighbour Ethiopia.)[1]

In the eighteen years from the 1991 World Athletics Championships in Tokyo to the 2009 World Championships in Berlin, Kenyan men won a total of ninety-three world and Olympic medals in middle- and long-distance running events. Thirty-two of those medals were gold. In the same period, which spans ten World Championships and five Olympic Games, Britain won precisely none, of any colour. Even the mighty USA only managed three gold medals, and two of those were won in Osaka in 2007 by a man who only became a US citizen at the age of twenty, having been born and raised and developed as an athlete in . . . yes, you guessed it, Kenya.[2]

---

1 In 2011, the top twenty fastest marathons of the year were all run by Kenyans.

2 In the 2011 World Championships in Daegu, Somali-born Mo Farah won Britain's first medals in the middle- and long-distance events for over twenty years, with gold in the 5,000m and silver in the 10,000m. Despite no medals in either of these two races, Kenya ended the championships with seventeen medals, its biggest medal haul ever.

As a teenager I used to imagine I was running across the plains of Africa as I skirted around the edges of the Northampton housing estates. I used to love to run on hot days, when the heat would visibly shimmer across the road, because it was how I imagined Kenya. The thought of doing it for real is intoxicating. Not just running the Lewa marathon, but to go and train with the Kenyans, too. To discover their secret, as Annemari Sandell did. Of course, first I'll have to sell the idea to Marietta. If I'm going to go, I want her and the children to come too.

I first met Marietta at university in Liverpool. She had her hair cut short in a boyish crop, ate a diet of nothing but rice and seeds, and liked techno music. I could never have guessed she was from an aristocratic Devonshire family. She had a self-contained air that intrigued me, and we ended up becoming good friends, before I finally realised I had fallen for her. It took one of my friends to point it out.

'I think you're in love with Marietta,' he said in a bar one night.

'What?' I said. 'Are you mad?' But he was right.

Breaking the news to her was awkward, as by then we were both living in the same shared house with three other friends, and she had a boyfriend. At first she wasn't keen, but I was consumed with teenage love, staring forlornly out of rain-splattered windows, sitting up late at night writing poetry. For about a month I couldn't get her out of my head, I was thinking about her constantly. And then, suddenly, it was gone.

I felt relieved, like a weight had been lifted from me. I walked into the house that afternoon and saw her standing in the kitchen. It's OK, I wanted to tell her, I'm cured. But she ran over and kissed me. Eight years later, Lila, our eldest daughter, was born.

Ever since we've had children, Marietta and I have wanted to take them off travelling, to give them an adventure, open their eyes to the immensity of the world.

When I first met Marietta, she had just come back from travelling around South America for a year. I was impressed. I'd never been outside the British Isles. After we got together, we took time out from university to travel to Venezuela together, and a few years later we both went back there again. So we figured South America was our stomping ground. Marietta was always suggesting we take the children there. 'You mean for a holiday?' I'd ask. 'No, for longer. Six months. A year. Imagine it, they'd learn to speak Spanish, it would be an incredible education for them.' It was always me coming up with the excuses, afraid to leave the safety blanket of my job, our little house, our families.

So I don't think Marietta will be fazed by the idea of an extended trip. And why not Africa? Her brother lives in Tanzania. Her sister lives in Kenya. In some ways our visit is overdue. The only snag may be when I tell her I want to go there to run.

Marietta has no interest in running. In our last year at university I tried to get her enthused about it. We lived beside a park, which was about 2 miles around the outside. I used to take her out every few nights, at a slow jog, and by the end of a few gruelling weeks we made it the whole way around without stopping.

That night Marietta developed a huge migraine and lay in bed cursing me and my training regime. Her running career, it seemed, was over.

Years later I decided that perhaps she would be better at middle distances, such as the 800m. Perhaps the lap of the park was just too far. By then we were living in London, so I somehow managed to convince her to come to the local track for a 400m time trial. If she could run it in under 90 seconds, I thought, we'd have something to work on. She obviously thought I was mad as I took her through the warm-up routine and got her to stand with her toes just behind the start line. I held the watch up. Ready? Go.

We started off, jogging. 'It's only one lap,' I said. 'Can you go any faster?' She looked like she was going to punch me.

No, running is not for her. Sometimes we sit across from each other at the table in the evening and I find myself recounting some new world record and telling her how the athletes were lapping in under 60 seconds, or how the winner ran a 52-second last lap, and I see her eyes glazing over. So I'm not sure what she's going to make of my plan to move us all out to the land of runners.

That night, after the children are in bed, I put forward my idea. Six months in Kenya. We'll have an adventure. She'll get to visit her sister. We'll see elephants, zebras, go riding across the bush in the back of a jeep – the kids will love it. And I'll get to run. Really run. With the greatest runners on earth. And if I find their secret, I can bottle it and make a fortune.

She looks at me across the table. 'Are you serious?'
'Yes,' I say. 'What do you think?'
'I think it's a brilliant idea.'

3

In Kenya, there are only athletes.
Vivian Cheruiyot

'You're brave,' says a neighbour in our village when she hears we're off to Kenya. 'But then, you lot are like that.'

She's trying to be nice, saying brave, but she means mad. We get quizzical looks from people whenever we mention our plan. But we're pressing on with the preparations. The children, of course, take it all in their stride. One evening, as I'm putting them to bed, I conduct a mock television interview with Lila and Uma, pretending that they're famous explorers. Ossian, picking up on the general sense of excitement, is running around in his sleep suit yelling like a lion and laughing. I ask Uma what she thinks it will be like in Africa.

'Hot,' she says.

'And what else?' I probe.

She pulls a thoughtful face, looking up at the ceiling. 'And not cold.'

Right now, that's about as much as any of us knows.

As well as all the travel arrangements, I need to get as fit as I can if I'm going to stand a chance of keeping up with the Kenyan athletes. One evening, I read an article in the newspaper about a group of Kenyan runners who live and train in Teddington, in south-west London. I decide to look them up. Perhaps they can give me a few insights before I head out to Kenya.

So a few days later, at eight o'clock on a Tuesday morning, I find myself standing outside a small suburban house. I check the details again. It's definitely number 18, opposite the Tesco car park. An unassuming 1960s terrace house with grey blinds pulled across the windows. Weeds are coming up through cracks in the concrete parking spot in the front.

The front door is set back into the wall, so I have to venture into the dimness of the brick doorway to ring the bell. I wait for a few minutes, stepping back outside onto the quiet street. The athletes' manager, an Irishman named Ricky Simms, told me that they would be expecting me. He even said they'd take me for a run. I try the bell again. After another few minutes, the door opens slowly. A slim man in a tracksuit opens it and looks at me with sleepy eyes. I explain who I am. He nods and lets me in.

He takes me upstairs to an untidy living room and spends about five minutes absently pointing the remote control at the TV before it finally turns on. He doesn't say anything other than that his name is Micah. Once the TV is on, he turns and leaves the room.

Micah, it turns out, is Micah Kogo, the 10K world record holder and bronze medallist at the Beijing Olympics. He has gone to get changed.

Heads appear intermittently in the doorway behind me as I sit there watching the news. There are six Kenyan athletes living in the house, and they seem to be finding my presence amusing. I can hear them talking to each other on the landing. Eventually Enda, another Irishman who works for

Ricky, the manager, turns up and introduces me to everyone. They offer me limp handshakes and smile at each other as I'm told who has broken which world record, or won which World Championship medal.

'Are you going for a run with them?' Enda asks me.

I nod, unsure whether it's a wise thing to do. 'You think that's OK?'

'Sure,' he says. 'If you want.'

I try to act calm as we head out through the small backyard of the house, a couple of bikes leaning up against the fence, the old bulldog in the next-door garden barking at us hoarsely. We walk to the end of a small cul-de-sac and then on to the main road. The athletes talk and joke with Enda about their recent races. Nobody seems to be in a hurry to actually start running. One of the athletes explains to me that they don't like to run on concrete, so they walk until they get to the grass. In Kenya, he says, they run only on dirt roads.

The nearby Bushy Park is a large expanse of flat grassland, complete with deer and a maze of gravel pathways and tracks perfect for running. It's one of the reasons the Kenyans use this corner of London for their base while they're away from home.

Once we get inside the park gates, there's a lot of standing around and talking, and some half-hearted stretching. And then, without warning, we're off.

The pace is surprisingly easy, and, initially at least, I can keep up without too much trouble. Because they're all in between competitions, they're only doing easy running. I'm secretly hoping people will stare at us in wonder as we run past. *Wow, look, Kenyans. And did you see that white guy? He must be some runner.* But the park is virtually empty save for a few dog-walkers who don't even give us a second glance.

After about two miles, Mike Kigen, a former Kenyan 5,000m champion, Micah Kogo, and Vivian Cheruiyot[1], the women's world 5,000m champion, all suddenly speed up. None of them says anything, it just seems to happen. Within seconds, like startled animals they're gone, their heads bobbing away into the distance. The rest of us keep an easy pace (at least for the Kenyans it's easy), running in a pack, until we get back to where we started. I'm blowing hard but I just about manage to keep up.

Back at the house Micah cooks up some ugali and green vegetables for everyone's lunch. Ugali is the runners' favourite food. It's basically maize flour and water boiled up to make a white, sticky dough. Micah cuts me a huge slab with a knife and lays it on the plate on top of the vegetables. It has a soft, moist texture, but doesn't taste of much. The athletes, however, love it. They tell me, only half-joking, that it's the secret to Kenya's running success. On the floor of the kitchen, packets of maize flour brought over from Kenya are piled up in the corner.

Micah tells me, as we eat, about the day he broke the world 10K record. He says he remembers warming up and feeling light, but strong. 'So light, but so strong,' he says, almost reverential of the memory. All the athletes perk up

---

1   In 2011, Vivian Cheruiyot retained her world 5,000m title, as well as winning the world 10,000m gold medal and the world cross-country championships.

when they talk about running. Vivian, a tiny woman who can't weigh more than six stone, tells me about the day she won the World Championships, beating the supposedly unbeatable Ethiopians. 'It was so much fun,' she says, grinning.

Later that afternoon, after they've all slept and had a massage, Richard Kiplagat, an 800m specialist, and Vivian head out for another easy run. I decide to join them again. Afterwards, as we stand in the park stretching, a man in his mid-forties, slightly overweight and drenched in sweat, jogs past.

'In Kenya, do you have runners like that?' I ask them, pointing at the jogger. 'People who are just running to get fit?' I assume that's what he's doing. Hoping to lose some weight, too, no doubt. He doesn't look like he's running for the pure joy of it. And he certainly isn't hoping to make a living from it.

Richard, who a few months later will go on to win a silver medal in the Commonwealth Games, grins at me and shakes his head. 'No,' he says, definitely.

'In Kenya,' says Vivian, 'there are only athletes.' It isn't a boast, but merely a statement of fact. In Kenya, it would seem, if you are an athlete, you run. If you aren't, you don't.

'Maybe in some areas in the big cities,' says Richard, wanting to be clear, 'where rich people live, you may see a runner like that. But not in the rest of the country.'

It is the rest of the country I'm headed to. When I made my plan, I envisaged running hard across the plains in the midst of a group of Kenyans, the pounding of our feet shaking the dry earth. But seriously, who am I kidding?

'How fast is the slowest athlete in Kenya?' I ask, looking for a crumb of hope. Maybe I am an athlete. I won the

Powderham Castle 10K race. My time was 38 minutes and 35 seconds. 'For the 10K, for example, what would be the slowest time?'

They both look at each other. This is obviously a tricky question. 'Are we including juniors?' Richard asks me. That's eighteen- and nineteen-year-olds. I nod. I could train with juniors, why not? Perhaps that's the solution. 'And girls?' I nod again. The more the merrier. 'About 35 minutes,' he says.

So, I'm three and a half minutes slower over 10K than the slowest junior girl in Kenya. I've got less than six months to go before I get there. I've got some work to do.

Things start off well when, a few months later, I manage to finally lower my half-marathon time to under 1 hour 30 minutes with a barnstorming 1 hour 26 minutes in a hilly race in Dartmoor in Devon. But just as my fitness is improving, I set myself back by embarking on an experiment.

It all begins, like it does for many people, when I read Christopher McDougall's book *Born to Run*. The majority of the book is about a race in the Copper Canyons in Mexico with a tribe of ultra-runners called the Tarahumara. It's a fascinating tale, but the most intriguing part of the book, and the thing that has catapulted it onto bestseller lists across the world, is its revelation of the concept of barefoot running.

McDougall talks about a theory developed by Harvard scientists that humans evolved in the way we did partly because we hunted by running animals into the ground. While we are painfully slow at sprinting compared to most four-legged creatures, say the cheetah, horse, rabbit, or a thousand others, when it comes to long-distance running, we are the Olympic champions of the animal kingdom. Our key advantage is our ability to shed most of our heat through sweating. This means we can cool ourselves down on the move, while most other animals need to stop when they get too hot in order to pant their heat away. Our ancestors could chase even the swiftest runners like antelope until they literally dropped dead from overheating, and the book recounts a story about bushmen in the Kalahari Desert in Namibia who still do this today.

The scientists claim, in effect, that humans are born to run long distances, that our bodies are designed specifically for the purpose. It's why we have Achilles tendons, arched feet, big bums and a nuchal ligament at the back of our necks (to keep our heads still as we run). And we are designed to run, they say, in bare feet. Running shoes only mess things up.

A few weeks before reading all this, I bought myself a new pair of trainers. The shop in London was kitted out with a high-tech system for assessing your running gait. I was asked to put on some trainers and hop on a treadmill. The man in the shop then filmed my feet and played the footage back to me. I was, like 80 per cent of runners, he told me, landing heel first. This made my legs 'pronate', which meant they were basically buckling under me with each step. To remedy this, he told me, I needed running shoes with added support on one side.

I thanked him for his useful advice and bought a pair of shoes with added stability as he suggested. A week later I broke my half-marathon best time. Unfortunately, I also developed a slight injury at the top of my left calf muscle. Injuries are a common part of being a runner, so I didn't panic.

Depending on which study you read, somewhere between 60 per cent and 80 per cent of runners get injured at least once every year. So I'd have to be very lucky never to get injured. A small muscle strain was getting off quite lightly.

McDougall, however, disagrees. The reason runners get injured so often, he says, is because they land heel first. And the reason they land heel first is that they wear stability trainers. It sounds like a Catch-22, but according to both McDougall and the Harvard scientists, there is a simple way out: take off the shoes. Our body is the perfect running machine, they say, developed over millions of years of product testing and fine-tuning. We don't need the modern invention of running shoes to do something we've been doing perfectly well for millennia.

Like most people, at first I think this is an interesting theory, but really, you can't go around running in bare feet. What about broken glass? What about dog poo? But then I read something that makes me prick up my ears: one of the key scientists cited by McDougall, Daniel Liebermann, developed his ideas through studying Kenyan runners.

Because they grow up running barefoot, Kenyans have a completely different style of running. Rather than landing heel first, they land forefoot first. Not only does this reduce the risk of injury, but it is a more efficient way of running. In effect, by landing heel first, most Western runners are braking with every stride. No wonder we can't keep up.

I decide to try barefoot running out one evening in the local park. I run there in my shoes, but once I get to a clear grassy patch, I take them off, hide them in some bushes, and then set off around a field of football pitches. My running style instantly changes to a shorter, faster stride pattern, as though my feet are afraid to touch the ground. I go for about ten minutes, before deciding I've done enough. It's fun, but afterwards it's nice to put my shoes back on. They feel warm and comforting, like big soft pillows.

To find out more about barefoot running, I decide to track down the biomechanic expert Lee Saxby. He's one of the men who taught McDougall to run barefoot. Can he teach me to run like a Kenyan? I wonder.

Lee works out of a boxing gym by the railway tracks in north London. I struggle to find it at first, walking up and down the road, evening commuters dashing around me to catch their trains home. I turn my map up the other way, but it still doesn't make sense. Then I realise his place is tucked down a back alley between two tall, four-storey houses. I walk down a narrow passage and find a black, unmarked door. This must be it. I ring the buzzer and the door opens automatically. I step inside a huge room, with an empty boxing ring in the middle. High up on a small balcony along one wall I spot a man looking down. He gives me a nod and points to another door at the side of the gym. I walk over and a skinny boy opens it.

'I'm here to see Lee,' I say. He nods and points up some stairs. At the top is Lee's office. Lee stands at the door smiling.

'Come in,' he says.

I enter, full of questions. I leave, a few hours later, convinced I have discovered the secret of Kenyan running.

'With any other sport, to get good you need to learn about technique,' he says. 'But with running, people think they can't change their style. Well that's rubbish.'

He has a certainty it's hard to argue with. Why don't the top African runners actually run barefoot in races? I ask. 'A top runner can't afford to hurt himself standing on a sharp stone,' he says. 'But they wear racing flats. There is no stability or cushioning on running flats. They allow you to run in a barefoot style. They don't force you to land heel first like most running shoes.'

He has a mischievous twinkle in his eye. 'Sometimes I feel like the Che Guevara of running,' he says. 'I'll show you.' He tells me to hop up on his running machine. First he films me running in my normal style. Then he tells me to take off my shoes and films me again. I immediately and instinctively start landing forefoot first.

'Your body won't let you run heel first if you're barefoot,' he says. 'It would be too painful.' With shoes on we have a false sense of security, and feel that we can hammer the road as hard as we want. But the impact from landing heel first is still shooting up the leg, juddering the knees, the hips, the back, regardless of how much cushioning you put under your feet. McDougall describes it as akin to putting an oven mitten over an egg before hitting it with a hammer. In fact, because you can't feel the ground, with shoes on you're forced to land even harder as your body instinctively looks for stability and a harder surface. Without shoes, however, you're forced to tread lightly, skipping gently over the ground. Your body just does it naturally.

According to Lee, however, it's not only about the forefoot strike. He tells me to keep my head up, lead with my chest, and pull my legs through, as though I'm on a unicycle. If

that isn't enough to think about, he starts a metronome going at a rapid-fire tack tack tack. I have to match it stride for
tack. Then he plays the three films back to me.

It is quite shocking to watch. With my trainers on I look
like an overweight office worker out for a slow jog. (Admittedly, that's perhaps what I am, but it isn't how I imagine I
look when I'm running.) I seem to be sinking backwards at
the waist, as though I'm half-slouched into an invisible armchair. With the shoes off it looks a bit better, but after Lee's
lesson I look like a proper runner. 'You look like a Kenyan,'
he says, though that may be pushing it.

Outside the window the evening commuter trains are rattling in and out of London. Do I even need to go to Kenya?
Have I found the secret right here in this West Hampstead
gym? Part of me is mad that I didn't discover this years ago,
when I was still young enough to put it to good use. In that
moment, watching the videos, I have no doubt that this is
a key reason the Kenyans are so good at running. It makes
complete sense.

In the following weeks, as the initial excitement of my
discovery begins to die down, I realise that the proof will be
in the running. The whole notion of barefoot running ap-
peals to me. I love it when, after years of research, we realise
that the most natural and primitive way to do something,
the way we always did it before scientists and corporations
got their hands on it, was actually the best way after all.
I love the fact that despite all our technological advance-
ments, poor Kenyans running barefoot have the edge over
us. As a notion, it's brilliant. But as a reality? The only way
to find out is to try it.

One of the reasons so few athletes have tried to change their style, according to Lee, is that it involves relearning how to run from scratch. Because it uses different muscles, you need to start with short one-mile runs. Once you can do that without it hurting the next day, you can start to increase the distance slowly.

I had hoped to combine barefoot running with my usual style, to hedge my bets and to avoid losing any fitness. But that's not an option, according to Lee. 'It's all or nothing,' he says. 'Your mind will slip into the style it's most used to. If you're running heel first most of the time, your body will do that automatically.'

Before I leave, Lee promises to send me a pair of barefoot shoes to run in. It may sound like an oxymoron, but the barefoot style of running is less about actually being barefoot and more about the way you run. Barefoot shoes have minimal cushioning or support, but they have a firm undersole to protect your feet from the glass and dog poo. Once I've got used to my new style, I decide, I'll switch to running flats, just like the Kenyans. These have a little more support than barefoot shoes, but none of the bulk and weight of the conventional trainers usually worn by Western runners.

So for the next six weeks I start learning how to run again. Running short distances has its advantages. Runs take a fraction of the time they used to, which means I can fit them in more easily.

'Don't worry,' I tell Marietta as I head out the door, 'I'll be back in ten minutes.' Lunchtime runs at work are also less of a mad panic to get back to my desk within the regimented hour.

As Lee predicted, my legs feel sore after the first few runs, but the more I do it, the further I can run, and the more natural it begins to feel. I even find myself spontaneously running around the street in my new style. Where before I used to feel wary about breaking into a trot without my running shoes on, I'm now happy to run in any footwear. In fact, running shoes seem to be the singularly worst possible shoes to run in. My normal office shoes have very little heel, and I find I can run barefoot-style in them quite easily. And the more I do it, the zippier it feels.

The only problem with embarking on this experiment is that by the time our bags are packed ready to go to Kenya, I'm still only up to three-mile runs. I've obviously lost quite a lot of fitness, and my waistline has visibly expanded. I'm hardly in the shape to keep up with the Kenyans. But the experiment has to go on. If it really is the secret to their success, I'll soon catch up to where I was, and then, well, who knows where I'll end up?

4

It's opener there
in the wide open air.
    Dr Seuss, *Oh, the Places You'll Go!*

Our plane touches down in Nairobi on a bright late December morning. As we fold ourselves out of the cramped cabin, the warm African air feels soft on our frazzled skin. It's almost twenty-four hours since we drove away from our cottage in Devon, leaving the garden and surrounding fields covered in a thick blanket of snow.

We plan to spend most of our time in Kenya up in the Rift Valley, in a town called Iten. I've read so much about Iten that it has become an almost mythical place in my mind. Before we left England, I watched a local news report on the internet in which the town's taxi drivers were complaining that they couldn't do their job properly because the roads were so clogged up with runners. It's only a small town, with about four thousand residents, but I've read that at any one time you can find around a thousand top athletes living and training there.

But before we get to Iten, we head off to spend a week with Marietta's sister in Lewa, where I will run my first ever marathon at the end of the trip.

Jophie first came to Kenya in 2004 to do some voluntary work on a monkey conservation project. One night, in a bar on the coast, she met Alastair. Of Scottish ancestry, but born and bred in Africa, Alastair is a tough man. Marietta's brothers joke that he is like 'Crocodile' Dundee, at home in the wildness of the bush. In Kenya they call them KCs, or Kenyan Cowboys. Big, strong men in leather boots and denim shorts who sit around drinking Tusker beer and talking in slow, deliberate voices about things like boreholes, hunting, motorbikes. But even among the KCs, Alastair is tough.

Jophie and Alastair have two small daughters and live in a tented camp in the middle of the bush. On New Year's Eve, after the children are asleep, the four of us sit around the fire drinking Tusker. The trunk of a tree lies across the flames, burning in the middle. Alastair said he was going looking for firewood, and came back with an entire tree across his shoulders.

He is sitting there silent with that wild, quizzical look in his eyes he gets after he has had a few beers.

'So those guys up there, they can really run, you know,' he says, talking about the athletes in Iten.

'I know,' I say.

'How are you going to keep up? They're not messing around up there. Those guys can run.'

I still haven't worked out how I'm going to keep up. At the moment I can barely walk after hurting my calf running on a treadmill in the hotel in Nairobi. But after a few drinks, Alastair doesn't wait around for answers. His question has already drifted off into the darkness. He is telling a story about when he was a safari guide in Botswana.

'One time I went on this trip with a wealthy American couple. We're talking rich, man. Gold Rolex watches dripping from their wrists. The three of us were walking through the bush when from nowhere this bull elephant is charging at us. So I push them both to the ground.' He almost falls out of his camp chair demonstrating how he pushed them. 'I pushed them and then I turned and I charged at the elephant.'

I look over at Jophie. She isn't telling him to shut up.

'What happened?' I ask.

'If you have a bull elephant charging at you, your best hope is to charge back. I had my arms waving around in the air and I was roaring as loud as I could.'

He stops to sip on his beer. The fire crackles in the night. The stars spill across the sky above us.

'It stopped,' he says. 'Turned on its heels and ran.'

The next evening, we get our own close encounter. At night in the camp you have to walk quickly from tent to tent, using a flashlight to look out for snakes or other wild animals. However, our cheap wind-up torches from TK Maxx in Exeter can barely light up the ground in front of us, let alone pick out a lion from the engulfing blackness. 'Look for the eyes,' says Alastair, swinging his torch's huge light-beam across the darkness. 'There.' A pair of staring eyes hovers unblinking in the beam less than 30 yards away.

'Buffalo,' he says.

Later, as we're walking to our tent to go to bed, we hear a terrible grunting sound. It starts off far away, but with each grunt it gets louder and fiercer. It sounds like something running at us. We rush for the tent and I throw Lila through the opening before Marietta and I both dive in and zip up. Uma and Ossian are already fast asleep in their beds.

'What was that?'

'A lion,' says Marietta. She has heard the noise before on other nights, but from much further away. It starts again. It sounds far away to start with, but by the end of its roar you can almost feel the air vibrating. Lila is terrified, but is trying not to cry.

'I'll get into your bed with you,' I say, as if I could fight off a lion.

Alastair has told us that lions don't know the difference between a tent and a rock, and that we are quite safe once we're inside. But with all the ferocious grunting noises going on just outside, I start having doubts. Surely the lions can smell us? There are no people inside rocks. Then I remember that the zip at the back of the tent is broken. The tent is actually open, partly, at the bottom. I try to forget I've just remembered that.

It's a ten-hour taxi ride from Lewa to Iten, so we decide to stop for the night in Nyahururu, another big running centre. We book ourselves in at the town's most exclusive hotel, the Thomson's Falls Lodge, which employs a local athlete to take guests out running. His name is John Ndungu and he agrees to take me for a run at seven the next morning before we continue our journey. I get the impression it's a little late for him, but he gives me a crooked smile and says it's fine.

So, on a bright, crisp morning at 8,000ft, I head out for my first run with athletes in Kenya. I find John waiting for me at the main entrance to the lodge with another man, a serious-faced eighteen-year-old from his village called Lucas Ndungu. The two are not related, they tell me, surprised that I think they might be.

I need to go slow and not too far, I tell them. I'm not only worried about keeping up, but I'm also concerned that my new barefoot running style might give me an injury if I push it too far too soon. To give my calves some added protection, I decide to wear racing flats rather than my barefoot shoes. It also means I won't have to feel embarrassed wearing new-fangled shoes designed to mimic Kenyans running without shoes. Somehow, now that I'm here, that seems an odd thing to want to do.

As we jog out along the hotel drive, two baboons ambling across the lawn turn to watch us briefly, before scuttling away. The security guard on the gate gives us a salute. Once we're out of the hotel complex, we turn onto a dirt track and head up into the town towards the main road.

The first thing I notice is that Lucas is wearing big, chunky running trainers and is landing heel first. John is wearing racing flats a bit like mine, and is landing forefoot first. It's far too soon to be drawing any conclusions, of course, but Lucas's heel-first footstrike is unexpected.

As we run, we pass streams of other athletes coming in the opposite direction, and none of them is barefoot. Most of the runners are wearing normal training shoes with lots of support around the heel. It's hard to tell, running towards them, if they're landing heel first or not, but it looks like some of them might be. I'm confused. Where are all the barefoot runners?

In the end the run feels surprisingly gentle, considering the high altitude. We run for 30 minutes, with the pace picking up slightly over the last mile or so. I'm just congratulating myself for keeping with them when they tell me they've already run six miles from their village to meet me, and that they plan to train again a few hours later.

'You?' they ask.

I'm not planning on running again for a few days.

'I'm still adjusting to the altitude,' I say. 'I don't want to overdo it and get injured.' My calves feel fine, however, even though it's the longest run I've done since I switched to my barefoot style.

After we warm down, Marietta and the children come out to find us. Lila and Uma are all sleepy smiles and sticking-up hair, shaking hands with the two men and showing off their dolls. John turns to me and tells me I now have four children. I give him a confused look. 'Me,' he says, smiling. He's older than me.

5

Every day in Africa a gazelle wakes up. It knows it must run faster than the fastest lion or it will be killed. Every morning a lion wakes up. It knows that it must outrun the slowest gazelle or it will starve to death. It doesn't matter whether you are a lion or a gazelle. When the sun comes up, you better be running.

Abe Gubegna, Ethiopian author

At the bottom of the Rift Valley the road to Iten crosses over a deep gorge. The driver stops for a rest and we all get out. Far down below, basking on a sandbank, their mouths fixed wide open, are four crocodiles. Ahead of us the road shimmers in the baking heat. On the roadside is a rickety honey stall, the bottles lined up in rows, glowing in the sun. In the distance the land rises up over 4,000 feet to Iten, which sits perched on the edge of the Kerio escarpment.

'Dad, I'm thirsty.' We've been on the road for about five hours, the children bumping around in the back, clambering over the seats, spilling their pens and sandwiches all over the floor. But we're nearly there.

From the bottom, the road winds up, twisting back and forth, twirling around cone-shaped foothills, the land changing colour, turning greener the higher we rise. The driver keeps pointing at the thermometer gauge, which drops down another degree every few minutes. The cooler it gets, the more houses we see, and the more people sitting beside the road, or walking along it. They glance over at us, the engine straining with the slope. At a sign for the Lelin Campsite, the car swings off the road onto a dirt track, bumping along, the underside scraping on the stones, until we come to a large elaborate gate painted in blue and yellow, the word 'Karibu' ('Welcome') in an arch above it.

Before we left England I tried to arrange somewhere for us to live in Iten, but finding a house to rent in a small Kenyan town from the other side of the world was not easy. Most people who travel to the town stay either at an upmarket athletics training camp run by Lornah Kiplagat, the holder of four world records, or the Kerio View, a hotel perched on the edge of the escarpment overlooking the valley.

However, both of these places are beyond our budget, so instead we've decided rather apprehensively to stay at the Lelin Campsite about five miles down the side of the valley.

We arrive in the early afternoon. The campsite owner comes down from his house on a nearby hill to greet us. He shakes hands with everyone and shows us to our rooms. We have three rooms in his newly built cottages, two to sleep in and one to cook in. The kitchen room has a camping stove on the table and a few pots and plates on the bed. He is obviously delighted to have us to stay, so I try not to look disappointed as he shows us around. The bedrooms are just about big enough to fit the beds in, the pillows are tatty bits of hard foam, the toilets have no seats, and there is no basin in the bathroom, just a tap on the wall. His smile drops when I ask him where the basin is. I mime brushing my teeth. Washing hands. He points to the tap.

'Oh, you use that?' I say. 'Of course. Perfect.'

Although I didn't manage to find a house, I did get hold of a contact in Iten, a former athlete called Godfrey Kiprotich. He phoned me a few days before we left Lewa to tell me he had found us somewhere to rent. I'm hoping he can come and get us and take us to see it, but when I call him he says he doesn't have a car.

'It's in the garage,' he says. 'But let me see what I can do.'

He calls me back to say he has arranged a lift for us. Sure enough, twenty minutes later a low-slung white car with tinted windows rolls into the campsite and a neatly dressed man with a gold watch steps out.

His name is Christopher Cheboiboch, he says, looking around warily at the campsite, as though it might make his clothes dirty. 'Are you a runner?' I ask, thinking he might be too old. He smiles. 'Yes,' he says. 'I have the fifth-fastest time ever in the New York marathon.'

He drives us very slowly up the final stretch of the escarpment to Iten. We glide past a steady stream of people walking along the road. Children with sticks stand watching their cows grazing on the grass verges, or run, barefoot, disappearing into the long grass and undergrowth. At the top of the valley, a rusting sign over the road welcomes us to Iten.

As we drive into the town and up along the main street for the first time, we gaze out of the window at the half-collapsed wooden market stalls, carts pulled by donkeys, ladies sitting on top of piles of clothes for sale. It's market day and the place is full of people. Cows and sheep seem to wander around freely, poking their noses into piles of rubbish left on the dirt verges beside the road. People ride by with their bicycles stacked ten feet high with mattresses, crates of chickens, firewood. Ahead of us a small bus is driving off with two people still hanging out of the door.

Christopher calls out to a man in the street, who comes over to the car. They shake hands. Christopher gives the man some money, and then drives on. We sail slowly up the road, past a small supermarket, two speakers placed outside blaring crackly music. On the other side of the road sits a pristine white mosque. Red dirt roads cut through rows of rusted tin roofs rising up the slopes on either side. It looks just like any other roadside town we passed through on the way from Lewa.

We seem to pass through the town before we realise it, emerging out the other side and pulling off the road, down a rutted track past a boarded-up wooden bar, to Lornah Kiplagat's training camp. Christopher pulls in regally as the gates are swung open by the security guard. This is the most state-of-the-art training camp in town, with a gym and a swimming pool. There are no Kenyan athletes living here. Instead it caters for foreign runners. As soon as we get out of the car I spot the British international runner Helen Clit-heroe sitting at a table going over her training schedule on a laptop with her coach. A Greek athlete with a long goatee beard walks by lost in the music from his iPod. A man with long blond hair who looks more like a surfer than an athlete bounds out of the gym. It's Toby Tanser. I was reading about him in the newspaper in Lewa last week. I've also got his book, *More Fire*, about how to run like a Kenyan, in my bag. I stop him and say hello.

Toby has an encyclopedic knowledge of Kenyan running and is friends with just about every athlete here. He also heads up a charity, called Shoe4Africa, which is building a school and a children's hospital near Iten. He is full of optimism about everything. When I tell him we're looking for a house to rent, he says, 'Finding accommodation in Iten is not a problem.' As he says it a group of young Kenyan men walk by.

'Erastus,' Toby calls to one of the men, who ambles over. Erastus is wearing a neat leather jacket and a big grin. In his hand he has an expensive mobile phone.

'What's happening with your house?' Toby asks him as they shake hands. 'Is it free to rent?'

The man nods.

'There you go,' Toby says to me. 'This man has the nicest house in Iten. What did I tell you?'

Before he rushes off, Toby offers to take me on a running tour of the town. It's an offer I can't refuse.

While we're talking, Godfrey, my contact with the other house to rent, turns up. He's dressed in jeans and a T-shirt and must be in his mid-forties. I call Marietta and the children over. While I've been talking, they've been wandering around, trying to keep out of the way of the athletes. Godfrey greets us like long-lost friends, crouching down to shake the children's hands. He's full of apologies for not having a car. It's in the garage, he says. Instead he has hired a taxi, and he's with another former runner called William Koila. Between Godfrey, Koila, the driver and the five of us, it's a bit of a squash, but we all bundle in and head off.

Godfrey tells us the house is in a 'very nice neighbourhood', as we drive along over a bumpy dirt track resembling a dry mogul ski run. It's the sort of road I wouldn't even attempt to drive on in England. The weighed-down taxi scrapes over the bumps as we pass some small houses with smashed windows and overgrown gardens. We stop outside a black corrugated iron gate. The driver beeps his horn. Outside in the street, two men sit on the counter of a small wooden kiosk staring at us. To the other side, a two-storey house is penned in close behind a high wooden fence. Pairs of eyes peer out between the gaps. Lila and Uma, leaning out of the car window, peer back.

'See what a nice area this is?' Godfrey says as we wait. He's sitting squashed in the front seat with Koila. I don't know what a bad area looks like, so it's hard to judge. I look over at Marietta and the children. They all look slightly breathless, as though everything is happening too fast suddenly. Marietta holds my hand. Ossian, standing on her lap like the captain of a ship, watches out the front window, an anxious look on his face.

The gate is pulled open by a workman in overalls, revealing a large, sweeping garden, with a bungalow about halfway down. It's painted in blue and white and has a red tin roof. It looks quite nice. Behind the house is a view out across the valley.

'They've built it the wrong way around,' says Marietta, as we walk around it. 'Surely the house should face out towards the view?' Instead, all the windows overlook the garden and the eight-foot corrugated metal fence that runs around the perimeter. To one side is the roof of a neighbouring house.

'That house belongs to Ismael Kirui,' Koila tells me. That's the athlete who won my favourite race, the 1993

World Championships 5,000m, by sprinting away from the field with seven laps to go. Before I get too excited, Koila tells me that Kirui doesn't actually live there, but rents the house out.

Lots of the houses in Iten are owned by former athletes, but, like Kirui's house, they are all surprisingly small and unglamorous. The late Richard Chelimo, a former 10,000m world record holder, was the first athlete to invest in Iten. His legacy is a few rows of concrete one-bedroom units now falling into disrepair. Later we go to look at the house Toby Tanser found for us to rent. 'The nicest house in Iten,' he said. It is actually owned by Erastus's wife, Sylvia Kibet, a world 5,000m silver medallist. Tucked behind a petrol station, it has three small bedrooms with views onto brick walls, some old chipboard cabinets in a dark sitting room, and a tiny shared yard.

Godfrey's backward-built house is sumptuous by comparison, with its ample garden and views across the valley. When we see it the first time, it is being redecorated and is in a bit of a mess, but we're assured it will all be ready within a few days. In the garden are four sheep and an angry dog tied to a post. The house is split in two and we're told that the man who owns the dog lives behind the dirty polyester curtains covering the windows in the other half, but that he will be moved out.

'The landlord is a man who has travelled,' Godfrey reassures me. 'He understands privacy.' Koila is more succinct: 'And mzungus.' The implication is that we're too finicky and uptight to share our house with a strange man with a wild dog. To be honest, I think we are. But where will he go?

'He will still be your neighbour,' says Godfrey, pointing to where he will live somewhere vaguely over the back fence behind a large plantation of passion fruit plants. It turns out the man has been squatting in the house and growing passion fruits for some time. We agree to let him back in once a week to spray and harvest his crop. The day we eventually move in to the house, he shows up. He has an unsettling grin and tiptoes around me like an unpredictable pony. He tells me he wants to be a runner, if I sponsor him. I have to admit, I'm a bit worried about letting him into the house even once a week. Godfrey seems to think he's harmless, though, and jokes with the man while helping himself to some passion fruit.

'He says you can eat the fruit whenever you want,' Godfrey tells me, as the man grins his approval.

We agree to rent Godfrey's house, but are told a few days later that it won't be ready for another week. I get the call while we're in the larger, nearby town of Eldoret. We've come here to visit the European-style Nakumatt supermarket. Nakumatt is a big glossy store that opens twenty-four hours a day and sells everything a homesick European could dream of, from buggies to bathrobes, Barbie dolls and ice cream.

After a few days in our little campsite, cooking rice on the camping stove and sleeping on dirty pillows, it's like stepping back into the comfortable, ordered world we left behind. I realise, suddenly, how tough life has been for the children over the last few days. Although Alastair, my brother-in-law, has now lent us a car, we've been ferrying the children back and forth in it, from house to house, back to the campsite, then off to visit athletes in training camps, all in the heat, meeting lots of people who talk about running. They also get stared at wherever they go. Sometimes they embrace it, waving at everyone, laughing and shaking hands with all the other children, who shriek with excitement and run along beside us. But sometimes it's too much.

They keep telling us they like England better. 'It will be different when we have our own home,' says Marietta, chopping up an onion with a blunt knife in our kitchen bedroom. 'They're just unsettled.'

When the children are unhappy, the whole venture seems like a folly. I feel I've dragged them away from their friends, from their home, all for some whimsical goal of running a fast time in a running race? It seems so trivial. I begin to think I should take them home to England.

As we drive back from Nakumatt, through the outskirts of Eldoret, the road is lined with collapsing houses and tiny shops built from scraps of metal, cardboard boxes, anything people can find. Children play in puddles black with grime, or sit among stray dogs on piles of rubbish, as men whip threadbare and overladen donkeys into a slow, painful trot.

Then, as we reach Iten, we pass a group of European runners. With their fair skin and pristine clothes, they look like creatures from another world. It seems ridiculous that they have come all this way to preen themselves for some competition. Amid the chaos and poverty, where people struggle to make enough money to buy even the simplest things such as bread and water, here are some of the world's best athletes doing drills, back and forth, along the side of the road.

Yet, ironically, they have come here to be inspired. To live among people who don't think that running is ridiculous, no matter how hard their lives are, but who value running, and the opportunity it brings, who revere it, almost. Even if you never become an Olympic champion, or even manage to race abroad, just being an athlete here seems to lift you above the chaos of daily life. It marks you out as one of the special people, who have chosen a path of dedication and commitment. You can see it in the runners' eyes when they talk to you. Even the slowest of the runners talk about their training with an almost religious devotion. They may live in makeshift houses, without running water, and sit by candle-light each night, but their best times for the half-marathon are recalled with reverence. Running matters.

6

No race begins at the start line.
   Haile Gebrselassie

Toby Tanser tells me to meet him at the gates to Lornah's training camp, where I first bumped into him, at 6.30 a.m.

I wake up at dawn, feeling a thrill of excitement as I pull on my running kit, which I left ready and laid out on the floor. Lila and Uma are sleeping soundly curled up on their beds, their heads fallen off the hard pillows. I slip out of the room. The awakening Rift Valley drops away outside the door, the sound of cockerels echoing over its majesty. This is it, the first run in Iten. Let the show begin.

The car starts with a purr, and I drive it carefully out through the campsite's elaborate entrance gates and up the bumpy road to Iten. Toby is there waiting for me when I arrive, bouncing around on his toes. We head out on a very gentle 30-minute jog, down through the town, past the famous St Patrick's school and out along a dusty red track into the countryside. The trail we follow is actually a road, snaking its way through farmland and green fields dotted with cedar trees. The only vehicle we pass, though, is a motorbike with two men and two children on it, beeping at us as it bumps along.

We see fewer runners than I was anticipating. Toby says we're a bit late, that most of them start earlier. The few we do pass are running alone or in small groups of two or three. I don't see any large groups blocking the way of taxi drivers.

Every couple of minutes Toby points to a house and tells me the name of an athlete who lives there and the incredible times they have run or the championship medals they have won. He also has a personal story about some wild escapade he once got up to with each one.

I ask him why the people here are so good at running. Could it be because they run barefoot?

'They don't,' he says. 'The children run barefoot, but it's not what makes them fast.' I don't press him. I wasn't expecting the barefoot theory to be widely held, even here. I ask him what he thinks it is, then, that makes them so fast.

'It's not one thing,' he says. 'You'll meet lots of people. You'll get lots of answers. And they will all be right.'

As we run, schoolchildren run along beside us. A few call out: 'How are you?', but most seem to be running regardless of us. One of the theories often put forward as to why Kenyans are so good at running, often by the athletes themselves, is the fact that they run to school each day.

'Are they already hoping to become athletes?' I ask Toby, assuming he will know the answer. 'Is that why they're running?'

'No,' he says. 'They're running because if they're late they get caned.'

Despite the fact that corporal punishment was officially banned in schools in Kenya in 2001, lots of Kenyans later verify that Toby is right. A few weeks later the national newspaper carries a story about one of the country's brightest junior runners, Faith Kipyegon, who has been so badly beaten by her teacher at school that she is unable to train because of her injuries. With the world cross-country championships coming up, it's bad timing, the newspaper reports. There is a distinct lack of outrage in the article.

But surely school beatings can't be the secret behind Kenya's running success? It's not as romantic a secret as barefoot running. Godfrey later tells me that when he was young he ran the six kilometres to school each day because he felt better when he ran.

'I noticed I felt better in my body during the day,' he says. 'I was able to concentrate much better. When I didn't run, I felt tired and lethargic all day.' Perhaps he only felt more awake because by running to school he could sleep in longer, but it's interesting to hear him talk about how good running made him feel. It's this sense of well-being that gets people out running in the West, rather than necessity, but I wonder how many runners here even think about how it makes them feel.

Godfrey admits to me that I'm the first person he has ever told this to. In fact, he says, he has only just realised it now, as he was saying it. We're sitting in the cheap Hill Side Hotel café in Iten and Godfrey has a look of excitement on his face, as though he has just realised something profound. I don't know if it is coincidence or not, but later that day he tells me he wants to run the Lewa marathon with me. He hasn't run for years, but suddenly he's full of the joys of running. He wants to be my training partner, and keeps saying thank you to me as though I've done something other than listen to him and nod.

*

A few days after we arrive in Iten, the national cross-country league comes to town. It's the last leg of a seven-race series and it's all brilliantly organised, with runners doing laps in and around the playing fields in the centre of the town. It's a warm day and a big crowd has turned out, lining the hills on two sides of the playing fields. There is even a sound system booming out from the back of a lorry, with two women on the stage grinding to the jumped-up music. By the start and finish area a few gazebos have been put up by the corporate sponsors, KCB, a Kenyan bank. We make our way over. Marietta initially sits down with the children on the front row, where someone is handing out free bottles of water. But after a few stern looks and badly disguised coughs she realises she is taking up the prime viewing seats in the VIP tent – seats reserved for dignitaries such as the head of the army and the head of the Kenyan Olympic Committee.

Milling around by the start, I bump into both Toby and Godfrey. They introduce me to endless runners and coaches. Rather than telling me their names, each person is introduced by a time or an achievement – often a world record or an Olympic title. One man in particular seems to be getting handshakes from everyone. He's a short, white man with a ruddy face shaded by a baseball cap. He has his arms folded tightly across his round body as the leading junior girls come by. Quietly, with a strong Irish accent, he tells the girl in second to 'stay there, stay there'. I know who he is without being introduced.

In the late 1970s, an Irish priest with no background in athletics came on a two-year placement to teach at Iten's Catholic boarding school, St Patrick's. At that time there were no runners training in Iten. Even though the school had already produced an Olympic medallist, Mike Boit, who won the bronze medal in the 800m in 1972, it was the influence of the new recruit from Ireland, Brother Colm O'Connell, that was to turn St Patrick's into one of the most successful athletics schools in the world, and turn Iten into the running centre it is today.

Soon after he started teaching, the school's track coach returned to Britain and Brother Colm stepped into the vacant role. His teams began to do well in national competitions, and in 1986 he was asked to select the Kenyan team for the first-ever world junior championships in Athens. He picked nine runners, seven from St Patrick's. Having never competed internationally, he didn't know what to expect from his team, but to his surprise they won nine medals, including four golds.

'It was then I realised we had something special going on here,' he later tells me. Three years later, in 1989, he started the first running camp in Kenya. It was in the school holidays, and initially it was just for girls.

'I just wanted to give athletics a bit more focus,' he said. But the idea caught on. St Patrick's went on to produce numerous world and Olympic champions, and today there are more than 120 training camps in and around Iten. Brother Colm has since retired from teaching at the school, but he still lives within the school grounds. Tucked behind his modest house is his training camp – a small house where the runners share rooms. He only currently has four athletes in the camp, but they're all people he has coached since they were very young. One of them, twenty-two-year-old David Rudisha, has just been crowned the IAAF World Athlete of the Year after he twice broke the thirteen-year-old 800m world record. The person who held the record before him was Wilson Kipketer, another St Patrick's old boy and former charge of Brother Colm.

At the race in Iten, Godfrey, yet another of Brother Colm's former prodigies, introduces him to me as a legend in Kenyan running. Brother Colm, though, is quick to dampen down the hyperbole.

'The legend is bigger than the man,' he says, looking away as though he's in a hurry to be somewhere else. Godfrey tells him I'm writing a book on Iten and the runners, and that I'd like to talk to him at some point.

'What do you want to talk to me for?' he says. 'There are lots of other more interesting people.' Every article I've read about Iten talks about the influence of Brother Colm. The athletes themselves talk about him as the godfather of Kenyan running. As Godfrey says, to them he is a legend. But I guess he doesn't like the limelight, because before I've had a chance to say a word, he's gone.

I bump into him again the next evening at the bar in the Kerio View hotel, sitting with a young Kenyan woman. 'I'm stalking you,' I say, only half joking. He warms to me a bit more when I tell him my parents are Irish and that my dad is from Galway. 'I went to university in Galway,' he says, and starts telling his companion about the beautiful wildness of Connemara. He talks with the wistful tone of a man who has spent a long time away from his homeland and remembers only the most cherished of moments, like little treasures in a box, taken out occasionally, held delicately, turned over, and then placed carefully back again.

Back at the race in Iten, a long line of men stretches out across the dusty field. A few officials are rushing along the front of the line, trying to keep order. I've gone to stand at the first corner, to take pictures of the start, so it's hard to see what sets everyone off, but suddenly half the runners are charging across the field towards me. A shout goes up from the crowd as marshals rush onto the course to halt the runners. Some of them don't want to stop and have to be virtually pulled to the ground. Eventually they all return to the start line to try again.

With all the incredible runners here, competition is stiff, so getting a good start is vital. The second time they get it right and the line quickly becomes a swarm of athletes fighting to get ahead. I hold my camera up as the field arrows towards me and darts around the corner. It is like they're sprinting for their lives, but they still have over 7 miles to run, in almost 30°C heat.

This is one of the fiercest races you could hope to witness anywhere in the world. At the world cross-country championships, for instance, there are only six Kenyans in each race, most of whom usually finish in the top ten. Here there are three hundred Kenyans in each race. It is quite a sight.

Unlike open cross-country races in Britain, where you will always see a fair sprinkling of grey hair and bandy legs, and many runners who are clearly doing it purely for fun, in Kenya, everyone is under forty and fast. I briefly contemplated running, but after watching, I'm glad I didn't. Next time I'll run, I tell myself, not realising the next race is only a few weeks away.

There is one foreigner in the race. A fair-haired man wearing a Winchester AC running vest. He trails in just a few places from the back and I'm thinking he is a brave man even to be out there. Later, I find out that his name is Tom Payn and that he is the fourth-fastest marathon runner in Britain.

The large crowd watches mostly in silence, except at the end when it occasionally rises to an excited cheer at the prospect of a sprint finish. In the women's race, people scream and yell as the world 5,000m silver medallist, Sylvia Kibet, who was almost our landlady, produces a barnstorming sprint at the end – to finish third. The race is won by one of Godfrey's friends, Lineth Chepkurui.

The men's race is won by Geoffrey Mutai, who a few months later will go on to win both the Boston and New York City marathons, setting course records in each, while the winner in the junior men's race is Isaiah Koech, who just weeks later will smash the world junior indoor 5,000m record by an incredible 40 seconds. Finally, the junior women's race is won by Faith Kipyegon, just days before the reports of her school beating, and a couple of months before she becomes world champion. And this is just a national league race.

The quality of the running is slightly lost on my children, who initially enjoy watching, but soon find the sun too hot and the races too long.

'Daddy, is it nearly finished yet?' Uma keeps asking me. Eventually Marietta has to take them back to the car.

Ossian may not have been paying close attention to who was winning the races, but later that day he starts playing a new game. He stands at one end of the long veranda that runs across the front of our three rooms at the Lelin Campsite, and says 'ready, steady, go'. Then he starts running, his arms up in the air, and a big grin on his face. The Kenyan magic, it seems, is already starting to have an effect.

A week later, our house in Iten is finally ready to move in to. When we turn up, the only person there is the builder, still working on a few last jobs. The place smells of paint and dust. The rooms are bare, save for unmade beds and an elaborate hand-made sofa set in the sitting room. The new lino floors have been badly sellotaped down and are already curling up at the edges.

In the section of the house where the man with the passion fruit was squatting, a half-made bed without a mattress fills a tiny, bleak room. The main room is completely empty, while a third room is filled with junk – an old television, bits of wood, some frayed leads. Flora, a young woman Marietta's sister has hired to work for us, is supposed to live in this half of the house. It feels a bit desolate. The toilet is black with grime and the flush doesn't work.

About an hour after we arrive, the landlady turns up carrying lots of sheets and blankets for the beds. She's an elderly, kindly woman in a big patterned blouse who gets straight into mopping the floors and making the beds. Like all women in Kenya she wants to hug and pick up the children, but they back away shyly. This only makes her persist more, giggling to herself as she chases them around the room.

While the rest of the house is put in order, we leave Lila and Uma with Flora and head back to the supermarkets of Eldoret to kit ourselves out with spoons, plates, knives, pots, pans and all the other household items. It's quite a job and we don't get back until after dark. On the way home we start worrying about the girls. They seem too small suddenly to spend the day in an empty house, in a small Kenyan town, with a twenty-two-year-old woman they hardly know looking after them. As we pull in through the gate, though, they're standing smiling at the front door, a warm glow of yellow light behind them. They run out into the night to meet us. Inside, on the table, is some soup they've made. We all sit down, and family life in Iten begins.

7

'Well, in *our* country,' said Alice, still panting a little, 'you'd generally get to somewhere else – if you ran very fast for a long time as we've been doing.'

'A slow sort of country!' said the Queen. 'Now, *here*, you see, it takes all the running *you* can do, to keep in the same place. If you want to get somewhere else, you must run at least twice as fast as that!'

Lewis Carroll, *Through the Looking-Glass*

'The time is five thirty-five. It's time to get up. The time is five . . .' I switch off my alarm before it wakes Ossian up. I look over. He's sleeping soundly. I creep out of bed and put on my running kit: tights and a long-sleeve top. The door bangs as I open it, but no one in the house stirs.

I step out into a moonlit night. Dogs and cockerels are already doing their best to wake the valley, but there's still no sign of the dawn as I walk through Iten towards the meeting point: a junction between one of the many dirt roads and the main paved one. I've been told that athletes meet here just after six every morning.

Despite the thousands of runners in Iten, when you first arrive there is no programme you can join or centre where you can go to put your name down to start training. Many international athletes come here, stay at Lornah's camp and run every day by themselves or with other international athletes they meet at the camp. So far I've run a few times with Godfrey, who is just starting to train again after a few years, trying to get himself into shape for Lewa. But if I want to run with the big groups I see zipping by everywhere, I'm going to have to do what any Kenyan hopeful turning up in Iten has to do, and that is simply stand by the side of the road, wait for a group to come by, and join in.

The town is quiet at this time of the morning, and I slip by unseen in the darkness. Already there are people out running. I don't know how they can see well enough to negotiate all the bumps and potholes without twisting an ankle. There are also children running to school already, racing past with their pencil cases rattling in their school bags.

I'm the first to arrive at the junction. I do a bit of stretching and jogging up and down to keep warm as the occasional matatu drives slowly by, beeping for customers.

After about ten minutes, runners start appearing from everywhere, materialising out of the darkness. Within minutes there are about sixty Kenyan athletes standing around. Some of them are talking quietly and stretching. The runners are mostly men, their long, skinny legs wrapped in tights, some wearing woolly hats. I suddenly feel out of my depth, panicking as more athletes bound down the slopes or appear out of the trees. But it's too late to turn back now.

Without any announcement, we start running, heading off down the dirt track. Here we go, I tell myself, following them off into the darkness. Buckle up and hang on. The initial pace is quick without being terrifying, so I edge myself into the middle of the group and try to stay calm, focusing on my style, feeling the gentle pat, pat, pat of my feet skipping through under me. Up ahead the full moon lights the way, while behind us the dawn is creeping across the sky, making it easier to see. The last few stars go out as we hurtle along out of the town and into the African countryside.

I love running like this, in a group. You often hear commentators on television saying that an athlete is getting an easy ride running in the pack. In one way it doesn't make sense. You're still running under your own power, using the same energy to propel yourself forward. Wind resistance isn't usually a big factor in running. But somehow, in a group it is easier. It can feel as though the group is running, not you. As though the movement around you has picked you up and is carrying you along. The switching back and forth of legs focusing the mind, synchronising it, setting a rhythm for your body to follow. As soon as you become detached from the group, its power evaporates and it feels harder to run.

When I run on my own in England, particularly in a town or city, I feel like I'm constantly negotiating obstacles, such as the kerbs, pedestrians, parked cars, lamp-posts. Here it is potholes, cows, bicycles. In a group, though, they all whizz by almost without registering. In the group, everything is swept up and spat out as you pass.

A few of the runners around me are chatting quietly, but mostly we run in silence, passing small settlements of round mud huts, following the red dusty trail as it winds its way further and further from anywhere I recognise. The children who usually call out and get excited when I go by just stand and watch. I'm lost in the blur of the charge.

It doesn't last long, though. After just a few miles, the pace begins to pick up. I feel it most up the hills, and soon find myself drifting to the back of the group. I ask someone how far we are running.

'One hour ten,' he says. We must be moving at about 6-minute-per-mile pace now, and getting faster with each stride. I'm going to have to have the run of my life not to get lost.

Luckily for me, two women also begin struggling with the ever-increasing pace and I end up sticking with them for the rest of the run. They kindly encourage me whenever I start to fall behind. Up one particularly steep hill near the end, as my legs finally start to rebel, refusing to match the patter, patter rhythm of the two women, one of them turns to me and says simply: 'Try.'

I can't help but respond, and I manage to stay with them until the end. We finish at the top of the hill outside Lornah's camp back in Iten. The other runners are all standing around in the bright sunshine, joking and stretching. Some are walking home. I'm exhausted, but still standing. It's as much as I could have hoped for.

After thanking my two companions, I make my way slowly through Iten back to our house. The rest of the town is waking up now. Men walk around selling newspapers by the side of the road, while boys on bicycles deliver bread to the various wooden kiosks dotted everywhere around the town. Outside the big black gates to our house is a tiny kiosk with a grille-covered window across the front. It sells tea and rice and other things that last a long time even if nobody buys them. There are always men sitting on the counter outside, as though at a bar, passing time, watching us as we come and go. I walk over and shake their hands. Inside I can just about make out the face of a man. 'Fine, fine,' he says, coming out through a side door to greet me.

His name is Geoffrey, he tells me, smiling. He thought we were German. One of the men sitting languidly on the shop counter is his brother, Henry, an athlete. 'Half-marathon,' he says.

The other, shorter man is wearing a ripped yellow tracksuit. He gives me a big buck-toothed grin. His name is Japhet.

'Are you an athlete too?' I ask him.

'Yes,' he says. His torn running shoes and old clothes suggest he isn't the most successful athlete in Iten, but I imagine he's still probably pretty fast.

'Two hours twenty-eight,' he says. He's talking about the marathon. It's a surprisingly slow time for a Kenyan. Most marathon runners in Iten have a best time of under 2 hours 15 minutes at the very least. Even 2 hours 10 minutes is fairly average. But Japhet says it was his first marathon, and he ran it in Kisumu here in Kenya. He says it was very hot when he ran. 'But I ran all the way,' he says, smiling. 'Position 27.'

I ask him if he trains full-time, or whether he has a job, too. He shakes his head.

'If you have a job, you can't run,' he says. 'You get tired. Too tired.'

I tell him that I'm running a marathon in Kenya, too. Perhaps we could train together.

'The Lewa marathon,' I tell him. 'Do you know it?'

'Lewa?' he asks. 'Yes. Very hard. Very hot.'

'Perhaps we could go for a run together, all three of us?'

'Yes,' says Japhet, looking at Henry, who nods his approval. 'That would be good.'

A small herd of cows ambles past along the rutted road, followed by a young girl in a gold silk evening dress, torn across one shoulder. Her bare feet are caked in mud, and her hair is cropped short. In her hand she carries a stick for prodding the cows. She stares at us as she passes.

'I see you have a soldier,' says Geoffrey.

He means our nightwatchman. Everyone has told me that Iten is a safe town. But they also said that we should get a security guard. Just in case. I'd heard enough terrible stories of foreigners being robbed in other parts of Kenya to make sleeping in the house the first few nights an hourly ordeal of hearing a noise, waiting to see if it would happen again, and then, if it did, jumping up to look out of the window. At four o'clock in the morning on the first night, Lila woke up shouting. I went in to see her.

'What's that banging noise?' she asked, almost hysterical.

'Shhh, it's nothing,' I said, listening to see if there was any banging. There was. 'Quiet,' I said, urgently enough to make her quiet. She looked at me. I looked at her. 'Wait here,' I said. The banging seemed to be coming from the kitchen. I opened the door quickly, but there was no one there. It was coming from above.

Marietta called from the bedroom. I went in to see her. 'It's just the birds on the roof,' she said. 'They've been making noises all night.'

The problem with not having a watchman is that you can't reliably call the police if something happens.

'What do we do if someone tries to break in?' I asked Godfrey. 'Call the police?'

'Yes,' he said. Then, thinking about it, he smiled. 'No,

first call Koila.' Koila lives near our house. 'Or call me.'
Godfrey lives 30 miles away, near Eldoret.

In the end we hired a watchman. He arrived in an armoured car with about eight other uniformed men who all
jumped down and saluted me like members of the A-Team.
Deliberately last out of the van was a smooth-talking manager in a shirt and tie. He was all reassuring smiles as he
pointed at the armoured car.

'If anything happens, we send the car from Eldoret,' he
said.

'How long will that take?' He smiled at me. 'This is your
guard,' he said turning to the smallest of the men, who gave
me a worried salute. The others looked strong and sturdy,
like soldiers. Our man, Alex, looked more like a runner.

That evening he turned up punctually at seven o'clock
and started snooping around the garden like a comic-book
guard with his uniform and watchman's hat, his big white
truncheon held out in front of him. He checked the fence
and noted things down on a big clipboard.

Later that evening I looked out of the window and saw
his torchlight skirting the ground by the fence. Checking
it again.

He might not be particularly effective, with his truncheon
and his back-up team all the way in Eldoret, but that night
I have the best sleep since we moved in. I leave the worrying
about noises to our man in the garden.

'Yes,' I say to Geoffrey, the kiosk owner. 'You saw him?'

'Yes,' says Geoffrey. He smiles, friendly. 'It's best to be
safe,' he says.

*

For the next few weeks I find myself running mostly with Godfrey, or with other foreigners in the town, in an attempt to ratchet up some fitness before joining in with another group run. But everyone here is fast. One guy I meet is a young American student called Anders. Godfrey seems to have taken him under his wing.

'His mum', Godfrey tells me, 'ran the first-ever marathon. In the Olympics. She just jumped in with the men and beat them all.'

He repeats this jumbled story to people countless times and each time the result is a puzzled expression, rather than the look of impressed surprise Godfrey is hoping for. Eventually I work out that Anders's mother is Joan Benoit. The story Godfrey was trying to retell was her victory in the marathon at the 1984 Olympics. It was the first women's Olympic marathon and she didn't jump in with the men, there was a separate race. As well as being an Olympic champion, Joan is also a former world record holder and a two-time winner of the Boston marathon. She's basically America's greatest-ever women's marathon runner.

Anders is no slouch himself and has a 10K time of 33 minutes – 5 minutes quicker than my best. One morning I head out with him and Godfrey on a steady run through the forest. After a few minutes, Godfrey, the one training partner I can keep up with, stops, complaining of sore knees. Godfrey was once a great athlete, but at forty-five years old he is struggling to get back into shape.

'Sorry guys,' he says as we leave him to hobble back to town. As we run, Anders tells me that he's not sure Godfrey will really run the Lewa marathon. Godfrey must be the world's most friendly, helpful man, but sometimes that can be a problem. He says yes to everything.

'There's been a change of plan' is his famous refrain, just when you're expecting to do something with him. He's usually on the other end of a long-distance call from Nairobi or western Kenya, where his wife works as a police officer. So I'm not surprised when Anders says he might not run Lewa, but it leaves me without a training partner. It suddenly feels lonely to go there on my own. I should form a team, I think. It would give me a ready-made group to run with. It would be a great way to get closer to some of the athletes, to find out what makes them tick. And if Godfrey doesn't run, perhaps he could be the coach.

When we get back, I mention the team idea to Godfrey. He thinks it's a great plan. 'Chris will run too,' he says. He means Christopher Cheboiboch, the runner who picked us up from the Lelin Campsite on our first day in Iten. The man with the fifth-fastest time ever in the New York marathon.

'Really? You think so?'

'Sure,' he says. 'We want only the best.'

8

If you want to win something, run 100 meters. If you want to experience something, run a marathon.

Emil Zátopek

For years I've been saying that one day I would run a marathon, and now, in a few months, I will.

I'm slowly getting in shape. Every time Godfrey sees me he mentions the fact that I've lost weight – I must have had a lot to lose. Whenever I mention the Lewa race to any of the other runners, however, they grimace. 'That is tough,' they say. It's hot, hilly, and run on dirt tracks. Kenyans generally prefer courses where they can run fast times. A fast time can mean an invite to a big-city marathon. A slow course is in many ways simply a waste of effort.

My neighbour Japhet, though, says he would like to run it with me. He keeps telling me how he is always at the front on the early morning group runs.

'I'm forming a team,' I say. 'Would you like to join?' He grins. 'Yes,' he says.

Japhet, it turns out, is from the same village as Christopher Cheboiboch, who has also agreed to be part of the team. The village sits on a ridge just below the top of the escarpment, caught between a chiselled rock face rising up behind rolling fields, and the vast Rift Valley falling away to the front. It's a beautiful place. Chris says he remembers when Japhet was born. Their family homes are practically next to each other.

Every Kenyan runner has a story. To go from a small *shamba* – plot of land – on the side of a mountain in rural Kenya to winning big-city marathons in Europe and America is inevitably a tale filled with drama and adventure. Chris told me that the first time he ever visited Iten, he was fourteen years old. It was the first time he had ever seen even a small town. He walked through the streets agog at all the people and buildings. Ten years later he was almost winning the New York City marathon, racing past huge skyscrapers, being cheered on by hundreds of thousands of people.

Chris took me home to his village one time to meet his family. He looked completely out of place among the raggedy farmers, with his neatly ironed shirt and easy smile. Everywhere people waved to him, or stopped to talk. The one who had made it. The prodigal son, returning to see his people. But a distance had grown between them. He spoke to most people through the window of his gently purring car. After we'd spoken to one labourer, reaching in to shake my hand, his clothes covered in dust and mud after a hard day's toil, Chris turned to me.

'He was a classmate of mine,' he said, aware of the contrast in their fortunes. Letting it linger as he drove on.

Chris's family home was a simple mud hut like all the others, but he had bought lots of the surrounding fields. It was hard to keep tabs on how much he owned.

'Those cattle are mine,' he said, pointing into the distance.

'I bought those two fields for my brother.' At his homestead, his sister had prepared a feast for us. Inside it was like a shrine to Chris, with newspaper clippings about his successes and photographs of him on the walls, all framed and surrounded in tinsel.

After we'd eaten, his mother turned up. She was a tough woman who grunted an unimpressed hello at me. After Chris's father disappeared when he was very young, she started farming the land, bringing her six children up on her own. But Chris was clearly a little embarrassed by her, with her tired scowl and woollen Manchester United hat. They hardly spoke to each other. A few muttered words and then we were gone, heading back to Iten.

Chris is now forty-two, although, like virtually all male Kenyan runners, his official age is much lower, in this case thirty-four. I never get to the bottom of why they are all older than they say they are. Each person has a different story, although it usually involves someone else, such as a manager, getting the date wrong. Strangely, around half of Kenya's runners were born on 1 January according to their official records. When I fill Japhet's Lewa entry form in with him, I ask him what his date of birth is.

'1987,' he says.

'What day and month?' I ask him. He looks at me and starts shuffling around on his seat.

'Let me go and find out,' he says.

In 2002, when Chris was thirty-three (official age twenty-five), he came second in both the Boston and the New York City marathons. He was flying, one of the top athletes at the illustrious training stable of the Italian agent Dr Rosa.

Almost immediately, though, he became distracted. He used his money to build a school, named after his home village, Salaba.

Like all Kenyan runners, when he was young Chris had to run to school, 4 km, back and forth twice a day every day.

'Unknowingly, we were already training,' he says. 'But it was hard.' He says he built Salaba Academy so that his own children didn't have to suffer as he did.

'It's also an investment. It's his retirement,' says Godfrey.

A fee-paying boarding school just outside Iten, Salaba Academy takes up a lot of Chris's time. He seems to do everything, from buying the flour for the ugali to attending meetings with education officials in Nairobi. One day we arrange to leave for an early morning run at 5 a.m. and he asks if we can pick him up at the school.

'Why will you be at school at that time?' I ask.

'I'm always at school early,' he says.

'But is anyone even awake?'

'They are in class already,' he says, affronted, as though I'm suggesting his children are lazy.

'At 5 a.m.?'

'They have exams coming up. They must work hard.'

Once his school was up and running, Chris never reached the same level of performance in his running again.

Chris's story of short-lived glory is common among the athletes here and shows just how vital focus and dedication is to Kenya's running success.

The most famous example of a great athlete becoming distracted by success is Sammy Wanjiru, who blazed away to win the 2008 Olympic marathon at the tender age of twenty-one. A few months after I set up my Lewa team, Wanjiru, one of the most precocious and successful of all Kenya's runners, is killed in a fall from a balcony at his home in Nyahururu. Wanjiru was well known among the athletes as a heavy drinker. I was told that if I wanted to meet him, I should go to a bar in Eldoret and ask around. According to the stories, he would regularly go into a nightclub and buy everyone there a drink. On the night he died, his wife came home to find him in bed with another woman. What happened next no one knows, but Wanjiru ended up dead.

One warm, still afternoon, as a paraglider circles in the sky above, I find the legendary Italian coach Renato Canova sitting in his seat by the vast windows that span one side of the Kerio View hotel, a glass of milk on the table in front of him. He's the only person there apart from a team of waiters hovering by the kitchen door talking quietly to each other. I ask him if I can sit down.

'Please do,' he says, moving the chair out for me. Renato has a permanent room at the hotel and spends much of the year sitting here, perched above the sky, reading a newspaper or gazing out the window. Since he first came to Iten in 1998 he has been training Kenyan athletes. Virtually all of his charges have gone on to win world titles.

One of the waitresses comes over and asks me what I want to drink. I order a passion fruit juice. She doesn't ask Renato. He has his milk. He'll be back later for supper, at the same time as always.

'So, what did you want to know?' he says. I ask him why the Kenyans often have short careers. Unlike the great Ethiopian runners such as Haile Gebrselassie and Kenenisa Bekele, most Kenyans run well for a few years and then disappear.

He looks at me over the top of his fingers, held in a prayer position on the table.

'The runners all come from poor backgrounds, with less education,' he says. 'When they win, the whole village celebrates their victory, and everyone asks for support. The successful athlete becomes like the chief of the village, so then everyone goes to him with their personal problems.'

He says he once had an athlete at the World Championships who was being phoned up every two hours by people back in Kenya asking where they should put the windows in a building they were constructing.

'The athletes need to concentrate on their training,' he says. 'They need to educate their villagers about their life.'

This is why the training camps were started, to remove the athletes from the distraction of their families and relations, and the rest of the outside world. But once they become successful, often the athletes decide they don't want to live in the camps any more, where daily life is stripped down to the bare essentials of run, sleep and eat, so they move out. 'They start dealing with building projects, borrowing money,' says Canova. 'This is normal behaviour for a Kenyan.' It is normal behaviour in most other countries, too, even for athletes. It is the ones who live in the camps who are unusual. But the difference it makes is huge. Without the same intense levels of dedication and focus, and the time to rest, when an athlete leaves a camp it often signals the beginning of the end. Wanjiru isn't the only great athlete who ended up propping up the bars of Eldoret. Chris, at least, kept running. He tells me that for the month before the Lewa marathon he will move away from home, to a hotel, to concentrate on his training.

'Of course,' he says. 'You have to be focused.'

I can't imagine this level of intensity, living away from home in basic training camps for months at a time, being considered normal among athletes in other parts of the world. Yet there are hundreds of these camps in Kenya, all filled with dedicated athletes. Under the heading 'secrets' in my notebook, I jot down the words 'focus, dedication, training camps'.

Godfrey calls a Lewa team meeting at a hotel in Iten. Japhet turns up wearing a sleeveless safari jacket that hangs way too big from his shoulders. He sits shyly on the edge of his seat, listening intently as Godfrey talks about what an honour it is to be in the team, that the race will be live on television, that the whole world will be watching. As he's talking, Chris arrives with another runner.

'This is Josphat,' he says. 'He wants to run, too.'

Josphat shakes my hand and gives me an amused smile. Like Chris it's hard to put an age on him, but it turns out he's Chris's childhood friend and is also from the same village.

'OK,' I say. 'So altogether we're five, if Godfrey runs.' He has been telling me his knees are too sore. 'Otherwise, Godfrey has agreed to be our coach.'

Godfrey and Chris take turns to make the most grandiose speech about what the team means, and they keep thanking me profusely for setting it up.

'We are representing Iten,' says Godfrey. 'When you are

interviewed afterwards,' he says, looking at Japhet, 'you must speak well. You mustn't be shy.'

'Josphat, what have you got to say for yourself?' says Chris, turning on his friend. 'What will you say after the race?'

Josphat, who hasn't spoken since he arrived, looks unwilling to join in the game. The hotel waitress brings over five cups of tea, buying him some time. She places them down on the table in slow motion, without speaking or looking at anyone.

'So, Josphat,' says Chris, sounding like a teacher.

'I don't know,' he says.

'Ah, that's no good,' says Chris, annoyed.

Later, after the others have gone, Godfrey seems concerned.

'I don't know why Chris brought Josphat along. He doesn't add anything to the team. He's way too old. We need a winner.'

A week later I get a call from Godfrey. 'Finn,' he says. 'I think I've found our winner.' I'm not sure we need a winner. I've agreed to pay the race entry fees and arrange some accommodation for the night before the race. Suddenly everyone wants to be in the team.

'How good is he?' I ask.

'Are you kidding me? He's good. Come and meet him tomorrow. There's a homecoming for some athletes who ran in the African championships. Komen will be there.' He means the great Daniel Komen, the 3,000m world record holder.

'OK,' I say, not realising what is in store.

After driving for about two hours along the edge of the escarpment, we swing in through the drive of a school in the village of Kamwosor. 'Can we stop?' Godfrey asks. I pull the car to a halt. 'I think this is it,' he says, 'but let me check first.' He gets out of the car and disappears out through the gate behind us.

'Where's Godfrey going?' Lila asks me, as though I ever know what is going on when Godfrey is around.

'I don't know,' I say. We all sit staring out through the front window. A long corrugated metal building sits at the end of the dirt driveway. I presume it's the school. A few heads appear around the edge of one wall, and then disappear. Suddenly the whole school is running up the drive towards us, a huge swarm of red jumpers. We sit trapped in our car as the children clamber around, laughing and chattering to each other, peering in at us. They reach in through the half-open windows, looking for handshakes, money, sweets, anything. Lila and Uma are not sure whether it's funny or terrifying. Uma is standing up on the back seat, while Lila climbs into the front and curls up on my lap. The car is rocking in the frenzy.

'Finn, Finn.' I can hear Godfrey outside, but I can't see him. He manages to push his way through the crowd. Where are the teachers? 'Finn, start to come back,' he says. I turn the engine on to a big cheer, and start edging the car backwards. Godfrey is pulling children out of the way. Finally we make it out, back onto the street. The children stand in the open gateway, held back by some invisible force, waving and laughing as we turn the car. Godfrey gets in.

'Sorry about that,' he says. 'Let's go this way.'

We drive up into the village, a single strip of road with painted wooden shops on either side, a few flimsy vegetable stalls, women with big skirts holding long knives, standing staring at us. We park the car and Godfrey takes us into a tiny blue building with the word 'hotel' painted across it. It's actually a café. Inside, a few men sit at wooden tables. They look at us in silence as we sit down. Rickety chairs, benches along the walls, a dusty red floor. A wooden counter stands in one corner, with a pile of rock-like buns on a shelf behind a glass front. In the other corner is a butcher's shop, the skinned and headless body of a cow hanging from a hook.

Godfrey asks us what we want to drink and then disappears out through the front door when we tell him, leaving us sitting there.

'Where's he gone now?' Lila asks me quietly, leaning across the table.

'I don't know,' I say, looking at Marietta. She shrugs, amused at his constant comings and goings. Ossian climbs onto her lap and starts banging the table and singing, happy to be out of the car. The other men in the room give up watching us and turn back to their conversations. Eventually Godfrey comes back with a bag full of sodas. He has two men with him. One of them is Shadrack, the runner he has been telling me about.

'Hi,' I say, after Godfrey introduces us. 'I hear you want to run Lewa?'

'Huh?' He looks at me as though I'm mad.

'Lewa. You know, the marathon?'

'Yes,' he says.

'You want to run?'

He nods, staring at me now with unblinking eyes. 'Yes,' he says.

About three hours later than planned we make our way back down the road to the village school, where the homecoming ceremony is finally about to begin. Four of the children from the village have just come back from the African cross-country championships in Cape Town where Kenya won every single medal on offer, despite only sending a second-string team.

The appearance of the teachers means we don't get such a raucous reception this time, but are free to park the car and walk over to where the festivities are taking place. As guests of honour we are each given tinsel wreaths to wear around our necks and directed to sit under the shade of a small marquee. The schoolchildren sit on the ground around the tent in the hot sun.

One of the speakers is Daniel Komen. The chairman of the local athletics board, he sits sullenly through the speeches by the other dignitaries, not laughing when everyone else does. Occasionally he calls Godfrey close and whispers something in his ear, his eyes looking around to make sure nobody else is listening.

Tall and smartly dressed, Komen is one of the greatest runners that has ever lived. In 1996, at the age of twenty, he burst onto the international scene like a fireball. The great Ethiopian Haile Gebrselassie was the dominant force in distance running at the time and was breaking world records for fun. Suddenly he had a challenger. Upset at not making the Kenyan team for the Olympics, at the end of the 1996 season Komen went out and ran one of the most staggering performances ever seen on a track. On a cool September evening in Rieti, Italy, he flew around seven and a half laps like a man possessed, breaking the 3,000m world record by over four seconds. Despite all the great names that have tried, nobody has since been able to get even close to the time he ran that night.

However, less than two years later, his career was virtually over. Those who knew him blame the money he won. Komen is often held up as the prime example when people talk about athletes winning money and then becoming distracted. Komen himself, however, blames the shortness of his career not on money but on injuries. I corner him one day at the exclusive Eldoret Golf Club, where he often sits on a Sunday, under the shade of an umbrella, brooding while his children dive-bomb each other in the pool.

'I had many injuries,' he says, looking away. He seems annoyed.

'What injuries did you have?'

'From high school. The teachers wanted the points for the team, so they made me run all the races. Sometimes I had to run two races on the same day. The Ethiopians don't have so much pressure on them in high school, but it's a big problem in Kenya.'

Despite his ill feeling, Komen is heavily involved in junior athletics in Kenya. As chairman of the local athletics board, he seems to show up at every school event I go to, although he says he is stepping down next year to focus on his own school he has set up. He also sponsors talented athletes to go and study in the US.

'But we have many problems,' he says, scowling. 'People don't run. They take the money.' Just a few months before, one of his sponsored athletes in Alaska hanged himself. There's not a lot of light in Komen's world right now.

He sits glowering at the homecoming ceremony as the speeches rumble on, the gold tinsel wreath hanging uncomfortably around his neck. After about three hours Godfrey is called up to speak. He talks in English, telling the schoolchildren that education is important. That they should work hard at their studies. Marietta has taken our three children off behind the marquee to play, but a queue has formed of people wanting to be photographed with them. It's starting to get dark, so we decide to make a break for it. We bundle out as the town's mayor takes up the microphone. Heads follow us as we make our way back to the car. Godfrey, shaking hands with everyone, is dragged on by Lila. A man from a local radio station comes over, wanting to interview me, asking me to talk into his tape recorder as I climb into the car, reversing as someone leans in through the window, alcohol on his breath, telling me he is a great runner.

And then we're off, following the road back along the edge of the escarpment, past round mud huts, flickering wooden fences, bicycles, people walking, the sloping green fields full of the late afternoon, children laughing and chasing each other. And all the while, to one side, the great open space of the Rift Valley falling away below us.

9

The human foot is a masterpiece of engineering and a work of art.

　Leonardo da Vinci

When I can't find anyone to run with, I put on my racing flats and head out on my own. Although I prefer running in a group, here in Kenya sometimes it is a relief to run alone. At my own pace, I can simply enjoy the trails, the country-side, the sense of motion, the earth trundling by under my feet, without having to feel slow and hopeless at the back of the pack, always bursting my lungs to keep up, just waiting to see how long I can survive until I'm cast aside.

On one of these solo runs I strain a toe landing on a stone. I get it massaged by one of Iten's many physios and it's fine a few days later. But it makes me re-examine the wisdom of doing all my running in racing shoes.

Lee Saxby, the barefoot expert in London, told me that was what the Kenyans ran in, but this clearly isn't the case. Like all runners, it is what they race in. But mostly they run in big, chunky cushioned trainers, just like your average plodding Western jogger.

Oddly, though, contrary to Lee's theories, these big shoes don't force the Kenyans to run heel first. They virtu-ally all run in a lovely, smooth forefoot-first style – what Lee would term 'barefoot style'. The shoes, it seems, make no difference.

'Your feet are not used to the terrain here,' the physio tells me, pressing my toes to a pulp as I lie on the treatment room table in Lornah Kiplagat's training camp. Lornah actually walks in mid-grimace and shakes my hand.

'You need more cushioning on your shoes, because of all the stones,' the physio tells me.

So I've come full circle. To run like a Kenyan, it seems, I need to go back to where I started, and get myself a big, padded pair of trainers.

I can't quite bring myself to do it, though.

That afternoon we all walk down to the local mitumba, a weekly market selling mostly second-hand clothes shipped over from Europe and America by aid charities. The clothes are piled high on sacks laid out on the floor. Everything from European high-street names to designer labels. For bargain hunters it's a bonanza of cheap clothes, a jumble sale of epic proportions. Marietta loves it, and she and the children head down most Saturdays to rummage through the bounty.

'I could clothe us all for the next two years,' she says, not joking.

All together they cause quite a stir, my family in the mitumba. Marietta disappearing under armfuls of clothes, bartering hard with a woman sitting high like a queen on a throne of piled-up clothes, Lila drawing giggles as she tries on a pink faux-fur waistcoat, looking at herself in a shard of broken mirror, Uma, following on, holding tightly to a Barbie tracksuit, folding it up and squashing it under her arm. Even Ossian likes to get in on the act, sitting down on the ground and kicking off his shoes so he can try on endless pairs of high heels and flip-flops.

This being Iten, a couple of the stalls at the mitumba are selling running shoes. Lines and lines of scrubbed-up trainers, glistening in the sunshine. I scan along them looking for the pair with the thinnest sole. I stop on a pair of orange Asics.

'Yes, my friend,' says the seller, sensing I have my eye on a pair. 'Which country are you from?'

The trainers are slightly worn down, but that's all the better, right? I'm confused now. Do I want to be near the ground or protected from it? They're the only pair in my size that don't have a huge wedge of sponge stuck on under the heel. I buy them.

But on my very first run in my new trainers, I land heavily on another stone. I feel the pain shooting up my leg. After a few minutes it subsides, but the whole barefoot issue is clouded yet further. Clearly my feet are still not tough or strong enough to run forefoot first, even in trainers. But I can't go back now. I've got to the point where forefoot first feels completely natural to me. And I'm still convinced it's a more efficient way to run.

I remember the day, back in Exeter, when I went to buy my racing flats, just before we left for Kenya. I'd been practising my barefoot style for a few weeks and had managed to run two miles without my legs aching too much, but I was nervous about the shop assistant asking me to get up on his treadmill so he could analyse my gait. He might tell me that I shouldn't be buying flats as I needed more support, padding and everything else. I tried to be as inconspicuous as possible as I picked out the flattest shoes

I could find, with the least support. But I was the only person in the shop.

'Do you have these in a nine?' I asked.

The man took the shoe from me. 'Do you pronate?' he asked.

'Er . . . I don't know,' I said, wary of lying outright in case he could tell that I did just by the way I walked.

'Hop up on the treadmill and we'll take a look,' he said.

I considered bolting for the door, but decided against it. Instead I obediently put the trainers on and clambered aboard the treadmill.

The machine whirred slowly into action. Lead with your chest, I told myself. Legs like a unicycle. It started to get faster. Pad, pad, pad. He was crouching down trying to look under my feet. I tried to look casual, like this was my natural running style, not something I was working hard to maintain. He was checking me out from the side now. After about thirty seconds, I hit the stop button and the machine came to a halt.

'You're lucky,' he said. 'You have a lovely forefoot style. It's the most efficient way to run.'

Occasionally, during my solitary runs here in Kenya, I try changing back to heel first, just for old times' sake. It's like a car changing down gear suddenly, as I feel my whole body slumping back into a slower motion. No, I'm convinced the barefoot style has to stay. I just need to strengthen my feet. Toby Tanser told me that it was too late, that the Kenyans' ankles and the arches of their feet were so much stronger and more flexible from years of running barefoot, that we couldn't hope to compete. But I'm not trying to compete with them. And I'm not actually running barefoot. Just in a forefoot style. Surely that's possible.

Once an aspiring runner arrives in Iten and finds a group to train with, his next aim is to run fast enough to attract the attention of a manager, who will sign him up and send him abroad to race. In return for his services, the manager takes a percentage of the prize winnings. Virtually all the managers are foreigners who have set up training camps in Iten and the surrounding area. Once an athlete gets signed up, he usually lives in the manager's training camp, where he receives food and lodging and gets to train with the other athletes in the camp. Most camps also have a masseur on hand to revitalise tired limbs and treat any niggling injuries. It's amazing how some heavy-duty thumb pressing can usually fix an injured athlete, as though he's simply made of plasticine.

Although I'm never going to impress a manager, after a few weeks running around Iten I've gradually got to know some of the other athletes, and one invites me to spend a day at his camp. The Run Fast camp, as it's imaginatively named, is one of Iten's newest training centres. There are ten athletes living here, in five small dormitories, each with a shower, a sofa and a bunk bed. Nine of the athletes are Kenyan and one is the British runner whom I saw competing in the Iten cross-country race.

Tom Payn was a technical sales engineer for a filtration company in Portsmouth when he decided to give it all up to come out to train in Kenya. With a best marathon time of 2 hours 17 minutes, he's hoping to get himself into shape to make the British team for the Olympics.

To start my day in the camp, I'm told to meet Tom and the other athletes at 6.20 a.m. outside a hotel on the main road in Iten. There's quite a big group gathered there when I arrive. As well as the ten athletes in the camp, Run Fast has a group of second-string runners who live outside the camp but come to the training sessions. A few days before I turn up, two of the runners in the camp were told that they had to leave because they weren't training or racing as well as expected. They got quite upset. Two runners from the outside group were invited in to take their place.

The Run Fast manager is an Englishman called Peter McHugh. He has told the group that by the end of the week he will pick six of them to travel to Europe to run a series of races. Once they get there, all they have to do is run like Kenyans and watch the money start rolling in. Last year, the camp's star runner won enough prize money to buy himself a plot of land in Iten when he got back.

There's a lot of tension in the group right now as the runners wait to find out if they will be among the chosen six. Most of them have never raced abroad before. They stand on the threshold of the door to the promised land. This is what they've been training for, dreaming about. But if their name is not on the list, they'll be left standing outside in the cold, watching as their friends head off without them.

One of the athletes, Eliud, has been running for twelve years and has made a total of 1,000 Kenyan shillings – or about £8 – in his entire career. Even a small race abroad could net him £1,000. But only if he gets picked.

The problem is, Peter tells me, that finding races for

Kenyans is getting harder and harder. With the global recession, prize money at races is down, and people are getting bored of watching Kenyans win everything. Race organisers are desperate for top runners from other countries. When a manager calls up a race director with the offer of a few unknown Kenyans, the response is usually a bored shrug. 'Is that all you've got? More Kenyans?'

Peter only set up his Run Fast camp recently, but the other managers I speak to don't think he has much chance of making it a success. It's not that he doesn't know what he's doing, but that the landscape is dominated by a handful of über-managers.

'The governing body passed a new rule recently,' explains one US manager, who is pulling out of Kenya after twenty years working with athletes here. 'Contracts need to be renewed every year. It's good for the athletes, because it means they can move on if they're not getting a fair deal. But it makes it easy for athletes to get poached by other managers.'

He says that once a smaller manager like Peter discovers a promising talent, the bigger names will simply move in, offering short-term incentives to the athlete to switch.

'There's no loyalty any more,' he tells me. 'The Kenyan runners don't understand the longer-term view. So if you offer them $500 up front, they'll jump at it, even if the terms of the contract mean they'll lose out in the long term.'

Peter just shrugs when I mention this to him. 'Hopefully that won't happen,' he says. 'If they're happy with me, I don't think they'll feel the need to change.'

Despite promising murmurs, Eliud doesn't get picked to travel. It's all too much for him. 'An athlete can't keep in good shape for ever,' he tells me. 'I'm in good shape, but what for? I don't have a race.' He looks close to tears. A few days later he leaves the camp, and sends a message to Peter to tear up his contract. But where else can he go? He moves in with some friends and continues training.

'He's an idiot,' Tom Payn tells me. He likes Eliud and is sad he has left the camp. 'I think Peter was about to give him a race, but now he has no chance.' It may be sod's law, that he left just as he was about to get a race, or perhaps the race would have remained forever a mirage, always about to happen. Eliud was too proud to sit and wait any longer. He would rather face the impossible route of going it alone. Unless he wins a big race in Kenya, though, it could now be game over.

Although the Run Fast camp is fairly second-rate by the immense local standards – there are no Kenyan internationals in the camp, for example – through my eyes it's still a formidable bunch of athletes standing around outside the tiny hotel in the morning half-light. Each person who arrives shakes hands with everyone else and then stands waiting for the runners from the camp to turn up. I spot my neighbour and Lewa teammate Japhet among the crowd. He shakes my hand nervously, his usually big smile slightly terse this morning.

We all travel together to the university track in Eldoret squashed in the back of a pick-up truck. It's still only 7 a.m. when we arrive, but already there are a few groups of runners hurtling around in mid-session.

The Run Fast schedule is for them to run twelve lots of 600m and twelve lots of 400m. I decide to run 400m with them when they're running 600m, and 200m when they're running 400m. Hopefully, with the shorter distances and the longer rest between them, I'll be able to keep up.

It's evident right from the first one, however, that that won't be the case. I find myself almost sprinting around the dirt track, stumbling all over the place trying to run in the trench that has been worn all around the inside lane. A Russian man back in Iten told me that if you run on the track with Kenyans, you feel disabled. I now know what he means. I manage to stick just behind Tom, but the others are far ahead.

Tom is the slowest runner in the group. But, perversely, he is the only one who is sponsored, by Adidas. And he has the best chance of anyone in the group of making it to the Olympics. It seems unfair, but the Kenyans just grin ruefully when I mention it to them. They're just here to run. They don't seem to dwell on whether it's fair or not.

Peter, who has come to watch the training, says that the British runners are usually the ones claiming an injustice.

'I've been getting a hard time back in the UK,' he says. 'The British runners don't like me bringing Kenyans over there to race. They complain that the Kenyans are taking all the prize money. But it's an open race.'

He's talking to me as I sit on the grass watching as the other runners carry on without me. I struggled around less than a quarter of the session, getting further and further behind. Determined to carry on, I switched over to the women's group: three runners, toiling around at what looked like a much slower pace. They nodded shyly, hardly glancing up, when I approached and asked if I could join them. But they were also too fast. I managed to keep close to the slowest of them for a few intervals, even battling to overtake her once or twice. But she just kept going, lap after lap, until I had to drop out, exhausted.

After she has finished I go over to shake her hand.

'You're too fast,' I say. She grins. 'What's your name?'

'Beatrice,' she says, looking away.

The men's group is still charging around the track. A few others drop out, and Tom doesn't get any further behind. Little Japhet seems to be struggling with the pace, dropping off from the main group. Even Tom is almost catching him. It's amazing that he has chosen to live and train as a full-time athlete when he clearly has little chance of success. Hope, or optimism, or a lack of alternatives, drives many of the Kenyans on. But you can't eat hope.

As well as the large groups of Kenyans, I spot the odd Italian athlete and another British runner training. The Serbian team is also here, stocky men with big hair grinding their way around the track.

Finally, the Run Fast group stops. Time to head back to Iten for breakfast.

At the camp we get a mango and a banana each. Then we sit down and drink tea and eat dry bread. The food is doled out by the camp cook as people find themselves a chair to kick back in. The remainder of the day, until the afternoon run at 5 p.m., is dedicated to resting.

For Kenyan runners, rest is a serious business. None of the athletes has jobs. Even the athletes who don't live in the camps rarely do anything other than run, sleep and eat. I met one athlete who had worked for a while in the Hill Side Café in Iten, but he told me he had to give it up because it made him too tired to run. Without a job, most of them rely on the kindness of relatives, or other successful runners, to see them through. They don't require much, living frugal lives, with no electricity or running water, and eating a simple diet of rice, beans and ugali.

The athletes in the camps, who don't have to worry about finding and cooking food, sit for hours every day on plastic garden chairs talking or just staring into space. And when they get bored, they go to sleep. Lornah Kiplagat famously sleeps sixteen hours a day when she is in serious training. I spoke to some top British athletes who had come to Kenya to train and I asked them what they thought the biggest difference was between the Kenyans' training and their own.

'Rest,' they all said, unanimously.

'In England when we're not running we go shopping, cook food, meet up with friends. Here they just rest.'

It could also be called focus or dedication, and like barefoot running, the scientific research is playing catch-up with the intuition and simplicity of the Kenyan approach. If you ask a Kenyan athlete why he sleeps so much, he won't quote the recent paper from Stanford University in the US that found that its basketball players ran faster in time trials and had a 9 per cent improved shooting accuracy after increasing the amount of time they spent sleeping. No, he'll tell you that he needs to sleep more when he's in training because his body gets tired.

The Stanford researcher Cheri Mah says that this wisdom isn't unique to the Kenyans.

'Intuitively many players and coaches in the US know that rest and sleep are important,' she says. 'But it is often the first thing to be sacrificed.' But in Kenya, where the daily schedule is simply run, sleep and eat, there is nothing to sacrifice it for. I note 'rest' down on my list of secrets. 'Barefoot running, training camps, running to school, rest . . .' The list is growing.

At some point in the mid-afternoon, after we've eaten lunch, I find I'm the only person still sitting out in the garden. One by one the athletes have got up and wandered off, disappearing into the short row of dormitories. I get up to see where they've all gone. Some are sleeping. In Tom's room I find four of the runners watching music videos.

After lounging around all day, by 5 p.m. the Run Fast athletes don't seem too keen to do their evening run. A few of them decide they are too tired, while the rest of us head out for a forty-minute run. It's a lovely time of day out along the lanes around Iten, the air just cooling, the light turning yellow. It's a rare thing for me to train twice in one day, but I feel surprisingly good. For the others, of course, it's only an easy run, but in my head we're racing along, the wind in our hair. People watch as we fly by, tightly bunched. I may be bursting my lungs, but here I am, a month after arriving in Iten, running with the Kenyans, and keeping up.

Gradually, achingly, but just about perceptibly, I begin to get fitter. Shortly after my day with Run Fast, I return to one of the big early morning group runs.

I meet Japhet again one evening while I'm watching over Lila and Uma playing with the other children from the neighbourhood in the dirt strip of a street outside our house. Uma, who loves to unbolt the gate and run outside like a celebrity mingling with her fans, has caused great excitement and charging around by bringing out an inflatable beach ball.

Japhet sidles over with an arm outstretched, his other hand resting on his wrist as a sign of respect. We shake hands. 'They are having fun,' he says. 'It is good.' He asks me when we'll go on our first training run with our Lewa team. I tell him I'll talk to Godfrey. I'm still not quite sure how the team training is going to work, so for now Japhet offers to join me on one of the early morning group runs. He says he will stay at my pace the whole way. It's a kind offer. It means I won't have to worry about getting lost. We agree to meet at the kiosk at 5.50 the next morning.

It's pitch black as Alex, our guard, unbolts the gate and lets me out. In the darkness I can just about make out two figures standing waiting. It's Japhet and his friend Henry, the brother of the man who owns the kiosk. They look cold as I walk over and shake their hands.

There's no moon, so we walk carefully and slowly along the bumpy path down to the meeting point, feeling the way with our feet. Today we're going to run with a group known as the *mwisho wa lami* group, or the End of the Road group, because they meet at the point where the paved road ends. Wilson Kipsang, one of the fastest marathon runners in history, is part of the group, they tell me. I stop, and pretend to turn back, making them laugh.

'It's OK,' says Japhet. 'Today is easy.'

Henry nods. 'Easy,' he says.

A few runners jog past us out of the blackness, calling out in Kalenjin to Japhet and Henry. Cockerels, somehow spotting the imperceptible paling in the eastern sky, call out among the scattering of tin roofs.

About sixty people have gathered for the run, stretching long arms in the air, shaking hands, or standing huddled in silence. Someone starts speaking to the group, explaining the route. Japhet nudges me. 'Kipsang,' he says, nodding towards the man talking. A few people ask questions. I'm sticking to Japhet like glue. Despite his small stature and tatty clothes, he's bubbly and friendly with everyone, even making a joke about the route that gets a few chuckles from the other runners. I remind him that I'm slow, and not to forget about me amid the banter, but he says it's OK and that he is happy to run as slow as I want.

It's still dark as we shunter off. '*Pole, pole,*' ('Slowly, slowly') says Kipsang, as we begin running up the main road into town.

At St Patrick's school we turn right down a side track. The first seepage of light is beginning to pick out trees, silhouettes. As I run along beside Japhet in the midst of the group, something strange happens. I don't get left behind. Even as the pace begins to increase, my breath remains steady. Strong almost.

Occasionally a car coming the other way forces everyone to slow down and bunch together, and I get to catch up any lost yards, gather myself. And then we're on again. For the first forty minutes I'm motoring along amid the scattering of feet and swishing of tracksuits, feeling fine.

Eventually, as the charge to the finish begins to gather pace, I start to lose ground, but, good to his word, Japhet sticks with me, and we run the rest of the route within sight of the main group. At the end we're standing stretching by the side of the road when Henry, Japhet's friend, comes dawdling up the track. He's dripping in sweat as he stops next to us.

'You're fast,' he says, clearly out of breath. I look around to see who he's talking to, before I realise it's me.

10

When the Missionaries arrived, the Africans had the land and the Missionaries had the Bible. They taught us how to pray with our eyes closed. When we opened them, they had the land and we had the Bible.

Jomo Kenyatta, the first president of Kenya

Foolishly buoyed by my run with Japhet and the End of the Road group, two days later I find myself standing on the start line of a local cross-country race.

It's a hot but windy day in Eldoret. We've all woken up early so that Lila and Uma can run in the children's race. Memories of the fun run at the Great West Run in Exeter have prompted their enthusiasm. That day Uma refused to run and Granny Bee had to carry her around the two-mile loop. But today's race is only one kilometre, and she's now five – she was only three and a half then.

They get dressed in their best racing outfits – shorts, trainers and Hello Kitty T-shirts – and we talk tactics in the car on the way to the course. As we enter the gates to the Eldoret Sports Club it's still only 8.30 a.m., but the place is heaving with excitement, people in race numbers and bare feet darting around everywhere. Heads turn to look at us as we enter, children giggling and passing comments behind cupped hands. Seeing Lila and Uma, a man at a desk ushers us over. Lila, though, has changed her mind. She doesn't want to run. Uma, in a blur of bodies and early morning chaos, lets me register her. The race is about to start, so I guide her through the crowd – a parting sea of staring eyes – and out onto the course. The sun is hotting up. Announcements are blaring out over the PA. There are children zipping around everywhere. Skinny, bony children, light on their feet. Uma is one of the youngest. She looks confused.

'It's OK,' I say. 'Look, that girl is smaller than you.' A little girl watches us from the side with unblinking eyes. She has a race number on her chest, but doesn't appear to be heading to the start.

'If you don't want to run, you don't have to,' I say. Uma looks at me and leaps up into my arms, burying her head in my neck. It's an intimidating atmosphere for two little English girls just turned seven and five. I sympathise completely. In three hours' time, it will be my turn.

Instead of racing, we take the girls and Ossian to sit in the small stand by the clubhouse. Inside, we find Godfrey with some friends. He is in his element, chatting with former runners, reminiscing about old times. He introduces me to a man in a smart brown jacket and sunglasses who won the silver medal in the marathon at the 2001 World Championships, finishing just one second behind the winner.

'I was that close,' he says, holding up his thumb and forefinger.

Also sitting in the stands is the Chinese national team. They're here to watch and learn, their coach tells me. This is no ordinary local cross-country race. The whole thing is sponsored by Nike and is used as a way to unearth emerging talent.

As the event organiser, the legendary manager Dr Rosa gets to pick a few of the most promising young athletes to invite to train at his camp.

As stewards hand out water to everyone in the stand, two announcers tag-team on the PA. They say everything twice, in Swahili and English, and take turns to talk, so there's no let-up in the noise booming from the speakers that have been set up just in front of the stand.

Meanwhile, the races are trundling by. Every now and then a crowd of barefoot children flies past. Interestingly, in each race there are a few children wearing running shoes, but they all invariably finish near the back of the field, particularly in the younger age groups.

A week later I find myself watching a race at Chris Cheboiboch's school, Salaba Academy. Again the same pattern is evident: the children wearing shoes are all at the back of the field. I seem to be the only one noticing it. Whenever I point it out to people, they smile and say 'Oh, yes, how funny' as though it's a quirky coincidence. They don't seem to make the connection, that running barefoot could actually be a key part of the Kenyan secret.

But the evidence is mounting. At one training camp in Iten, a top marathon runner tells me that when he was at school his parents had a bit of money so they bought him some running shoes. But the children without shoes kept beating him, so he took his off and started winning the races.

Ironically, the prize for the winners at Chris's school race is a pair of running shoes. It's as if the organisers not only don't appreciate the benefits of barefoot running, but see it as some kind of disadvantage. It seems ridiculous to be giving the fastest runner in each race something to help him run which, on the face of the evidence in front of us, will only slow him down. In one race, the further back in the field the girls finish, the better their shoes, to the absurd extent that the girl with the newest, sleekest running shoes of all comes in last, while the girl whose shoes are only slightly worse finishes second to last. Each time, the runners without shoes seem light and graceful, while those with trainers on seem to be plodding, burdened by heavy weights tied to their feet.

At the cross-country race in Iten a few weeks before, the junior girls' winner, Faith Kipyegon, tried on a pair of running spikes for the first time.

'They felt uncomfortable,' she said. 'Even though they were very elegant, they felt very heavy to run in.' So she stuck to what she knew best, and ran in bare feet. She won. A few months later she would go on to win the world cross-country championships, also barefoot. To Faith, used to running barefoot, even running spikes, the lightest shoes imaginable, seemed heavy.

Despite the recent boom in barefoot running in the West, it is not a new idea. In 1962, a young Briton called Bruce Tulloh won the European 5,000m title running without shoes on. The same Bruce Tulloh who would later train the Kenyan national team in the run-up to the 1972 Olympics. I met him just before leaving for Kenya and asked him why he chose to run barefoot.

'I ran a lot on grass tracks in those days and it was just much easier in bare feet. I could adapt more quickly to changes in the uneven surface. Also, when I ran barefoot, I had a shorter stride and a faster leg turnover.'

Tulloh agreed to be a guinea pig for Dr Griffiths Pugh, a leading exercise physiologist of the time. 'He managed to plot a straight-line relationship between the weight of the shoe and the energy cost of running,' said Tulloh.

Few men have looked as closely at the phenomenon of Kenyan running as the sports scientist Dr Yannis Pitsiladis, from the University of Glasgow, who has spent the last ten years trying to work out what it is that makes East African runners so good. Across many trips to Kenya and Ethiopia he has become close friends with many of the athletes and is now a visiting professor at both Moi University in Eldoret and Addis Ababa University in Ethiopia.

Yannis was recently asked by the great Ethiopian runner and marathon world record holder Haile Gebrselassie[1] to give a seminar on how to get a human to run under two hours for the marathon. He went through a whole predictive lecture on what would be required, and one thing he thought would help would be if someone such as Haile, who had not run with shoes until he was in his late teens, didn't move on to shoes but remained barefoot.

Even Haile, Yannis says, couldn't now run a marathon barefoot if he wanted to because his feet had become used to running in shoes. But he says that if he put him on a treadmill without his shoes on and measured his oxygen uptake, he's confident from his previous studies that he would be at

---

1 Haile Gebrselassie's marathon world record of 2:03:59 was broken by the Kenyan Patrick Makau on 25 September 2011, when he won the Berlin marathon in 2:03:38.

least 5 per cent more economical than with his shoes on.

But surely someone running a marathon barefoot on concrete roads would be risking injury?

'These kids we study in Kenya,' Yannis retorts, 'the soles of their feet are as strong as any shoes. They can walk on glass and it doesn't hurt.'

As well as being lighter, Yannis says that running barefoot gives you stronger feet, which allows you to train harder with less chance of getting injured.

Yet if running barefoot is such a clear advantage, why do all the adult athletes in Kenya run in trainers? It's an interesting conundrum. Abebe Bikila, from Ethiopia, broke the world record on his way to winning the 1960 Olympic marathon, running barefoot through the streets of Rome. But in Tokyo four years later, he won the gold medal and broke the world record again, this time wearing shoes. So was he better off with shoes or without them?

The biggest advantage running barefoot gives you is that it forces you to adopt a better running style. Without shoes on, all the senses in your feet are suddenly activated, and your inbuilt running software, developed over millions of years, is switched on. You instinctively start to control your impact on the ground, landing lightly on your feet. You quickly learn that the energy you put into the ground will return and propel you on. I've seen it happen, to me. It really works. The problem for those of us not used to it is that our feet are soft, our arches are flat, and the muscles we need to run like this, both in our feet and in our calves, are out of shape. If we try it, we're likely to end up with sore feet and calves after even a short run.

So we have to start slowly. Barefoot shoes can help protect the soles of our feet from abrasions, but we still need to start with short, gentle runs. It takes time, and we lose fitness. But if we stick at it, our muscles will strengthen, and our style will start to change. And as our foot muscles strengthen, our arches will rise. Arches are like springs, and the higher they are, the more spring we have in our step.

It's interesting to note, in trying to determine how much of a factor all this can be, that Kenya's dominance is greater in one particular event than any other: the steeplechase. This is a 3,000m track race where the runners have to hurdle five 91cm barriers on each lap, including one with a pool of water on the other side. To be good at this event you clearly need to have good springs in your feet, probably more so than in any other event. Yet despite the fact that there are virtually no facilities to practise steeplechase in Kenya and very little steeplechase-specific coaching, Kenyans have won every single men's steeplechase Olympic gold medal since 1968 (except for the two Olympics Kenya boycotted, in 1976 and 1980).

Once you have it, bounce and good running form are not lost the minute you put on conventional running shoes. So the Kenyans may wear shoes, but they're still running in what would be called a 'barefoot style'. Essentially, the key advantages of barefoot running are retained.

Lee Saxby, who taught me to run barefoot, said the Kenyans wore shoes so they didn't hurt themselves standing on sharp stones. The roads in Kenya are made of dirt, but every now and then you land on a stone half-buried in the ground and it can really hurt – my two sprained toe injuries testify to that (and I was wearing trainers). But that's not a reason to ditch the shoes completely. You could still do what people like Bruce Tulloh did and run barefoot in races and when the conditions underfoot were conducive to it, such as in track races and on grassy cross-country courses. But it is rare to see a top Kenyan runner racing anywhere without shoes on. Tulloh tells me that during his time in Kenya he sometimes ran races in bare feet.

'I was the only one,' he says. 'They all just thought I was a crazy mzungu.'

One reason the adult runners give for wearing big shoes is to make their training harder. One runner tells me they always look for the biggest, heaviest trainers they can find.

'Then, when you put on your racing flats, you feel so light,' he says, as though it's a magic trick.

But why do they even want to wear racing flats? According to Nicholas Leong, a cycling coach based in Iten, the real reason is cultural.

'Kenyans have too much respect for Europeans,' he says. 'They don't have enough confidence in their culture to say, you know, I've grown up running barefoot, I've been winning races, I'll keep running barefoot.'

Nicholas is from Singapore. A sports fan, he says he remembers watching as gradually more and more black athletes began to flourish in sport after sport.

'I remember the first black footballers in England,' he says. 'Then you had the dominance of the African runners. Then the Williams sisters in tennis, and even Tiger Woods in golf.' But Nicholas was a cycling nut.

'It never happened in cycling,' he says. 'To this day, there has never been a single black rider in the Tour de France.[1] I thought to myself, if no one is doing anything about this, then I will.' He decided the best place to start would be Kenya. If they were so good at running, he thought, then perhaps they would be good at cycling too.

He hatched a mad plan to find the Kenyan runners. He booked himself a flight to Nairobi on the same night as the Singapore marathon, figuring that some top Kenyan runners would be on the plane. Sure enough, as he waited to board, he saw a group of Africans in running kit milling around. He went over and asked them if they'd just run the marathon. They had.

'Who won?' he asked. One of the men grinned as the others pointed him out.

'Where do you live?' Nicholas asked the man, who said he lived in Eldoret.

'Do you mind if I come home with you?'

He eventually ended up in Iten, where he started a cycling team. To recruit his cyclists he tried some unusual tactics. One was to place a sign at the bottom of the Kerio Valley offering a prize of 200,000 Kenyan shillings (about three times the average Kenyan's annual income) to anyone who could cycle 25 km up the road to Iten 4,000 feet above in under 1 hour 8 minutes. Only one man ever achieved it, but Nicholas signed up anyone who came close, giving them a good

---

1 In 2011, a few months after I spoke with Nicholas, France's Yohann Gène became the first black cyclist ever to compete in the Tour de France.

monthly salary and board and lodging while they followed his training programme.

'In the past people have looked at African cycling and said, the big problem is that they don't have the right bikes.' Nicholas has the harassed look of a prospector, as though he's in a race to find the golden formula that will produce Kenyan cyclists on a par with the Kenyan runners.

'There are so few things from Africa that generate such genuine awe, fear, unreserved respect, like a Kenyan runner on the start line of a marathon,' he says. 'It is such an achievement. We need to tap into that.'

Instead of tapping into it, of empowering them, though, he says giving them brand-new bikes makes them helpless.

'Here we have guys straight from the shamba who can hit 5.8 watts per kilo. That's cycling talk, but trust me, that's good. That's the same power as a top cyclist. Yet you give them a new bike, and they don't know what to do with it. They don't know how to use it, so they feel helpless. You're imposing a European system on them. You're saying, right, now you should do what we say. And it simply doesn't work.'

It's just like giving them shoes to run in, he says.

In the short time I've been in Kenya I've been frequently taken aback by the levels of respect we've been afforded simply because of the colour of our skin. At every event we've been to we've been immediately afforded VIP status and given the best seats to sit in. Sitting in the sun in the Run Fast camp that afternoon, one of the athletes told me that Kenyans needed European coaches and managers 'because you have more brains than us. We need to learn from you.'

At one school I visited, the head teacher started telling the children about all the great things the British had done, and about how the British had brought civilisation to Kenya. It's a view I hear frequently, when I was expecting the opposite, that the British had stolen their lands and destroyed their cultures.

So when Westerners turn up and see their bare feet and think, oh, look at the poor kids running around without shoes on, we must do something to help them, the Kenyans, too, begin to believe that running barefoot must be wrong, or inferior. Something to frown upon. Ironically, they see the Western runners wearing shoes, and want to emulate them.

'Have you spoken to Brother Colm yet?' Nicholas asks me. 'Briefly,' I nod. 'Has he done his Yoda thing on you?' I'm not sure what his Yoda thing is, but I don't think so. 'When he talks about feeling the earth through your feet?' Nicholas says Brother Colm is the only coach who gets his athletes to train and do drills barefoot. This is a man with no European coaching experience, a man who works prin-cipally with youngsters, a man who says he learned all he knows 'from watching the athletes'. He is also one of Kenya's most successful coaches. I make a note to ask him about it the next time I see him.

11

Boy: Do not try and bend the spoon. That's impossible.
    Instead . . . only try to realise the truth.
Neo: What truth?
Boy: There is no spoon.
    The Matrix

So here at the Nike-sponsored cross-country race in Eldoret, barefoot children streak away at the front of each race. In the girls' under-twelve race, the first two runners across the line are not only barefoot but are wearing frilly silk dresses. They are quite a sight, sprinting away at the front in their Sunday best outfits, like two shaven-headed Cinderellas racing home after midnight. It obviously isn't a marketing ploy – they probably didn't have anything else to wear – but the scouts at Nike seem to like it, as the winner is one of the two athletes 'discovered' on the day and invited to train at Dr Rosa's camp in nearby Kaptagat. She collects her award wearing the event's free Nike T-shirt pulled on over her dress. She stares ahead throughout the ceremony, looking more annoyed than anything, as photographers snap pictures and dignitaries hand her bits of paper. When it's over, she scuttles away into the crowd.

The races tick slowly by: under-fourteen boys and girls, junior boys and girls . . . my race is the last one. To register to run I have to join a long queue of athletes. They all have the bearing of serious runners. I couldn't feel more out of place, with my pasty white skin, shaggy beard and my few excess pounds of fat. Not for the first time since I arrived in Kenya, I have to ask myself what on earth I am doing. It is like I keep volunteering to fly an aeroplane, only realising once I'm at the controls that I don't have a clue what to do.

The longest queue of athletes is at the table for the under-twenty junior boys' race. Kenyan runners seem to take a flexible approach to age, basing the category they enter more on how they feel their career is progressing than how old they are. 'I'll run the 12 km [senior race] when I'm ready. Maybe next year,' many of them tell me, despite the fact that they are openly in their mid-twenties.

The officials take a slightly different view, however, and it is someone's job to walk along the line and pull out people who look too old.

Once I've registered, I head back to the grandstand. Ossian has dragged Marietta up to the highest seats, which are empty, to play with his toy cars. Uma says she is hungry, but there's nowhere to buy any food. Lila's sitting on Godfrey's lap, pulling him around while he tries to talk with his old running friends. When I sit down, she clambers across on to my lap instead. Then Uma starts handing from my neck, telling me she wants to go home. It isn't ideal preparation for my race.

Finally the time comes for me to start warming up. I take off my tracksuit and hand it to Marietta. The girls look concerned.

'Wish me luck,' I say and trot off to the start.

Behind the start area, hundreds of athletes are jogging around in a large circle, like a parade ring. I slip in and join them. The hot sun is already making me sweat. I feel like a carthorse that has somehow wandered into the wrong en-closure.

Someone is talking about me. I can tell because I hear the word 'mzungu'. I look over.

'Where are you from?' the runner asks. He's friendly really. He asks me how I'm hoping to run today. Flush with confi-dence, I tell him my aim is not to come last. To beat at least one person. He looks at me as he pins his number to his vest.

'I'm sure you can beat two,' he says.

Soon we're called over to the start. I try to hide at the back, out of the way of the impending stampede, but one of the organisers walking along the line spots me. It's not hard.

'Yes, my friend,' he says, as a hundred faces turn to look at me. 'Where are you from?'

'England,' I say. He's writing it down.

'And what is your name?'

'Finn,' I say – it's just easier.

'Vin?'

I spell it out for him.

'F for Freddy. I. N. N.' He writes it down.

'And?' He wants another name. OK, you asked for it.

'Adharanand.'

My parents were hippies in the early 1970s when I came into the world. They followed a thirteen-year-old guru from India called Maharaji and, getting swept up in the peace and love swirling around them, they named me Adharanand. It means Eternal Bliss in Sanskrit.

The organiser looks at me, mock-startled, when I say my name, and then puts the pen away without writing anything down. It gets him a few laughs. A few minutes later I hear the PA announcing that Finn from England is here racing today. If only they knew how good I was.

I don't hear the starting pistol, but suddenly we're off. My plan is to stick at the very back of the field, but it's as though I've been shot and I'm falling backwards through the air as they all charge off. I'm sprinting, trying to stay upright, but it's no good. It's like a bad dream where your legs won't move.

At the first corner there's a lot of congestion in front of me, so I manage to catch up with the tail end of the field. As we head past the stand for the first time I'm nicely tucked in. There are almost 400 runners ahead of me, but I'm sure some people have started too fast and that I'll soon begin picking them off. But it's me who has started too fast, and soon I'm struggling to stay with anyone. I battle to keep up with an elderly man in front of me, but he's too strong and I'm soon drifting on my own. I think there's a runner behind me, but everyone else is disappearing into the distance.

The course is six laps of a route that doubles back on itself constantly so that people watching can see nearly the whole race. Once we get to the only part of the course where there are no spectators, I find myself running past about fifteen athletes standing around looking at each other sheepishly. They've all dropped out already, after less than a mile. If I can just keep going, I'll have beaten them at least.

The crowd that lines most of the route watches me pass in silence. Have I shocked them into dumbness with my ineptitude? I get the odd patter of applause, for trying I presume, and hear the odd muttering of 'mzungu', but otherwise it's just faces watching. I try to focus on my running, but I'm not feeling great. My legs are heavy, sinking into the dirt that seems to get softer with each step. I don't know if I'm running heel or forefoot first. I don't care. Near the end of the first lap I try to swallow and nearly get sick. This is going to be a long race.

I trundle on in a blur. The soft dirt, the watching faces, the fluttering of the tape marking the course. I keep hearing the word 'mzungu'. People seem to be laughing. Someone somewhere says 'Finn'. I raise my hand to thank whoever it was.

Halfway around the third lap the leaders hurtle by to lap me. One after another after another after another they fly by. It makes me feel even slower. I'm sure people are laughing now. There's a fine line between humbling and humiliating, and I think I've just crossed it.

As we pass the stand for the third time I see Marietta and the children watching. They look concerned. I'm still only halfway around, but I'm finding it hard to will myself on. It's too easy to stop. I've seen enough. I wave both hands as though something is wrong. It's not me, it's the engine. I jog to the side and sit down. I'm dropping out.

It feels blissful to just sit on the grass. I pull off my shoes and socks, releasing my feet. They look so white. I watch as a slow runner struggles past among all the charging athletes. Then another, a man who must be in his seventies. So there were two runners behind me. But they're still going. Suddenly I feel bad. My body feels fine now. I could have kept going. I briefly contemplate joining in again. I could even run barefoot. But it's too late. The two runners are gone, off on their weary way. I hoist myself up and walk back to the stand. People smile at me as I sit down.

'Thank you for trying our race,' says one man. I can't answer, so I just shrug and shake my head. 'Next time you will do it,' he says.

My sense of failure is tempered slightly when I later find out that the three-time London marathon winner Martin Lel finished in 33rd position, and the reigning 1500m Olympic champion, Asbel Kiprop, like me, dropped out. That's some serious competition.

After the race I sit with Marietta and the children in the venue's clubhouse eating chips. The Kenyan version of MTV plays quietly on the screen in the corner.

'Dad,' Uma asks me, with one eye on the TV, 'did you win?'

Just over a year ago, in England, I did win a race. But here in Kenya's Rift Valley, things are very different. I feel as though I've fallen into a cultural chasm, and it's one that right now I'm not sure I can get across. In England, running is largely a hobby, practised gamely by enthusiasts who squeeze in training runs where they can amongst all the other things in their lives. A handful of people dotted here and there take it more seriously, training regularly, turning out on freezing winter mornings for races with their local athletics club. But here in Kenya, anyone who can run dedicates their life to it. And that dedication seems to be spreading. There are more training camps than ever before. More runners. All pushing each other, training harder, every single day. Here, athletics is like a religion. On the way to the race, Marietta commented that in such a fervently Christian place, it didn't seem a good idea holding the race on a Sunday. But it didn't stop thousands of people from turning out, arriving in busloads from the surrounding villages, both to run and to watch.

In a land where running is so revered, my goals of running a marathon, or beating my personal best times, seem feeble and half-hearted. Here people are running to change their lives. To feed their families. To break world records.

'I'm not sure this is going to work,' I say to Marietta. 'I'm too out of my depth.'

She looks at me. We both know I'm just looking for some reassurance. It has been a tough day. 'You've only just started,' she says. 'You just have to give yourself a chance. You never thought you were going to win. You came here to learn from the Kenyans, not beat them.'

Of course I can't give up. I've come too far for that. Running is a simple activity. Just lace up your shoes and go, one step at a time, like each breath. But the question is, where do I go from here?

12

Ask yourself, 'Can I give more?' The answer is usually 'Yes.'
Paul Tergat, Kenyan athlete

After the race in Eldoret I decide I need to ratchet up my training. I'm still in my old mindset, training every other day, treating running as a side activity. I need a dose of Kenyan dedication. That's what I came here for. But the weeks are ticking by. I call Godfrey up.

'Godfrey, we need to organise a run with the Lewa team. The marathon is in a few months.' But he's already onto it.

'I know, Finn,' he says. 'That's just what I was thinking. We need to do a long run this Saturday. 30 km. I've already spoken to Chris, and Shadrack says he will come. You just need to tell Japhet.'

To get myself ready for the long team run, I decide to brave Iten's weekly fartlek session. The other runners have been telling me about it for weeks.

Every Thursday morning in Iten, all the various groups and training camps come together in one huge force of runners. A common form of training around the world, fartlek involves alternating fast bursts of running with slow recovery jogs. It comes from a Swedish word and means 'speed play'. For most of the athletes it is one of the week's toughest sessions.

'Daddy, where are you going?' Uma asks me as I lace up my trainers. The sun is streaming in through the garden doors. Flora is ladling out the porridge into bowls on the table. Usually I'm back from my run at this time, but the fartlek sessions don't start until a leisurely nine o'clock.

'I'm going running,' I say.

'Why?' she asks. It's a good question, but right now, just before a run, is not the best moment to try to answer it. Right before you head out running, it can be hard to remember exactly why you're doing it. You often have to override a nagging sense of futility, lacing up your shoes, telling yourself that no matter how unlikely it seems, after you finish you will be glad you went. It's only afterwards that it makes sense, although even then it's hard to rationalise why. You just feel right. After a run, you feel at one with the world, as though some unspecified, innate need has been fulfilled.

'Because it's fun,' I say. She smiles. It's an answer that makes sense to her. Fun is always a good reason to do something.

It takes me twenty minutes just to jog to the start of the 'speed play', at the bottom of a long hill heading out of Iten along the edge of the escarpment. All along the way, people emerge running from side streets, shops, doorways, joining the flow of runners, all going the same way, to the same starting point as though we're part of some mass celebration. By the time I get there, two hundred or so runners are gathered, milling around, chatting. The men stand to one side of the road while the few women that have turned up stand quietly on the other side. I walk into the crowd as it edges its way across to the start. Long skinny legs. An array of faded colours, rustling jackets, T-shirts. Then everything goes quiet. A team leader of some sort is standing up on a mound explaining the day's session to the runners like some biblical preacher. Even if I could speak Kalenjin, I can't hear what he is saying from all the way at the back. Someone tells me it's 'twenty-five one one'. That means we jog for a minute, then run hard for a minute, twenty-five times.

Before I know it, the floodgates have opened and I'm being carried off down the dusty road into the countryside. The pace is easy, for a minute. I'm jogging along in what feels like a sea of runners, people bobbing around in front of me like I'm heading into choppy waters.

By the sides, up on the banked earth, farm workers stand taking a break, watching us pass. It feels like it should be an incongruous sight, this huge mass of Lycra-clad runners streaming by amid the hand-ploughed fields and mud huts of this rural African outpost. Things seem even more unlikely when two hundred watches start beeping simultaneously. But here in Iten, it's the most natural thing in the world.

The watches set everyone off like wound-up toys being released, zipping and flying away. I attempt to keep up, working my arms, trying to find the smoothest part of the track to run along. But I'm rapidly slipping backwards, runners nipping past me on both sides.

A minute later the scattering of beeps catches the galloping herd, pulling it to a halt. As the group slows to a jog, it begins to bunch up again. A few stragglers like me have become detached already. Behind me there are others: mostly, if not all, women, their arms working side to side, trying to catch back up.

But it's a cruel game. Before we can make contact again

with the group, the swarm of watches goes off, and the main group is gone, stringing its way out along the distant track.

At the back, we team up in twos and threes, for support. I find myself running next to a tall girl with short hair. I hope she doesn't mind me running next to her.

'I don't have a watch,' I say, by way of explanation.

'Three – two – one – up,' she says, and we're off again.

I must be the only runner here without a watch. Before I came to Kenya, I had naively imagined everyone racing along without a thought for anything as controlling and analytical as a stopwatch. It would just be them and the open road, I thought, their bare feet pounding on effortlessly, the wind in their hair. It turns out that's not the case.

However, while in the West we time everything so that we can measure and analyse it afterwards, or keep track of what pace we're running, so we can calculate whether we need to slow down or speed up, Kenyans use their watches in a completely different way.

In their daily life, most Kenyans are fairly relaxed about time. If someone arranges to meet you somewhere at 2 p.m., it's always a loose arrangement. There's little point pacing around at 2.05 p.m. wondering what can have happened. But when it comes to running, Kenyans are as punctual as the well-oiled cogs of Big Ben. If they say a run will start at 6.10 a.m., you will miss it if you arrive at 6.11 a.m.

By running their intervals according to the regimented beeps of their watches, Kenyans are actually taking the thinking and analysis out of their running. When the watch beeps, they speed up. When it beeps again, they slow down.

Although they say they are doing twenty-five sets of intervals, in reality they just run on, speeding up and slowing down, until they get to the end of the route. Afterwards, no one could honestly tell you how many intervals he had run. Nobody keeps a training log or adds up their weekly mileage. Each session is forgotten as soon as it is done. The timing is just a way of structuring the training, of telling them when to start and when to stop.

When Kenyans do hill training, again, they run up and down for a set amount of time, usually an hour. This saves them having to count the number of hills they've run, which may not sound that difficult, but as you get tired your brain becomes easily addled. I've often done hill sessions on my own and even by the third one I'm struggling to remember how many I've done. I have to keep repeating the number over and over to myself, which can get tiring. Having a watch doing the counting means you can just run, unthinking, back and forth, up and down, until the beeps tell you to stop.

'In the West we break it all down and analyse everything,' says Brother Colm when I track him down again, standing on the playing fields at St Patrick's High School watching David Rudisha going through his warm-up routine. 'But sometimes by doing that you lose the bigger picture. Kenyans might wear watches, but they're not using them to analyse their training. They just take it as they see it. It's a simpler approach.'

Most of the athletes in Kenya follow virtually the same training schedule. Toby Tanser told me it was set up by Bruce Tulloh when he was in Kenya in the early 1970s. Other people date it back further to the British system of the colonial days. An integral part of the schedule is the regular

6 a.m. run. I often ask the athletes why they always have to start at 6 a.m. when it's still dark. If they waited even thirty minutes, it would be light and they would be able to see.

'It is best to run early' is all they can say, laughing when I try to debate the point.

Accepting the schedule, rather than questioning it, makes things simpler. They don't have to lie in bed trying to convince themselves to get up in the morning. At 5.45 a.m. when their alarm goes, like a barking sergeant major, they just get up and, like disciplined soldiers, they run.

Even if it is just a slow jog, the routine needs to be kept. 'If you train hard all the time,' Brother Colm tells me, 'your body will become tense at the thought of training. But if sometimes you go easy, then your body becomes more accepting. Then when the time comes to push, you are ready. It is easier.'

Of course, you don't break world records, like Rudisha has done, without some analysis and careful thought going into your training. But this process is usually kept from the athletes.

'I might spot something in his training that needs changing,' says Brother Colm, 'but I won't discuss it with Rudisha. I'll just alter the training a bit without him knowing.' For those without a coach, it is the watch that does all the thinking.

'Three – two – one – up,' says my companion, and we're off again, her watch beeping along.

Eventually we catch up with groups of people walking slowly along the road like stunned survivors making their way from the scene of some terrible catastrophe. All along the dusty road we pass people in sweaty T-shirts, leggings and running shoes, hands on hips, not talking. They've all finished the fartlek, it seems, and are walking the rest of the way back to Iten.

My companion doesn't stop, though.

'Three – two – one – up,' she says as her watch beeps again. We weave through the bodies, that turn to watch us, the mzungu and the girl, still going.

Up the final hill back into Iten I drop back. She is too strong. The altitude still zaps me when I try to run up hills. At the top, she stops and I catch up. She's walking now. That must be the end.

'*Asante sana*,' I say, shaking her hand, catching a glimpse of her face for the first time. She looks young, still a teenager. I wonder if she would like to join our Lewa team. She's about the same speed as me.

'Do you run marathons?' I ask. Her eyes skirt away when I talk, looking down at the ground. I feel like I'm crossing some forbidden barrier. I'm being too friendly.

'No, track and field,' she says. Others, intrigued, are walking next to us now. They're looking hard at me, as though trying to fathom whether I'm real. We walk in silence the rest of the way back into town. The sun is hot on the back of my neck. I'm tired, but still standing, my first fartlek session done.

13

If one could run without getting tired, I don't think one would
often want to do anything else.

C. S. Lewis

'It's like we're going to war,' jokes Godfrey as we pile out
from the back of the pick-up truck and start stripping down
to our shorts and T-shirts. Marietta is scooting around taking photographs, while the children watch sleepy-eyed from
the truck cab, piles of water bottles on their laps, a bunch of
bananas up on the dashboard.

We're about to set off on our first Lewa marathon group
training run. We're now officially the Iten Town Harriers.
The rest of the team didn't fully join in the debate about
choosing the name, looking at me blankly as I offered up a
number of alternatives. They liked them all, they said. Godfrey tried to humour me and get involved, but his sugges-
tions, the Iten Runners, or the Iten Warriors, were made
tentatively.

It was like asking hardened farmers what colour they
would like the handles of their shovels. These were serious
runners and I was drifting into the territory of fun running,
coming up with team names. Next I'd be asking them what
colour vests we should wear.

In the end I made that decision by myself: yellow.

Secretly, I'm amazed this team run is happening at all.
The night before, Godfrey rang me to say the truck he was

hoping to borrow was being used by someone else, but that Chris was going to find another one. I get nervous when Chris is organising things. He is always telling me to relax and to trust him the whole time. But good as his word, the black gates to our house swing open at 6 a.m. and a big, shiny pick-up truck comes waltzing through, a grinning Godfrey at the wheel, Chris running in after him having opened the gate.

The truck actually belongs to a top runner called Isaac Songok, one of Brother Colm's athletes. He needs it back by 9 a.m., so we've got to get moving.

Our newest team member, Shadrack, has come all the way from Kamwosor for the run, travelling to Iten the night before. It's a big effort for a training run. Godfrey tells me that Shadrack has been running with David Barmasai. The two have been best friends since they were children. However, Barmasai has just won both the Nairobi marathon and the Dubai marathon, one of the richest races in the world, where he collected over $250,000 in prize money. Shadrack, I suspect, is feeling a little left behind.

'But they say Barmasai can't keep up with him in training,' Godfrey tells me.

If that's true, then he has huge potential. It's exciting having him on our team, although I can tell that Chris is less thrilled. He nods towards him, looking at me for an explanation. 'Godfrey knows him,' I say. 'He says he's good.'

'Ah-kay,' he says, in that clipped way he does it when he's not entirely happy.

The two runners shake hands, not saying anything to each other. All around us, Iten is waking up, stretching and yawning in the yellow glow of morning. Godfrey gives us a little pep talk.

'No racing,' he says. 'Take it nice and easy for the first 15 km and then push on. I'll be in the truck with water and I'll give you your splits every 5 km. Everyone OK? Japhet, you OK?' Japhet grins at being singled out. 'Finn, ready?' I nod. 'OK, let's go.'

The plan is to run 30 km, although I'll be happy if I can keep with them until 15 km. Marietta, Flora and the children are to ride with Godfrey in the truck.

We set off at a gentle pace (we go through the first 5 km in 24 minutes), and I run at the head of the group with Chris. We follow the path that runs along beside the main road, down and up and out of town towards Eldoret. My legs are feeling fresh after a massage the day before, and I'm even able to chat with Chris as we run.

After about ten minutes the truck drives past us along the paved road, the children waving, Marietta crouched in the back snapping away like a war photographer.

'It's good how much support you have,' says Chris. 'Your whole family is here supporting you.'

Marietta later tells me how much she enjoyed coming along. I realise that through running I have been able to explore the surrounding countryside while she and the children have been largely confined to our compound and our tightly packed neighbourhood. We occasionally attempt to venture off further for a walk, but at every corner we are stopped by people wanting to chat to us, to shake hands with the children, or invite us home for tea. It's nice to feel so welcomed, but it means we rarely get very far.

Soon after the 5 km mark, the route turns off the main road and we head out through the lush patchwork of fields that surround Iten. The dirt road wanders gently through small homesteads, clusters of huts dotting the landscape like huge kilns. Occasionally a car or motorbike will come by in a cloud of red dust, beeping at us to get out of the way.

At 10 km Godfrey stops the truck and Lila and Uma hand out the water bottles, which we grab on the run as Godfrey shouts out that we've completed the last 5 km in 22 minutes. Things are speeding up.

'Keep it up,' says Godfrey. 'Finn, you're looking strong. Just maintain. Maintain.' He's a good coach.

'Where's Chris?' We look around, but he's not in sight. We carry on running, hitting a long hill that rises up through fields back to the main road. I push on. Although I struggle with the hills out here, I've decided the best approach is to attack them. If I give in to them and slow down, they grind me into the ground, sucking at my legs until I'm shuffling like a dead weight on sticks.

If I shoot up them, I'm past before they get a chance to grab me. Of course, it's a risky strategy. If the hill is too long, it wakes up while I'm only halfway there, spying me with a wry grin, and then, as though it has tipped up suddenly against me, I'm done for.

But today I'm feeling fine and I lead the charge up the hill, passing my water bottle to Shadrack as we go. He keeps coughing and blowing his nose as we run, and sweating hard. He doesn't seem, right now, like a Lewa champion.

At the top of the hill I spot Tom Payn, the British marathon runner, chugging along behind his pacemaker. We're like busy trains heading this way and that, runners crossing the endless network of roads and tracks.

On we run, over the main road and into the countryside on the other side. Behind us we hear the quick patter of feet. We all glance behind as, without a word, Chris comes past. We follow on, close to him, but the pace has increased. I don't know if Chris is trying to assert his authority, but suddenly the talking and joking stops.

The route seems to be heading slightly downhill, so the pace has no chance to slacken. Josphat, who is running up at the front with Chris, beckons me to take his place on the front line. I oblige, but we're really on the charge now. I'm not sure how long I can keep this up. Chris turns to me with a grin.

'You OK?' he asks.

Surprisingly, I am. I'm quite enjoying the new pace, even. But I feel as though I'm pushing my luck. Chris's question sends doubts, excuses pinging around in my head. Before I've fully made the decision, I'm blurting out: 'I'm just going to run 15K.'

'Sure,' says Chris. I feel like I've given him the answer he was expecting. 'We're nearly at 15K,' he says. 'Just two more corners.'

I should go on, but the pronouncement has been made. Once you decide where you're going to stop, it takes a reckless surge of energy to overrule yourself. You've done enough, I tell myself, you've kept up this far. This is just a first run. Reasons, reasons, reasons. The decision is final. Up ahead I see the truck stopped at the 15 km point.

'I'm stopping here,' I announce, just to be clear, as I move into a sprint. I hear a few chuckles as I leave them behind for a moment, charging to little Lila who is running to meet me with a bottle of water.

It feels good to stop. The others run past, and on, following the dusty road disappearing into some trees.

'That last 5 km was just under 20 minutes,' Godfrey tells me. 'That's fast.' It's not bad, but I can't help feeling I bailed out too early. I clamber into the open back of the truck and sit down on the spare tyre next to Uma.

Godfrey starts the car and we drive on to catch up with the others. About two miles further on we see Chris walking along the track. He hops into the back of the truck.

'I twisted my ankle,' he says.

'Does it hurt?'

'No, man. It's fine,' he says, giving me his million-dollar smile. 'I just didn't want to push it.'

As we pass the others, Godfrey holds out their water as he drives along beside them. 'Time to push,' he says. 'Just 5 km to go.' They're flying now. Little Japhet is hanging on, his ripped shoes almost falling apart on him as his feet pound back and forth.

Along the last stretch, Shadrack, the young buck, pushes on, but Japhet matches him stride for stride. Josphat, to Chris's annoyance, starts to drop off the pace.

'Come on, Josphat,' he says. He turns to us giggling. 'Josphat is too slow,' he says.

A few minutes later and they're done. We gather by the truck as they catch their breath. Godfrey hands out bananas while Marietta, getting into her role as the official team photographer, gets us to line up beside the truck for a group photograph. Then we jog the last 1 km back to Iten for a warm-down. Inspired by watching the run, or perhaps just fed up with sitting in the truck, Lila joins us, skipping along up and down the banks at the side of the road like the Kenyan children on their way to school.

By the end she's feeling very pleased with herself, her face beaming as Chris lifts her back into the truck. Godfrey drops us all off back in Iten and we head our separate ways, resolving to meet up again for another group run in a few weeks. The Iten Town Harriers, it seems, are up and running.

Later on that afternoon, Chris arrives at my house with a friend. A few days before, he called me to ask if there was a prize at Lewa for the first masters runner (one who is over forty years old). It turns out there is, for the first three over-forty finishers, though it doesn't say on the forms what the prizes are. Never mind, Chris has found a runner who, unlike him, is officially over forty, and he wants him on the team. As I've offered to pay the entry and accommodation for everyone, I'm concerned about the rising costs, so I tell him I think we've got enough runners already. With Shadrack, we're five. That's a good number. But, as Godfrey would say: 'You know Chris.'

I open the gate and he slinks his car in. He gets out, wearing a neatly pressed shirt. The children, getting to know him now, run over and give him a hug. Another man gets out the other door.

'This is Philip,' says Chris. 'The masters runner I told you about.'

'Hi,' I say. He has a friendly face.

'Hi,' he says.

It turns out Philip is actually fifty-one, but due to the usual Kenyan age-stretching techniques, he's officially only forty-two. Still, it's old enough to put him in with a shout of winning a prize.

'You going to run Lewa with us?' I ask.

'Yes,' he says, watching me closely. Philip has run around fifty marathons, many of them in Europe, and has a best time of 2 hours 8 minutes. He's an experienced man. It'll be good to have him around.

'Do you need any more runners?' Chris asks me, as though I'm collecting them. Still, I'm thinking it might be good for balance to have a woman on the team. Someone not too fast, who I can keep up with perhaps.

'Maybe a woman?' I suggest.

'OK,' he says, thoughtfully, nodding his head. I realise it's a done deal. He'll find me someone.

14

The little space within the heart is as great as the vast universe.
  The Upanishads

'How are you?' a small voice somewhere calls out. It's a sound we're used to now, a childish, precise call, with all the stress on the 'you'. It's a greeting, not a question. There's no expectation of an answer. Ossian is the only one who still reacts, running out the doors to look up the garden towards the gate. The flap is open and a little face peers in. 'How are you?' it calls.

'Somebody here,' says Ossian, chugging back into the house.

'Why don't you see who it is?' Marietta suggests to Lila and Uma. But they're not interested. They carry on with their game, ignoring her. All the attention is becoming too much for them, and they are beginning to withdraw more and more from the world outside our garden fence. That is until the day Flora takes them both to the local salon to get braids put in their hair.

It has been both my daughters' dream, ever since they were old enough to entertain such dreams, to have long flowing locks like the Disney princesses in their books. Unfortunately, their hair grows very slowly, if at all. Sometimes it seems to be getting shorter. But once they hear that you can actually 'make' long hair, they want to know how. And more importantly, when.

So one bright morning we head out of our gate, along the dusty dirt road into town. Down a small backstreet, through a broken gap in a stick fence, we find a sign for Limo's hair salon. We duck through the gap and walk along a narrow track through what feels like someone's backyard, with an upturned bucket for washing and an empty clothes line. At the end of the track are three small salons arranged in a square. Small wooden benches, painted blue and yellow, sit outside. Doors with draped ribbons hanging across them. On the wall outside is a painted picture of a woman in hair braids. We pull back the ribbons in the first doorway and enter the salon. Inside, four women are sitting drinking tea and listening to a crackly radio playing Kalenjin music. They get very excited when they see us, asking the children to shake their hands and giggling when they refuse – Lila and Uma are too agog at the rows and rows of wigs and hair extensions to be greeting people.

The walls are covered in pictures of women with different hairstyles, as well as the obligatory portrait of Kenya's president. Despite the cabinets full of hair accessories, the salon doesn't have enough light brown extensions to do both Lila and Uma's hair, so they have to send someone out to buy more. The two girls sit down quietly on plastic chairs in front of cracked wall mirrors, looking around as we wait until a woman comes back with a plastic bag full of extensions.

'Right,' she says, handing them out to the other women, who pull up their chairs, and the plaiting begins. It takes four hours, with two women working on each head. Uma sits happily talking to herself in the mirror most of the time, but for Lila it all goes on too long. By the end she is crying and begging to be set free as four women work frantically on her to get it done.

'It's finished,' she says, looking at me all teary-eyed. 'Tell them it's finished.'

Despite the tears, they run home, bouncing along the path, desperate to show Marietta and Ossian. Flora and I watch them go. 'I think they like it,' says Flora.

From that day on, something changes. I don't know what it is about the braids, whether somehow this crossover with the local fashion has broken down some barrier, or whether they just feel invigorated to have long hair, but suddenly they want to play with the other children again. Every evening, from then on, when the other children come home from school, Lila and Uma rush out to meet them, skipping around in their flowing plaits. I have to wander along the rows of tiny wooden huts, ducking under washing lines, poking my head into lace-walled rooms, looking for the girls.

'Sorry, have you seen my daughters?'

I'll find them curled up on a velvet sofa with eight other children watching Catholic sermons on TV, or drinking tea and chatting away on someone's front step. They can be gone for hours.

They become particularly good friends with three girls from the neighbourhood, Maureen, Hilda and Brenda. Maureen is a livewire of a child with a little shock of electrified, fuzzy hair and a permanently mischievous grin. Every time I ask her how old she is, she gives me a different answer. Hilda and Brenda are sisters and, as far as I can work out, nieces of Japhet, who lives in the adjoining house. Brenda, who is twelve, is the eldest. Slow-moving and easily confused, she is always the last to arrive and the last to leave. Hilda, who is ten, is as bright as a pin and has taken a particular shine to Uma.

'When will they come to our school?' the three girls ask as they sit with Lila and Uma making passion fruit juice on the back step of our house. Between them they have virtually stripped the passion fruit plantation of its bounty, leaving the poor man who cultivated the plants with nothing left to sell at the market. He hasn't complained, but he has stopped coming so frequently.

'Would you like to go to school?' I ask my two daughters. They both nod at me, only half sure. Marietta is nervous about them going. We've seen classrooms in other schools, with up to a hundred children crammed in, sitting in long rows, learning by rote, repeating their lessons lifelessly. We've heard stories of children being beaten for getting low marks in a test, or for being two minutes late for class. We're not great advocates of school at the best of times. In England they go to a Steiner school, where formal learning doesn't even begin until age seven. 'And they'll be the centre of attention all the time,' Marietta says. She's right, it won't be easy for them. But it is part of community life here, and they seem to want to go. We decide they can try it for a day.

So a few days later, at 6 a.m., I wake the girls up for school. They packed their bags the night before and even laid out their clothes in anticipation, but as I pull back the curtains, Lila hoists the covers up over her head and says she doesn't want to go. Uma is already up and bustling around, getting dressed, saying 'Come on, Lila, I'm not scared.'

I promise Lila that I'll stay with her if she wants me to, and so at 7.30 a.m. we arrive at the gates of Sunrise Academy. Most of the children are already in school. A few late-comers, who can't be more than three or four years old, scuffle in behind us, staring as they go, their heads corkscrewing around as they pass us.

The head teacher comes out of his office to greet us. Hilda and Maureen emerge to take Lila and Uma off to their classroom to prepare for assembly. Another student brings over a couple of white plastic chairs for me and Marietta to sit on. Corrugated metal classrooms surround a small grassy square. From behind the closed doors comes the busy sound of chattering and laughter. Then the doors open and from everywhere children parade out into the square. I spot my children, two little blonde heads among the mêlée.

After the assembly, the children all return to their classrooms: windowless sheds, the light streaming in from gaps between the walls and the roof, pairs of wooden desks arranged in rows. Lila and Uma squeeze into small spaces on the benches between their friends. They seem fine, so we leave them unpacking their pencils and notebooks from their bags.

I return at lunchtime to see how they're doing. As I walk into the school, one of the eldest classes is lined up along one side of the small playing field. They all have their arms in the air and are kneeling down in front of their teacher, who has a big red stick under one arm. In unison, they chant out a chilling refrain: 'We will not fail again. We will not fail again.' Over and over.

I walk past them and into the courtyard, where the head teacher, the deputy and another teacher are sitting on plastic chairs in the sun. They have the slow, unhurried aspect of people who have been there a long time.

'How are they?' I ask.

'They're doing fine,' says the head teacher. 'They'll be out in a moment.' Lila is the first one out. She walks over to me looking a little dazed and buries her head in my jumper. Uma, however, is in the swirl of a big gang, trying to ignore me. She's the youngest in the class by about five years and all the other children are swooning around to look after her.

'Dad, I want to stay for lunch,' she says.

'OK.' But she's already gone, carried in the flow of children towards the lunch barn. The head teacher smiles happily.

'And you, Lila?' he asks. But Lila is burrowing deeper.

'You want to come home for lunch?' I ask her. I can feel the nod in my side.

On the way out we peek into the barn that houses the dining hall. Among the sea of black hair and grey uniforms bustling around sits a little blonde girl in a pale blue dress, her face flushed, a fork in one hand, laughing and joking with the other children. We leave her there and head home.

When we return after lunch, the other children bring Uma out of the classroom. She's crying and looks lost. She gives me a big hug as Lila slips back into the dark classroom, finds her desk and takes out her books.

Uma wants to come home. On the way out of the school, she holds my hand like a captive being led to freedom. I can feel the relief in her step, her voice, which gets almost giddy as we head out through the gates.

I don't go back to collect Lila until five o'clock. Rather than rush to me though, she walks straight past with Maureen, Brenda and Hilda. I end up following her home at a distance, trying not to cramp her style as she walks along holding hands with the others, her rucksack on her back. The people in Iten stand and watch as she walks by in the midst of the other children, just part of the gang, coming home after another day at school.

When she gets home, though, she collapses on the sofa, exhausted. Uma hovers around her intrigued to know what the rest of the day was like. But Lila looks shell-shocked and just stares straight ahead, not speaking. I get the feeling she will remember this day for many years to come.

Later that night as they sit in bed, I ask them if they'd like to go back to school again.

'Yes,' they both say. But they don't sound sure.

'Tomorrow?'

'Maybe not tomorrow,' they say.

A few days later, Chris's car is rolling back through my gates, this time with a woman athlete. She is in her early twenties and has just run a local half-marathon in 76 minutes, which is pretty fast for a race at altitude. She looks familiar as she gets out of the car. Her name is Beatrice. I ran with her on the track one day with the Run Fast camp. I seem to remember being able to keep up with her, which suggests she's not as fast as she says. Chris has her half-marathon time written down in pen on a scrap of paper, as though that's proof that she did it. But Beatrice has a winning smile, and is soon playing with the children on the grass and chatting to Marietta, already part of the team.

She tells us she has only been running for two years, and has never done a marathon before. She says she knows that the Lewa race is tough, but she's confident she can do well.

'Are you a runner, too?' she asks Marietta as we all sit down at the table.

'No,' says Marietta, holding up her hands, making it clear she won't be joining the running craze any time soon. 'I just like to watch.'

'You look like a runner. You should try,' Beatrice insists. 'You are slim. I think you would be good.'

Unlike most athletes, Beatrice didn't run at school. She says she didn't like running. After she finished primary school, at fifteen, she lived at home for the next five years, helping her mother.

'I was big,' she tells me one day as we sit facing the gas stove in her tiny house. 'This big,' she says, holding her hands out wide. Bored of sitting at home with her mother, she decided to follow her brother who had moved to Iten to become an athlete. She found a small room behind a noisy café. To get there you have to walk in through the café and out into the backyard. As well as a few wooden rooms, there is also a shed where they show English football matches and big running races on a screen.

One evening I sit there in the darkness, squashed on one of the long wooden benches between Japhet and Beatrice, watching the Boston marathon. Less than a month before he is found dead, Sammy Wanjiru is sitting on one of the benches in front of us, going wild along with everyone else as the Kenyan Geoffrey Mutai wins in 2 hours 3 minutes 2 seconds, the fastest marathon time ever run.

When she moved to Iten, Beatrice started running early in the morning, at 5 a.m. when it was still dark, so that people wouldn't see her. Slowly the weight started to drop off. Now, two years later, she's a 76-minute half-marathon runner (at least, that's what she says). She's still quite big compared to the typical Kenyan runner, but extremely slight by the usual parameters.

Despite her initial lack of promise, Beatrice's mother agreed to fund her running, giving her what little money she could to cover the cost of her rent – which is about £4 a month – her fuel and her food. There can't be many countries in the world where you can leave your poverty-stricken family saying that you want to become an athlete, spending most of your days resting and sleeping, and they will reply, great, let us give you the tiny amount we have to help you. But like their children, the parents in Kenya are aware of the bounty that running can bring.

Many people in Kenya mistakenly assume that all athletes are wealthy. One moderately successful runner told me that when he runs, children shout out to him 'Buy me a car'.

'Who has told them that just because I'm a runner, I'm rich?' he says. 'Where do they get that idea from?' But it's an assumption that drives many poor men and women towards running. Training is regarded not as some frivolous way to spend your time, but as serious work, even by those struggling to put food on the table. All around the Rift Valley there are role models proving that running can bring you your fortune. Virtually every village has its running star, someone who has packed a bag and gone off to win world titles or big road races abroad, returning rich, at least by Kenyan standards, driving a big 4×4 Land Cruiser, building a brick house, and buying a cow, and some land to plant maize.

As Bruce Tulloh pointed out to me, the great expansion in Kenyan running coincided with the rise in financial rewards. While running was still an amateur sport, Kenya produced a few great athletes who had come through the military system, or via track scholarships with US universities, but once professionalism took off in the mid-1980s, with prize money and appearance money being offered to the fastest athletes, that was when Kenyan runners really started to dominate.

Recently, Kenya's success on the world's road racing circuit, where most of the money now is, has far outstripped its performances on the track. At virtually every big-city marathon or half-marathon, from Brussels to Bogotá to Boston, the winner is almost always a Kenyan. However, over the last two world athletics championships, Kenyan men have won only one bronze medal in the 5,000m and 10,000m events.

Of course, a desire to escape poverty is not unique to Kenya or East Africa. And all over the world people are running barefoot to school. The difference is that here in Kenya there is an established running culture ready to take advantage of it. The origins of that culture are hazy, built on the folklore of Kipchoge Keino, who won gold medals in the 1968 and 1972 Olympics, and developed through the running camps set up by Brother Colm and others.

As Yannis Pitsiladis says: 'How many athletes' training camps are there in India or Bolivia?'

Now that running is firmly established as the way out, as football is in Brazil or cricket is in India, all over the Rift Valley people like Beatrice and Japhet are taking it up in their thousands, and the result is that Kenya is now dominating long-distance running even more than ever.

15

Harambee.
Kenya's official motto ('All pull together' in Swahili)

Iten wasn't always the home of Kenya's conveyor belt of running talent. When Kenyans first started to raise eyebrows with their running exploits, it was mainly the runners from the Nandi Hills further south who dominated.

'When I came here in 1976,' says Brother Colm, 'there were no runners in Iten.' I'm sitting in his dimly lit living room, sunk back into an old armchair. In one corner is a small TV with piles of videos stacked up in the sideboard underneath. Godfrey tells me that Brother Colm records every race that gets shown on television. The room is sparsely furnished, with a clock and a picture of a saint on the wall, alongside a free tractor calendar. He doesn't offer me any tea. A packet of ginger nut biscuits on the table remains unopened.

It was the influence of Brother Colm and his St Patrick's boys' school, and to a lesser extent Singore girls' school just outside Iten, that was to turn the town into the running centre it is today. With the repeated success of their teams in national and international competitions, Iten began to build a reputation as the place to train.

'St Patrick's and Signore were the beacons that made Iten the running centre,' says Brother Colm, as he walks me back out to the school gate. He has his cap pulled down low over his eyes and walks, where he can, in the shade. 'We put Kericho [the Iten region] at the centre of the map. Now everything emanates from Kericho.'

As we stand at the gate a car pulls up and a man gets out and starts shaking Brother Colm's hand. 'Henry, how are you?' says Brother Colm. He looks at me. 'Henry was one of my students. He's now a university lecturer.' Henry turns to shake my hand.

'We are all his products,' he says, pointing at Brother Colm, clearly delighted to have bumped into him again.

Iten's influence is celebrated each year at its annual sports and tourism day. 'Iten is the factory of Kenyan running,' the day's organiser tells me as we stand in the sports field at the centre of the town. 'So we thought we should have a factory day.'

The proceedings begin, aptly, with a race. Starting down in the hot, cactus-pimpled belly of the valley, the route winds its way 21 km up to the cool freshness of Iten. A half-marathon, uphill all the way. I'm hurrying the children to get dressed. The race is supposed to start at 8.30 a.m., but I've just received word that not only is it starting on time, but that it is starting only half a mile down the road, so the runners will be passing through the town in about five minutes.

Uma says she doesn't want to come. I'm sensing her passion for running is wearing thin. Lila seems happy to tag along, though, so we leave Uma with Flora and hurry down into town.

There are very few spectators around, but we spy a couple of the men from the Run Fast camp standing by the side of the road. Before we've had time to shake everyone's hand, the runners are in sight and pushing up the hill. Somewhere among the heaving of bodies is Japhet, gamely throwing his hat into the ring. Organised by the local council, the event offers fairly small prize money, which puts most of the top runners off competing. For someone like Japhet, that's ideal, as it gives him a better chance of winning something. Even if he comes sixth he will win about 8,000 Kenyan shillings, which for most people here would be a decent month's salary.

We clap as the runners surge by. And then they're gone.

'They'll be back in an hour,' I say, wondering what we should do until then. We decide to amble up the street to see if anything is happening by the finish. As we set off, a 1970s school bus, with St Patrick's High School printed down the side, pulls up beside us. I get out my camera to take a photo. As I do a man in a tracksuit comes over and asks if we'd like to ride in the bus. A large group of women in tracksuits is starting to board it.

'OK,' I say. 'Where is it going?'

'To the start of the women's race,' he says. It turns out the courses have been altered at the last minute because the council couldn't find enough buses to take all the athletes down to the bottom of the valley. So this St Patrick's bus is taking the women 10 km down the flatter road towards Eldoret. From there they'll run straight back to Iten.

I'm not sure how the athletes are supposed to prepare for these races when things like start times, courses and race distances are decided at the last minute and news is spread purely by word of mouth. Somehow, though, they always seem to know what is happening.

Lila's thrilled to be on a bus.

'Is this a school bus?' she asks me as we sit down. 'It's like an aeroplane.'

A runner called Rose sits down next to Marietta and Ossian, who is peeking blearily out of his sling. She tells Marietta she has four children, but that her husband has left her. She can't afford to send her two daughters to school, she says.

'Where are they now?' asks Marietta.

'At home,' she says.

'But who's looking after them?'

'They're alone,' she says, looking out of the window. They're six and four.

Rose has come to Iten in the hope of becoming an athlete, but she has been injured for seven months, so she has been working as a house girl for Nicholas, the cycling coach from Singapore.

After about ten minutes, the bus pulls off the road. An army officer with a stick under his arm is standing by the roadside peering out from under the brim of his hat.

The women rush to get changed into their running kit and then all hop off the bus and run over to the start line. A man in a tracksuit is yelling instructions and waving his arms around. It's Chris Cheboiboch. He spots me.

'Hey, man. Want a ride?' he asks.

'OK,' I say. I don't know how else we're going to get back to Iten. Lila looks slightly confused as I bundle her straight from the bus into a car, but the race has already started and we're speeding off ahead of the runners. Chris's job, it seems, is to warn oncoming traffic about the race. He does this by driving at top speed headlong towards anything coming in the opposite direction. Once the oncoming vehicle is forced off the road, he stops briefly beside it and fires off a ream of instructions about being careful of the runners. It's a hellfire ride back into town.

The race finishes in the field in the centre of Iten. Chris arrives just in time to leap out of the car and get someone to hold up a finishing tape before the leading man comes sprinting across the field.

Chris seems to be organising the race single-handedly. He leaps back in his car and skids off, leaving the following runners with no obvious finish line. They have to keep running, charging past the people trying to record their times and hand them bottles of water. Someone eventually realises what's going on and puts a bit of tape down on the floor as a makeshift finish.

Japhet ends up in around 25th position. He seems happy enough when I see him afterwards, holding his free bottle of water like it was a gold medal.

'Did you enjoy that?' I ask him.

'Yes,' he says, beaming with happiness. 'I enjoyed it, yes.'

After the men come the women. Rose, unfortunately, limps in way down the field, almost at the back. It doesn't bode well for her career prospects. This is easily the slowest race I've seen since I arrived in Kenya.

As the last runners come through, a truck drives onto the field and pulls up beside the finish. Two men get out and begin unloading a marquee and stacks of white plastic chairs. It seems a bit late to be setting up a spectators' area, but the men press ahead, working without haste, lining the chairs up in neat rows.

Afterwards, I meet lots of familiar faces milling around. Godfrey's friend Koila is there. The marquee and chairs, he tells me, are for events later on. The race, the actual running, is just the appetiser. However, before anything else happens we have to wait for the guest of honour to arrive. The rumour going around the field is that it's the deputy prime minister of Kenya, Musalia Mudavadi.

It's now 11 a.m.

'I'd better go back and see how Uma is getting on,' says Marietta, clearly not enthused by the prospect of a political rally. The sun is coming out and people are beginning to congregate. It has all the rumblings of a long, drawn-out occasion, the sort of event that leaves the children hot and flustered. 'I'll take Lila and Ossian with me,' she says.

By midday, Godfrey has shown up and has taken a pew on the front row of the VIP tent. But the deputy prime minister is still not here. I decide to head back home for some lunch.

At 2 p.m. I call Godfrey to see what is happening.

'I advise you to come now,' he says, not elaborating. Crestfallen after missing out on a bus ride this morning, Uma wants to come with me. Lila, worried she might miss out on something else, is coming along, too.

When we get to the field, groups of schoolchildren are performing traditional songs and dances. We sit down next to Godfrey and settle in for the show.

The children are drilled to perfection, pulling eye-popping faces as they perform. Lila and Uma watch, fascinated, particularly when their friends Hilda and Maureen stand up to do a performance. The guest of honour, however, has still not arrived.

As we sit waiting, I spot, on the road running along the far end of the field, about fifteen shiny 4×4s zipping by, one after the other. 'The deputy prime minister,' Godfrey tells me as the convoy of cars zooms onto the field. One by one the cars stop, the doors swing open and large men in suits step out.

It's instantly clear which one is Mr Mudavadi. He has a large, self-satisfied smile across his ample face. He has people crowding around him, and he's waving cordially in all directions.

The announcer is suddenly very excited and starts trying to organise the schoolchildren into lines so they can all perform again for the guests. As well as the deputy PM, there are about thirty civic officers and local politicians in tow. Once they're all seated and have finished congratulating each other, the children begin their songs again.

Each time, one of the honoured guests gets up and starts dancing along with the children. Then another one joins in. Sometimes the deputy PM himself gets up and shimmies around to the music, smiling for the cameras snapping pictures of him. Someone is handing sheets of paper out around the tent. It's a schedule of the day's events. According to the timetable, the whole thing was due to end at 2 p.m. It's now 3.30 p.m.

The announcer is hurrying the singers on. 'We have a lot of speeches,' he says. 'So, please, just one song each.'

By now a few thousand people have gathered to watch the proceedings, among them Marietta and Ossian, who were wondering what was keeping us. It's almost 4 p.m. Time, finally, for the speeches to begin.

On and on they go, one politician after another, talking

in a haphazard combination of Swahili and English about corruption, the coalition, the political parties, and many things I can't understand. At one point, Daniel Komen bravely stands up and starts berating the politicians.

'You politicians,' he says. 'You take the money from Kenya and put it in foreign bank accounts. Then the athletes have to go and win it back.' The politicians don't look amused.

After a couple of hours we take the children home. But, curious to see how the day ends, I return alone to the field.

It's now past 6 p.m. and they're still talking. I sit down next to Komen. 'They're still talking?' I ask.

'This is Kenya,' he says. 'It's twenty-five laps. There are two more to go.'

Eventually, the deputy PM says '*Asante sana*' and it's over. The crowd claps politely. The faint sound of a tractor can be heard struggling along up a hill somewhere. The prizes for the runners, who finished running over nine hours ago, are handed out. The curtain comes down.

As I cross the field back towards my house I spot Beatrice. She stops, surprised to see me. In the darkness I'm not sure it's actually her.

'Hi, Beatrice?'

'Hi,' she says, holding out a limp hand for me to shake.

'Did you run today?'

'No.'

'Why not?' She doesn't answer, but just grins bashfully as though I've asked her a personal question.

'You might have won a prize,' I venture, still unsure how fast she really is. 'There were prizes for the top ten.'

'Top ten?' She looks surprised, shaking her head. 'For the women too?'

I nod. She looks thoughtful, but doesn't say anything else. The headlights of a matatu swing around into my eyes for a second and then drive on.

'I should get back,' I say. She just nods shyly. 'Well, good night. I'll let you know when we're doing our next run.' She wanders off into the night. There are no street lights in Iten and once night falls it can be very hard to see where you're walking without a torch. I scamper off home while I can still see the ground.

Beatrice may not say much, but she is actually quite outgoing for a Kenyan athlete, particularly a woman. Despite the country's incredible dominance of one of the world's most popular sports, if you stopped a stranger in the street in any Western city and asked him to name even one Kenyan runner, he would probably struggle. One reason for this is the shyness of the athletes. Their awkward looks and monosyllabic answers when placed in front of the media can drive their agents mad. Marketing a Kenyan runner in a saturated field is already hard enough.

Unlike athletes from other parts of the world, such as the Jamaican Usain Bolt, Kenyan runners rarely seek out the limelight. Even when they win gold medals, they always bring their teammates with them on their lap of honour. The teammates, who may have finished in last place, can often seem just as happy as the winner. Kenyan runners will also often race as a team, with one of the athletes sacrificing his chances of winning to act as a pacemaker for his countrymen. All this selflessness is simply a reflection of how Kenyans are raised.

'Very few of the Kenyan champions come from a sheltered family unit,' Toby Tanser explains to me one day, sitting on the grass in our garden. 'Instead, they are brought up as part of the wider community of a village, almost like pieces of a bicycle chain. They soon learn about harambee.' Harambee is a Kenyan tradition, in which a whole community will come together to help itself. It literally means 'all pull together' and is the official motto of Kenya.

'When a Kenyan wins a medal, or a large amount of money,' says Toby, 'he reflects on the journey that took him to that moment, and he realises, perhaps better than we do, that no person achieves without the help and support of those around him.'

One of the fastest runners around right now is Mary Keitany, yet she's also one of the shyest. I first meet her at the cross-country race at Salaba Academy, Chris Cheboiboch's school. She is there as a guest, sitting along with everyone else under the flapping gazebo as the winners are presented with their prizes. Dressed in a purple suit, she could easily be one of the many school administrators who are also sitting with us on the rows of plastic chairs.

When I see her again at the Iten race, she is wearing the same purple suit. She has just broken Lornah Kiplagat's half-marathon world record, winning $75,000. I ask her if I can come and visit her. As one of the fastest female athletes in the world, perhaps she can add another piece to the puzzle of why Kenyan runners are so good.

*

One of the runners from the Run Fast camp, Raymond, is Mary's brother-in-law. His brother Charles is married to her. When Raymond hears that I'm paying a visit, he says he wants to come too. It's only about five minutes outside Iten, but he says he wants us to drive there. He's been coveting my car since he first saw it. To me it looks just like any other car in Kenya, a slightly beaten old white Toyota. But to most Kenyan men I've met it's a gleaming dream on wheels. Wherever I go, they stand staring at it, shaking their heads in disbelief. 'You don't often see a car like that,' they say. 'You can tell it's a mzungu car. Mzungus know how to look after their cars.' Raymond asks me to sell it to him. But it's not mine. It was lent to me by my brother-in-law Alastair. And I've already promised Godfrey that he can buy it if Alastair wants to sell it. But Raymond isn't giving up. He tells me not to tell anyone that he wants it. I'm not sure what his strategy is, but I agree to keep it as our secret.

We drive out of town and then immediately turn off the paved road and down a dirt track, clouds of red dust billowing behind us. The car is hot like a sauna after being parked in the midday sun with the windows shut. Up ahead a woman in tracksuit bottoms and a bright yellow T-shirt, and a small boy holding her hand, stand by the side of the road. They watch us as we pass.

'That was Mary,' says Raymond, after we've gone by.

'Really? Should I stop?'

He doesn't say anything. I look over at him. He's grinning at me. He nods. I pull the car to a stop and wait. In the mirror I can see that she's walking back towards us. I wind the window down.

'Hello,' I say as she comes over. But she's looking past me, to Raymond. They talk hurriedly, as though there's a problem. I lean back in my seat so they can see each other. Raymond looks at me and points ahead to the gate.

'In there,' he says. I look at Mary. She smiles, stepping back to let me drive.

'She was going to a neighbour's house. She forgot we were coming,' Raymond tells me. We drive through into the small compound. To one side is some farm machinery and two men. One of them, her husband, Charles, watches us suspiciously as I park the car. I get out and wave to him.

'Hello,' I say. He gives me a small nod, not returning the smile, as Mary and the boy follow us in and then disappear inside the house. Raymond gets out and stands by the car, stretching his hands in the air as though we've just been on a long journey. I'm not sure where to go.

Charles eventually comes over and shakes my hand and gestures towards the front door.

'Karibu,' he says. 'Welcome.'

I step through into a small living room so crammed with sofas and coffee tables that there's almost no space to stand. Mary, who still hasn't spoken to me, is fixing up two glasses of toxic-coloured orange squash. I sit down in one of the armchairs. Raymond, following along behind, sits in the far corner of the room. Mary gives us both a drink and sits down somewhere midway between us.

I look around the room. The walls are full of photographs. Most of them are of Mary or Charles running. The biggest pictures are all of Charles. Medals hang from the corners of a few of the pictures. A shiny gold Happy

Christmas sign hangs over the door.

'You must have been happy to break the world record last week?' I say. She looks at me confused, perhaps surprised by my accent.

'Did you know you could break the record, or was it a surprise?'

'A surprise,' she says, looking away. Charles comes in with their son and sits down beside her. He picks up the remote control and clicks the TV on. It's just behind my head, so I can't see it. They all stare at it. It feels like they're staring at me. Mary is running the London marathon in a few weeks. I ask her if she thinks she can win. She laughs. I'm not sure if it's in answer to my question or at something on the TV.

Our stilted conversation goes on for about ten minutes, Mary looking away shyly every time I ask her a question, while Charles and Raymond sit watching on silently, their eyes flicking back and forth between me and the TV above my head.

'Well, I'd better leave you to get ready for your afternoon run,' I say at last. Mary just nods.

Once we're outside, Mary disappears. Charles takes me around the back of the house to see the cows. I ask him if they'll use the money from Mary's world record to build a bigger house. He looks at me confused. 'Why?' he asks. I feel like I've insulted him. Their place is nice, but it's fairly simple. It's not the house you imagine a world record holder living in.

Money is clearly an awkward subject. Mary has been a fairly late developer. She's twenty-nine but is only just starting to make a mark on the world stage. Up until recently, Charles was the star runner in the household. The house was probably built with his winnings.

A farmhand is milking one of the cows. 'Do you sell the milk?' I ask him. Again he looks at me as though I'm mad. 'No,' he says. 'It's for us.' The majority of the people in the Rift Valley are brought up as subsistence farmers, so when the athletes win any money, the first thing they do is buy a cow for milk. I can't help thinking it would be easier and cheaper just to go to the shop and buy it every day. Every street has a tiny kiosk selling fresh milk for virtually nothing. But the mindset is to own a cow. A person without a cow is not really a person. You can judge the importance of someone by the number of cows he owns.

Charles tells me that when they were younger, they used to drain some of the blood from the cows to mix with mursik, a fermented milk drink. They would make a tiny hole in the cow's neck to get the blood out, and then seal it back up afterwards, leaving the cow to run off unharmed.

'It made us strong,' he says. The mixture of blood and mursik is often cited by runners as the Kalenjin secret, even though it is rarely drunk these days. Mixed with charcoal, it is an unpalatable but potent tonic. When triumphant athletes return home after winning a big competition, they are often met at the airport by a ceremonial gourd of mursik, which they drink to loud cheers.

Charles and Mary also have a small field of maize growing nearby.

'For ugali,' Charles tells me. Yet another Kenyan secret. Mary is certainly running fast on it. A few weeks later she does indeed win the London marathon, in the fourth-fastest time in history.

Raymond is standing by the car, waiting to go. We walk over. Charles wants to know where I got the car.

'KXE,' he says, referring to the number plates. 'It's a very nice car. You don't see KXE like that, in that condition.'

He asks if he can look under the bonnet. He stares at the engine, fascinated. 'Do you want to sell it?' he asks. I tell him it's my brother-in-law's car. 'Well, tell him', he says, 'that if he wants to sell it . . .'

I assure him I will. Raymond has climbed into his seat and is waiting like a moody teenager to go. I wave goodbye.

'Say thanks and goodbye to Mary for me,' I say, as we pull out through the gates and back up the bumpy road to Iten.

16

I don't even know what I was running for – I guess I just felt like it.

  J. D. Salinger, *The Catcher in the Rye*

The next day I hop back into our coveted Toyota Corolla and set out on the long, perilous drive down to Nairobi. Godfrey and I have a pilgrimage to make.

In some ways it's just another race. A bunch of people running around a field. But the Kenyan national cross-country championships is probably the toughest, most competitive running race in the world. The top hundred or so Kenyans in each age group come together, the very fastest of the fast, racing each other for a few coveted spots in the national team for the World Championships. It's the most densely concentrated gathering of running brilliance anywhere in the world. I simply have to be there. To witness the spectacle, and to hopefully learn more about the secrets of Kenyan running.

Godfrey had said he would give me a lift, but a few days before, he rang me to say there had been a change of plan. His car was still in the garage, he said. He was now going to get the bus to Nairobi a day early with Anders as he had to help an athlete to get a visa.

So that afternoon I find myself standing by my car in a hot, dusty town about 50 miles from Iten waiting for another runner and his wife. Godfrey has arranged for me to give them a lift, so that they can keep me company and help me find the way.

A man in a stripy shirt carrying a big jacket under his arm approaches me as I stand there, his hand stretched out.

'Yes, my friend,' he says as I shake his hand. 'Where are you going?'

'Nairobi,' I say.

'I'll come,' he says. It's only half a question. I can't tell if he has just decided to go to Nairobi because I've suggested it, or whether he was going there anyway. Spotting my concerns, he says: 'I am a police officer.'

I agree to give him a lift. He's heading home to see his family for the weekend. The runner I'm waiting for and his wife turn up soon after looking harassed and complaining about the matatu journey from their home village nearby.

As the mid-afternoon sun burns in patches of light across the town, we all climb into the car and head out along the potholed road into a land scattered with spiky cactus plants and dry, stony river beds.

It's a straight four-hour drive to Nairobi, past small, ramshackle crossroad settlements, big school gates, up into the hills, overtaking tractors, lorries, avoiding the matatus and smoking cars coming the other way. At one point we pass a group of baboons sitting right by the roadside grooming their young and watching the vehicles pass without interest. Finally the road drops down into Nairobi.

As we drive, my passengers make an effort to speak in English and include me in the conversations, but gradually they slip into Swahili. I let them go, my gaze drifting off into the rainy hills. The grass here is green and soft, with rows and rows of healthy-looking crops rising up the hillsides. People cycle by in rain jackets under grey, English-looking skies.

Once we get to Nairobi, we meet Godfrey and Anders as arranged at the YMCA. Godfrey has supposedly booked all three of us into a room, but it turns out it only has one single bed.

'It's OK,' he says, 'I know another place nearby.'

We park my car and climb into a vehicle Godfrey has managed to procure from somewhere. He drives us further and further out of town, past bigger and bigger houses, until we've been going for about 45 minutes. Finally, with night bringing its curtain down, he turns down a side road which leads us to what looks like a deserted conference centre. A sign at the entrance says 'KCB Bank Leadership Centre'. It doesn't look much like a hotel. Anders glances at me, doubtful, but Godfrey is as confident as ever.

'Trust me,' he says, 'you are going to love this place.'

The guard on the gate looks surprised to see us. Godfrey winds down his window with a big smile. But the guard is nonplussed. He seems to be telling Godfrey that the place is only used for conferences, that it's not a hotel.

Godfrey bids the man good night and reverses the car back out into the road.

'It's full,' he says. 'There's a conference on.'

Instead, a few minutes away, we pull in at the Shade Hotel. It has some cheap, quirky rooms and a restaurant. We're tired and hungry. We take it.

Half of Iten seems to be at the race in Uhuru Gardens in the centre of Nairobi, sprinting back and forth around the course to get as many glimpses of the runners as possible. As well as enthusiasts like myself, the coaches and agents are all here, encouraging their runners along with gruff shouts. When one of their athletes wins, they grin and high-five each other like City traders watching their stock rising in value.

A few thousand local fans have turned out to watch. For a cross-country race, this is quite a lot, but I can't help thinking that here in the capital city of the world's most passionate running nation, there should be a few more.

Some fans are appreciating it, though. One man turns to me with a big grin as the lead women go by, and says: 'I've just seen Linet Masai [the eventual winner] with my own eyes. Not on the internet.'

The athletes parade out to the start at the beginning of each race like warriors, their arms swinging, bouncing up and down on their toes. It's a warm, windswept morning and I spend much of the time rushing around trying to take photographs. I want to somehow capture the majesty of it all, the power and speed with which they charge around. But it seems to get lost amid the wide open space of the park. Occasional planes sink down across the sky, landing at the nearby Wilson Airport, dwarfing the runners still more. Perhaps it's because I want to be overwhelmed by it, because I've come so far to see it, that I'm straining to fully appreciate just how fast the runners are moving. Then in the last race, as the men's winner, Geoffrey Mutai, hurtles around the last corner right in front of me, he almost goes the wrong way. It's like trying to redirect a speeding train to get him back on course. We have to leap out of the way as he flies straight at us, heading off on yet another lap, as though he could just keep going for ever. Somehow the marshals manage to grab him and send him back along the funnel to the finish.

He completes the 12 km course, over rough, hilly terrain, on a windy day, at altitude, in a staggering 34 minutes 35 seconds.

To illustrate just how tough these races are, the four current world champions – senior and junior men and women – are all running, but none of them manages to finish even in the top ten. Leonard Komon, who in the previous few months has broken the 15K and 10K world records, can only manage sixth place in the men's race.

Before I leave, Godfrey introduces me to a young girl from a small village somewhere in the Rift Valley. She has her head shaven like any other Kenyan schoolgirl, her teeth are stained. She could have just arrived after a day planting maize in the fields. She offers me an embarrassed handshake as I'm told she is Mercy Cherono, the world junior champion from the year before. Today, though, she came thirteenth, herself outrun by a host of other girls from small, dusty villages.

My meeting with Mercy Cherono gets me thinking. Something about her seemed to encapsulate the Kenyan running phenomenon. There was something accidental, unconscious even, about her brilliance.

One evening, weeks earlier, in the Kerio View hotel in Iten, Marietta and I met a couple drinking wine on the terrace. The man was from the Eldoret area, but was now an executive with the country's biggest telecommunications company, Safaricom, in Nairobi. I asked him what he thought the Kenyan running secret was. He looked at me over his glass.

'Ask any top runner about his background,' he said, 'and you will find out he comes from a poor family.' At the time I thought it was a slightly crass observation, but the more I think about it, the more significant it seems. Talking to Mercy Cherono, it was clear that her success hadn't come as the result of years of dedication, being driven to training sessions and races by her parents. Her school probably didn't even have a track to train on. Instead, simply from the inherent physical toughness of her daily life had come a talent to outrun the world.

Brother Colm nods when I put this theory to him, that all the Kenyan runners come from a poor background. 'I'll add something else,' he says. 'They all come from a poor, rural family. We've yet to have a good runner from a city.'

The life of the rural poor in Kenya is tough. From a young age they have to work hard, herding goats or digging in the fields, and they run or walk everywhere. You see them at dawn shuffling along the trails on their way to school. It's the perfect groundwork for an endurance athlete.

I remember the day I had lunch with Daniel Komen in the Eldoret Golf Club. He wore a dark green suit. It was a hot day, children were playing in the swimming pool. A buffet barbecue was in full swing. Waiters in crisp white shirts carried trays of Sunburst drinks across the lawn.

'Every day I used to milk the cows, run to school, run home for lunch, back to school, home, tend the cows.' He didn't smile as he spoke. It wasn't a happy memory. 'This is the Kenyan way.'

Chris Cheboiboch once told me a similar story. 'We were training already without knowing it,' he said. 'Every day running, running, running.'

Not only are they training from a young age, but they're doing it at high altitude. There is a broad scientific consensus that training at altitude helps endurance athletes to run faster by increasing their blood's ability to carry oxygen around the body. Virtually every international distance runner will include spells of high-altitude training in their schedules. But the Kenyans are born and raised at altitude, running around everywhere from a young age, which gives them a big advantage.

I head back to the Kerio View in search of Renato Canova and find him sitting in the same seat, his glass of milk on the table. He motions for me to sit down when he sees me, and orders me a glass of passion fruit juice. I ask him about this theory that it is their tough rural upbringing that makes Kenyans such good runners.

He thinks for a moment, measuring his words as though he could answer the question in a hundred different ways. 'It's true,' he says. 'In the West, we have a good quality of life, no? But if you think about what "quality of life" means, it means less fatigue. Making things easier. Running, on the other hand, is about how much fatigue can you do.'

My list is growing, but all the reasons, the secrets, I'm discovering are also beginning to join up. The tough, physical upbringing, the barefoot running, the altitude, the running to school. They all arise naturally from the Kenyans' daily lives. None of it is done with the intention of becoming an athlete. It's just how they live. Simply through growing up on the slopes of the Rift Valley, far from cities and the technologies that the West has invented to make life more comfortable, they have found themselves excelling at the world's most natural sport.

When my children turned up in Eldoret for the cross-country race, it was unlike the fun runs they had enjoyed before in England. There were no podgy legs or flushed faces, children running at a cute waddle, happy to be doing something active for a change. In Eldoret, the children were all charged with energy, rushing around, darting back and forth on the start line. Something was already afoot, long before any athletic training had started to take place. Lila and Uma took one look and were terrified.

'To build your aerobic house, to have enough of an endurance base to run long distances, takes about ten years,' Canova tells me. 'By the time a Kenyan is sixteen,' he says, smiling, as though this, my friend, is everything boiled down to one small, neat point, a little sound bite that you can take away with you, 'by the time a Kenyan is sixteen, he has built his house.'

Meanwhile, in Nairobi, I'm preparing to set out on another run. I'm training almost every day now, as the Lewa marathon gets closer. Training is starting to become a daily practice, like it is for Japhet, Beatrice and all the other runners in Iten. Except that here in the city, things are very different.

'Right everyone, stop wanking and gather round.'

It's a motley crew that assembles around the big red 4×4

in the car park of the Nest hotel in Ngong, a satellite town just north of Nairobi. The majority of the forty or so people in the group are overweight. A few are drinking fizzy drinks. One lady, with a face like a snarling dog, is smoking a cigarette. Everyone is wearing running kit.

'Today's long route is 10 km,' says the man in charge. 'The short route is 8 km. Enjoy.'

Most of the people here look like they'd struggle to make it up the stairs to the bar. But with good-natured smiles and jokes, we all file out of the car park, onto the road, and start jogging.

Before I return to Iten, I've come to visit some old friends of Bruce Tulloh, Ray and Doreen Meynick. Ray told me he was good friends with two of Kenya's greatest running legends, Catherine Ndereba and Paul Tergat. They just live around the corner from his house in the leafy suburb of Karen, he told me. They often come around for dinner. I was hoping they would have something to add as to why Kenyans are such good runners, but unfortunately neither of them is answering the phone.

Instead, Ray is insistent that I meet up with some of the non-elite Kenyan runners that you can find here in Nairobi. Fun runners, mostly, which in Kenya is an unusual concept. 'Running with the Kenyans?' he says, giving me a pointed look. 'Well, they're Kenyans too.'

With over 1,700 groups meeting in most major cities around the world, the Hash House Harriers is an international phenomenon. More a social club than a typical running club – they like to describe themselves as 'a drinking club with a running problem' – they nevertheless head out on regular runs all across their respective cities. Rather than run along a set route, the Hashers follow a trail marked out in advance with white chalk.

The pace is excruciatingly slow at the back of the group as runners heave themselves along the Ngong Road, almost being knocked over by buses crammed full of commuters heading home after work.

At the head of the group, a few lean runners are getting away. I chase after them, but as soon as I catch them, they step behind a wall and stop. They're all grinning.

'What's going on?'

One of them, an elderly man with one of his front teeth missing, points at two white chalk lines on the ground.

'That means it's a false trail,' he says. But he doesn't want the others to realise, at least not until they too have come all the way down the dusty side road as we have. This is going to be very different from running in Iten.

Once we get back on track, returning en masse to the main road and taking a different chalk-marked side road, the same few runners hurtle off at the front again, and I stick with them. We soon find ourselves running through the backyards of some collapsing wooden houses, ducking under washing lines, leaping over small children playing in the mud.

But we seem to have lost the trail. As we stand around deliberating, a man in a doorway points down a narrow gap between two of the houses. Without thanking him, we rush down it, and sure enough, there are more chalk marks.

'On, on,' the others shout at the top of their voices, as the slower runners begin to catch up.

And so it goes on. Every time we get stuck at a turning, it gives the other runners a chance to catch up. When we find the right way, we yell 'on, on' and the charge resumes.

Despite having initial reservations, I'm finding it all quite exhilarating. We're running like loonies through tumble-down backstreets, looking for white chalk marks. I even find myself yelling out when I find one.

'On, on,' I yell. Two women sit in a doorway watching me run by. Behind comes a long line of plodding Kenyans in tracksuits and fluorescent bibs.

At about halfway we find a car parked with the boot open. Inside are cups of water, slices of melon and chunks of sugar-cane to suck on. Sitting in the front of the car is the woman who was smoking at the start.

I'm one of the first to arrive, but soon everyone has caught up. As we stand around eating and getting our breath back, someone says: 'Let's have a song.'

Spontaneously, they all break into a hearty version of 'Singing in the Rain', with actions like wiggling bums and sticking out tongues. The people living down this particular backstreet, with its dusty hair salons and mango stalls, stand around in groups, agog.

Although there are a few other mzungus in the group, the Hash is mainly made up of black Kenyans. They all drive big cars and are more than happy to hand over 150 Kenyan shillings (£1.10) just to run – more than many people here in Kenya earn in a day.

After the run, the Hashers drink the night away, with beers at specially reduced prices and rooms booked at the hotel for those too drunk to get home. I've heard stories about humiliating initiation ceremonies for 'virgins' like me, so rather than investigate further, I cowardly sneak off under the darkening sky.

In terms of the quality of the running, my sojourn with the Hash House Harriers is like taking a little space capsule back to a running club in the UK for the night. All the bandy legs and beer bellies setting off at 10-minute-mile pace. One contributing factor in East Africa's dominance of long-distance running is the fact that in the West we're getting slower. Despite all the advances in training technology, nutrition, physiotherapy, the increase in the quality and quantity of races, the introduction of prize money, in the West we're stuck on a conveyor belt going the wrong way. In 1975, for example, 23 marathons were run in times under 2 hours 20 minutes by British runners, 34 by US runners, and none by Kenyan runners. By 2005, however, there were 12 sub-2:20 marathon performances by Britons, 22 by Americans, and a staggering 490 by Kenyans.

For every reason for Kenyan success, we see the opposite trend occurring in the West. While Kenyans lead incredibly active childhoods, in the West we're becoming ever more sedentary. A recent study by the University of Essex found that even in the last ten years, the average English ten-year-old has become weaker, less muscular and less able to do simple physical tasks. They're not talking about running three miles to school twice a day, but the most basic activities such as hanging from wall bars in a gym. The academics who conducted the study pinned the blame on our modern lifestyles. The study's author, Dr Gavin Sandercock, said,

'It's probably due to changes in activity patterns, such as taking part in fewer activities like rope-climbing in PE and tree-climbing for fun.'

Back in the 1970s we weren't exactly running barefoot, but the majority of running shoes were thin-soled and light-weight, much like the 'barefoot shoes' selling like hot cakes today. And what's more, we were growing up wearing them, which meant we had good form, strong calves and higher arches.

Our diets, too, are getting worse. While Kenyans have their carbohydrate-rich ugali, we're eating more salt and more fatty foods than ever before. Obesity and diabetes are rising. According to the World Health Organisation, the obesity rates in the UK and the US have risen at least three-fold since 1980.

Kenyans also have an abundance of successful role mod-els, which encourages them to try running and makes them believe they can be good at it. The success stories are every-where. Nicholas, the cycling coach from Singapore, says he doesn't have this advantage when it comes to his cycling team.

'If we pick cyclists at fifteen or sixteen they don't want to join us,' he says. 'They don't have the role models like in running. They are no Paul Tergats in cycling.'

Of course, the more success Kenyans have, the more that runners from other countries are squeezed out, leaving fewer role models for everyone else.

Scientists have found that the ever-growing perception that Kenyans are better runners can also give them a psy-chological advantage during races. If a European runner automatically expects the Kenyans in the same race to be faster than him, this has the potential to affect his performance negatively, especially if the belief is supported by everyone else around him. Conversely, if a Kenyan runner believes the same thing, that he is faster because he is a Kenyan, it can have a positive effect on his performance.

When a runner from another country does break through, the impact can be significant on the following generation. When Kelly Holmes won the 800m and 1500m gold medals at the 2004 Olympics, for example, Britain hardly had an illustrious history in women's middle-distance running. But by 2009, five years later, it was a major force, winning 1500m silver and 800m bronze in the World Championships that year.

With fewer role models and less potential for success, fewer people are willing to give up everything for a career in athletics. The fewer full-time athletes you have, the fewer stars are likely to emerge.

Put altogether, it's a sliding scale of factors that has all the weights pushed over on one side. It's no wonder the Kenyans are better. The fact that someone like Paula Radcliffe can come through a field so skewed against her to shatter the world marathon record is in some respects a minor miracle.

17

He was alone. He was unheeded, happy, and near to the wild heart of life.

James Joyce, *A Portrait of the Artist as a Young Man*

There's a metal pole in the ground outside the post office in Iten which all the athletes use as the starting point for their long runs. We line up beside it, gazing up the road into the dawn sky. Two figures appear over the horizon running towards us. Marietta and the children look sleepy, sitting in the cab of the truck as we prepare to set off on our second Lewa team run. Godfrey tells us that we need to go faster this time. Last time, he says, was too slow. 'But no pushing, Chris,' he says. 'Just maintain.' Chris smirks like a naughty schoolboy not taking his lessons seriously. Godfrey and Chris are good friends, although both think they are the senior partner in their relationship. It means Chris doesn't like taking advice from Godfrey.

Chris starts off at the front, as if to make his point, but he's not pushing too hard. After a steady 5 km, we turn off the road, following the same route as before, and drop down into the fields. Beatrice, however, is already dropping off the pace. I look behind. She has a short, heavy stride, her arms held up high across her chest. Japhet drops back to check she's OK as the rest of us push on.

I'm determined to make it to 20 km this time, so as the pace starts ratcheting up, around the 12 km mark, I let them go. Marietta watches me from the back of the truck, concerned.

'Are you OK?' she asks as I drift further back.

'I'm fine,' I say. 'Tell Godfrey he doesn't have to wait.' She takes a few more pictures as the truck speeds up, chasing after the others in the main group.

I'm actually feeling strong, keeping my form, lifting my legs, relaxing my shoulders. I pass the 15 km mark three minutes quicker than the last run, in 1 hour and 3 minutes, and then push on. The last stretch up to the 20 km mark is all uphill. By the time I get there, my legs have gone. All I can manage are short, pathetic steps that edge me slowly along, past groups of watching children, calling each other from across the fields to come, quick, to see the mzungu running past. They sprint like excited puppies across the ploughed earth to see the strange sight. 'Fine, fine,' I manage to gasp in response to the singing chorus of 'How are you?' that follows me the whole way up.

At the top, Chris is already sitting beside Uma in the back of the truck. This time he doesn't give an excuse for why he has stopped. I put on my jacket and take a water bottle.

About five minutes later, an exhausted-looking Beatrice looms into view, her 76-minute half-marathon looking more questionable than ever.

'You OK?' we all ask as she puts on her tracksuit top. She breaks into her big smile, happy to have stopped. 'Yes,' she says, seemingly unperturbed by how far behind she was. 'That was good. Very good.'

We all hop in the truck and tear off after the others. Godfrey is supposed to give them water and time splits at each

5 km point, but we've become so spread out that he can't catch up with them until almost the 30 km mark. Josphat is the first to be caught. Then Philip. Finally we catch up with Japhet and Shadrack. They're sprinting now, flying along the lane. Godfrey hands drinks to them as he drives, which they collect calmly, without breaking stride, drink and then hand back. 'Only 1K to go,' says Godfrey, driving along beside them. 'Push now, push, the last 1K.' They race each other up the last hill, Shadrack still wearing his running jacket, drenched in sweat, and little Japhet, his matchstick legs, amazingly, keeping up, stride for stride.

'Welcome to my home,' says Japhet as I step in from the steady rain that has settled over Iten today, through the wooden door into a darkened room. Along the back wall is a bed, with clothes hanging from a string stretched above it. Sheets hung from the ceiling divide the room into sections.

'Sometimes my uncle stays here,' Japhet says, pointing at a covered area at the back. A small kitchen section with a camping stove, a few pots, pans, two thermos flasks for tea, lines another wall. The whole place is about half the size of my bedroom back in England.

Newspaper has been stuck all over the walls. Japhet has pinned athletics reports over the top here and there, and he points them out to me, recalling them fondly as though they were describing his own exploits. He has the customary agricultural calendar, and a few medals hanging from the cardboard ceiling. Behind the door is a huge container of water, which he uses for cooking and washing. When the tap in the yard outside works, he refills it from that. Otherwise he walks down to the river, or collects rainwater.

'Sometimes if I hear the rain at night, I get up and put my can under there,' he says, pointing to the roof gutter.

I sit on the only chair and he sits on the bed. From a folder he carefully slides out his application form for university. He never sent it off because he couldn't afford the fees. The form is kept, though, as testament to his ambition. It's even on his CV, which he pulls out and shows me. Under 'Talents And Achievements' it says, handwritten in blue biro, 'Form filled in for Moi University'.

He pours me a cup of millet porridge from one of the flasks. It's sweet and warm, bringing comfort from the rain outside.

Japhet gets the little money he has for food and rent from his uncle, who works at the petrol station in Iten. I ask him about his father. Does he help too?

'My father is very old,' Japhet says, smiling, perhaps surprised that I want to know, or perhaps because he hasn't thought about his father for a while. The memory makes him chuckle. 'He married six times,' he tells me. 'He wanted to have children, but his first five wives didn't produce.' Japhet's mother, though, wife number six, started to go mad when Japhet was very young.

'She killed my brother,' he says.

He refills my cup. The afternoon is quiet. People are in their houses waiting for the rain to stop.

'How did she kill him?'

'She lay on him. She used to burn houses, and attack my father. One morning we found my father bloodied on the floor. He was once a powerful man in the community, with many cattle, but he had to sell many things to pay for my mother's treatment.'

Once, when Japhet was just a baby, the neighbours caught his mother trying to drown him in the river. So they put her in a psychiatric hospital in Nairobi. She was there for seven years, receiving treatment. Eventually she was allowed home. The doctors gave the family handcuffs to tie her up with when she turned violent.

'One day she tied a bull up in the house and killed it with a machete.'

Driving or walking through the picturesque valley slope where Japhet was brought up, it's hard to imagine such madness lying under the peaceful surface: lush green hillocks, fluffy white clouds drifting through a blue sky, the air soft and warm.

Chris took us there one time to meet Japhet's family. He sat in his car while we ran down the track to a small, peaceful compound with a round thatched hut in the middle. An old man was lying asleep on the grass. When he heard us he leapt up as though he had seen a ghost.

'Who are these people you've brought?' he asked Japhet in Kalenjin, panicked, looking around as though he was trying to remember where he was. The only other people living there, in another small mud hut along one edge of the compound, were Japhet's sister-in-law and her baby. She came over to greet us, shy, but strikingly beautiful. A radio fuzzed away, hanging from a nail in the outside wall of her hut.

Josphat, who was also with us, told us we had to go. Chris

was waiting, he said. So we left them there, standing in the green fields, wondering what had just happened.

In 1999, either from her madness or from the drugs she had to take, Japhet's mother died. Japhet was twelve years old. It was then that he started running.

'I still have the school record for the 5,000m and 3,000m,' he tells me, pouring the last of the millet porridge into my cup.

One summer, Chris convinced Brother Colm to take Japhet on one of his training camps.

'I still do the exercises I learned,' he says.

Even though he couldn't afford to pay the school fees, the head teacher at his school let him stay because he was running well.

'Sometimes he sent me home, but then he called me back when the races were on.'

At race meetings, he tried to find a coach, but he says they didn't help him. He had no phone and lived in a remote area, so communication was a problem. When he was twenty-one, he decided to move to Iten to become an athlete.

'First I ran by myself to get into good shape,' he says. 'I was seeing the athletes, how they behave. I tried joining a few groups, but the End of the Road group was the best. They were talking, explaining the routes, bringing a vehicle for long runs. Kipsang was there.'

The rain has stopped. A small boy in a fleecy snow suit comes in, sees me, screams and runs off. Japhet seems keen to tell me something else before we're interrupted.

'Cheboiboch said he would help me. But he left me,' he says. He means Chris. The boy pokes his head back around the door, a woolly hat under his hood, snot running from his nose. When I turn to look at him he yelps and runs off again.

'Now I am learning how to run,' says Japhet. 'Before I used to go home too much to help my father on the shamba, with the cows. But I was wasting time. I keep correcting my mistakes. I saw Kipsang going to Paris and thought I could do that. Now I don't go home so much, I just focus. I see others going home, not serious.'

I imagine what it would mean for Japhet to win some-thing at Lewa. It would justify all these years of persever-ance. All those thousands of miles run in the belief that one day it will pay off. His dedication in the face of such odds is humbling. Perhaps Lewa will be his crowning moment. He has been outrunning some good athletes on our training runs. Godfrey has given him some new shoes.

'Hopefully you will do well at Lewa,' I say. 'There are prizes for the top five, remember.'

'I will do it,' he says, that big grin of his lighting up his face. 'I will do it.'

18

If you're young and talented, it's like you have wings.
Haruki Murakami, *What I Talk About When I Talk About Running*

The One 4 One camp is just a single grass courtyard surrounded by rows of small dormitories. A water tower stands high in the middle, offering some shade. In one corner are some sheds with the words 'toilet' and 'shower' painted over the doors. It is one of the top training camps in the country, housing some of the very best Kenyan athletes.

Godfrey and I arrive around midday when the runners are all resting. We walk in and sit down on the grass. Godfrey knows the coach, and a few of the athletes come over to sit and chat with us. I ask one of the more talkative runners what his speciality race is.

'Marathon,' he says.

'This is Emmanuel Mutai,' says Godfrey. 'Second in New York last year, and second in London.' He also came second in the World Championships.

Chewing on a piece of grass and watching me closely, his long legs folded up under him like a praying mantis, is a young man called Nixon Chepseba. Although he is only twenty-one and hasn't raced much outside Kenya, the coach is full of praise for him, telling me that he has recently broken the 1500m record at the local track by three seconds. In most places in the world, breaking a local track record is a relatively minor achievement, but considering the roll-call of athletes who have raced in the Kipchoge Keino stadium in Eldoret, it is worth noting.

'He was reading a book on the last lap, he was so easy,' eulogises the coach.

The athletes invite me to spend a few days training with them, and so, a few weeks later, here I am, driving my car back down the bumpy track to the camp, just off the main road between Eldoret and the town of Kaptagat. I drive past a tiny makeshift house built from sticks and plastic, stopping in front of two innocuous metal gates. Who would guess that behind this badly bricked wall live some of the greatest runners on earth? I'm a little nervous as I get out and push open the gate.

At first no one moves to help me. They all sit stopped in mid-conversation, watching. Then a few of them, realising who I am, or what I'm doing, come over to hold the gate open for me while I drive my little Corolla through and park it up beside a glistening Land Cruiser.

Some of the athletes are lying on old mattresses on the grass chatting. I spot Emmanuel Mutai sitting on a stool washing his running shoes in a bucket of water. I go over and sit next to him, hoping he'll remember me.

He nods a hello and carries on scrubbing away at his racing shoes. He has three pairs of them.

'Do you remember me?' I ask. 'I came here a few weeks ago. With Godfrey Kiprotich.' He nods, not looking up. One of the other athletes brings me a cup of tea and a full flask which he places on the ground by my chair.

'Thank you.' We shake hands.

'Thomas,' he says, and goes off to sit in a chair.

I turn my seat around slightly so I'm facing the courtyard. One athlete is hunched over the newspaper, peering into it like a man who needs glasses. Nixon Chepseba is playing cards at a small table with another athlete. Running kit hangs drying from lines around the edge of the courtyard. A dumbbell made from two old paint pots filled with concrete lies on the floor.

'You feeling ready for London?' I ask Mutai. In a few weeks he's running the London marathon again. He looks up. 'Yes,' he says. Then goes back to his scrubbing. He's not as gregarious as I remember.

'Are you running with us in the morning?' he asks suddenly.

I ask him what they're doing.

'Thirty-eight kilometres. We leave at five in the morning.'

'Yeah, sure. Sounds good.' Sounds terrifying, is what I mean. I've never run more than 21 km before. But hopefully they will start slowly, like on the Lewa team runs, and I can bail out when I run out of steam.

'Will there be a truck?'

'Yes,' he says, laying his shoes out on the grass to dry. And then he walks off and disappears into his room.

For the next few hours I sit listening to the runners chatting away in Kalenjin, the words drifting and bumping around in the still afternoon air, my face slowly burning in the sun. Only one of the athletes in the camp is not a Kalenjin. Daniel Salel is a Maasai 10,000m runner. When the other athletes talk to him, they speak in Swahili, Kenya's national language, but once they get chatting among themselves, he's left sitting, like me, unable to understand anything.

The afternoon sun is just beginning to weaken when I spot Chepseba and another athlete striding around in their running kit.

'You going for a run?' I ask. 'Can I come?'

'Sure.'

We walk out through the gate, two of Kenya's finest athletes, and me. We make an odd threesome as we set off slowly towards the forest. They're both long and sinewy, gliding along through the trees. I feel like a clown stuttering along beside them.

They have just come back from racing indoors in Europe for the first time. Chepseba ended the season with the fastest 1500m time in the world. Luckily, however, this is just a recovery run and the pace never rises above a slow jog. The forest is quiet. Unlike on the trails around Iten, there are no children calling after me, or running along beside me. Just endless forest, the late afternoon sunlight dappling the trees, the trails soft under our feet as we run in single-filed unison.

At one point we come up behind a man herding his cows. At the sound of our feet, the cows start to run on ahead of us along the narrow pathway, and so we keep going, chasing them like a backwards version of a Spanish bull run. Eventually we come to a clearing and the cows skip and twirl out of our way, their big horns spinning around dangerously. We've run a long way with them, and I wonder how the owner is going to track them down again.

When we get back to the camp, the day is starting to cool. Chepseba, stripped down to his waist, hands me a bucket. He starts to fill his up from the outside tap. 'Is this the shower?' I ask, unsure. He grins at me, nodding, amused at my confusion. We take the buckets into the shower sheds and then use the cold water to splash ourselves, scooping it up with our hands.

Later I ask the runners why the camp has such basic facilities. The toilets are just holes in a concrete floor. This is typical in Kenya, but these are wealthy men, most of them. The collection of brand-new cars parked just inside the gate is proof of that. But the athletes even clean the toilets themselves, a handwritten rota on the wall in the common room listing when each athlete is expected to carry out his chores.

'It's what we're used to,' says Emmanuel Mutai. It is this way of life that has got him to where he is now. To change it would be to risk everything. The athletes know that those who choose to leave the camps to live a more comfortable life often lose their edge. And with so much competition in this one tiny corner of the world, edge is something that once lost is hard to get back.

Soon after darkness falls, the supper is dished out. We all sit in the common room, the strip light glaring along the ceiling, building rubble piled in one corner. The walls are bare except for an article cut out from a newspaper about why fizzy drinks are bad for children. Some twenty athletes are cramped into the room, sitting on white plastic chairs, talking excitedly. Almost everyone is wearing the same puffy black Adidas overcoat.

The cook passes a tray with a mound of ugali on it

through the window from the adjoining kitchen. Then a pot of sukuma wiki, which is basically stewed kale. Pages of an old calendar are used as place mats for the pots. While Chepseba acts as head distributor, handing around the food, slicing the ugali with a bread knife and then adding a side helping of stew, Mutai sets up a laptop computer on a chair beside the television. We're going to watch a film.

Someone turns out the strip light and quiet descends as we all sit eating with our fingers, watching as Mutai tries to get his DVD showing on the television. Finally it appears to a half-hearted cheer and the film starts.

It's about an American teenager and martial arts fan who somehow ends up in China learning kung fu from Jackie Chan. At first he is hopeless, way out of his depth and racked with doubts.

'Just don't forget to breathe,' Jackie Chan tells him. It's good advice. Gradually, with months of dedicated practice out in the woods, waking up at dawn every day to train, he becomes brilliant. Then he returns to his small town in the Midwest to duff up the bullies who had been giving him a hard time before he left.

It's engrossingly similar to my story. Will I, too, return home transformed, stunning people with my speed as I streak by like a Kenyan? I look around. I'm the last person still watching. One by one the others have gone off to bed. We have a 38 km run in the morning. I turn off the power and cross the courtyard to my room. Lightning flashes across the night sky. Mutai has left me an extra blanket in case I get cold, but there's no pillow. I make one using a sheet and my towel, and climb into the bed. One of the runners said he would wake me, but just to be sure I set my alarm for 4.30 a.m. and turn off the light.

There's a quiet knock on my door. I roll over and look at the time on my phone. 4.40 a.m. I must have fallen back to sleep.

'OK,' I say, swinging my legs out of the bed. It's still dark outside, so I switch on the light. It squashes my sleepy eyes back shut. I sit on the edge of the bed for a moment, trying to wake up, but it's cold so I start to get dressed. In ten minutes we have to leave.

We head out through the gate just before 5 a.m. and walk under the stars to the main road. Athletes stand around in the shadows while we wait for a bus to come and pick us up. A young man of barely twenty asks me how far I will run.

'It depends on the pace,' I say. 'How fast will you run each 5 km?'

'Probably 16 minutes, maybe 17,' he says, casually, as though that's a normal pace for a 38 km run. At 6 a.m. At 8,000 feet. A few months ago I ran a 5 km race on a flat course in Exeter. It took me over 18 minutes, running flat out.

A minibus pulls up and the door opens. Sleepy faces peer back at us. The bus is already full and there are about ten of us waiting outside. Somehow we all squeeze in, with people sitting on each other's laps, or standing bent over, heads squashed against the ceiling. I manage to get on the edge of a seat next to the window and peer out at the passing verge as the driver cranks up the skipping Kalenjin music. Nobody speaks.

Just before 6 a.m. the bus stops on a lonely dirt road in the middle of nowhere. A few people walk by in the darkness, looking over at us as we tumble out of the bus, some of the athletes disappearing off into the blackness for a last-minute pit stop. The rest of us stand around like early morning workers about to start a shift. I'm fretting about the pace. I won't even last the first 5 km. A thin sickle moon hangs in the sky as an orange glow starts to seep in from the east. It's a beautiful, still morning.

We seem to be waiting for something.

'What's going on?' I ask one of the other runners.

'We're waiting for the ladies,' he says, nodding over to the road where three women are standing holding their watches, getting some last-minute instructions from the two coaches. 'They get a 10-minute head start.'

A head start is what I need. I run over. 'Perhaps I should go with them?' I say to the coaches. 'Sure,' they say, and a few seconds later I'm running. The pace is gentle at first, but we're soon moving steadily along. Kenyans are brilliant at slowly cranking up the speed on long runs so you almost don't notice you're getting faster. By 5 km we're overtaking bicycles, as we pass streams of people making their way to work. At each corner the road stretches off again far into the distance, but we keep going, without speaking, our feet pat-patting, the miles passing as the day rises into the sky.

At about 17 km the men come past us. First the sound of rushing feet, then they go by, their strides strong, their shoulders leaning forward, little puffs of dust kicked up by their feet. One by one they go. At the front is Emmanuel Mutai and a Ugandan athlete called Stephen Kiprotich, who came sixth at the recent world cross-country championships. The others are not far behind.

As they race past I feel suddenly worse, as though the harsh contrast in speed has stripped away the belief that I was feeling strong. The women are also getting away from me now. They too are running 38 km, but the pace is still picking up. Behind me I hear the motor of the bus. As it passes me the side door slides open. The coach, a former Olympic silver medallist, grins at me.

'You want a ride?' he asks. It's a beautiful offer. I leap in through the door and sit down on a long empty seat. My heart is pumping, my body tingling to have stopped.

'You know,' says the coach, 'it is very high up here.' He's giving me an excuse, which is generous of him. But it's for him too. The offer of a lift was more of a command than a question. The bus has to keep moving from the back of the group to the front, handing out drinks, giving out times and offering encouragement. The further behind I get, the harder that is to do. But it's OK, I've done enough. In fact, I'm exhausted. I've run 17 kilometres in 1 hour 14 minutes, at altitude. That's slightly faster than my first runs with the Iten Town Harriers. Just over 3-hour-marathon pace. Could I keep it going for another 25 km over similar terrain? I doubt it.

I sit in the van doing my mental arithmetic as we skirt back past the leaders to the 20 km point. They're really flying now, yet they still look effortless. Mutai is racing away at the front, leaving behind at least five or six world-class marathon runners. As we drive along beside him and hand him his water, he seems calm, as though he's out for a morning stroll. He drinks some, pops the lid back on and hands it back. Only 18 km to go.

I've been reading previews of the upcoming London marathon and nobody is mentioning Mutai as a possible winner, despite the fact that he came second the year before. Why is that? I ask the coach.

'That's because people who write for newspapers don't know what they're talking about,' he says, turning around to me, grinning. He knows I work for a newspaper. 'But Emmanuel is ready. For sure.'

He gets to the end of the 38 km run before us, and is walking around beside some wooden buildings, hands on hips, when we arrive. The coach hands him his jacket. A gentle mist drifts between two picture-book hills rising up behind the wooden houses. The red road winds on beyond them.

The other runners come through one after the other. Bernard Kipyego, who a few weeks later will come second in the Paris marathon, followed by Kiprotich, the Ugandan. They all come to a stop and grab their drinks without saying anything. A 38 km run is a tough session even for these runners. One of the last to arrive is Thomas. Thomas is clearly a junior member of the camp, perhaps not in age, but in terms of success. He doesn't have a car, but when he's bored at camp he likes to wash the cars of the other runners.

'Do they pay you some money?' I ask him.

'No, I like doing it,' he says.

Thomas is excited to hear that I'm running the Lewa marathon.

'I ran Lewa in 2008,' he tells me. Confident he could do

well, he managed to scrape together the entry fee from family and friends. He then travelled to Lewa the night before the race and managed to stay in some community housing on the conservancy. In the race he came third, winning more than enough to pay back the money he borrowed. The One 4 One camp's manager, Michel, signed him up as a result.

Rather than stopping by the van, though, he runs straight past us and off between the two pointed hills. We catch up with him waiting by the road a few miles further on.

'I wanted to run 40 km,' he says, looking at me with serious eyes. He hasn't had a race since he joined the camp and is desperate to compete again.

Back at the camp, the athletes are in chirpy spirits. The day's work is done. All that is left now is to rest. Tea is served by the cook, but hardly anyone eats anything. After all that running, on nothing but the ugali from the night before, breakfast is a solitary cup of tea. For anyone who is hungry, like me, there are slices of dry white bread. It's not much, but it tastes delicious.

Mutai, more relaxed now after his run, stands looking at my car with a few of the other athletes. I walk over.

'Where did you get it?' he asks.

'It's my brother-in-law's. You like it?' He nods, thoughtful.

Bernard Kipyego is smiling. 'KXE,' he says, shaking his head.

To me, it looks like an old banger next to their collection of brand-new 4×4s. But it seems to hold grown men in thrall wherever it goes. The camp's track coach, Metto, didn't recognise me when I turned up the day before. Then he saw the car. He spun around, a delighted grin on his face.

'Oh, you, with the car.'

Mutai is still looking at it.

'Do you want to see the engine?' I ask. It sounds almost suggestive. He nods, so I pop open the bonnet. They all crowd around, talking to each other in Kalenjin. Then Mutai looks at me.

'Do you want to sell it?'

Just over two weeks later, I'm sitting in the Grand Pri restaurant in Eldoret waiting for the start of the London marathon. The owner, the former half-marathon world record holder and world 10,000m champion Moses Tanui, has promised a London marathon party, and the whole place is kitted out with red balloons and posters. Moses and his friends are all wearing red Virgin London Marathon jackets, smiling and handing out whistles.

Downstairs in the underground bar area, hundreds of people are sitting awaiting the start on the big screen. The only problem is that there is no power, and the race is about to begin.

Moses seems unperturbed. He has a generator, he says. Things will be up and running in a minute. But when the power eventually comes on, about forty-five minutes later, for some reason the only thing any of the TVs can tune in to is a programme called *Gospel Sunday*.

We sit and wait. Moses has invited me to watch the race in his personal office, which has the biggest TV I've ever seen in it. Also watching the race here is a host of other former star runners, including Emmanuel Mutai's coach.

Nobody else seems perturbed that we are missing the race. They sit chatting calmly as the minutes tick by. After a while I decide to see what the atmosphere is like downstairs in the packed bar. On the way down I pass Moses on the stairs.

'Sorry,' he says as he passes, talking urgently on his phone. He looks slightly traumatised. Inside the bar it's completely empty. The last man is just leaving.

'The Klique hotel,' he tells me. 'It has screens.'

I leave Moses fretting with a team of engineers and head to the Klique hotel around the corner. It is rammed to the rafters with people cheering and blowing whistles.

By the time I arrive, Mary Keitany has a big lead in the women's race. A few weeks ago I was sitting in awkward silence in her cramped living room drinking orange squash. Now here she is on the television, racing away to win the London marathon.

The men's race is just beginning to hot up, with Emmanuel Mutai still in the lead pack, running with the same fluid form and easy air he had on the dusty tracks of Kaptagat just weeks before. A big cheer goes up as he surges to the front of the field at around 30 km and starts leaving the others behind, and I find myself cheering and blowing my whistle like everyone else.

He seems to be floating through the streets of London. I can see the people standing by the road there, marvelling, wondering where he came from, how he can run so fast, so easy. His burst is quite spectacular. He puts in the fastest 10 km ever run in a marathon (28 minutes 44 seconds) to leave the rest of the field flailing far behind, winning the race in the fourth-fastest marathon time in history and a new course record. He really was ready.

After the race, I feel a warm glow of connectivity as I tumble out of the bar with everyone else. In the street outside I bump into a few of the other runners from the camp.

They smile and shake my hand. 'Emmanuel ran well,' they say calmly, as if it's what they expected. He has just run one of the greatest marathons ever, but to them it's just another day's work.

19

During the early days, the only measure of endurance was to catch an antelope.

Mike Boit

Brother Colm says he has been in Kenya so long that he feels Kenyan now. And like a Kenyan he can be difficult to pin down. One morning I ring him to see if I can come and watch his star athlete, David Rudisha, training. He says he doesn't know what time Rudisha will run, and when I push him to see if I can come by another day, he gets suddenly annoyed.

'I don't do schedules,' he says, spelling it out for me in the overly pronounced way he talks to his athletes. 'Rudisha told me last night he had a cold so probably won't train today. But maybe he'll run in Eldoret. Maybe he'll turn up here [in Iten]. I can't say "at ten o'clock we'll be doing so and so". My athletes are elite athletes. They don't need to be in peak shape until August [for the World Championships]. They're not like all those runners you see in Iten, running around hoping some eejit will see them and send them off to some race somewhere. I mean, it's a good thing they're out there running, it's better than sniffing glue in Eldoret, but half of them don't know what they're doing or when they're racing or what.'

He's less curmudgeonly about his Easter camp. He tells me to come along at 10 a.m. any time during the holiday.

These camps were among the first training camps in Kenya, and certainly the first in Iten, set up by Brother Colm in the 1980s to help develop the region's junior talent.

Japhet went to one of these camps when he was seventeen. He has a treasured photograph from it on the wall in his house. I ask him what he learned there.

'Form,' he says, without hesitating. 'He taught me about form.' It's a common answer. Nixon Chepseba, the 1500m runner at the One 4 One camp, also went to St Patrick's school and trained with Brother Colm. He says the same thing, that Brother Colm taught him about form.

It's an interesting answer. Most Kenyans have a lovely, fluid running form, which I assumed was because they all grow up running barefoot. So how is it that Brother Colm's secret is teaching form?

When I turn up at his house, he's just leaving, full of purpose. This, you can tell, is what he loves doing. Nurturing the champions of the future.

Before the training begins, he takes me around to the school kitchen where a man is cooking beans in an industrial-size vat. Brother Colm wants to check that the cooks received the ugali flour he sent them. I follow on behind, smiling and shaking hands with everyone we pass as we head on through the dimly lit dining hall. Along one side, beyond the rows of benches and tables, is the school's Wall of Fame. It's full of framed photographs of runners. If you look closely, you can spot an incredible array of Kenya's most celebrated athletes. There's the former St Patrick's student Wilson Kipketer (three-times world champion and former 800m world record holder) planting a tree in the school grounds, while

Richard Chelimo and Matthew Birir sit with Brother Colm on a sofa showing off their medals after the 1992 Olympics. Another grainy shot shows the 1988 Olympic gold medallist Peter Rono hurtling around a dusty track.

Brother Colm passes through the hall and out onto the field at the front of the school. Groups of young athletes are gathering, ambling across the grass from their dormitories. Waiting for everyone to arrive is a young man called Ian. Although he is only twenty-five, Brother Colm has signed him up as his assistant. Quietly spoken and baby-faced, he doesn't have the air of a coach, but once the athletes are ready, he stands before them and explains the session.

Brother Colm lets him talk, standing with me a few yards away.

'I chose Ian because he has a gymnastics background,' he tells me. 'He understands form.'

Ian sets the athletes off jogging around the small field. They jog slowly, in single file.

'We're looking to see which of them have rhythm,' Brother Colm explains. 'They should naturally fall into the rhythm of the athlete in front.'

'What if they don't have rhythm?' I ask, watching one girl who seems to be struggling to match the easy, synchronised flow of everyone else.

'Then we work on them,' he says.

Among the athletes I spot Rudisha jogging around in the middle of one of the groups. The world athlete of the year. The fastest 800m runner in history. Taking part in a school holiday camp. Not as a mentor, or teacher, but as one of the athletes. That's the level of professionalism that these schoolchildren are working to. Their faces are focused, serious. Each has been hand-selected for the camp by Brother Colm after he spent the winter travelling to school races across the region. An invite to the camp is an honour. But more importantly, it's an opportunity. So many have come here and then gone on to become professional athletes. Brother Colm says he has about a 60 per cent success rate. I look around, wondering which of these youngsters will be stepping onto the track at the next Olympics. No doubt a few of them will.

All the athletes, I notice, are wearing shoes.

'What do you think about barefoot running?' I ask. For some reason it feels like a naive, almost stupid question. As though I'm asking him if he thinks athletes run better with shorter hair.

'We do all our exercises at the school in bare feet,' he says, looking at me, making sure I'm listening. 'In the West we put children in shoes before they can walk. What are we teaching them? We're teaching them that the ground is dangerous, that they need to be protected from it. But Kenyan children can feel the ground, so they have a better relationship with it. They learn to place their foot carefully when they run, so they don't hurt themselves. They learn to land gently, lightly, gliding over the earth rather than pounding it.'

Brother Colm says he works on it not because he thinks the Kenyans have bad form, but because he wants to turn good form into perfect form. Breaking world records and winning gold medals requires fine polishing of talent. The running barefoot is one part of a formula that produces that talent, he says. A talent completely derived from their upbringing.

'It is a hard, physical life, one that makes them strong, disciplined and motivated to succeed,' he says. 'When the athletes come to me at fifteen or sixteen, they are 60 per cent already there.' What he is doing by working on their form is giving them the tools to nurture that talent, that strength, born out of hardship, and turn it into gold.

After the training we head back to the dining hall for a mid-morning snack of jam and Blue Band margarine sandwiches. I sit with Brother Colm and Ian, while the athletes sit at an adjoining table eating dry slices of bread.

'They don't like jam,' says Brother Colm, reaching for another sandwich and then leaning back against the peeling wall, his feet up on the bench. 'So these are just for the coaches.'

We sit for a moment in silence, munching on the sandwiches, the sound of pots clanking in the kitchen. I'm still mulling over his comments out on the field. I ask them both if they've heard about the Born to Run theory that humans evolved through running.

'We had Daniel Liebermann here,' says Ian. 'He was a nice man.' Liebermann was one of the Harvard scientists who developed the theory. He did it through studying Kenyan athletes. I feel like I'm at the very source of the story. This retired Irish priest and his twenty-five-year-old Kenyan assistant. They're an unlikely pair of sages.

'After Mike Boit won his Commonwealth gold medal,' Brother Colm says, sitting up and putting his feet back on the floor, 'they held a big celebration in his home village.' Mike Boit, a former student at St Patrick's, won an Olympic bronze medal in the 800m in the 1972 Olympics. In 1978 he won gold in the Commonwealth Games. 'At the celebration, his childhood friend came up to him. The two of them used to run around together as children. He shook Boit's hand. "That's all very well," he said, pointing to his gold medal. "But can you still catch an antelope?"'

He's leaning forward, watching me, a half-smile across his face. Chairs screech across the floor behind us as the athletes all get up and head back outside. They had been so quiet, I had forgotten they were there. Brother Colm sits back against the wall, as though snapping shut a book. That's it, my lesson is over. He has seen many people over the years coming to discover the secrets of the Kenyan runners. Even that morning, a camera crew from Ireland has been setting up, preparing to spend the week following him, no doubt wanting to discover the Kenyan secrets.

'We even had one man from Sweden who wanted to analyse the ugali,' he says, pulling the cling film back over the tray of sandwiches. 'I told him to bring some of the flour home to test it, but he said he needed to cook it at altitude, in Kenyan water, in a Kenyan pot.' Brother Colm is incredulous at the stupidity of it.

'Did he discover anything?' I ask.

'Absolutely nothing,' he says, almost spitting in delight. 'You people come to find the secret, but you know what the secret is? That you think there's a secret. There is no secret.' I haven't mentioned a secret, but he's fuming now, his arms folded across his chest.

Ian, sitting opposite him, as serene as a poet, suggests we head outside to see the athletes again before they disappear for their midday naps.

*

Brother Colm may be convinced that there is no secret to Kenya's running success, but it hasn't stopped endless scientists coming out to Kenya to conduct studies to try and unearth the magic formula.

What intrigues many scientists is the fact that most of Kenya's top runners come from one particular ethnic group, the Kalenjin. In 2011, 66 of the world's top 100 marathon runners were from Kenya, almost every one a Kalenjin. Long-distance running is one of the most popular participation sports in the world, and Kalenjins account for just 0.06 per cent of the global population. It's such a staggering dominance, one of the most remarkable in all the annals of sport, that most people, particularly casual observers, will just throw up their hands and say: it must be in the genes.

It is scientific fact that genes have a significant effect on athletic performance. One person can train for months, getting up at dawn every morning, sticking on the *Rocky* music, eating the right food, and will still struggle to break two hours for a half-marathon, while another person, with the same upbringing, can turn up with minimal training and breeze around in 1 hour 20 minutes. That's down to genetics, or, as we usually refer to it when we're not talking about East African runners, talent.

Genes determine how tall we are, how well we respond to training, the colour of our skin, and whether we are male or female. The effect of gender on athletic performance is so marked that we split the competitors up. So genetics makes a difference to how fast people run, that much is clear. That top athletes are all people with a genetic advantage towards their discipline is also fairly certain. What is less clear, however, is whether Kenyans, and more specifically, Kalenjins, have better running genes than people in other parts of the world.

So far, there is no scientific evidence that they do. Yannis Pitsiladis has been working tirelessly on this for at least a decade now, spending months on end conducting tests in a laboratory in Eldoret's Moi University, and after ten years he says he can't find a single gene or group of genes unique to East Africans to explain their phenomenal running success.

Without the hard evidence, but in light of the huge discrepancy between the size of the Kalenjin population and its dominance in running, many people have looked elsewhere for indicators of genetic advantage.

One theory is based on an outdated Kalenjin custom: cattle rustling. Before the British settled in the region at the beginning of the twentieth century, bringing with them new crops and agricultural techniques, the Kalenjin people were largely cattle herders and, often, cattle raiders. The Nandi and Kipsigi ethnic subgroups were particularly aggressive cattle rustlers. Their raids would often take them hundreds of miles from home, then they would run back with their stolen animals as fast as they could before the owners could catch them. It was a dangerous game that only the fittest, strongest and fastest runners survived. The better a young man was at raiding, the more cattle he accumulated. The Kalenjin were, and to a lesser extent still are, a largely polygamous society, and so the more cows a man had, the more wives he could buy, and the more children he was likely to father.

The theory is that this reproductive advantage may have

caused a significant shift in the Kalenjin's genetic make-up over the course of a few centuries, leading to them becoming better runners.

The US journalist John Manners, who was partly raised in the Rift Valley, believes that this is the case. 'If you weren't good at running,' he says, 'you were more likely to get killed. If you were, you were more likely to have children.'

A few years ago, John set up a programme called KenSAP (the Kenya Scholar-Athlete Project), which sends top students to elite colleges in the US, such as Harvard and Yale. The idea was based on John's belief that virtually all Kalenjins can run. He thought that if he picked the top students from the Rift Valley region, the ones with the best grades in their high-school exams, perhaps half of them would be good enough at running to interest the track and cross-country coaches at the US colleges, who might then help process their applications. The first year he managed to get scholarships for six students, two of whom he thought were good enough to pitch directly to the track coach at Harvard.

'But it didn't pan out,' he tells me. 'Once they got there, the students weren't committed enough to the training. They were scared of missing their studies. Essentially, they were duds.'

So the experiment failed? If anything, it showed that not all Kalenjins can run after all, right?

'Not quite,' he says. John didn't stop there. The next year he put his potential scholars through six weeks of training, and got them to run a 1500m time trial, so he had a better idea of which ones to pitch to the US colleges as runners.

'In seven years, we've sent seventy-six kids to top US

schools,' he says. 'Of those, twenty-eight were pitched as potential athletes. Fourteen didn't pan out, mainly through lack of commitment. To be on a team at a US college means around three hours of training a day.'

But, fourteen of his seventy-six A-grade students turned out to be decent enough runners to make the varsity track or cross-country teams. Of those, four were the best athletes in their college, three became All-Americans, an honorary title given to the best runners in a particular season, and one became a nine-time Division III champion.

'From what was essentially a random selection of Kalenjins, these achievements are pretty impressive,' John rightly points out. 'It leads to the conclusion that there is something special about the Kalenjin.'

He's right, of course, there is something special about the Kalenjin, but I'm not as convinced as he is that it necessarily suggests a genetic advantage. Although none of the students he sent to the US were athletes before they left – they were too busy studying – they all benefited from active childhoods, no doubt running to and from school, probably barefoot or in flimsy plimsolls. They were raised at altitude. They benefited from a carbohydrate-rich, low-fat diet. So they all came to John with a strong inbuilt endurance base – their house, as Renato Canova, the top Italian coach, would put it, was already built. So much so that when pushed into running, they were physically ready to go. Of course, some people just aren't great runners, but if we really were all born to run, as the scientists argue, then to get fourteen good runners from a selection of seventy-six fit, healthy teenagers is perhaps not such a surprise.

If you took a comparable group of English or American students, the chances are that they would have spent their lives doing very little physical exercise and probably eating bad food. Stuck on a track and asked to run 1500m, most of them would probably look at you as if you were mad. They would probably never have run that far in their lives, except perhaps on some forced cross-country race in first grade. Would it be such a surprise to find that only one or two of them, if that, could run?

Yannis Pitsiladis says he has heard the cow herding theory, but that it doesn't add up. 'There just isn't enough time,' he says. 'Genetic adaptations take thousands of years, and besides, the Kalenjin are not an isolated gene pool, they have been mixing with other ethnic groups. It's a nice story, but that's all.'

Of course, just because the hard evidence hasn't been found yet doesn't mean that Kenyans, and more specifically Kalenjins, don't have a genetic advantage. But I don't think we should hypothesise that they do simply on the basis of their performances in races. Not only is that unscientific, but it seems that there are enough other contributory factors that, when taken together, explain Kenya's running dominance.

Presuming a genetic advantage also diminishes the incredible achievements of the Kenyan athletes. If they do have an inbuilt genetic advantage, it changes the way we perceive their victories. It lessens our admiration for all their hard work, determination, fortitude.

It also changes the way other athletes feel about their chances of competing, of even trying to compete. It's dangerous to conclude that because so many people from one ethnic group win so many races they must therefore have a genetic advantage. If that's the case, the rest of the world might as well give up.

20

'Don't think. Feel. It is like a finger pointing a way to the moon. Don't concentrate on the finger or you will miss all that heavenly glory.'
    Bruce Lee, *Enter the Dragon*

'Finn,' says Godfrey cheerily when I call him up. 'Great to have you back.'

I've been to Ethiopia, Kenya's northern neighbour and the world's other great running nation. I ran a half-marathon there in the town of Hawassa, about 170 miles south of Addis Ababa. The race was organised by Haile Gebrselassie, arguably the greatest runner ever – from 1993 until 2000 he won every major 10,000m gold medal, including two Olympic Games, while during his career he broke an astounding twenty-four world records. The great man has a luxury hotel on the shores of Lake Hawassa.

The night before the half-marathon, I bumped into the former British marathon runner Hugh Jones in the hotel lobby. He told me he was now an IAAF official and was there to measure the course.

'It's not a PB course,' he told me when I said I was hoping to run a personal best time. 'It goes off-road along by the lake and the path is quite bumpy.'

Still, after all my training, even with the bumpy trail and the altitude (around 5,500 feet), I was hopeful. I'd been training harder than I'd ever done. I felt leaner than I had in years. I had visible calf muscles for the first time in my life.

At the start I was relieved to find the competition less intimidating than the cross-country in Eldoret. The field had been split into two races, an elite race and a mass race. I was in the mass race, along with lots of other foreigners, mainly aid workers based in Addis Ababa. The Ethiopians in the race were mainly aid workers, too, as far as I could gather.

Almost immediately after the horn sounded for the start, I found myself running on my own, a lead group of about six runners pulling ahead, and everyone else disappearing somewhere behind me. The course headed along a road into the town and then detoured down along a dirt track by the lake. Fishermen stopped their work as we ran by, frozen like photographs, their nets half drawn in. A herd of glistening horses hauled themselves up out of the water, crossing the path. The runners in front of me managed to skirt around one side, making the horses skip back. I spotted my chance and nipped through the same gap. I was feeling strong, and starting to reel in the leaders.

Halfway round the second of three large laps, I caught a glimpse of my shadow on the paved road and was surprised to see that I actually looked like an athlete, striding along the wide avenue. Twelve kilometres done and I was feeling great, running at a good pace. 'Good, good,' people said as I cruised past.

By the time I passed the same point on the third lap, however, it wasn't such a glorious sight. My stride length had shortened, my arms had stopped moving. I was struggling with a stitch, which forced me to stop for a moment along by the lake and do some stretching. It kept coming and going. The slower I ran, the better it was. Or was that just my mind playing tricks on me? I was caught in a battle of wills between my desire to run as fast as I could and my body's desire to slow down.

But the desire to run fast was being drowned out by the internal chatter that told me it didn't really matter what time I ran, or where I finished, that nobody really cared, not even me, that I should just enjoy the experience. I ended up virtually jogging the last kilometre, up the long road to Haile's resort, past a troupe of threadbare white horses grazing among half-built apartment blocks.

Here at the end, the road was lined with spectators, three people deep, who clapped quietly, or just stared out from under their shawls. The runner ahead of me was too far away to chase, and I couldn't see anyone else behind. As I reached sight of the finish I saw the excited faces of Marietta and the children. They were all smiling and clapping and I mustered a little surge to the line in their honour.

Despite talking myself down from pushing on too hard, I managed to finish in seventh place, in a personal best time of 1 hour 26 minutes and 47 seconds. The seconds were important, because it was a best time by just seven seconds.

The great man, Gebrselassie, was standing there waiting to greet me like a long-lost friend. I gave him a sweaty hug, and walked on to collect my medal and free T-shirt.

'That's great to run a PB,' Godfrey says when I tell him my time. It's hard to know how I feel afterwards. After four months of training with the greatest runners in the world, I'd knocked seven seconds off my best half-marathon time. With only six weeks left until the Lewa marathon, I was really hoping for a bigger improvement than that.

'You did brilliantly,' says Marietta when I suggest I'm not happy. 'You were right near the front.' It was certainly better than my performance in Eldoret, so at least I was moving in the right direction.

Sitting by the hotel's infinity pool the next morning, overlooking the dark waters of Lake Hawassa, I was still brooding on the race. I thought hard about how I had lost the psychological battle, running along that long, straight road, my resolve blown away like a silk scarf in the wind. I just wasn't ready, mentally, for when the crunch came.

'You've said this before,' said Marietta, trying to help. 'Is there anything you can do about it? Anything you can learn?'

She was right, it had happened to me before in other races, my mind whispering in my ear, 'What's the hurry? Who cares?' until I went, 'OK, you're right,' and I eased down.

Kenyans are not so flaky in races. Partly it's simply because they're usually nearer to the front. During my win in Powderham Castle, such thoughts didn't bother me. Driven on by the growing belief that I could actually win, I managed to stay focused until the end.

But it's not just that. For a Kenyan runner, driven on by a will to change his life, the stakes are much higher. Even for top Western runners, winning a race is unlikely to have the same impact on their lives as it will for a Kenyan runner. For someone who has spent years living at a subsistence level, even $1,000 can change everything.

Kenyans are also more used to hardship in their daily lives, so that when it appears rising up at them near the end of a race, they are less cowed by it. One theory about why Kalenjins are so psychologically tough, or the men at least, deals with the circumcision ceremony all Kalenjin boys have to go through as adolescents. They are expected to stand in front of the village elders and endure the pain unblinking, without betraying a single flicker of emotion on their faces. One wince and their passage to manhood is for ever incomplete and they are cast aside from the community as cowards. Many athletes have told me that after passing through such an ordeal, all other challenges they face in life, such as a sprint finish at the end of a race, seem easy.

Another reason Kenyans may be mentally tough is that they seem to spend less time analysing while they're running. If you ask a Kenyan runner what was happening in his head during a race, he will usually say something as simple as 'I felt good, so I ran faster' or 'I felt tired, so I stopped.' A Western runner, in contrast, will be able to tell you exactly what his thoughts were at each mile, what his time splits were, how his tactics changed during the race. Many of the Kenyan runners I meet tell me that they don't wear a watch when they're racing, that they prefer to run on feeling. For most Western runners, this would be a dangerous approach. It would be like going on a long car journey and switching off the speedometer and petrol gauge.

But as Renato Canova said after one of his Kenyan charges won a big-city marathon in the US recently: 'If you want to be a top athlete you have to be a little bit wild, not be an accountant.' Wild like Ismael Kirui in Stuttgart in 1993, who went with his feeling, spurred on to a crazy pace with seven laps still to go. He wasn't calculating his average lap times that night, he just felt good and went, and he ended up as world champion.

So what I learned from the race in Hawassa, or am now learning, is that next time I need to be mentally prepared, to find a way to keep my focus and will-power locked in on the target, and to keep my distracting, debilitating thoughts at bay. I don't want to end the Lewa marathon dawdling home like a tourist on safari, telling myself I'm too tired to run, that I should just watch the wildlife and not worry about the minutes rushing away, the people streaming past me. I didn't come all this way, and do all this training, to flake out right at the end.

But without the same driving forces pushing me on as the Kenyans, what should I do? I've heard people say they have their own special chant that they use. I remember Paula Radcliffe once saying that she managed to outrun the great Ethiopian Geta Wami to win the New York marathon by chanting 'I love you Isla' – Isla being her baby daughter – over and over in her head. Maybe I should try that next time, although I can already hear my mind reasoning that my kids don't really care about my race position or what time I run.

But then, I'm sure Isla didn't care either. What really pushed Paula on was her love for her daughter, not her daughter's approval. But why should love make her run harder?

The actor Sean Connery was once asked in an interview what, if anything, made him cry. After thinking for a few moments, he replied, 'Athletics.' I often feel the same way. Watching runners racing for the line, relying on nothing but themselves, their own will-power, fighting their own limitations, eyes fixed ahead in complete focus, the dedication of years of hard work etched across their faces, can bring tears to your eyes. Running is a brutal and emotional sport. It's also a simple, primal sport. As humans, on a most basic level, we get hungry, we sleep, we yearn for love, we run. Just watch small children left to play unsupervised. They can't stop running. It is part of what makes us human.

Perhaps it is to fulfil this primal urge that runners and joggers get up every morning and pound the streets in cities all over the world. To feel the stirring of something primeval deep down in the pits of our bellies. To feel 'a little bit wild'. Running is not exactly fun. Running hurts. It takes effort. Ask any runner why he runs, and he will probably look at you with a wry smile and say: 'I don't know.' But something keeps us going.

We may obsess about our PBs and mileage count, but these things alone are not enough to get us out running. We could find easier ways to chart and measure things. We could become trainspotters, or accountants. No, the times and charts are merely carrots we dangle in front of our rational mind, our over-analytical brain, to give it a reason to come along for the ride. What really drives us on is something else, this need to feel human, to reach below the multitude of layers of roles and responsibilities society has placed on us, down below the company name tags, even the father, husband, son labels, to the pure, raw human being underneath. At such moments, our rational mind becomes redundant. We move from thought to feeling.

Except our mind doesn't just stop. Many runners say

they become aware of their thoughts when they run. All day our thoughts churn away, turning us this way and that, but it doesn't bother us in the slightest. Yet the minute we start moving away from its carefully constructed world of reason, into the wild heart of existence, our mind panics. Our thoughts try to pull us back, to slow us down. But like the marathon monks of Mount Hiei in Japan, who run 1,000 ultramarathons in 1,000 days in the search for enlightenment, if we push on, we begin to feel a tingling sense of who we really are. It's a powerful feeling, strong enough to have us coming back for more, again and again.

Love, too, connects us with a primal feeling deep within us, far from the realm of reason. Which is why Paula's chant worked. The love she felt for her daughter and the raw emotion of running come from the same source. Evoking love helped push her on, even though rationally it shouldn't have made any difference. Her daughter couldn't hear her internal chant, and even if she could, at nine months old she was oblivious to the whole concept of marathon running. But by calling on such a strong emotion, Paula was able to bypass such reasoning. Her rational brain, which was telling her, no doubt, to slow down, was overcome.

I decide to try it the next time I'm struggling on a run.

21

It's precisely because of the pain, precisely because we want to overcome that pain, that we can get the feeling, through this process, of really being alive.
Haruki Murakami

It's a beautiful, lazy Easter Monday afternoon in Iten. All morning, the streets were deserted as the entire town crammed into the tin churches that sit on virtually every street corner. The preachers did their best to outdo each other, their sermons blaring through speakers placed out in the street in an effort to spread the gospel as far as possible.

It's the last day in town for Marietta and the children. For the next few weeks they are going to stay with Jophie and Alastair in Lewa, leaving me to immerse myself in my running. Marietta asks me to take a walk with her through the neighbourhood one last time, down to the viewpoint that looks out across the valley. Lila and Uma are off playing with their friends, running along the rows of houses, laughing and disappearing through doorways. So we take Ossian and wander off down the lane that runs along beside our high metal fence, past the little kiosk. A lady is digging a small square of earth with her daughter. She stands up as we go by, dropping her hand plough and mopping her brow.

'Marietta,' she says. 'Where are you going?'

'Just for a walk,' says Marietta. 'It's my last day in Iten today.'

The woman looks shocked. 'Why?' she says. 'You should stay and buy a plot here.' The woman is a single mother with two children who works at the hospital, runs a little shop, grows maize and owns two cows for milk. She asks us if we have a cow back home in England, and gives us a look of disbelief and pity when Marietta tells her that we don't. 'Then you must buy one when you get home,' she says.

One of her cows lumbers across the mud towards the fence, which gets Ossian excited. He has a stick in his hand and is poking it through the stakes and making a noise like a cow herder.

'Rarr, rarr,' he says, hitting the fence with his twig. The woman laughs as we start to walk on.

'Leave me to my struggle,' she says, waving us on our way.

All along the path we pass small homesteads with families sitting outside preparing food or just drinking tea and talking. Each time, the children run over, giggling and reaching out hands, while the mothers wave at us.

'*Iyamune?*' we say. It means 'How are you?' in Kalenjin. '*Chamage,*' comes the reply. Everyone is fine.

'It seems a shame to be leaving now,' says Marietta. 'I feel that we're just settling in. It's starting to feel like home.' We turn the corner and the sky opens out before us. Small houses continue to dot the landscape further down the slope, dropping away into the hazy distance.

'It's beautiful,' she says, stopping to admire it as Ossian ambles along behind us. 'I love the way that when you wake up in the morning here, the first thing you do is step outside. In England we're always cooped up in our houses and cars, like little bubbles, removed from everyone else.'

'You think you could live here?' I ask her. Even though she is right, there is something enviable about the simplicity of life here, I'm not sure I could make the leap to living here. I don't really know why, but somehow I feel tied to my life back in England.

'I don't know,' she says.

Despite feeling settled in Iten, we stick to our plan, and I return from Lewa alone, racing Alastair's little car up the Uganda highway, dodging the lorries and matatus, winding my way up the patchwork slopes, past the scenes of numerous accidents, back to the little town of runners.

As usual, the first sight that greets me on arriving back in Iten is scores of people running along beside the road. On and on they go, day after day, tearing up mile after mile, in the hope, as Brother Colm puts it, that some eejit will send them to a race. Well, for a few of them, that eejit is me.

I call up all the other Iten Town Harriers to see how they are and to arrange to do another long run that weekend. We're running out of days now, so it's time for me to make it to 30 km.

I'm going to spend my last few weeks in Iten at the Kimbia training camp. This is where Godfrey works, and he has invited me to stay. I've gradually realised, however, that he doesn't really work here. It's a complicated story and is different each time, depending on who tells it. The camp was originally set up by a US agent who employed a German coach to train the athletes. But the coach started to become an agent himself, so they split the camp in two. Godfrey was a multi-purpose operator, part coach, part scout, part facilitator. But the German coach took a dislike to his laid-back style, and banned him from the house. Neither of the agents lives in Kenya, however, and all the athletes like Godfrey, so he comes back surreptitiously now and then when he needs somewhere to stay in Iten. He also invites his friends to stay.

When I first arrive, the only person staying in the house is Anders. He seems happy to have some company, and shows me to my room.

'You've got the best room,' he says. 'It has a great painting on the wall.' The painting is a map of the world, painted by some Peace Corps volunteers who stayed here once. Otherwise the room is fairly sparse. A blood-red chipped concrete floor. Two single beds with mosquito nets tied up above them, and a piece of string running from one end of the room to the other for hanging clothes on.

A few days later, three of the camp's athletes return from a spell of racing in Germany. They come bustling in one evening, shaking my hand and settling down quickly in front of the television. They've been missing their Mexican soap opera. The TV room is more like a storeroom than a place to relax. There's a fold-up table right in front of the television, a massage table shoved into one corner, three stacks of plastic chairs, and piles of running trainers by the door, next to an empty glass cabinet. The athletes pull out enough chairs for everyone and place them in a circle around the television as Mama Kibet, the camp's cook, brings in a small charcoal stove, which she places on the floor in the middle of the room. The three of them are in heaven when she brings through the ugali.

As they eat hungrily, I ask them if they missed the ugali

while they were in Germany. They all nod vigorously, their mouths too full to speak.

While we had our own house in Iten, we ate a mixture of Kenyan food and food the children were more familiar with, such as pasta and soup. We had ugali occasionally, but now, in the camp, it is part of my daily diet. I tuck in, trying to will it on, telling myself to enjoy the frugal blandness of it. Mixed with the stewed kale Mama Kibet has given us it's nice, but on its own, especially after it has gone cold, it feels fairly pointless. The other athletes, in their excitement, try to get me to eat more, but really, I've had enough.

The Kenyans are always joking that it is the ugali that makes them so fast. It's not as far-fetched as it might seem. While alone it is not the secret of Kenyan running, it is a small part of the puzzle I'm gradually putting together. As Yannis Pitsiladis says, after years of research: 'It's not any one thing. But all of them.'

As well as the physical, active nature of a typical, rural Kenyan childhood, the altitude, the barefoot running, the intense dedication, the diet of the athletes plays a role, too.

In the Rift Valley, everyone grows up eating a diet full of carbohydrates, with very little fat. Beans, rice, ugali and green vegetables are the staples. Occasionally the runners will eat meat or drink milk. It is very hard, in Iten at least, to find cakes, ice cream, cheese, burgers, pizzas – all those fatty things we love so much in the West. They just don't exist. When our neighbour Hilda had a party for her tenth birthday, her mother had to get a cake driven in from Eldoret.

Yannis tells the story of a group of German scientists who

wanted to study the Kenyan physiology, but rather than conduct the research in Kenya, they brought some runners back to Germany. 'The interesting part for me,' says Yannis, 'is that after just two weeks in Germany, they all put on 5 kg.'

When I visited the house in Teddington before leaving for Kenya, one of the athletes, as he stood stirring the ugali, asked me how much I weighed. The others were sitting in the kitchen listening to our conversation. The last time I had weighed myself, I was 80 kg, but I'd been training quite hard, so I knocked off a few kilograms. '77 kg,' I said. The runner looked at me surprised, and even stopped stirring for a second. One of the other athletes said something in Kalenjin, but I could tell by the tone of his voice that he was asking for confirmation from his friend that what he had just heard was really true.

'77 kg?' the athlete asked me, to be sure. 'Yes,' I said. 'Is that a lot?' He nodded, still unsure he was hearing me right.

He said he was 59 kg, while one of the other athletes was only 51 kg.

Two weeks before we leave Iten for Lewa, I manage to find some scales in the petrol station where Japhet's uncle works. I'm 69 kg. I've lost 8 kg since leaving England. Of course, all the running is a significant factor, but so too is the diet. With hardly any fat in my diet, I'm now fighting weight.

Godfrey rings me that night to see how I'm settling in at the Kimbia house, and to tell me there has been a change of plan regarding our Lewa team's long run the next day.

The truck has been double-booked, and he doesn't sound as though he has the energy to find another one. I suggest that we just drive to Eldoret in my car and run back along the paved road. He sounds distracted as he agrees, telling me it's a good idea.

We decide to leave at 7 a.m. to mimic the start time of the marathon in Lewa, but when I call Chris, he's not happy.

'It's too late,' he says. He's also unhappy about the route. 'Only mzungus run along the paved road,' he says. But we don't have a truck to go off-road. Reluctantly he agrees to be picked up just after 7 a.m. outside his school.

At 6.30 a.m. my phone rings. It's Chris.

'Hello, sir,' he says. 'I'm at the school. I'm ready. We need to get started.'

Anders has decided to come along too, so after we get dressed and fill up our water bottles, we roll the car out of the gate and head off to find Japhet and Beatrice. Beatrice has turned up with a friend. I guess she's feeling a little out-numbered by the men in our team. Having a friend will also give her someone to run with, but it means we're now five in the car. Luckily, the team is depleted today, with Shadrack and Philip not running. Josphat also hasn't turned up.

'He's gone to the US,' Japhet tells us.

'What for?' I ask, surprised. 'Is he coming back?'

'He's gone to race. I don't know when he'll be back.'

Even though he's good friends with Josphat, Chris is also surprised when he hears the news.

'That is not good, man,' he says. 'He should have at least informed somebody.' Godfrey, too, is full of consternation. 'He must respect the team,' says Godfrey, shaking his head.

'It's not good.' Personally, I don't mind. He was a troubled character, Josphat. One time we went to visit his home down in the valley. He hadn't seen his wife or children for at least a week, but he just barged into the house, picked up a bag and left again without a word of greeting to them. His children stood around in bare feet and ripped clothes watching with their big, silent eyes as we climbed back into the car. I waved a solitary goodbye as Chris started the engine, and we left.

No, Josphat is no big loss from the team. In fact, everyone is already suggesting we replace him with a good mutual friend called Paul Tanui. Known as The Preacher because of his religious fervour, Paul is one of the nicest men in Iten. When you talk to him, everything is always 'fantastic'.

Like Josphat, Paul is a veteran journeyman athlete who has won numerous smaller races around the world. He is excited when I ask him if he'd like to run with us in Lewa.

'Yes,' he says, his voice swooshing the word like a balloon lifting off into the sky. 'Of course.'

Once we get to Eldoret, Chris starts remonstrating with Godfrey about the route. Why are we running along the road back to Iten? he wants to know. Godfrey isn't sure.

'Finn, do you really want to run on the road?' he asks. Kenyans very rarely run on concrete, and having driven along the road from Iten just now I can see that it's not the nicest run. But I'm worried about the car going off-road.

'I know another route nearby,' says Godfrey. 'Just a few kilometres along the road. It's very flat. The car will be fine.'

So we pile in and start out along another paved road. Unfortunately, this road is so potholed it's like trying to drive across stepping stones. I have to keep to a painful crawl, the morning sun rising higher into the sky with each passing minute. Chris grins at me. 'I told you,' he says, 'seven o'clock is too late.'

I slalom around the road, left and right, for around 20 km, with Godfrey telling me at each corner that we're almost there. His promises begin to become meaningless after an hour or so.

Eventually we get there. It's a relief to get out of the car. We're in a tiny settlement that has built up around the intersection between two roads: a few houses, a petrol station and a school. We all get ready as Godfrey talks us through the route. This time I'm doing 30 km – my longest run ever.

As we line up at the start, Godfrey gives us his now customary pep talk, with Chris doing his customary best to look like he's ignoring it.

'Right, as we all know, this town is called . . .' Godfrey begins, looking around. He looks at Chris. 'What's this town called?' he asks.

Anders, Beatrice, her friend and I get a ten-minute head start, running along a straight, flat road that stretches out before us like a thin pencil line, cutting the landscape in two. I'm wearing a cap given to me by Anders's mother, Joan Benoit. She has just been in Iten visiting him. Not really knowing much about her career, I looked her up on the internet and managed to find a video of her Olympic victory in 1984. Amazingly she broke away from the field with 22 miles still left to run and just kept ploughing on, a look of steel on her face as she kept on pushing, unrelenting, until the end. All the while she had her cap pulled down low over her eyes.

I pull my cap down, like blinkers, focusing, ignoring everything else but the rhythm of our feet. We run mostly four abreast, not talking. The miles tick by. Beatrice is doing a much better job of keeping with us this time. Occasionally Anders pushes the pace a little, but we claw him back each time with our steady, steady patter. We pass the occasional house, but mostly it's a deserted landscape. Drier here than in Iten. The sun is high now, soaking us with its heat.

Godfrey, in my little car, pops up from time to time, hopping out with his arms full of water bottles, telling us to 'maintain, maintain'. 10 km. 15 km. Somewhere around 17 km we hear a rushing of feet behind us as Chris and Japhet stride past. Nobody speaks.

Soon after, Beatrice starts to fall off the pace, and then at 20 km Anders stops. Chris has stopped, too. I run by, on along the dusty road. My head is too hot for the cap now, so I throw it to Godfrey. I feel released, as though everything up until now was only the warm-up. I push on, leaving Beatrice's friend behind, racking up the miles, feeling like a long-distance runner. The road is more hilly now, but my legs are strong. The car, with the others in it, passes me.

'Good job, Finn,' says Anders from the window as they pass, driving after Japhet who is off ahead somewhere on his own. I see Beatrice looking out of the back window of the car. She must have stopped at 20 km too.

The dust from the car lingers in the air for a while. It's just me now, in the middle of nowhere, running. I find myself smiling. It's like I'm on one of my childhood runs, imagining I'm running across the plains of Africa. I feel fine. The road slopes down and I feel myself striding strongly, faster than ever. I can see the car stopped ahead. They're all waiting. I sprint up to them, grabbing my water bottle as I stop. Thirty kilometres. And still standing.

'Well done, Finn. Good running,' says Godfrey. I stand by the car, smiling. 'Thanks.'

I ran the 30 km route in 2 hours and 7 minutes. Considering the altitude and dirt road, that isn't too bad. Another 12 km in under 53 minutes and I'd run a sub-3-hour marathon. It suddenly feels within my grasp. Even in Lewa. We've run late today. It won't be that much hotter in Lewa. And the altitude will be lower. I'm suddenly progressing quicker than I had expected.

Japhet walks over still looking fresh after finishing in 1 hour 48 minutes. We shake hands, the only two to make it to the end today.

Once I've recovered, we pile back into the car and begin our slow, bumpy way back to Iten. Once we're on the paved road it's better, although we still have to watch out for police checks. All around Kenya, police stand at the side of the road waving people to stop. Then they walk around the car looking for something wrong. Anything will do, a broken mirror, a bare tyre, too many people in the car. At first I never seemed to get stopped, or when they did wave me down, they'd usher me on when they saw that I was a mzungu. I don't know if perhaps it was because I began to look more like I belonged here, but after a few months I started getting stopped. One time I was driving with Anders and his mother when a policeman waved us down. He had a serious look on his face as he patrolled around the outside of the car. I sat still, not wanting to annoy him.

He circled around and then stopped by my window, and told me to get out. He said I'd been driving dangerously, overtaking a lorry on a black spot. The road was straight in both directions.

'How is that a black spot?' I asked, looking around at the road.

He gave me a tiny smile, as though that was hardly the point. As we were driving, Joan had been wanting to stop to use the bathroom, so when I saw her hop out of the car and scuttle away towards the bushes I knew what she was doing. The policeman watched her, a small, elderly white woman with short grey hair. Anders got out of the car and came over to help.

'We were trying to catch our friend who was driving too fast,' he said by way of explanation. It's true, we were following Godfrey in another car. But it wasn't exactly a good excuse. The officer looked at Anders's running shoes.

'Are you athletes?' he asked.

'Yes,' I said, noticing a tiny thaw in his demeanour. 'You see that woman who just walked off?' He nodded, hearing me out. 'She's an Olympic champion,' I said. He smiled, as though I was trying it on. 'That lady? In what?'

'Marathon.' He could tell I was serious. He was shaking his head, but in wonderment rather than disbelief. She was shuffling back now from the bushes.

'Joan Benoit. She won the gold medal in Los Angeles in 1984,' I told him. Joan walked up to us.

'Madam, can I shake your hand?' he said, bowing his head. Joan, unsure what was happening, shook his hand, looking at us for an explanation. 'It's an honour to meet you,' he said. Then, turning to me, smiling like a teddy bear now, 'I'll let you off with a warning.'

'Thank you,' I said, and we all hopped back in the car and drove off in search of Godfrey.

22

Stars of track and field are beautiful people.
  Belle and Sebastian

Time passes slowly at the Kimbia camp. After their morning training the athletes sit on plastic chairs as Mama Kibet stands in the kitchen cooking up the rice and beans for lunch. A cockerel struts around the garden letting out the occasional belated crow, while Mama Kibet's sheep forage nervously at the edges, pulling at the short grass with their teeth.

Mama Kibet is a kind-hearted woman, always laughing. You only have to tell her you enjoyed your lunch and she's off, giggling away. One day I ask her why Godfrey was banned from the camp. It seems unfeasible that anyone could take a dislike to Godfrey. He seems the most benign person on earth, always making sure everyone else is happy. In fact, without a real job, he seems to have made it his life's work to help people.

'You know, in Kenya, people are not straightforward,' she tells me. She doesn't want to elaborate further, but it adds another layer of mystery to Godfrey's character. Anders and I often sit in the garden and wonder if everything is as it seems with him. He tells us he has a wife in western Kenya who is a police officer. He has a son at the expensive Kip Keino school. He has a house and land just outside Eldoret, and another house down in the valley. However, considering

Godfrey is the world's friendliest man, neither of us has ever seen anything of his life. Three times he has invited me to have dinner at his house with his wife, and three times he has cancelled at the last minute.

The athletes in the camp are no help when I ask them about him. They just smile and shake their heads, saying, 'Oh, Godfrey, he's so funny.' So it is with a sense of intrigue that I set out with him one morning on a trip to visit his mother at the family home down in the valley.

As ever with Godfrey, the plan is a complicated one. We need to drive about two hours out of Iten along the edge of the escarpment, where we plan to meet with Shadrack's training partner, David Barmasai. The road down into the valley is too steep and bumpy for my car, so Barmasai is going to lend us the 4×4 truck he has just bought with his winnings from the Dubai marathon. Later we're going to meet him back at Shadrack's parents' house, where it sounds like I'm going to be the guest of honour at a big feast.

'They were going to slaughter a goat for you,' Godfrey tells me as we sit waiting for Barmasai. We've parked up beside a small row of wooden shops pegged onto the edge of the cliff. Behind and under them the sky stretches out above the valley. People stand outside the shops watching us.

'I told him,' Godfrey says, laughing, '"Before you kill that goat, you should know, Finn is a vegetarian." He was so happy he didn't have to kill the goat. He's going to kill a chicken instead.'

Godfrey tries ringing Barmasai, but there is no answer. He should have been here forty minutes ago. A man pulls up beside us on a bicycle. In his basket he has an upside-down sheep. He unties the legs and then hauls it out and ties the rope that's around its neck to a tuft of grass. Then he rides off.

'That must be strong grass,' I say, watching as the sheep, without hesitating, simply carries on with its interminable mission in life, to eat. Godfrey tries ringing Barmasai again. This time he gets through.

'He's on his way,' he tells me after he has finished talking. 'He said they ran later than usual today. I told him it's fine, we're athletes, we understand that training comes first.' The man on the bicycle returns with another sheep which he unties and places down next to the first one. Then he rides off again.

As we wait, Godfrey tells me the story of the time, years ago, when he took an American friend back to his house in the valley. He'd been away racing for quite a few months and arrived back at the house in the middle of the night.

'I tried to open the door, but it wouldn't budge,' he says. 'That's strange, I thought. Then I heard this noise, a hissing noise, and I thought, oh my God.'

'What was it?'

'I knew what it was. It was the hissing sound of termites. There was a termite mound behind my door. Inside my house. My friend looked nervous. I told him there could be a snake, because snakes like to sit on termite mounds. As soon as I mentioned snakes he started running away.' Godfrey chuckles as he tells the story. 'He got into the car and locked the door. When I went to talk to him he only rolled the window down a tiny bit, enough to hear, he was so nervous. Then he wound it back up again.'

Godfrey found a machete and managed to slide it around the door and knock the termite mound over. It crashed down across his bed. 'There was mud everywhere. When I went in I was scared because there could be a snake. I had to sleep on the floor in another room.' His friend was still in the car when he woke up in the morning.

'He wouldn't come out until he saw me,' says Godfrey, shaking his head at the memory.

Finally, about two hours later than arranged, Barmasai arrives, and after swapping cars, we set off.

The road down into the valley has to be one of the most spectacular drives I've ever experienced. A 4,000-foot descent down the side of a sudden, jagged cliff, giving way to steep-sloping fields that finally slide out into the dry valley below. The road passes through different climates, from thick jungle air down into the dry, baked sunshine of the Fluorspar mine at the bottom. Toby Tanser once told me that I couldn't leave Kenya without running Fluorspar. It's a rite of passage for any aspiring athlete. Moses Tanui claims he ran it every second week before he won the Boston marathon in 1996. From the mine at the bottom to the shops at the top where we met Barmasai is exactly 21 km. A half-marathon. Uphill all the way.

'Shall we do it with the team before Lewa?' I ask Godfrey.

'Sure. We have to.' It takes us almost an hour to drive down, the road is so bumpy. I can't imagine how long it will take to run up.

By the time we arrive at the gates to Godfrey's family home, it's almost three in the afternoon. The place has a still, lazy feel to it. People sit under trees watching as we drive past, too hot to be surprised. His gates open into a little oasis of green grass and tall pine trees, with two neat little houses that look like Swiss chalets nestled at the bottom.

'Welcome to my home,' says Godfrey as we drive in.

As we step out of the truck, Godfrey's mother walks over to greet us. She has a proud, weathered face, with sharp eyes. She's wearing a grey two-piece suit, a colourful headscarf and a pair of running shoes.

'She always likes to look smart,' Godfrey says. She gives me a firm handshake. 'Karibu,' she says, looking straight at me.

Mama Godfrey worked her whole life in the Fluorspar mine, initially smashing rocks with the men, but eventually as a messenger in the office. She lived with her family in a small company-owned house, and even though her husband had left her, she worked hard to send her first-born and only son to St Patrick's High School in Iten. He wasn't a runner, but once there he met Brother Colm and started doing well in races. One day his cousin, the athlete Joseph Chesire, turned up at the school and asked Godfrey for his identity card. Godfrey, not sure what was going on, handed it over.

'Right,' said his cousin. 'I've got you a place in the army.' Godfrey didn't really want to join the army, but it was a chance to live as an athlete and get paid. 'He thought it was the best thing for me,' Godfrey explains. Unfortunately, unknown to any of them, Godfrey's scholarship to study in America had just come through. But it was too late. He was a soldier now.

'Brother Colm was so mad,' Godfrey tells me. 'He's still mad with me today.' It seems a shame, he would have made a good student. But as an athlete Godfrey ended up spending a lot of his time in the US winning many road races. He also ran for Kenya numerous times and once finished fourth, ahead of both Paul Tergat and Moses Tanui, in the world half-marathon championships. The boy from the Fluorspar mine did good.

Inside his house, which was the first thing Godfrey built with his race winnings, the table is laid out with an array of food. Mung bean stew, rice, chapattis, beans, bananas, ground nuts, freshly made mango juice. I'm starving.

Piled up in one corner of the room are six old suitcases.

'This is my old stuff,' says Godfrey, opening up the top case. Inside it is full of magazines, running kit still wrapped in plastic, medals, trophies. Among the early 1990s Puma vests and tights he finds an old copy of *Athletics Weekly* magazine. I skim through it, thinking he must be in it somewhere. I find a page listing the year's world rankings. There he is, Godfrey Kiprotich, ranked ten in the world over the half-marathon.

'So funny,' he says, pulling out an old Kenya tracksuit. 'This is from when I was a junior.'

His mother comes in and speaks to him. He looks around.

'Come on, we must eat,' he says, realising where he is. 'My mum is worried that we're not eating.'

By the time Godfrey has taken me to visit the local school and the mayor of the town, it's getting late. To get to Shadrack's home we need to wind our way up another dirt road that seems to skirt endlessly along the edge of the valley, going up and then down, passing through settlements lost in time, colourful wooden houses basking in the late afternoon sun. Finally the road careens across a clacking bridge and then up an incline so steep we have to attempt it three times, the truck's wheels spinning and sliding on the loose gravel.

Shadrack's house is back at the top of the escarpment, perched on a narrow ridge sticking out into the vast skyscape. It clings to the edge of the world like the home of a wizard in some fantastical painting. All around it the land falls away so it feels as though it's almost floating in the air. The curves of the distant hills, faded now in the last light of the day, push up from below.

It looks like we've arrived too late to eat. I don't know if the chicken was saved, or has already been eaten. Children and neighbours crowd around to meet Shadrack's exotic visitors. His mother, pretty despite a few missing teeth, wears a dirty overcoat, shaking hands shyly, looking down. His father, older, grinning, proud of his son for bringing such visitors, walks over. He looks as though he has come straight from the fields, dust and sweat dried to his tough skin. He has a wispy beard and is also missing some teeth.

We stand there awkwardly as the night closes in, chasing away the day's warmth. The children run around giggling, touching my clothes. Shadrack, not used to being a host, stands to one side watching. Smoke is rising through the grass roof of one of the small, round huts.

Two car lights come swinging around at us from the nearby field. It's Barmasai with my car. We walk over, followed like Pied Pipers by hundreds of children. I'm ready to get back to Iten. We still have about three hours of driving to do, and I've got a morning run to think about.

I shake hands with everyone, and then clamber into my car. Shadrack gets in the front beside me. For some reason Godfrey is with Barmasai in the truck. I follow them out of the field, leaving Shadrack's parents and the children peering after us at the disappearing tail lights, their faces glowing red for a second before the darkness closes in, reclaiming them.

We follow Barmasai until he pulls in to a familiar-looking roadside settlement. A single dirt road with wooden shacks up along either side.

'Why are we stopping?' I ask Shadrack.

'Yes,' he says, nodding.

Barmasai is at the window. I wind it down.

'Take tea,' he says. Men stand around, their shoulders hunched against the cold, looking at me as I get out of the car.

'It's tradition,' says Godfrey, appearing out of the darkness, excited as a child. 'You must never leave without having chai.'

We're led into a tiny café. It's the same one I came to with Marietta and the children on the day of the homecoming ceremony over three months ago. The butchered meat hanging in the window. The low rumble of conversations, the lights from mobile phones floating in the darkness. The whites of eyes looking over at me. The electricity has gone off, Godfrey tells me. We all sit down at a corner table. A man comes over and puts a cup in front of each of us. Then, using the light from his phone to see, he pours the tea from a large flask.

Suddenly the lights come back on. Everyone looks around, silenced for a second. The place is packed. Roughly hewn wooden tables. Cups of tea. 'Half cakes'. A framed quotation on the wall. 'Failure is just a setback on the road to success.' And then the delicate strings holding everything snap, and the sound of conversations, of the Mexican soap opera on the television, come tumbling in over one another, filling the room with noise.

A week later I'm back in Fluorspar, standing with the Iten Town Harriers posing for a photograph. The road stretches off innocently ahead of us, beginning up a gentle slope. From there, though, it winds and switches back again and again, snaking its way up the side of the valley for 21 km. My aim is to keep running the whole way.

On the way down, the other runners discussed the Fluorspar record. It's only a training run, so there are no official records, but they seem to think the fastest time ever is in the region of 1 hour 26 minutes. That's for a half-marathon that rises over 4,000 feet.

Godfrey, as ever, starts us off with his pep talk. He will be right behind us in the truck, he says, handing out water every five kilometres.

'It's hot, so it's very important to drink water all the time.'

Chris seems more impatient than ever to get going this morning. He called me at half past four in the morning to tell me he was ready to go. I still had another thirty minutes' sleep planned before my alarm was due to go off. A few minutes after I spoke to him I heard Godfrey's phone ringing in the other room.

As well as the full Lewa team, David Barmasai has joined us for the run, which should be a good test for young Japhet. Barmasai has just been selected to run the marathon for Kenya at the upcoming World Championships.[1]

'OK,' says Godfrey, 'let's go.'

We start off easy, in a big group. Beatrice, looking feisty, seems to be pushing the pace at the front. She has a doggedness that's hard not to admire. She rarely speaks when we meet, but when she does it is always with certainty that she will run well in Lewa. In every training run she starts off at the front, full of confidence. And no matter how far back she drops off the pace, she remains undeterred.

Hill running has never been my strong point, so I'm not expecting to stay with the others long, but to my surprise I make it around the first two switchbacks in the middle of the pack. Then suddenly they change gear, and they're gone.

Sure and steady, I tell myself as I pitter-patter along, avoiding the biggest stones, trying to take the shortest line around the innumerable corners. I manage to edge my way past Beatrice and her friend, who has joined us again, but the others are further and further ahead every time I look up, until they disappear completely.

People stand stopped at the side of the road to watch me as I pass. At first they're friendly and I greet them happily. I'm feeling fine, just taking my time. But as we go on, I start to feel faint. Godfrey hasn't appeared yet. We must have passed the 5 km point. The more tired I get, the more

---

1 A few months later, Barmasai ended up finishing in fifth place in the World Championships in Daegu.

piqued I become. Where is he? I imagine Barmasai thinking this is all very unprofessional. Come on, Godfrey. I'm not even that thirsty, but it's becoming a distraction. I keep expecting to see him before the next switchback, but he never appears. I don't know if I'm imagining it, but everyone I pass now seems to be laughing at me. It's like a bad dream: the manic laughter, the endless dirt road, the aching in my legs, the pounding sun. And still no sign of Godfrey.

At one point a slow-moving lorry comes up behind me. It's barely moving any faster than I am, and so for about five minutes it feels like it's following me, its straining engine grunting at me to move aside. I keep running, glancing up at the driver as the lorry finally grinds past. He looks at me from his cab, expressionless. At least he's not laughing. Up and up I go, until the mountains that towered above me when I began now look like small hills down below. Up and up, back and forth, into the cooler air. Ahead, the clouds cling to the rock face that holds back the highlands.

As I run, my mind keeps estimating how far I have left to go, and suggesting that I slow down. I decide to try Paula Radcliffe's chant. I tell myself that I love my daughter. 'I love you Lila,' I say to myself. 'I love you Lila.' Amazingly, I feel suddenly lighter, as though I've thrown off a heavy cloak. My feet start picking up their pace, switching back and forth under me with an easy flow. 'I love you Lila.' But then I feel bad for singling out Lila. 'I love you Uma,' I say. 'I love you Uma.' But now something has changed. I'm slowing down again. I've been tricked. My mind, like a double agent, has stolen in, undermining the power of the sentiment by distracting it, mimicking it. I look at the hill rising up, endlessly up. I try again. 'I love you Lila.' But it feels too calculated now.

For a second, though, the chant worked. Maintaining it against such a slippery adversary, however, was not easy. Perhaps I just need to save it up for the crucial moments, when all hope seems lost and I'm about to give in.

And still the road goes on, turning round and back, round and back, up and up. Just before the end Godfrey finally appears. A woman, who turns out to be his sister, hands me my drink from the passenger window. I've no idea where she has come from.

'Godfrey, what happened?' I manage to gasp, handing back the water.

'I couldn't start the car,' he says, looking distraught. 'Sorry.' I push on, refreshed now, until finally I reach the top. My legs are wobbly as I stand there feeling like Edmund Hillary on the peak of Everest. The other runners are all sitting on the grass drinking lemonade and eating peanuts and boiled eggs as though they've just been out for a gentle stroll.

Japhet, it turns out, was the first one to the top. Ahead of Barmasai. Little Japhet. We're going to have to start taking him seriously, I think. He smiles his toothy smile as I tell him how hard I found it.

'It is hard,' he says.

In the end it took me 1 hour 58 minutes. The other runners kindly tell me that anyone who can run it in under two hours is 'very strong'. They, of course, all ran it much quicker, in just over 1 hour 30 minutes. After all this time in Kenya, I still, really, have no idea how they do it.

As we stand talking, Godfrey pulls up. He has Beatrice in the truck with him. She ran out of steam at about 18 km, he tells me later. 'I'm worried about her,' he says. 'How can she run a marathon if she can't do that?'

Back in Iten, there's a buzz going around. The circus and pageantry of the Athletics Kenya track series has come to town. For weeks we've been reading about the results of the other races in the newspaper, stories of Olympic champions being beaten by barefoot upstarts. The biggest race, the last one on the calendar, is a two-day extravaganza in the Kamariny stadium in Iten.

I'm sitting up in the stand, ready to watch the action. Godfrey is milling around talking to all his old athlete friends. I'm sure they all come to races just to chat and socialise, as they rarely seem that interested in watching the running.

The meeting itself is a mixture of haplessness, improvisation and brilliance. In some of the field events it feels like the organisers have simply plucked a few random passers-by to compete. Men in trousers and wellington boots fling the discus, while at the pole vault mat, the marshals sit chatting and waiting to see if anyone turns up. Nobody does.

The high jump features a host of tall, skinny athletes who rush at the bar and karate kick themselves over. Despite all lack of conventional technique, they manage to reach the impressive height of almost two metres, contorting and twisting their bodies somehow up and over the bar.

It all feels a bit like a school sports day, a commendable effort, a bit of fun. That is until the distance athletes file onto the track. Then, suddenly, this sodden track that sits on the edge of the clouds, the vast Rift Valley spread out far below, becomes the stage for some of the most fiercely competitive racing you could find anywhere in the world.

In the men's 1500m, there are nine heats with around twenty athletes in each one. When the starting gun fires, they charge off like sprinters in a panic. In the 5,000m they seem to start just as fast. And there are just as many runners.

Despite this race being the highlight of the series, none of the most famous Kenyan athletes have turned up.

'They know you can't run fast times on this track,' one former runner tells me. The dirt track sits at an altitude of over 8,000 feet, and, by all accounts, is about ten metres too long. So the stage is left to those looking to make a break-through – the hundreds of Iten hopefuls, filing in through the gates, string shoe bags on their backs carrying borrowed spikes, weaving through the crowds to sign up at a small table.

The 800m heats, eight of them in all, are run at a break-neck speed, each won in around 1 minute 49 seconds. The 5,000m is won in just over 14 minutes. These are times that would put these athletes near the front in the British na-tional championships – although, of course, those are run at sea level and on an all-weather track that measures precisely 400m in circumference.

Japhet runs in one of the 5,000m heats, after arriving too late to enter the 10,000m. He looks like a child beside the other runners, his short legs moving twice as fast just to keep up. He seems to be holding his shorts the whole way around, and I hope he's not injured. He finishes around the middle of the field in 15 minutes 33 seconds. I go over to talk to him.

'Are you injured?' I ask him. He seems dazed. Surprised to see me.

'My shorts are too big,' he says. 'I had to hold them up.' Not owning a pair of shorts, he had borrowed some from a friend. Chris spots us and comes over.

'Hello, my friends,' he says. 'What time did you run, Japhet?' Japhet looks at his watch.

'Fifteen thirty,' he says.

Chris looks at me in surprise. 'Oh, man,' he says, laughing. 'That's a girl's time.' Japhet smiles, but I can tell he's hurt by the comment.

'Don't mind him,' I say. 'That's a good time on this track.' But Chris is already gone, off to talk to another of the former athletes hanging around in the infield. I spot Daniel Komen striding around, looking worried, trying to keep the show on schedule. Japhet, keen to get some clothes on, hurries off, too, leaving me to watch the next race from the inside of the track.

Interestingly, some of the athletes at the back of the races trail home in fairly slow times. I'm amazed to see 1500m runners finishing in times slower than I used to run at school. I know the track is slow, but surely not that slow.

The reason is that every athlete sets off as though he is going to win. Even after just 200 metres, some athletes have started so fast they are already dropping out, sheepish grins on their faces, disappearing off the track and into the crowd. If they don't drop out, those who went off too fast at the beginning end up jogging around to the finish.

Most Kenyan runners I meet have a strong belief that they can win almost any race they enter regardless of the opposition. They will make outlandish predictions about the times they hope to run, and afterwards, when they don't run them, they will just laugh and say: 'Next time I will do it.'

Among the crowd, I bump into Brother Colm's assistant, Ian. I ask him why everyone starts off so fast.

'It's OK,' he says calmly. 'They already know how to train, but here they are learning to race. After this, they can run in Rome or Oslo.'

This is the breeding ground for the great Kenyan runners of tomorrow. They may have natural talent – I see that every day on the roads in Iten – but now, here on the track, the final piece of their apprenticeship is taking place: racing. And it's interesting to see that this is one area where they still have a lot to learn.

On my way home I bump into Paul Tanui, the runner who has replaced Josphat in the Iten Town Harriers. He has been at the track to watch the racing.

'Hello,' he says, shaking my hand.

'Are you ready for Lewa?' I ask. It's only a few weeks away now.

'Yes,' he says. 'But, listen, what are we doing about visas?'

'Visas?'

'Yes, when are we getting them?'

'Lewa is in Kenya,' I say. 'We don't need visas.'

'In Kenya?' I feel like apologising. He obviously thought I was taking him abroad to race. One last pay day. The problem with racing in Kenya is that the competition is so much tougher. It's harder to win.

The outrageous depth of talent just milling around in this tiny corner of the world is illustrated by a telephone conversation I have that same afternoon. I've been trying to pin down Wilson Kipsang, who leads the End of the Road early morning runs. He's a fairly decent runner even in these parts, ranked in the world all-time top ten in the marathon with a time of 2:04.[1] Godfrey, who knows everyone, gives me his number, except that by mistake he gives me the number of a completely different person, someone called William Kipsang.

Not knowing that, I call up the number.

'Hello.'

'Hello, Kipsang?'

'Yes.'

'It's Finn here, the mzungu writer.'

'Eh?'

'We've met a few times. I was talking to you at the track yesterday.'

'Eh?'

'Is that Wilson Kipsang?'

'No, William.'

'Oh, I thought your name was Wilson. The 2:04 marathoner, right?'

'No. 2:05.'

Even if you dial a wrong number here you can end up speaking to a person who has run a time three minutes

---

1 On 30 October 2011, Wilson Kipsang ran the second-fastest time in history, 2:03:42, narrowly missing the world record by four seconds, in the Frankfurt marathon in Germany.

quicker than the British record, set over twenty-five years ago. No wonder Paul was hoping to race abroad.

23

Running is freedom, it is expression, it is a pouring out of the
life-force within us.
    Bruce Tulloh

'I guarantee that it's nothing,' Anders tells me. 'It's just because you're getting nervous about the race.' I've got a sore
foot. I've tried to ignore it for a few days now, but every
time I run it feels worse. I can hardly even walk on it. And
this time it's not a bent toe from standing on a stone, it's
the whole side of my foot. 'Then again, it could be plantar
fasciitis,' he says.

Plantar fasciitis is every runner's worse nightmare. It
strikes out of nowhere and the only remedy is to stop running. But I've only got a week now until the race. I can't
stop. If the worst comes to the worst, I'll just run through
the pain. I have to make it to that start line in Lewa, no
matter what.

The athletes at the Kimbia camp are in no doubt about
what I need: a massage.

One of the great things about Iten is the ready supply of
masseurs. Some of the former runners retrain in massage
after their careers end, or after they fail to take off, and every
camp has a man on hand to give the athletes a regular rub-
down. With very few physios around to treat injuries, the
Kenyans are keenly aware of the value of massages in pre-
venting problems in the first place. Massages release built-up

tension in overworked muscles and stimulate the circulation of blood and lymph fluids. Afterwards, all the little aches and pains from training are gone, leaving you with a clean pair of legs to punish all over again.

If an injury does set in, a good masseur can work on certain trigger points, pressing on them like crazy until you want to scream, to break down knots in the muscles and release tightness. It doesn't always work, but often it does.

The athletes outside the camps, such as Japhet, who can't afford to pay for a massage, have to improvise. Often when I see Japhet he tells me how he's feeling good after his weekly treatment.

'Who gave you the massage?' I ask him one day. He looks a little downcast, as though I've broken the illusion that he is just like one of the top athletes with a masseur on hand.

'Henry,' he says. His friend from the kiosk. They massage each other, he tells me. And if Henry is not around, Japhet massages himself. Still, as long as you don't press too hard, even a backstreet massage, or a self-massage, can help drive fresh blood into tired muscles and rejuvenate them. For runners like Japhet, it's better than nothing.

At the One 4 One camp, the athletes would go in gingerly one at a time to see the masseur and spend an hour or so yelping in pain. At one point when I was there, I went in to see what was happening. The masseur was climbing on the table trying to exert as much pressure as he could on Emmanuel Mutai's calf.

Since I've been in Iten I've been mostly avoiding massages, mainly because they're so painful, but I'm worried, now that I'm hobbling, that that was a big mistake. I call up the masseur who was torturing Emmanuel Mutai. He says he will come over straight away.

Over the next three days I get two intensive treatments. During the first treatment, in the Kimbia camp, my feet come out feeling as though they've been in a medieval torture chamber. He presses and presses, chuckling to himself when he hits a pressure point. As I grit my teeth and try to hang in there, he asks me about England or my family as though he's simply giving me a haircut. Just when I think I can't take any more, he finally stops. I feel mentally exhausted, and my foot still hurts. He tells me not to worry, that it will be fine for the race. I hope he's right, because a few days before we're due to leave, I'm still limping.

For the second massage, he asks me to come to a house in Eldoret near to where he lives. I've arranged a goodbye lunch with the athletes in the Kimbia camp on the same day, but I'm sure I can fit it all in. Mama Kibet is cooking up pots of beans when I leave. 'I'll get back as soon as I can,' I tell her as I reverse the car out of the gate onto the muddy road.

The house he wants to meet me at belongs to a runner. It's a small concrete box down a waterlogged side road. They usher me into a small sitting room, chasing the runner's sister and a young child out the back door at the same time. We all sit down around a table.

'First we must eat,' says the runner. 'As you are the guest in my house.' One by one his sister, mother and wife carry in large pots of beans, rice, meat, and place them on the table. I'm hosting my own lunch in an hour and I haven't had the massage yet. Next come the plates. A flask of tea. Cups. Forks. Napkins.

By the time we eat and I get my massage, lying face-down on the sofa, the runner sitting on a chair talking to me between my grimaces, it's past 1 p.m. I make my excuses and head out, refusing, reprehensibly, another round of tea.

As I leave, the masseur gives me a small jar of Menthol Plus balm to rub on my feet. On the box it has a picture of a man in glasses rubbing it on his head.

'This will help?' I ask sceptically.

'Yes, yes,' he smiles. 'You will be fine. For sure.'

And so, with my hobble and my jar of headache balm, I get back in the car and return to Iten.

The Kimbia garden has been laid out with a long table surrounded by white plastic chairs. Japhet and Henry are there, wearing puffy overcoats and sitting awkwardly among the other athletes. They both get up as soon as I enter and shake my hand. They seem a little star-struck to be in the camp, even though none of the athletes here is particularly well known. Beatrice is also there, sitting in the corner sheepishly, trying to blend into the background. She gets up and shakes my hand and then sits back down.

There's a knock on the gate. I open it and Tom Payn walks in with Raymond, Mary Keitany's brother-in-law. Anders is helping Mama Kibet bring out the food. I'm still full from my first lunch, but I can hardly refuse to eat at my own farewell meal. Mama Kibet piles the food up on one of the biggest bowls and hands it to me.

'Thank you,' I say, raising my eyebrows at the size of it, which sets her off giggling as she starts ladling the food out for the others.

Tom asks me what time I'm hoping to run in Lewa. After

my last few training runs I'm secretly hoping to get somewhere near 3 hours, but after my half marathon in Ethiopia, and with the heat, the hills, the altitude and the off-road terrain in Lewa, perhaps I'm being too optimistic. Tom thinks 3 hours 30 minutes would be a more realistic goal.

The other Iten Town Harriers are less circimspect about their chances, of course. When they hear that the race is usually won in around 2 hours 21 minutes, they look happy. 'Two hours 25 minutes will probably win you some money,' I tell them, having studied the previous years' results in detail. 'I will try,' says Japhet, struggling to contain his excitement. They all think they can run at least 2 hours 15 minutes, even in Lewa.

Beatrice, too, is hopeful when I tell her that anything under three hours could win her a prize. It seems a very slow time for a Kenyan athlete, but I'm doubtful she can do it. One evening just a few days before, she joined me, Japhet and Henry on a slow jog. It was the sort of easy run that is not meant to be testing, but is just to keep the body ticking over, to ease out any stiffness. Sometimes on these runs the pace gets quite fast for me, but that evening it was very gentle. We chatted as we jogged along past endless small fields, Japhet asking me about England, and how slow people run there. After a while, though, Beatrice started to drop behind. We slowed down but she told us to go on. She had a stitch, she said, holding her side. She was still smiling, but it was the first time I'd ever seen a Kenyan athlete struggling with a stitch, or at least admitting to it. As we ran on, I told Japhet that I was worried about Beatrice, that she might struggle even to finish Lewa. But he was as optimistic as ever.

'She is strong,' he said. 'She will be fine.'

Mama Kibet is bringing out a huge bowl of fruit salad for dessert. She has made us quite a feast.

'Where's Godfrey?' Japhet asks, putting down his half-finished bowl of beans.

It's a good question. I call him up on his mobile. 'Finn,' he says. 'I'm just coming.'

'Where are you?'

'I'm in western Kenya,' he says. 'My wife has got malaria.'

'Is it bad?'

'Yes,' he says gravely.

'Shouldn't you stay with her?' I've been worrying for weeks that Godfrey won't make it to Lewa, that something else will happen at the last minute to prevent him coming. With Godfrey, something else always happens.

'Yes, I might not make your lunch,' he says.

'That's fine,' I say. The food would be cold, anyway, as he's about a three-hour drive away. 'But what about Lewa?'

'No, no, I can't miss Lewa,' he says. 'No way.'

'But what about your wife?'

'She will be fine.' It's only two days until we leave. I hope he's right.

I go back to the lunch. It's a happy scene, even without Godfrey. Beatrice is chatting with Raymond, who is dressed neatly in a white shirt, holding his bowl carefully so as not to spill anything. Japhet is chatting with runners from the camp. I'm glad he's getting a decent meal a few days before the race.

Someone outside is beeping for us to open the gates. Two

of the athletes from the camp unbolt the lock and hold the gates open as Chris's car slides into the garden, almost bashing into the table. He climbs out of the car, a big, mischievous grin on his face.

'Sorry, man,' he says. 'I had to sort some things out at school.'

24

Strength does not come from physical capacity. It comes from an indomitable will.

Mahatma Gandhi

My alarm goes off at 5.45 a.m., as it has many times over the last few months. I reach out from under the mosquito net and switch it off. I get changed into my running kit and head out into the darkness. Although I felt I should rest my foot until the race, everyone has recommended that I go for one last run before we leave for Lewa. It's a fitting way to say goodbye to Iten.

My foot feels fine as I walk between silent houses, past stinking piles of rubbish, down to the main road. It has rained in the night, but not too much. A shadow passes by me in the darkness. Down in the town the matatus are already circling, lights on, looking for passengers. 'Yes, mzungu,' one conductor says as I walk by. 'Eldoret?' I shake my head. I walk up past St Patrick's school and start off on a slow jog. Ahead of me, the half-moon glows in a lightening sky, flicking between the trees as I run. Some children in school uniform, walking the other way, watch me pass.

I head out past the edge of town, into the countryside. Mist hangs blue in the dips, thick and magical. Pointy-roofed huts and neatly sown fields rise up here and there, the red track stretching out before me. I run on, like Dorothy, through a strange, Technicolor world. And who is that I see now, running towards me, his bright yellow jacket glowing in the first rays of sunlight? The scarecrow? It's Japhet, grinning to see me. He turns and runs beside me, back the way he came.

We run together, easy, passing bigger groups, people running hard, the sweat beading on their anxious foreheads, pushing themselves on in search of the elusive Oz, sure that some day, if they just keep running, they will get there.

Japhet tells me he has a calf injury. He doesn't seem too worried about it.

'I've had it for a long time,' he says. 'But it will be OK.' I guess you have to be prepared for a few niggles if you're going to train for a marathon, even if you're a Kenyan. It's interesting to note that the runners here still get injured despite their barefoot upbringing, but that the types of injuries they get are different.

'I don't see many impact injuries,' the physio at Lornah's camp tells me one day. These are common injuries in the West, and are usually the most serious and debilitating: things like runner's knee, shin splints, plantar fasciitis and stress fractures. In my time in Kenya I haven't met a single athlete suffering from any of these problems. If someone is injured, it is always something less serious such as a tight hamstring or a pulled calf muscle. Or a cut leg. Chris turned up at my goodbye lunch at the Kimbia camp with a huge gash in his leg. He said he fell while out running. It looked nasty and was heavily bandaged.

After showing me his leg he started telling me he had been getting up at 4 a.m. to train. It's a strange thing to do. At 4 a.m. it's too dark to run. No wonder he fell over. And why did he need to run so early? 'To get extra training. I might surprise you and finish in the top ten,' he said, as though it was some wild boast. When we first started training he was talking about winning the race. This is a man who has run the New York marathon in 2 hours 8 minutes. He doesn't need to prove anything to me.

A few nights earlier he invited me to his house for dinner. He lives in a small compound near St Patrick's school in Iten with his wife and five children. Inside it's like any other Kenyan runner's house. The walls are covered in Christmas decorations, bright posters of Alpine landscapes and inspirational quotes, and free calendars. On the shelves are bulbous, supersize trophies from Boston, San Diego, and other places.

He takes me out into the yard to show me his room for relaxing. It's a former garage with a few battered old sofas in it, a massage table and a beautiful mahogany chaise longue. Next door are the house staff rooms, although they all seem empty. All the buildings are on top of each other, crammed into his small bit of land, with little space outside. He shows me one of the rooms. A grotty bed is hidden behind a huge cabinet that has been left standing in the middle of the room, its back to the door.

'You see how nice it is kept?' he says.

As we sit waiting for supper, he hands me his photo albums. Pictures of him and his wife in Nairobi. He looks young and innocent, his tracksuit waistband pulled up too high as he poses proudly beside some tall buildings. For all his slipperiness, Chris is a good man. His talent for running has lurched him from a simple life of farming into an infinitely more complex world where he is expected to be a role model, a picture of success. It's a tough act to hold together.

He sits under the flickering strip light like a king on his big armchair, the pink velvet curtains folded up behind his head. His kids bustle around the cramped room, dark, handsome faces, polite and quiet, wearing thick overcoats. His wife serves up a feast of rice, lentils, baked bananas, meat, and freshly made mango and pineapple juice.

'I might surprise you, man,' he says, grinning. 'You never know.'

After the last morning run, I pack up my things, say good-bye to Anders and the other athletes at the Kimbia camp, and roll the car out of the drive to collect Chris.

'You're late, man,' he says when he sees me. Then we head back into town to find Japhet and Beatrice. Japhet is nowhere to be seen. We try calling him on his phone but there's no answer. Chris spots him in the garage. He's getting some last words of encouragement from his uncle.

'Come on, you're late,' says Chris, pretending to be annoyed. Japhet looks at us both, his eyes shot with worry. 'It's OK,' I say, sensing that he's too nervous for jokes. Chris laughs, sniggering to himself.

As we arrive to pick up Beatrice, she seems to be walking off in the opposite direction.

'Beatrice,' I call out. 'Where are you going?' When she sees me she runs back into her house and comes out with her bag. She gets in the back next to Japhet. The plan is to meet the others in Eldoret.

'OK, let's go,' I say, driving up the hill past Lornah's camp for the last time. 'Goodbye, Iten. Thanks for the memories.'

Chris has managed to hire us a matatu for the journey, but he decides that he and Philip will travel with me in my car, while everyone else can go with Godfrey in the matatu. I had planned to travel with Japhet, but I decide there's no point arguing.

Philip is dressed in a white suit with a Panama hat, while everyone else is in running kit. We sit waiting in the car while Godfrey arranges the luggage in the bus. His wife seems to have fully recovered from her bout of malaria.

'Let's go,' says Chris, impatient as ever.

'We might as well wait for them and all go in convoy,' I say.

'No, let's go,' says Philip. 'They can catch us up.' I don't have the conviction to argue, so I pull the car out of the garage and start off on the road to Lewa. I drive slowly, waiting for Godfrey to catch up, but after half an hour he still hasn't appeared in my mirror. I decide to call him.

'Finn,' he says. I can hear that he's driving.

'Where are you?' I ask.

'Sorry. Paul said we had to pray before we left. But we're right behind you.'

The journey takes most of the day. Chris sits in the front, excited, reading all the signs as we pass. Philip, like a wise old owl, sits in the back twirling his moustache. He used to live near Lewa when he was in the military in the late 1980s, he tells us. As we drive, he explains things to Chris, who sits there excited like a child taking it all in.

In the van, Godfrey later tells me, they were also staring out the window in wonderment.

'It's like a holiday for them,' he says. 'Especially Japhet. You should have seen him. Shadrack and Beatrice, too. They've never seen this side of Kenya before. They keep saying, "Wow, look."' He chuckles to himself, enjoying their excitement.

We finally arrive in Isiolo, the nearest town to Lewa, at about 5 p.m. As soon as we arrive at the hotel, they all get changed and head off for a run. I'm too tired from the journey to join them, and besides, I feel like I need to rest my foot. Instead I take a stroll into town.

Isiolo is a dusty, bustling settlement, with people in ripped T-shirts and flip-flops, hustling, looking for money, motorbikes skirting past. It has an aggressive edge far removed from the relaxed air of Iten. It feels like a frontier town, and in many ways it is. Even though it's 500 km from the Somali border, it's the last major town on the road and there are many Somalis living here.

It's almost dark when through the chaos, like six arrows, come the Iten Town Harriers. They seem like creatures from another world, mythical beasts, their muscles rippling as they glide effortlessly over the bumpy surface. Chris leads the charge, unsmiling as he shoots past. Beatrice, her arms swinging high across her chest, chases after him, closely followed by Paul and Philip. Japhet and Shadrack, relaxed, follow at the rear, Japhet waving when he sees me.

We've arrived in Isiolo a day early to give everyone plenty of time to recover from the journey. It means we've got the whole next day just to rest. It's not as easy as it sounds. I'm lying on the bed in the hotel room staring at the bright peach walls, the sound of the street rattling by outside the open window. Rather than feeling rested, though, my legs are inexplicably starting to feel tired. Aching, almost. It could be nerves, or the fact that I'm thinking about how tired they feel. I should go to sleep, but I'm too awake. Instead, I lie there thinking.

For six months I've been piecing together the puzzle of why Kenyans are such good runners. In the end there was no elixir, no running gene, no training secret that you could neatly package up and present with flashing lights and fireworks. Nothing that Nike could replicate and market as the latest running fad. No, it was too complex, yet too simple, for that. It was everything, and nothing. I list them, the secrets, in my head. The tough, active childhood, the barefoot running, the altitude, the diet, the role models, the simple approach to training, the running camps, the focus and dedication, the desire to succeed, to change their lives, the expectation that they can win, the mental toughness, the lack of alternatives, the abundance of trails to train on, the time spent resting, the running to school, the all-pervading running culture, the reverence for running.

When I spoke to Yannis Pitsiladis, the man who has delved deeper into this than anyone else, I pushed him to put one factor above all the others. 'Oh, that's tough,' he said, thinking hard for a moment. Then he said pointedly: 'The hunger to succeed.'

'Look,' he said. 'My daughter is a great gymnast, but she probably won't become a gymnast. She'll probably go to university and become a doctor. But for a Kenyan child, walking down to the river to collect water, running to school, if he doesn't become an athlete then there are not many other options. Of course, you need the other factors, too, but this hunger is the driving force.'

The will to succeed not only motivates Kenyans to become athletes, it helps them when they are racing, too. When the crunch comes in a race and your body is shouting at you to slow down, it is the drive to win that pushes you on.

I once complained jokingly to Brother Colm's assistant, Ian, that when I ran with a group of Kenyans, whenever we'd get to a hill they would all speed up, while my natural inclination was to slow down.

Ian smiled at me. 'That's because they want it more than you,' he said. 'When they see a hill, they see it as an opportunity. An opportunity to train harder, to work harder.'

When people in the Rift Valley decide to become athletes, they don't fit their training in around a job or college course, as we might in the West; they dedicate themselves to it completely. A daily diet of run, eat, sleep, run. In Iten alone there are around a thousand full-time athletes living like this – in a town with a population of just four thousand people. Every morning the lanes are full of people on the move, like commuters in any other city, but all of them in running kit, flying up hills, training, training, training.

Brother Colm once remarked to me, as we stood watching a team of his athletes charging repeatedly up the long hill leading to St Patrick's school, that 'This is the bit people miss when they look for the Kenyan secret.'

Humans evolved as runners over millions of years in order to survive, not because it was a fun thing to do. Catching the antelope meant the difference between life and death. So it makes sense that even in the twenty-first century, if you're running to survive, then you'll become better at it.

I've immersed myself in the world of Kenyan runners, living and training with them, sharing their commitment and following their almost monastic lifestyles, in the hope that some of their magic would rub off on me. Hopefully it has, but in truth, at thirty-seven, after years of living an easy, Western lifestyle, and without anything driving me other than the joy of running, and the desire to use my talent, my genetic advantage, I never stood a chance.

There's a knock at the door. Godfrey comes in.

'Finn, it's getting dark. Shall we go and find some supper?' This is it, the last supper before Lewa.

'Yes,' I say, sitting up. 'Where are the others?'

'They're all downstairs waiting. Chris says he has found the best place. He says it's cheap, clean, and has lots of vegetarian things.'

'Great. Let's go.'

They all stand in the lobby, dishevelled and bleary-eyed, like they've just woken from a deep sleep. I follow Chris and Philip out the door. Godfrey, smiling at everyone, is clearly the only person not running tomorrow. He is relaxed, chatty, while the rest of us walk along in silence.

Chris's restaurant has two small plastic tables in one corner. The rest of the room is bare concrete. A man with a pencil behind his ear comes over as we crowd around the two tables. He hands us a colourful laminated menu with about a thousand different dishes on it.

'Do they have rice and beans?' I ask Godfrey, feeling too dozy to ask the waiter myself. Godfrey speaks to the man. They seem to have a long conversation.

'They only have rice,' Godfrey says to me, looking concerned.

'Anything to go with it? Any vegetables?' Godfrey asks the man in English, but he shakes his head. 'Do you have anything vegetarian? Anything that is not meat?' He looks at me, thinking hard. It's a painful pause as he rifles through the list of dishes in his head. Then he shakes his head. 'Just rice,' he says.

Shadrack is looking more startled than usual. He mutters something to the waiter in Swahili, but the man shakes his head. Another waiter brings two plates of meat over to Chris and Philip, sitting on the other table.

'Godfrey, I can't eat just rice the night before the race,' I say.

More plates of meat are arriving. They place one down in front of Shadrack, to his horror. He pulls Godfrey's hand. There's a commotion as they discuss Shadrack's meal. Godfrey tells me that Shadrack wants ugali, but they don't have any. He suggests I take him to another restaurant beside the hotel where they might have something vegetarian.

'What's going on, man?' says Chris from the other table, his moustache glistening with the juice from the meat.

'It's OK,' I say. 'We'll meet you back at the hotel. Come on, Shadrack, let's go and find some ugali.'

Shadrack keeps two paces behind me as we dodge our way through the busy street, avoiding the motorbikes and buses blazing their headlights at us, watching out for holes in the rutted road. I ask him why he wants ugali so badly.

'I always eat ugali before a race,' he says, his eyes fixed ahead.

The other restaurant is quiet, with rows of sculpted concrete tables, and artworks on the walls. The woman behind the counter thinks hard when I ask if they have ugali, before finally nodding. And vegetables? She nods again. I order two plates and we sit in the window. Outside people in Somali robes stroll by, one man with a goat tied across his back. We eat in silence. This is it. It feels more like the end of the world than just the end of my journey. A bedraggled landscape of broken vans, trucks, a small wind picking up the dust, swirling it in the light from the window. Opposite me sits a lone warrior. Our champion. Preparing for the battle ahead. The time has finally come.

He looks up at me mid-mouthful. 'It's good,' he says.

'Good.' Eat well, my man, for the moment is nigh.

25

'And where does the power come from, to see the race to its end? From within.'
Eric Liddell in *Chariots of Fire*

Uma and Lila are waving to me from the sidelines, held aloft by Marietta and Godfrey. A small rope held by security men in bright jackets presses against my legs. Ahead of us lie the empty grasslands, the course narrowing up ahead through a small cluster of trees. Beyond that, 26 miles of wilderness. A man with a microphone is talking, telling us about the great work the race does for local charities. He's buying time. Occasionally the helicopters skirt across the sky.

'I think we're getting the all-clear signal,' he says. There are lions on the course. The helicopters are trying to scare them away, so they don't start picking us off like a herd of migrating wildebeest. But I guess it's not a simple job, getting lions to move by swooping at them in a helicopter.

'We have a few famous athletes in the field today,' the man says. I've been telling Chris that he's the star runner at the race, trying to make him feel special. The whole project has never quite had his seal of approval. At one point, after I returned from Ethiopia, Godfrey told me that Chris was talking about quitting. I wasn't surprised. In every long run he seemed short of training. His enthusiasm for the race was always fragile. He kept asking me questions about it, looking, I always thought, for reasons to drop out. So I kept building it up, to keep him on board. Godfrey told us all that the race would be shown live on national television. 'Of course,' he said. 'It's a big race. They always show it live. Everyone watches it.' I told Chris the organisers were excited that he was running. He was a big name, I told him. They had given him a complimentary place in the race. They were even mentioning him in their promotional materials. That last bit was not quite true, but I was getting carried away, wanting to satisfy his need for approval. Godfrey was as bad as me, trying to make Chris happy. He went even further. He told us he had met two film-makers from the US TV channel ESPN who were filming the race for a newsreel. They were so excited to hear that Chris was running, he told us, that they wanted to film him before the race and interview him afterwards. Chris grinned happily. *Really? Me?* I said I was sure the announcer would call out his name at the start. I emailed through the details of our team, with Chris's name at the top, his achievements in bold type.

The day before the race, we found out that it wasn't being televised live on Kenyan TV after all. Then, when I went to collect the race numbers, they told me they didn't have a complimentary place for Chris. I had to call up the race director on her mobile phone. She was obviously busy with other things.

'Hi,' I said. 'You agreed to give Christopher Cheboiboch a free race entry.'

'Who?'

'Christopher Cheboiboch.'

'Who is he?'

'He's a big-name runner. He came second in the New York and Boston marathons.' I felt like the agent of a D-list celebrity trying to get him an invitation to the opening of a local supermarket.

'Sorry, we can't do that.'

'But you've already agreed. I can send you the emails to prove it.'

'Did I? OK, he can have a place.'

With so many amazing runners in Kenya, finishing second in New York ten years ago ranks about as highly as being a man who was once interviewed on the street about the price of petrol. Unless an athlete wins the Olympics, he is soon pretty much forgotten in Kenya, even among race organisers.

On the start line the ESPN TV crew is there, panning along the line, shuffling through the dry grass, a big camera catching these last moments before we head out on our odyssey. They don't linger as they pass Chris. 'We have a team of elite runners here called the Iten Town Harriers,' says the announcer, coming good. 'They are: Chris' (he hesitates as he reads the name, unsure how to say it) 'Cheboych, who came second in the New York marathon.' He's said it wrong. I don't look across at Chris. The announcer is reading the rest of our names out, but nobody is listening. People are talking, preparing to run a marathon. The announcer is a background noise, an outside interference. It's time to focus. Only when he tells us, finally, that we're ready to go, and starts the countdown, from five, do we actually hear him. It's as if all the world, all the other sounds, everything that ever existed or happened is being sucked down into

[265]

those tumbling numbers, until three, two, one and the rope is dropped, and we're off.

The race starts off at a charge. People are sprinting. For some reason I wasn't expecting this surge of runners. I feel myself being swarmed, left behind like a boat still tied to the dock. I catch Chris out of the corner of my vision, streaking away at the front, but the others, like me, seem to have been caught out by the fast start. They're running just in front of me as a sea of bodies converges through the trees, the path narrowing, strides chopping, arms out so as not to crash into other people. Philip squeezes past me, but the leaders are already far, far ahead. We've got some catching up to do.

The race is both a marathon and a half-marathon run together at the same time, with the marathon runners lapping the course twice. We'd talked the night before about how some of the people running the half-marathon might go off fast, but that we shouldn't panic because they wouldn't be in our race. But we're already a long way behind. Surely they can't all be half-marathon runners.

After about a mile I start passing people. Some of them seem already spent, slow, thudding strides, big, thick legs, heavy, sweating T-shirts. I'm skipping past them, hopping up on the grass verges when the dirt track is too congested. I'm in a hurry, I seem too far behind. But I need to calm down, I tell myself. This is a marathon. I pull my cap down, over my eyes, recalling the steely gaze of Joan Benoit in those YouTube clips, settling into a steadier pace. Beatrice is a few yards ahead of me now. The others have gone off on the chase, somewhere among the long line of runners zigzagging towards the horizon.

After about ten minutes the race seems to settle down. The people around me are now running about the same speed as me. The soft, grey dirt underfoot puffs gently as we run. Everything else is silent. Up ahead I spot another mzungu. I start reeling him in, without pushing too hard, just keeping my pace steady, passing him calmly, pressing on along the track. I'm feeling light on my feet, my barefoot style gentle on my racing flats.

At the 3 km marker, we turn sharply and head up the first hill. My legs feel strong as I keep up the same pace, not slowing, passing other runners hitting their first difficult patch. At the top of the hill is the first water station. It's manned by a team of white women in khaki safari clothes, leaping around and cheering everyone on.

'First mzungu, first mzungu,' they shout, going wild as I run by. 'Well done, well done.' They hand me some water. I take a few sips and discard it like a man in a hurry. The first mzungu. Where are all the half-marathon runners?

As I run on, I spy a herd of zebra in the distance. I want to point them out to someone, but I'm running on my own now. I pull my cap down and press on.

At 5 km I begin to wonder how fast I'm running. I made a late decision not to wear a watch. Anders thought I was mad. But I've done every training run without one, and the Kenyan runners at the Kimbia camp didn't think it was a problem. Just run how you feel, they said.

The course dips down suddenly into a narrow valley. It feels like the sort of sheltered, shady place you might find wild animals resting. I try not to think about it. The field is more spread out now, but I'm still passing people, people who went off too quickly. I cruise by, discarding them, one by one, in my wake.

At one point, a man battles back past me. His persistence disrupts my ruthless rhythm, making me feel as though I'm working hard for the first time in the race. We're at 8 km, heading up a steep slope back out of the crevasse. I surge hard to drop him as we rise up, twisting through the rocky grassland, up and up. It's not steep, but every time I think we're at the top, it rises up more. To make matters worse, the ground here is even softer, sand-like, sapping energy from my legs with each stride. I keep crossing over from one side of the track to the other, because it keeps looking firmer on the other side. But it never is. My mind is playing tricks on me, I think, half-joking with myself. I'm becoming delusional. Up ahead, the heat is beginning to make the plains shimmer. It's getting hotter, 80°F and still rising.

For the next few kilometres the course goes up and down, up and down like a roller-coaster, except one you have to push along yourself. I try to stride down the slopes, but I'm getting a stitch now. I press my stomach with my fingers, which helps, but mainly it just comes and goes with the slopes, returning whenever I go downhill.

At each water stop, the stewards tell me I'm the first mzungu. They've been waiting to see how long it would take, I can tell. Well, finally, here I am.

At about 15 km, I see Marietta and the children for the first time. They're cheering, come on Daddy, Ossian peering out at me with his indifferent, what-are-you-doing? look.

Jophie, Marietta's sister, is also there. She looks as though she might cry.

'Come on, Dhar, you're the first mzungu,' she says disbelievingly. Godfrey is there, too.

'Come on, Finn, you're doing great.'

I stride through the water station like I'm leading the London marathon, swiping a bottle of water, grinning at my kids and heading back out into the silent, open plains. I've got a job to do, kids, I'll see you soon.

They all pop up again at the 18 km point. Godfrey looks at his watch as I pass.

'Eighteen kilometres. One hour 16 minutes. Looking good, Finn.'

It sets my mind off, trying to calculate how fast I'm going. But the heat is pounding on my brain now. I figure I'll hit halfway in under 1 hour 30 minutes, which is pretty fast. I may get that sub-3 hours, yet. As we come up to the halfway point, however, ready to set out on the second lap, I imagine for a moment that I'm only doing the half-marathon and that I'm gathering myself to sprint to the end. I'm not sure that if I wanted to I could actually go any faster. I feel totally spent.

Beatrice is still ahead of me, but I'm starting to catch her. If I'm feeling this tired, she must be really struggling. I fear she has gone off too hard. I feel sorry for her. She was so confident, her big smile, telling me she would do it. Two women have passed me in the last few minutes, running strongly. Now they're chasing Beatrice, moving in like two lions for the kill. It's hard to watch.

At the halfway point, I pass Ray, the man I stayed with in

Nairobi and who sent me along to run with the Hash House Harriers. His job is to make sure the half-marathon runners go one way, to the finish, and the full marathon runners head out on another lap, to do it all again. I can tell he's excited to see me because he stands up from his plastic chair.

'Come on,' he screeches. 'Get a bloody move on.'

A few corners later I pass a glum-faced Chris negotiating with a motorbike for a lift. He has dropped out. The gash on his leg is the official reason.

'Bad luck, Chris,' I say, holding out my hand as I run past.

'OK' is all he can muster, barely looking at me. We go to slap hands, but miss. It feels symbolic, somehow.

Meanwhile, Shadrack and Japhet both started off way too slow, but are making steady progress through the field. At halfway they are up into the top fifteen, running together stride for stride. Paul and Philip are strung out some way behind them.

As I run through the start line again to head out on the second lap, everything is eerily quiet. Just 90 minutes ago this place was buzzing with runners, spectators, the announcer on his microphone, the air humming with anticipation, the sense that something epic was about to begin. Now it is just me. It's as though the show has gone home, but for some reason I'm still running.

I head on, leaving the start line behind. Every step now feels nearer to the end. The balance between what I've done and what I still have to do has tipped. I'm on the downward slope. All I have to do is cruise in to the finish. Or so I think. The reality, of course, is that I've only just passed base camp, and instead of going down, the slope keeps rising, getting steeper. The real climbing is only just about to begin.

Up ahead, Beatrice isn't getting any closer. In fact, she seems to be pulling away from me, her shoulders swinging from side to side, pushing on. Good for her, I'm thinking. I can see the two women still chasing her. Can she hold out? There is still a long way to go.

At the same time, the fact that I'm not catching her is slightly concerning. I usually pass her at some point, but my legs are tiring. The ground feels softer now than it did on the first lap. The long straight lines cutting across the parched landscape seem to stretch on further than before. The gentle wind and the soft pat, pat, pat of my feet are the only sounds. I swing a few glances behind me, but there is no one as far as I can see. Just the long path already travelled, empty, as though I'm the last runner on earth.

I have an energy gel in my back pocket. I had planned to take it at 30 km, but now, at 24 km, it's all I can think about. It's like magic, someone told me. I pull it out, the yellow tube glistening in the sunlight. I rip it open and squeeze it into my mouth. It tastes of lemon-flavoured sweets. Sickly sweet. I suck on the packet. I'm in a hurry to finish it, squeezing out the last globs. Even holding it seems a waste of my precious, fast-depleting energy. I shove the packet back into my pocket as I turn and start to head up what was once the first hill. This time, however, I can't seem to move myself beyond a slow grind, churning my body up the hill with my arms, my feet taking short little steps.

At the top, the excitable women at the water station have also run out of energy. 'Well done,' says one, quietly, as she hands me a bottle of water.

I guzzle it down, the whole bottle. I'm suddenly insatiably thirsty. But the water station is gone. I'll have to wait until the next one.

Spurred on by the gel, and the downward slope, I begin to pick my speed back up. But it's so quiet out here. For the first time, as I dip down into the narrow valley again, I start looking around. I'm out in the bush. Alone. There are lions, cheetahs, leopards out here. I remember the roar of the lions outside the tent in our first week in Kenya. That was only a few miles from here. Out of the corner of my eye, I spot a man sitting beside the road. I almost don't see him. He's dressed in green uniform, with a gun across his lap. He gives me a friendly wave, as though I just happen to be passing.

Soon I'm running through another water station at around 30 km. A man with a bin bag is collecting up the discarded bottles from the first lap. I grab a full water bottle from a young boy and drink it up.

On I go, beginning the series of steep climbs. They continue, up and down, but mostly up, for about 10 kilometres. I can barely jog up the slopes now, instead getting my head down and shuffling as sure and steady as I can. At one point a woman overtakes me.

'Come on,' she says, urging me to run with her. 'Don't give up.'

I haven't given up, but I really can't go any faster. My legs feel as though they've been drained of life and refilled with lead. I can barely move. I almost need to use my hands to pull my legs along.

'Come on,' I tell myself. I try chanting. 'I love you Lila. I love you Lila.' But it's no use. The heavy debilitating tiredness swamping me swallows the chant whole, sucking it away until I can't even remember what it was. This time it's not a question of will-power. This time I haven't lost the psychological battle. No, my focus is intense. I'm pushing myself as hard as I can. This time it's purely physical. I'm struggling just to keep moving. At each water station I drink more. Two bottles of water. Lucozade. But my thirst is unforgiving. I squeeze sponges of ice-cold water over my head and for a blissful second I feel refreshed. But the burning road stretches on.

The kilometre markers become my only sanity, the only evidence that I'm actually still moving forward, and not just drifting aimlessly across a dry ocean. I begin to call them my little magic markers, talking to myself, to the little signs hammered into the ground.

'Ah, there you are, my little magic marker. What took you so long?'

Suddenly Godfrey is standing alone on the horizon, calling my name. At least, I think he is. I squint to see if I'm dreaming. When I reach him, he runs along beside me.

'Marietta was worried. How do you feel?'

He barely has to jog to keep up with me.

'How are the others doing?' I ask him, my voice sounding surprisingly composed, as though we were just walking along the road in Iten. My breathing is steady. It's just my legs that are holding me back, and my overpowering thirst.

'Shadrack is pushing on in about eighth. He can still catch the leaders, but I told him he has to push hard now.'

'And Japhet?'

'He's just behind him.' He looks at me, worried. 'How do you feel?'

'I feel exhausted. My legs just won't move.'

As we crawl over the brow of the hill, I see Lila standing at the water stop, holding out a bottle of water. When I reach her, I grab it. 'Thank you,' I say, smiling at her.

'First mzungu coming through,' Jophie announces to everyone gathered there. I don't know how much longer I can hold out. I'm getting slower and slower, surely someone must be catching me. But I push on, refreshed, for the moment at least, feeling back in control of my senses. I try to focus on my form, keeping my legs in order, leaning forward. It's as though my body is desperately trying to shut down and I have to do everything I can to keep it in operation.

Between each magic marker I lose track of how far we've gone, and I'm not sure which number to expect next. They seem to count erratically: 34 km, 36 km, 35 km, 36 km. But even if I'm losing count, each one represents progress, proof that I'm still moving.

And still no other mzungu passes me. Beatrice has long since disappeared into the distance, but amazingly nobody else comes by. I'm passing the slowest half-marathon runners now, still on their first lap, walking, most of them. I try to weave past them, but I'm barely moving faster than they are.

At 39 kilometres we reach the last water stop. I don't know what happens. I reach for a drink, and then stop. Completely stock-still. My legs, charged with sweet relief, feel as though they're singing hymns. I pick up a Lucozade and suck it down. Half-marathon runners, their big bellies hoisted up over their shorts, are standing around drinking and joking. This is the greatest party ever. I feel like a gatecrasher, my eyes wide. This is where it's happening. At the back of the field. This is where the real action takes place. Just when I think life couldn't get any sweeter, a man comes over and squeezes about eight wet sponges over my head. Ice-cold water. I'm in heaven.

But I have to get on. I tell myself to stop having fun, to pull myself together. I start off again, into the dry wastelands, the dust sticking now to my wet shoes. The taste of dirty water running into my mouth. I wonder whether I could walk the rest of the way and still be the first mzungu. No, it's too risky. I have to keep going. Just one foot in front of the other, no matter how slow, just keep running. I look down, watching them, my feet moving back and forth.

Finally, miraculously, I make it to where Ray is sitting on his plastic chair. He leaps up.

'Come on,' he bellows. 'What's wrong with you?' I can't help grinning at him. It's less than a kilometre to go from here.

'Thanks, Ray.'

Then Godfrey, the omnipresent, appears. 'Come on, Finn, you're going to win.'

He means the mzungu race. It's a victory of sorts, I suppose, although it's hard to fathom how right now. I feel more pathetic than heroic as I lumber along. Godfrey, the real hero of the piece, runs beside me, encouraging me. Somehow, with his help, I begin to get moving again, to move my legs once more like a runner. As I round the last corner, the beautiful arched finish rises up to meet me. The clock ticks on to 3 hours 20 minutes. And then I'm there. I've done it. I've won. I've finished. I've survived. I've finally stopped.

Marietta is there, smiling, proud, holding my hand. The children are there. It's beautiful. I want to cry. I can hardly stand. A man is moving me on, directing me to a chair. I hold on to it, to stop myself collapsing. The girls are buzzing around me, offering me a cupcake they've baked for me, a beautiful mess of melting chocolate. But I need water. Lucozade. Anything liquid. I collapse into the chair. Hands are reaching down, wanting to shake mine. Paul is there, his big grin. 'Fantastic,' he says. Chris walks over. Lila runs up and gives him a big hug. Godfrey is smiling under his hat. I have to look away, to stop myself crying. I'm overcome with emotion. I get up, to try walking around. Alastair comes over.

'Man, that was some run,' he says, offering me a big hand-shake. I can't look. I totter off, unstable, towards a sign that says Recovery Tent. Inside it's like a war zone, with exhausted people collapsed everywhere. Those on bales of hay are getting massages, while those on the floor have simply been left to die, it seems. I slide down next to a hay bale, out of the sun, among the pungent smells of sweat and Deep Heat, hidden from the emotions running wild outside. I need a moment to breathe.

I hear a voice I recognise. It's Ray. I owe him to stand up, at least. He wants me to meet someone from the charity that runs the event, but when he introduces me, I can't speak. I can barely blubber my name. I'll come back, I tell the man. I just need to get my breath back. He smiles knowingly. He's seen it before, of course.

When I finally re-emerge, composed, the others are all still there. Beatrice is talking and laughing with Flora. She ended up finishing fourth. In her first-ever marathon. She won a prize. Forty thousand Kenyan shillings. Enough to pay her rent for more than three years. Where did she get the strength from?

'It was very hot,' is all she can say when I congratulate her. From just after halfway, which was around the last time I saw her, she managed to stick with a Maasai runner from Isiolo. His encouragement kept the other women runners chasing her at bay, until, at around 26 km, amazingly she began to pick up the pace.

'I left the Maasai runner,' she says. She can't stop smiling. 'But it was very tough. At 40 km my legs felt so weak.' She had no idea that she was in the top five, but she kept on pushing.

'I thought I was number ten,' she says, which makes Flora laugh. They say something to each other in Swahili and start giggling.

Japhet and Shadrack are not there. Godfrey says they've gone off to get showered and changed. I ask him how they did.

He shakes his head. 'Not good,' he says, disappointed. 'It's my fault. I should have told Shadrack to drink more.' Shadrack and Japhet spent most of the race moving up through the field, but they had left themselves too much to do. Shadrack had not taken on enough water, and despite getting up to eighth, he almost fainted from dehydration with a kilometre to go.

'Japhet passed him, and told him "Let's run together,"' Godfrey tells me. 'But he was doubled over. "Go on without

[277]

me," he said.' In the end, Japhet finished in tenth place in 2 hours 28 minutes, with Shadrack struggling home in eleventh a minute later. Paul, who had malaria only a few weeks before the race, ran 2 hours 45 minutes, while Philip was the first over-forty runner after all, and won a brand-new mobile phone.

We stand by the bus, waiting for Beatrice. They've decided to head straight back home to Iten, while I'm staying here in Lewa with Marietta and the children. Little Japhet, our star man, gives me a hug. 'When are you coming back to Iten?' he asks. I shake my head. 'I don't know.' Chris, impatient to leave, slides open the minibus door. 'Finn, it has been an honour,' he says, his voice as smooth as ever. The saga is over, he can get back now to his school, to building his legacy. Philip shakes my hand and climbs into the bus. Paul talks to me in a hushed, wistful voice, telling me to greet my family, and to come back to Iten one day. Beatrice is here now. 'Thank you so much,' she says, the envelope of cash tucked into the waistband of her tracksuit.

'Look after that money,' I tell her. Her life is going to change after this, at least for a while. Everyone is going to want a piece of her prize. 'Talk to Godfrey if you need some advice.'

She smiles. 'I will,' she says. 'Thank you.'

The last one is Godfrey. 'Goodbye, Finn,' he says, quiet, a tear in his eye.

'Godfrey, we couldn't have done this without you. I'll be in touch, I promise.' He nods.

'Goodbye' is all he can say. He climbs into the driver's seat, and reverses the bus back. They all look out, waving. I wonder if I'll ever see them again. It has been an honour to have known them and to have run with them.

I stand watching as the bus drives off through the dust, bumping along the track, taking them back to Iten, back to the land of runners.

Epilogue

Four months later

It's eerily quiet as we chase like ghosts across the sky, 130 feet up on the Queensboro Bridge. If I could lift my head long enough, I'd see the skyscrapers of Manhattan jutting up along the edge of the East River below me. But I'm focused on the patter of feet, on my breathing. Eventually the steep climb tips and we start running down the other side of the bridge. Making use of the slope, I start snaking my way through the other runners. I went through the halfway point in 1 hour 23 minutes, a half-marathon personal best by over three minutes, and I'm still feeling strong. A sign up on the bridge reads: 'If easier means ten miles to go, welcome to easier.'

Up ahead the sounds of the crowd are building. As we come off the bridge, we emerge into sunlight, warm on my neck. A huge cheer goes up from a crowd five people deep. I feel a surge of energy and can't help smiling. Around the next corner the course turns onto First Avenue, a wide, empty street that seems to stretch on for ever, a huge space cut through the middle of everything, opened up for me to run along. People cheering line both sides, waving flags and handwritten cardboard signs. It's a long way from the silent heat of Lewa.

After returning from Kenya I want to see what I can do in a race at sea level. Toby Tanser manages to get me a place in the New York marathon, running for his Shoe4Africa charity team. But first I have a showdown with my 10K personal best down by the river in Exeter.

The race is flat and I spend most of it running on the heels of two other athletes, feeling comfortable, gliding over the ground, riding light on my toes. As I turn the last corner, a big clock over the finish shows 35 minutes, the seconds ticking along to 50 as I cross the line. It is a best time by almost three minutes. In one fell swoop I've moved to a whole new level. I can feel it as I walk around after the race, glowing with satisfaction, shaking hands with the other finishers. Thirty-five minutes. The Kenyan training has paid off after all. I'm now a 35-minute 10K runner. I feel excited as I head off for a warm-down jog. This is just the beginning. Next a half-marathon. Then New York.

But the next morning I wake up and can hardly walk. I seem to have injured my thigh muscle.

It's four weeks before I can start training again, so I turn up in New York two months later, on a bright November morning, worried about my fitness. In the few days before the race I head out to Central Park for a few last easy runs. The place is swarming with runners. There are more here than Iten.

'This city is running-crazy,' Toby tells me. He lives in New York and two nights before the race he holds a pasta party at his friend's apartment for all the Shoe4Africa team runners. I arrive at the building and look again at the directions. He hasn't given me the apartment number, I realise. It just says eleventh floor. I tell the doorman I'm here for a pasta party.

'Eleventh floor,' he says, opening the lift. There is no apartment number. It's the entire eleventh floor. Toby's friend is a famous actor. His apartment is huge.

In the kitchen a group of Kenyan women are cooking ugali. Toby is full of life, hopping around talking to everyone. I walk into another room and there among the clinking of glasses and excited New York chatter are three Kenyan athletes. They're still wearing their coats and sit in silence, waiting patiently for the ugali. I go over to say hello.

The man in the middle is Geoffrey Mutai. I tell him I saw him win a cross-country race in Iten back in January. He looks surprised. 'How?' he asks me.

'I used to live there,' I tell him.

It seems a long time ago now, even though it was just a few months back. Those long red trails full of runners, the children laughing and racing along to school. A few days before leaving for New York, I called Beatrice to see how she was doing.

'I am good,' she said. She sounded happy. I asked her what she had done with her winnings from Lewa. She said she had bought a TV and paid her rent for five months.

'The rest I gave to my mother,' she said.

Someone comes in and whispers in Geoffrey Mutai's ear. He looks at me. 'The ugali is ready,' he says, getting up. The woman beside him, Caroline Kilel, gets up too. Both Geoffrey and Caroline were the winners of the Boston marathon back in the spring. The third Kenyan, another woman, stays where she is. I don't recognise her. She says her name is Caroline Rotich. She's a Kenyan runner, so she must have won something, I suspect.

'What races have you won?' I ask her.

'I won the New York half-marathon this year,' she says. But of course.

I decide to wear a watch for the first time in my life and set it to beep every 6 minutes and 40 seconds – the average mile pace for a 2 hour 55 minute marathon. That would mean running close to my half-marathon PB twice in a row, but I feel I can do it despite the injury. That half-marathon time predates Kenya. Things are different now.

The first two miles of the race are up and down the expansive Verrazano-Narrows Bridge, downtown Manhattan basking in the sunshine on the horizon. By the second mile I'm already ahead of my schedule, but I feel fine so I decide to go with it. I don't want to be controlled by the watch, I think, wondering why I'm even wearing it. But at each mile I check it again, and at each mile I'm further ahead of my 2:55 schedule.

All along the course the crowds cheer us. They love it when one of the runners responds, with a high-five or a wave or anything. I'm trying, though, to stay focused on my running. The city's comedians have been out writing signs. One says: 'What are you all running from?' Another says: 'You've got great stamina. Call me. 1-834-768756.' Yet another reads: 'In our minds, you're all Kenyans.'

As I truck along at a good pace, far, far ahead, the Kenyans are putting on another show for the world. Geoffrey Mutai, fresh from his ugali at Toby Tanser's pasta party, streaks away at the front to win and smash the course record by over two minutes. It completes a stunning year in which every major marathon has been won by a Kenyan in a new course record. If they were good before, they're even better now.

My old friend Emmanuel Mutai, from the One 4 One camp, finishes second, also beating the old course record. I wonder what Chris is thinking back in Iten. He is no longer the fifth-fastest man ever in New York.

In the women's race, Mary Keitany, who once sat shyly talking to me in her cramped living room, sets off like a crazed matatu driver, running at world-record pace, pulling ahead of the women's field by over three minutes before being caught and passed just before the end. It's a brave run and wins the hearts of many people watching.

I'm still well under my target time as we head along First Avenue. The huge buildings rising up on each side make me feel tiny, but it's good to have firm ground below my feet, and cool air to breathe. Mindful of how thirsty I got in Lewa, I've been taking on plenty of water, and at the 18-mile point they hand us all energy gels. I take two.

As we run on, the mile markers keep coming quicker than I'm expecting, but gradually I start to slow. I'm losing my time cushion, the beeps of my watch getting closer to the mile markers. I treat them like reminders to keep pushing. 'Come on,' I tell myself, speeding up, passing a few other runners, finding someone at a good pace to draft behind, trying not to tread on his heels. I'm saving my chant of love until I really need it, but before I realise it we're into Central Park and nearing the finish. Around the last corner I can't stop the grin beaming across my face. I close my eyes and look to the heavens, holding my arms out. I can't help it. The crowd cheers me, embracing my moment of triumph.

I know I've done it. The sub-3-hour marathon is conquered as I cross the line in exactly 2 hours 55 minutes.

And then the emotions begin. I can hardly stand, my calves are in agony. A woman takes my arm, hauling me off to the VIP area by the finish – Toby is a good man to know. It's not much, a few chairs, a box of apples and some drinks. But the sun is shining. I've just run the New York marathon. Bliss is surging like a drug through my veins. A man standing by the gate like a joyous town crier sums everything up, the reason we do it, the reason I've put everyone through all this, gone so far, pushed so hard, for so long. In his big New York accent, he looks at me struggling to walk, and declares grandly:

'Welcome to heaven.'

Acknowledgements

My first and biggest thank you goes to Marietta. In some ways it feels like we wrote this book together. She was a steadying influence throughout, and her sense of adventure, her perseverance and her kindness were all invaluable.

Second, to my wonderful children for taking everything in their stride like three little superheroes.

Also, to my guide and mentor, Godfrey Kiprotich, the most helpful man in the world, a true friend.

To the rest of the Iten Town Harriers, particularly to Chris and Japhet, for all their help and for coming along for the ride.

To Jophie and Alastair for encouraging us to come to Kenya, for looking after us when we first got there, and for lending us the most coveted car in East Africa.

To Ray and Doreen, for their immense hospitality, letting us stay in their wonderful Flea House in Nairobi, and for putting me in touch with Godfrey.

To Anders for all the time spent loafing around in the Kimbia camp, Mama Kibet for the constant supply of rice, beans and ugali, and to Isaac Arusei for making me feel so welcome.

To Michel Boeting and all the incredible athletes at the One 4 One training camp.

To Flora for hand-washing all those clothes and for being such a friend to Ossian.

To Hilda, Brenda, Maureen, Linda and all the other children of Kapshow in Iten, for their kindness and friendship with Lila, Uma and Ossian.

To Jeff and Carey, Uhuru and Apollo for Iten training runs, pasta and kids' playdates.

To Kelly Falconer, a former editor who took the time to point me in the right direction even though she had never met me.

To my agent, Oliver Munson, for seeing the book's potential and taking it on, and for doing such a good job in selling it.

To my co-editors, Sarah Savitt and Ryan Doherty, for sharing my vision and for their skilled pruning of the original manuscript.

To Betty and Robin, for being so supportive right from the beginning.

To my parents, Val and John, for bringing me up with a sense of wonder and adventure.

And to Prem Rawat, for showing me the place from where everything else begins.

Finally, to all the other people who helped me out along the way, especially Stewart and June Vetch at the Muthaiga Club in Nairobi; Chris and Caroline Thouless; Willie and Sue Roberts at the Sirikoi Camp in Lewa; Nancy and Rosie at Lewa; Samani Samwel Indasi and his team of horsemen; Terra Plana; Pieter at the Kerio View; Lornah Kiplagat and Pieter Langerhorst at the HATC; Marguerita North-Lewis; Brother Paul at the Eldoret Golf Club; Geoffrey the kiosk owner, his brother Henry and the rest of our friendly neighbours in Kapshow, Iten; Alex the nightwatchman; Ken,

Edwin, Raymond, Eliud and the rest of the Run Fast camp; Tom 'Kiprop' Payn; Brother Colm and Ian Kiprono; Phillip Kipchumba and the rest of his training group in Ngong; Tara and Neil; Petra; the Nairobi Waldorf school; the Regency Hotel in Addis Ababa; Tadele Geremew Mulugeta; Mr and Mrs William Koila; Simon Biwott; Sunrise Academy in Iten; Braeburn school in Nanyuki; Sarah Watson; Simon the masseur at the One 4 One camp; Tom Ratcliffe; Ricky Simms; Micah Kogo and the other athletes in the house in Teddington; Toby Tanser; Ann and Herb Cook; and my two brothers Jiva and Govinda.